APR 2 1 2021

P9-DHJ-038

PRAISE FOR

THE DIARIES OF EMILIO RENZI

FORMATIVE YEARS

"Splendidly crafted and interspliced with essays and stories, this beguiling work is to a diary as Piglia is to 'Emilio Renzi': a lifelong alter ego, a highly self-conscious shadow volume that brings to bear all of Piglia's prowess as it illuminates his process of critical reading and the inevitable tensions between art and life. . . . No previous familiarity with Piglia's work is needed to appreciate these bibliophilic diaries, adroitly repurposed through a dexterous game of representation and masks that speaks volumes of the role of the artist in society, the artist in his time, the artist in his tradition. . . . Piglia's 'delusion of living in the third person' to 'avoid the illusion of an interior life' transmogrifies us as well, into the character of the reader, and 'that feeling is priceless.'"

MARA FAYE LETHEM, *THE NEW YORK TIMES BOOK REVIEW*

"When young Ricardo Piglia wrote the first pages of his diaries, which he would work on until the last years of his life, did he have any inkling that they would become a lesson in literary genius and the culmination of one of the greatest works of Argentine literature?"

SAMANTA SCHWEBLIN, AUTHOR OF *FEVER DREAM*

"A valediction from the noted Argentine writer, known for bringing the conventions of hard-boiled U.S. crime drama into Latin American literature. *L'ennui, c'est moi*. First-tier Argentine novelist Piglia's (*Money to Burn*, 2003, etc.) literary alter ego, Emilio Renzi, was a world-weary detective when he stepped into the spotlight in the claustrophobic novel *Artificial Respiration*, published in Argentina in 1981 and in the U.S. in 1994, a searching look at Buenos Aires during the reign of the generals. Here, in notebooks begun decades earlier but only shaped into a novel toward the end of Piglia's life,

Renzi is struggling to forge a career as a writer. . . . The story takes a few detours into the meta—it's a nice turn that Renzi, himself a fictional writer, learns 'what I want to do from imaginary writers. Stephen Dedalus or Nick Adams, for example'—but is mostly straightforward, reading just like the diary it purports to be. Fans of Cortázar, Donoso, and Gabriel García Márquez will find these to be eminently worthy last words from Piglia, who died at the beginning of 2017."

KIRKUS REVIEWS, STARRED REVIEW

"In this fictionalized autobiography, Piglia's ability to succinctly criticize and contextualize major writers from Kafka to Flannery O'Connor is astounding, and the scattering of those insights throughout this diary are a joy to read. This book is essential reading for writers."

PUBLISHERS WEEKLY

"Where others see oppositions, great writers see the possibility of intertwining forking paths. Like kids in front of a stereogram, they are able to shift their gaze in ways that allow them to read the history of literature otherwise and, in doing so, write beyond the dead end of tradition. Ricardo Piglia, the monumental Argentine writer whose recent death coincided with increasing recognition of his work in the English-speaking world, was without a doubt one of these great visionaries. . . . It was said that there lay hidden something more impressive than his transgressive novels or his brilliant critical essays, a secret work of even more transcendence: his diaries. . . . In the tradition of Pavese, Kafka, and Gombrowicz, the diaries were the culmination of a life dedicated to thinking of literature as a way of life."

CARLOS FONSECA, LITERARY HUB

"It almost seems as though Piglia has perfected the form of the literary author's diary, leaving in enough mundane life details to give a feeling of the messy, day-to-day livedness of a diary, but also providing this miscellany with something of a shape, and with a true intellectual heft. In these pages we see the formation of a formidable literary intelligence—the brief reflections on genre, Kafka, Beckett, Dashiell Hammett, Arlt, and Continental philosophy alone are worth the price of admission—but we also see heartbreak, familial drama, reflections on life, small moments of great beauty, the hopes and anxieties of a searching young man, the endless monetary woes of one dedicated to the literary craft, and the drift of a nation whose flirtation with fascism takes it on a dangerous course."

SCOTT ESPOSITO, *BOMB MAGAZINE*

"As a fictionalized autobiography, it is, like the work of Karl Ove Knausgaard, of *My Struggle* fame, part confession and part performance. Renzi meets and corresponds with literary luminaries like Borges, Cortázar, and Márquez, and offers insightful readings of Dostoevsky, Kafka, Faulkner, and Joyce. . . . Fans of W. G. Sebald and Roberto Bolaño will find the first installment in Piglia's trilogy to be a fascinating portrait of a writer's life."

ALEXANDER MORAN, *BOOKLIST*

"In the long history of novelists and their doubles, doppelgängers, and alter egos, few have given more delighted attention to the problem of multiplicity than the Argentine novelist Ricardo Emilio Piglia Renzi. . . . Under the name of Ricardo Piglia he published a sequence of acrobatic, dazzling novels and stories that consistently featured a novelist called Emilio Renzi. . . . The larger story of *Formative Years* reads something like a *roman d'apprentissage*: the romance of a writer's vocation, in all its hubris and innocent corruption. . . . [T]he book's real subject is more delicate and more moving than the simple story of a literary vocation. It is the process of textualization, of the stuttering, hesitant way a writer tries to convert life into literature. In these diaries, Piglia is dramatizing not only the writer's split between a public and private self, but also the time-consuming, exhausting, delicious, compromised effort to construct that textual self: the self that exists only in words. . . . *Formative Years* is one of the great novels of youth: its boredom, powerlessness, desperation, strategizing, delusion . . . this journal impassively records not only a novelist's self-creation, but a society's unraveling."

ADAM THIRLWELL, *THE NEW YORK REVIEW OF BOOKS*

ALSO BY RICARDO PIGLIA

RICARDO PIGLIA

THE DIARIES OF EMILIO RENZI

Formative Years

Translated by Robert Croll

Introduction by Ilan Stavans

RESTLESS BOOKS
BROOKLYN, NEW YORK

Copyright © 2017 Estate of Ricardo Piglia
c/o Schavelzon Graham Agencia Literaria
Introduction copyright © 2017 Ilan Stavans
Translation copyright © 2017 Robert Croll

First published as *Los diarios de Emilio Renzi: Años de formación*
by Editorial Anagrama, Barcelona, 2015

Work published within the framework of "Sur" Translation Support Program of
the Ministry of Foreign Affairs and Worship of the Argentine Republic

Obra editada en el marco del Programa "Sur" de Apoyo a las Traducciones del
Ministerio de Relaciones Exteriores y Culto de la República Argentina

All rights reserved.
No part of this book may be reproduced or transmitted
without the prior written permission of the publisher.

First Restless Books paperback edition November 2017

Paperback ISBN: 9781632061621
Library of Congress Control Number: 2017944631

Cover design by Daniel Benneworth-Gray
Set in Garibaldi by Tetragon, London
Printed in Canada

3 5 7 9 8 6 4 2

Restless Books, Inc.
232 3rd Street, Suite A111
Brooklyn, NY 11215

restlessbooks.org
publisher@restlessbooks.org

CONTENTS

INTRODUCTION

The Reading Life of Ricardo Piglia

ILAN STAVANS

"Do not read, as children do, to amuse yourself,
or like the ambitious, for the purpose of instruction.
No, read in order to live."

GUSTAVE FLAUBERT

Ricardo Piglia was an assiduous reader, that most embattled of today's pastimes. He published a book called *El último lector* (*The Last Reader*, 2005), in which he celebrates not speed in reading, as often done in schools, but slowness. In the epilogue, he quotes a line from Wittgenstein: "In philosophy the winner of the race is the one who can run most slowly. Or: the one who gets there last." Piglia called sharp readers "private eyes," in honor of his obsession with detective fiction, the style in which he wrote most of his work. (He loved W. R. Burnett's *The Asphalt Jungle*, James M. Cain's *The Postman Always Rings Twice*, and Dashiell Hammett's *The Dain Curse*.) He often invoked a famous photograph of Borges, who became blind in his thirties, taken while he was director of Argentina's Biblioteca Nacional, holding a book a few inches from his nose. Borges said, "I am now a reader of pages my eyes cannot see." Piglia writes, "A reader is also one who misreads, distorts, perceives things confusingly." For him, it was crucial to read idiosyncratically, against the current.

A cornerstone of contemporary Latin American letters, Ricardo Piglia taught at Princeton until he moved back to Argentina after he was diagnosed with amyotrophic lateral sclerosis, known as Lou Gehrig's Disease, of which he ultimately died on January 6, 2017 at the age of seventy-five. He didn't spend his entire life only reading; he also invested a prodigious amount of time writing about that life: his education, his relationship with his grandfather Emilio, the upheaval of Peronism, his early attempts at writing, publishing, and teaching. He loved to write about his responses to favorite books, especially Argentine classics (by Macedonio Fernández, Roberto Arlt, Borges, Julio Cortázar, Manuel Puig, and Juan José Saer), his thrill at mapping various national traditions (American, Italian, Polish), and his fascination with the *Rezeptionsgeschichte* of certain authors (Joyce, Kafka, Faulkner, and Dostoevsky).

Piglia identified himself as a critic who writes and as a writer who critiques, stating that "criticism is a modern form of autobiography." Early on in *The Diaries of Emilio Renzi*, he speculates, *"How I Read One of My Books* could be the title of my autobiography (if I ever wrote it)." He wrote stories, novels, operas, screenplays, and several volumes of essays (including *Crítica y ficción* [*Criticism and Fiction*, 1986], *Formas breves* [*Brief Forms*, 2000], and *Escritores norteamericanos* [*North American Writers*, 2016]). Yet his most enduring effort, the one likely to earn him a place in posterity, is the 327 notebooks he crafted day in and day out between 1957 and 2015 in which he imagined himself not as Ricardo Piglia but as his alter ego, Emilio Renzi. As it switches from the first to the third person and back, *The Diaries of Emilio Renzi* generates a sense of alienation, wonderment, and displacement in the reader. The first volume starts, "'Ever since I was a boy,' I've repeated what I don't understand,' laughed Emilio Renzi that afternoon, retrospective and radiant, in the bar on Arenales and Riobamba. 'We are amused by the unfamiliar; we enjoy the things we cannot explain.'"

In *The Symposium*, Plato's mouthpiece Aristophanes suggests that each human individual is made of two halves. At birth, these halves are divided, resulting in the vertigo and sense of incompletion that define us as humans. That division is solved through the quest to "find the other half," in love. In the case of Piglia, his solution came through fictionalization: the chronicling of his life as if it belonged to *el otro*, the other—that is, to Renzi. This strategy is often called "autofiction." *The Diaries of Emilio Renzi* is not a loyal distillation of what Piglia experienced, but rather a recreation, or even a revision. He started the notebooks just as the alter ego Emilio Renzi began to materialize.

It isn't surprising that Piglia loved other people's diaries. There are reactions to a handful of them—by Goethe, Stendhal, Flaubert, Kafka, Woolf, Gadda, and Pavese—spread throughout the volumes. What attracts him in them, it seems, is that adulterated mode called "fiction-alized autobiography." In that regard, *The Diaries of Emilio Renzi* is Latin America's response to Scandinavian Karl Ove Knausgaard's *My Struggle*. Yet Piglia's "autofiction" is different: the notebooks don't present their protagonist's state of being as a fait accompli but as an experiment. The reader catches Renzi in an ongoing state of gestation, writing, as he himself puts it, "an imaginary version of myself." In the end, he inscribes himself as a palimpsest, made of evanescent stories that are "told over and over again, and through telling them and repeating them they improve, are refined like pebbles honed by water in the depths of rivers."

The name Emilio Renzi isn't arbitrary: Piglia's birth name was Ricardo Emilio Piglia Renzi. Emilio Renzi is the name with which he signed his first publications. It is also the name of the detective in a number of his books, from *Artificial Respiration* (1980) to *Burnt Money* (1997) and *El camino de Ida* [*One Way Road*, 2013]. These, however, are tangential paths to appreciating Renzi's plight. The notebooks are his true habitat. In them his *argentinidad*, indeed his *latinoamericanidad*, come to full view. "How could one write about Argentina?" Renzi wonders. His answer is complex. It isn't the content of a book that makes it Argentine because the Argentine writer can write about anything. So what is it? "We write our books, publish them," Renzi posits. "We are left to live, we have our circles, our audience. To say it another way, everything must be centered on the use of language. In this way, the content will have different effects. The subject does not matter so much as the particular type of structure and circulation of our works."

In a conversation with Roberto Bolaño in the Spanish newspaper *El País* in 2001, Piglia describes *Latin Americanism*, the identity of Latin Americans, as made of misbegotten dictators and clairvoyant prostitutes, "a kind of anti-intellectualism that tends toward simplifying everything, and which many of us resist." Bolaño responds that, "to our disgrace, we continue to be Latin Americans," a condition that, he argues, is the result of economic and political forces. The two authors were disruptors rather than endorsers of this condition. Their fiction is a commentary on the merchandizing of stereotypes. Disruption for them meant laughing at how Latin America is exported abroad: a tropical, half-baked, exuberant landscape that is at once magical and anti-European.

Like Bolaño, Piglia plotted that disruption meticulously. Aware of his end (also like Bolaño), he devoted his remaining years, from 2011 until his death, to adapting the 327 notebooks into three ample volumes and seeing them to publication. Rumors about this magnum opus circulated long before the volumes were released, and they were greeted with enormous enthusiasm upon publication in the Spanish-speaking world, one each year between 2015 and 2017. Respectively, the volumes cover Renzi's "formative years," from 1957 to 1967, "happy years," from 1968 to 1975, and the years 2011 to 2015, under the subtitle *A Day in the Life*. He explores every detail of himself through Renzi, who serves as filter and intermediary, and perhaps also as demiurge.

Call the notebooks *Portrait of the Writer as Invention*. In them Renzi isn't an empiricist like Hume; he is closer to Spinoza. His interest isn't in reality itself but in the ways the brain imagines it. In *The Diaries of Emilio Renzi*, we witness Renzi's thought processes, his anxieties, his response to crucial actors in his life (such as his tyrannical father), even the way he constantly mocks his own seriousness—"I'm a trickster!" he enjoys saying. David Foster Wallace argued that fiction is where loneliness is not only confronted and relieved but also "countenanced, stared down, transfigured, and treated." Renzi articulates principles, faces boredom, scoffs at platitudes, and shifts restlessly in his own views.

A descendant of Italian immigrants (and immigrants are forcibly aware of the division of selves), Piglia was born in 1941 in Adrogué, in the south of Buenos Aires. The family eventually moved to Mar del Plata, and in 1965, Piglia, by then already a passionate reader, moved to Buenos Aires on his own. "It is what you read when you don't have to," Oscar Wilde said, "that determines what you will be when you can't help it." Like many of his generation, Piglia found Borges, who in turn opened up Argentine letters in full.

Renzi meets Borges during his student years. "He had an immediate and warm way of creating intimacy, Borges," he exclaims. "He was always that way with everyone he talked to: he was blind, he did not see them and always spoke to them as if they were near, and that closeness is in his texts, he is never patronizing and gives no air of superiority, he addresses everyone as if they were more intelligent than he, with so much common understatement that he has no need to explain what is already known. And it is that intimacy that his readers sense." If one doesn't know how to distill his work, Renzi argues, Borges's influence on others—and Cortázar's, too—becomes "a plague." Yet it is Borges who tells Renzi that "writing... changes the way of reading above all." Indeed, such was the allure of the author of "The Aleph" that much of Renzi's readings are built as digressions on Borges's ideas; he wrote about him and taught his work profusely.

The universe of signs is at the core of the Hispanic world, which is populated with books that address reading, from *Don Quixote* to much of Borges's work to *One Hundred Years of Solitude*. Piglia's oeuvre aims at that same insistence: living is reading and vice versa. In photos we have of him he is always caught looking at a book, with his thick glasses at center stage, or else toying with a magnifying glass, or—the trickster again!—giving the viewer (i.e., the reader) the middle finger. Clearly, reading isn't a metaphor for him.

Piglia's apologia for reading doesn't turn him into a hero whose mission it is to salvage an entire civilization, like Guy Montag and Clarisse McClellan in *Fahrenheit 451*. His quest is at once simpler and more complex: it is a defense of self-consciousness.

THE DIARIES OF
EMILIO RENZI

To Beba Eguía, reader of my life
To Luisa Fernandez, my Mexican muse

He had begun to write a diary at the end of 1957 and continued writing it still. Much had changed since that time, but he remained faithful to the obsession. "Of course, there is nothing more ridiculous than the conceit of chronicling one's own life," he would contend. "One automatically looks like a fool." Nevertheless, he is convinced that if he had not begun to write his diaries one afternoon, he would never have written anything else. He published some books—and perhaps will publish some more—solely in order to justify this writing. "And so, to speak of myself is to speak of this diary," he said. "Everything that I am is in there, but there are only words. Changes in my handwriting." Sometimes, when he reads through it again and surveys the things he has lived through, it costs him something. There are episodes narrated in those journals that he has forgotten completely. They exist in the diary but not in his memory. And, at the same time, certain scenes that survive in his memory with the clarity of photographs are absent there, as though he had never experienced them. He feels the strange sensation of having lived two lives. One written down in his notebooks and one in his memories. They are images, scenes, fragments of conversation, lost remnants that are born anew each time. The two never coincide, or coincide only in minute details that dissolve amid the confusion of days.

Things were difficult in the beginning. He had nothing to say; his life was absolutely trivial. "I like the first years of my diary precisely because, at the time, I was struggling against the void," he said one afternoon, in the bar on the corner of Arenales and Riobamba. "Nothing happened; in reality, nothing ever happens, but it worried me back then. I was very

5

naïve, always looking for extraordinary adventures." Then he started to steal experiences from the people he knew, stories of things he imagined they experienced when they were not with him. He wrote very well in those days, as it happens, much better than he does now. He had absolute convictions, and style is nothing more than the absolute conviction of possessing a style.

There are no secrets; it would be ridiculous to think that secrets exist, and he would, therefore, gladly disclose the first ten years of his diary in this book. He included stories and essays because they formed part of his personal journals in their original version.

The publication of his diaries was divided into three volumes: *I. Formative Years, II. The Happy Years*, and *III. A Day in the Life*. It was based on the transcription of the diaries written between 1957 and 2015, not including travel diaries and what he had written while he lived abroad. At the end, he recorded his final months in Princeton and his return to Buenos Aires, so that this trilogy thus finds a (rather classical) way to conclude an extensive story, organized along the succession of days that make up a life.

For anyone who is interested in such details, he insists on mentioning that the notes and entries from these diaries occupy 327 notebooks, the first five of which are Triunfo brand and the rest of which are notebooks with black covers that can no longer be found, from a brand called Congreso. "Their pages were a light surface that for years drew me to write on them," he said. "I was attracted by their whiteness, altered only by the elegant series of blue lines that summoned phrasing and prose, as if I were writing on a musical staff or Freud's mystic writing pad."

BUENOS AIRES, APRIL 20, 2015

I

1

On the Threshold

Ever since I was a boy, I've repeated what I don't understand, laughed Emilio Renzi that afternoon, reflective and radiant, in the bar on Arenales and Riobamba. We are amused by the unfamiliar; we enjoy the things we cannot explain.

At the age of three, he was intrigued by the image of his grandfather Emilio sitting in the leather armchair in a circle of light, off somewhere else, with his eyes fixed upon a mysterious rectangular object. Motionless, he seemed indifferent, reserved. The boy Emilio did not truly understand what was going on. He was prelogical, pre-syntactical, pre-narrative; he registered gestures, one by one, but did not string them together; he only mimicked what he saw being performed. And so he clambered up onto a chair in the library that morning and took down a blue book from one of the stacks. Then he went out the door into the street and sat down on the threshold with the open volume on his knees.

My grandfather, said Renzi, left the country and came to live with us in Adrogué when my grandmother Rosa died. He left the page of the calendar open on February 3, 1943, unturned, as if time had stopped on the day of her death. And that terrifying thing, with the block of numbers fixed on that date, remained in the house for years.

We lived in a quiet neighborhood, close to the railway station, and every half hour the passengers who had arrived on the train from the capital passed before us. And I was there, on the threshold, making myself seen, when a long shadow leaned over me and said that I was holding the book upside down.

I think it must have been Borges, laughed Renzi that afternoon in the bar on Arenales and Riobamba. He used to spend the summers in Las Delicias Hotel back then, and who but old Borges would think of admonishing a three-year-old boy like that?

How does one become a writer? Is one *made* to become a writer? For the person that it happens to, it is not a calling, nor is it a decision; it seems instead to be an obsession, a habit, an addiction; if he stops doing it he feels worse, but to *need* to do it is ridiculous, and ultimately it becomes a way of living like any other.

Experience, he had realized, is a microscopic profusion of events that repeat and expand, disjointed, disparate, in flight. His life, he now understood, was divided into linear sequences, unfolding series that flowed back toward minor incidents in the remote past: sitting alone in a hotel room, seeing his face in a photo booth, climbing into a taxi, kissing a woman, raising his eyes from the page and looking out through the window, how many times? Those gestures formed a fluid web, sketched out a journey. On a napkin he drew a map with circles and crosses. Let's say this is the trajectory of my life, he said. The persistence of themes, of places, of situations is—*figuratively* speaking—what I want to perform. Like a piano player improvising over the tenuous form of a standard with variations, changes in rhythm, harmonies from some forgotten music, he said, and settled back into the chair. I could, for example, recount my life based on the repetition of conversations with friends in bars. La Confitería Tokio, Ambos Mundos café, El Rayo bar, Modelo, Las Violetas, Ramos, La Ópera café, La Giralda, Los 36 billiards hall . . . The same scene, the same subjects. Each time I have found myself among friends, a series. If we do something—open a door, perhaps—and later think about what we did, it seems ridiculous; on the other hand, if we look at the same actions from a distance, there is no need to extract from them a sense of continuity, a common form, even a meaning.

His life could be narrated following that sequence of meetings or any similar one. The films he had watched, the people he was with, what he did when he left the theater—he had recorded everything in an obsessive manner, incomprehensible and foolish, with detailed and *dated* descriptions, in his laborious handwriting. Everything was notated in what he had now decided to call his *archives*: the women he had lived with or the ones with whom he'd spent a night (or a week), the classes that he took notes for, the long-distance phone calls, annotations, signs. Wasn't it incredible? His habits, his vices, his own words. Nothing of his interior life, just facts, actions, places, circumstances that, once repeated, created the illusion of a life. An action, a gesture that persists and reappears, saying more than everything that I could ever say about myself.

In El Cervatillo, the bar where he settled in the evening, at a corner table beside the window, he had placed his cards, a folder, and a couple of books, Painter's *Proust* and *The Opposing Self* by Lionel Trilling, and to the side a book with a black cover, a novel from the looks of it, with quotes of praise from Stephen King and Richard Ford in red print.

But he had realized he must start with the leftovers, with what had not been written, to move toward things that had not been recorded but persisted and twinkled in his memory like dying lights. Minuscule events that had mysteriously survived the nighttime of forgetting. They are visions, flashes sent from the past, images that endure, isolated, without frames, without context, cut loose, and *we can't forget them*, right? Renzi laughed to himself. Right, he thought, and he watched the waiter crossing between the tables. Another glass of white? he asked. He ordered a Fendant de Sion . . . it was the wine Joyce drank, a dry wine, which had made him go blind. Joyce called it the Archduchess, for the amber color and because he drank it like someone—like Leopold Bloom—sinfully drinking the golden nectar of a nubile aristocrat girl bent low, crouching, over an eager Irish face. Renzi came to this bar—which used to be called La Casa Suiza—because, in the cool air of the cellars, they kept several cases of this Joycean wine. And with his customary pedantry he quoted, in a low voice, the paragraph from *Finnegans* celebrating that ambrosia . . .

The diary was an X-ray of his spirit, of the involuntary construction of his spirit, to put it better, he said, and paused. He didn't believe in such *nonsense* (with emphasis), but he liked to think that his life was made up of small incidents. In this way, he could finally begin to think about an autobiography. One scene and then another and another, no? It would be a serialized autobiography, a serial life . . . From this multiplicity of senseless fragments, he had started to follow a line, to reconstruct the series of books, The defining books of my life, he said. Not the ones he had written, but rather those he had read . . . *How I Read One of My Books* could be the title of my autobiography (if I ever wrote it).

The defining books of my life, then, are not simply all of the ones I have read but rather those for which I clearly remember the setting and the moment in which I read them. If I can remember the circumstances under which I was with a book, that proves to me that it was decisive. They are not necessarily the best or the ones that have influenced me most; they are the ones that have left a mark. I am going to follow this mnemonic criterion, as if I had no more than these images to reconstruct my experience. A book only has an intimate quality in memory if *I see myself reading it*. I am outside, at a distance, and I see myself as though I were someone else (always younger). Because of this, I think perhaps, now, that image of myself reading on the threshold of my childhood home is the first in a series, and here is where I will begin my autobiography.

Of course I remember these scenes after having written my books, and therefore we could call them the prehistory of a personal imagination. Why, after all, do we apply ourselves to writing? Well, because we have read before . . . The cause doesn't matter, of course, but the effect does. More than a few should repent, myself for one, but in any bar in the city, in any McDonald's there's a fool who, in spite of everything, wants to write . . . Really, he doesn't want to write: he wants to be a writer and wants to be read . . . A writer is *self-appointed*, he self-promotes at the flea market, but why does this position occur to him?

Delusion is a perfect state. It is not an error; it cannot be confused with a mistake, which is involuntary. It is a deliberate construction conceived to deceive the very person who has constructed it. A pure state, maybe the purest of all the states that exist. Delusion, like a private novel, like a future autobiography.

At first, he declared after a pause, we are like Valéry's Monsieur Teste: we cultivate nonempirical literature. A secret art whose form will not allow itself to be discovered. We imagine what we are trying to do and live under that delusion . . . In short, these stories are what everyone tells themselves in order to survive. Thoughts not to be understood by strangers. But is a private fiction possible? Or must there be two? Sometimes perfect moments only have the one who experiences them for a witness. We can call this murmur—illusory, ideal, uncertain—our personal history.

I remember where I was, for example, when I read Hemingway's stories. I had gone to the Ómnibus terminal to say goodbye to Vicky, who was my girlfriend at the time, and on the side of the platform, in a glass-enclosed gallery, on a bargain table, I found a used copy of the Penguin edition of *In Our Time*. How that book happened to end up there I don't know; maybe a traveler had sold it, an Englishman with an explorer's hat and a backpack traveling south had exchanged it, perhaps, for a Michelin guide of Patagonia—who can say? The truth is I went back home with the book, threw myself down in an armchair, and began to read. I went on and on as the light changed, and finished it almost in darkness, late in the evening, illuminated by the pale reflection of the light from the street that entered through the window's thin curtains. I had not moved, had not wanted to get up to light the lamp because I was afraid of breaking the spell of that prose. First conclusion: in order to read, one must learn to *keep still*.

The first reading, the *notion*, he stressed, of first reading is unforgettable because it is unrepeatable and unique, but its epiphanic quality does not depend on the *content* of the book but on the emotion that remains fixed in memory. The associations with childhood, for example, in the Combray section in *Swann's Way*; Proust returns to the forgotten landscape of his childhood home, transformed once more into a boy, and revives memories of the places and the delightful hours dedicated to reading, from morning to the moment he went to bed. Such a discovery is associated with innocence and childhood but lingers beyond them. It lingers longer than childhood, he repeated; the image lingers with the aura of discovery, at any age.

Argentine writers always say, well, the defining books of my life, let's see, the *Divine Comedy*, of course, the *Odyssey*, Petrarch's sonnets, Livy's *History of Rome*. *They* navigate these deep ancient waters, but I *am not* referring to the importance of these books, I refer simply to the lived impression that is there, now, picked up without a return address, without a date, in memory. The value of reading does not depend on the book in itself but on the emotions associated with the act of reading. And often I attribute things to those books that really belong to the passion of that time (which I have now forgotten).

What is fixed in memory is not the content of memory but rather its form. I am not interested in what can obscure the image, I am interested only in the visual intensity that persists in time like a scar. I would like to recount my life by tracing these scenes, like a man tracing the markings on a map in order to guide himself through an unknown city and orient himself within the chaotic multiplicity of streets, not really knowing where he wants to go. In reality, he only wants to get to know that city, not to arrive at a certain place, to mingle with the whirlwind of its traffic so that one day he may remember something of this place. ("In that city, the names of streets reference the martyrs who died defending their faith in primitive Christianity, and as I walked down those alleyways, I imagined a city, this one perhaps, with streets that bore the names of the activists who died fighting for socialism, for example," he said.) I was there, I crossed a bridge over the canals to the zoo. It was a light spring afternoon, and I sat on a bench to watch the polar bears' circular pacing. That, for me, is constructing a memory, being open and surprised by the fleeting gleam of a reminiscence.

Primary School Number 1 in Adrogué. A lecture class. Miss Molinari has created a sort of competition: we read aloud, and whoever makes a mistake is eliminated. The tournament of these readings has begun. I see myself in the kitchen at home, said Renzi, the night before, studying "reading." Why am I in the kitchen? Maybe my mother is helping me with the lesson, but I don't see her in my memory: I see the table, the white light, the tiled wall. The book has illustrations, I see it, and I still know the first sentence I was reading by heart despite the enormous distance: "Ships arrive at the coast, bearing fruits from beyond . . . " The fruits from beyond, the ships that arrive at the coast. It seems like Conrad. What book was that? The year was 1946.

"We learn to read before we learn to write, and women are the ones who teach us to read."

It is my birthday. Natalia, a friend of my grandfather's, Italian, has recently arrived. Her husband died "on the front . . . " Beautiful, sophisticated, she smokes blond "American" cigarettes, speaks with my grandfather in Italian (Piedmontese, really), about the war, I imagine. As a present, she brings me *Heart* by Edmondo de Amicis. I can clearly remember the yellow book from the Robin Hood collection. We are on the patio of the house, there is a canopy, she is wearing a white dress and hands me the book with a smile. She says something affectionate to me that I don't quite understand, in a deep accent, with those burning red lips.

What struck me in that novel (which I have not read again) was the story of the "little Florentine scribe." The father works as a copyist, the money is not enough, the boy gets up in the night, when all are sleeping, and without anyone seeing him copies in place of his father, imitating his writing as well as he can. What fixed the scene in my memory, thought Renzi, was the weight of this unwitnessed goodness, *no one knowing* that he is the one writing. The invisible nocturnal writer: he moves in the daytime as if sleepwalking.

There is a series with the figure of the copyist, one who reads foreign texts by writing: it is the prehistory of the modern author. And there are many imaginary amanuenses in the course of history who have lingered until today: Bartleby, Melville's spectral scrivener; Nemo, the copyist without an identity, whose name means "Nothing," from Dickens's *Bleak House*; Flaubert's François Bouvard and his friend Juste Pécuchet; Shem (the Penman), the delusional scribe who mixes up letters in *Finnegans Wake*; Pierre Menard, faithful transcriber of *Don Quixote*. Wasn't copying the first exercise in "personal" writing in school? Copying came before dictation and before "composition" (theme: *The defining books of my life*). I study English with Miss Jackson, the widow of an upper-level railway worker from the south, who lives alone in a two-story house and has published two or three translations of Hudson in *La Prensa*. She gives us private lessons. (She earned her living in this way, because the pension, she complained, comes to her reluctantly.) The first thing we read with her was Hudson's book about the birds in La Plata. One afternoon she took us to visit Los Veinticinco Ombúes, the author's birthplace, which was a few kilometers away from Adrogué. We rode on bicycles; she, in her pretty skirts, seemed to move in profile, as if she were riding a horse sidesaddle, her dark mourning overskirt flapping in the wind. Oh imagination, oh memories, Renzi recited, already slightly drunk by this stage.

The Englishwoman is nostalgic for London, but most of all for South Africa (Rhodesia, she says), where her husband was for a couple of years. The infinite savanna, the white-faced monkeys, and the pelicans with graceful reddish feet. She showed us photos of her large house built of logs close to the river, beside a pier; we had to describe what we saw in English.

She was a kind woman, but irascible and not at all conventional. If one of us passed wind (*sorry*), she would make us stand in line and smelled our *arses*. One by one until she discovered the culprit, who was immediately led into the courtyard by an ear. It seemed like a scene from Dickens, a sudden change of tone in a Muriel Spark novel. I still have the old edition of *Birds of La Plata*, with notes written in the margins by Miss Jackson. A circle surrounds the word "*peewee*" and beside it, in her diminutive, ant-sized writing, she gave the definition: "*A person of short stature.*"

I'm on the train and have the book open on a little table beside the window. I'm reading Jules Verne's *The Children of Captain Grant*. I don't remember how I managed to find this novel, which describes a voyage through Patagonia, just as I was voyaging across the same Patagonia.

At the end of primary school, my grandfather takes me with him on a long journey to the south. We take a sleeping car, the bunks convert into seats. There is a little sink that folds down from the wall, silver-plated, tiny, with a mirror. In the neighboring compartment, alone, travels Natalia. A sliding door connects the two cabins. We have breakfast and lunch in the dining car—English silverware, silver tureens.

Natalia caresses my hair in the dizzying corridor of the train. An unforgettable scent comes from her body; she is wearing a flowered sundress and her armpits are unshaven.

In Verne's novel, Scottish aristocrat Lord Edward Glenarvan discovers a message in a bottle, thrown into the sea by Harry Grant, captain of the brigantine *Britannia*, which was shipwrecked two years before. The main difficulty is that the information in the message thrown by the castaways is illegible except for the latitude: 37° South.

Lord Glenarvan, the children of Captain Grant, and the crew of the yacht *Duncan* leave for South America, since the partial message suggests Patagonia as the site of the disaster. In the middle of the voyage they discover an unexpected passenger: French geographer Santiago Paganel, who has come aboard by mistake. The expedition circumnavigates the 37° South line and crosses Argentina, exploring Patagonia and much of the region of La Pampa.

As we crossed an old steel bridge over the Colorado River, I read in the novel that just as Patagonia began an old steel bridge crossed over that mighty river of reddish waters.

Verne's book explained to me what I was seeing. The erudite French geographer classified and defined the flora and fauna, the waters, the winds, the geographical phenomena. Popular literature is always educational (that's why it is popular). Meaning proliferates, everything is explained and made clear. On the other hand, what I saw through the window was arid, windy, scrubland, crushed weeds, volcanic rocks, emptiness. There will always be an insuperable rift between seeing and describing, between life and literature.

"We must remember," said Jean Renoir, "that a field of wheat painted by Van Gogh can arouse more emotion than a field of wheat *tout court*." It may be so, but it depends what you're doing in that wheat field . . .

At night I leaned out of the window and saw, in the shadows, a car's headlights on the road, the houses illuminated in the towns passing before me. I heard the slow and anguished sighing of brakes in barely visible stations; the leather curtain, once lifted, revealed a deserted platform, a porter pushing a luggage cart, a circular clock with Roman numerals, until finally the pealing of the bell announced the train's departure. Then I lit the little light at the head of my bunk and read. My grandfather was in the compartment next door.

The fleeting vision of Natalia alone, at dawn, digging among glass objects in her *nécessaire* on the plush gray cloth of her illuminated compartment, is unforgettable.

We traveled two days and two nights to Zapala and from there took a rental car to a house on a ranch in the desert. We visited one of my grandfather's friends who had been with him in the First World War. He was a tall and ungainly man, with a burning red face and pale blue eyes. He called my grandfather "the Colonel," and together they remembered the slippery combat positions on the frozen slopes of Austrian mountains and the interminable battles in the trenches. The man had a large mustache, like a Cossack, and was missing his left arm. "This guy," said my grandfather, "is a hero; he saved me, wounded, from no-man's-land and lost his arm in the attempt."

Several times I've thought of going back to the ranch in Patagonia to see the man who had lost his arm. "Well fine," he might have said to me, "I'm going to tell you the true story of your grandfather in the war." But I never went and have only isolated traces of that personal war: a photo of my grandfather dressed as a soldier and the papers, books, maps, letters, and notes that he left me as his only inheritance when he died. Nevertheless, sometimes, I can still hear his voice.

In 1960, 1961, when I was studying in La Plata, I spent a lot of time with my grandfather at the house in Adrogué. He even hired me, which was in a sense both comical and touching. I had no money at the time, and he thought I could help him organize his papers and recreate his experience in the war. He was afraid of losing his memory with age, and he had organized his documents *spatially*: in one room there were the maps and drawings of the battles ("The Map Room," he had written on the door); in another, he had the glass cabinets and tables covered with letters from the war; in another, hundreds of books dedicated exclusively to the worldwide conflagration of 1914–1918. He had fought on the Italian front; they'd hit him in the chest, and his friend and companion (whose name I don't know; my grandfather sometimes called him "the African" because he was born in Sicily) had saved his life at the price of losing an arm. My grandfather had a deep scar on his chest from the war. He spent three months in a hospital tent, and then he was sent to the Second Army's post office (because he knew English, German, and French) to the section for letters from soldiers killed or missing in action. His work consisted of gathering personal effects—watches, wedding rings, family photos, unsent or half-written letters—and sending them, along with letters of condolence, to their relatives.

"Many died, so many every day, the offensives against the Austrian defenses were a massacre." What task could be more oppressive than sorting through letters of the dead and answering a mother, a son, a sister?

Incomplete letters, interrupted by death, messages from those missing, shot down, killed in the night, never knowing the dawn, said Grandpa. Pity for those who fell, frozen stiff, alone, sunken into the mud. "How can we give voice to the dead, hope to those who died without hope, relief to the phantoms that wander among the barbed-wire fences and under the white glare from the floodlights?"

Little by little, after months and months of struggling with these remains, he began to lose his mind: he clung to the letters and stopped sending them; he was, he told me, paralyzed, without willpower, without spirit, remembered almost nothing from that time, and, when they finally sent him home to Argentina with his family, he carried with him the words of those bound to die. I still have a French officer's binoculars, which Grandpa gave me when I turned eighteen; on the side you can make out "*Jumelle Militaire*," but the number of the regiment is scraped off with a knife or bayonet so that their fate cannot be discovered. In the metallic circle of the two smaller lenses is engraved "*Chevalier Opticien*," and, when you turn it around, there is a tiny compass between the two larger lenses that finds true north even now. Sometimes I lean out of the tenth-floor window and look out at the city with these magnifiers: a woman with her hair wrapped up in a red towel is talking on the telephone in a lit room; the minuscule and agile owners of the Korean supermarket on the corner move boxes and speak among themselves in shouts, as if they were arguing in a distant, incomprehensible language.

Why had he stolen these letters? He said nothing, looked at me, serene, with his clear eyes, and changed the subject. For him, I imagine, they were a testament to the unbearable experience of the endless frozen battles, a way of honoring the dead. He kept them with him, like someone saving letters written in a forgotten alphabet. He was furious, and his delusional speech still rings in my ears because sometimes, even today, I seem to hear him, and his voice returns to me in the most desperate moments.

"'Language . . . language . . .' my grandfather would say," said Renzi. "That weak and frenzied material, without a body, is a thin thread that intertwines the tiny ridges and superficial angles of human beings' solitary lives; it ties them up, why not, he would say, sure, it binds them, but only for an instant, before they once again sink into the same darkness in which they were submerged when they were born and howled unheard for the first time, in a far distant white room where, in darkness once again, they let loose their final cry before the end, from another white room, although once again, of course, their voices reached no one . . . "

In the room at the back of my grandfather's house was the library where I had found the blue book, which I now connect to Carlo Emilio Gadda's *Giornale di guerra e di prigonia* [*Diary of the War*]. I discovered it back in the time when I was studying in La Plata and would came to visit him. It was an edition of *La cognizione del dolore*. Gadda had lived in Argentina, and in his novel, which is set in a town in Córdoba, the inhabitants, terrified in a lawless setting, hire a team of private security and it is they, the guardians, who murder those Argentines in their insular community, one after another . . . A prophet! Gadda had understood everything at once in a novel from 1953.

How could one write about Argentina? It could be seen clearly in *The Seven Madmen*, in *Trans-Atlantyk*, and in *La cognizione del dolore*. The three are by extravagant writers, untranslatable, who do not travel well. They don't use much literary language, said Renzi. They look at everything with crossed eyes, obliquely; they are dyslexic, guttural stutterers: Arlt, Gombrowicz, Gadda. As for me, I, who was the son and grandson of Italians, have sometimes felt myself an Italian-Argentinian writer above all; I don't know if that category exists . . . but I see that the secret line of my life goes backward from the book, to *Heart* and to *La cognizione del dolore*, passing through "Ships arrive at the coast, bearing fruits from beyond." I would have liked to have been Carlo Emilio Gadda's nephew, but I have to resign myself, Renzi would say, to being only his voluntary but illegitimate and unrecognized descendant . . .

I will have to conclude the first part of the so-called story of the defining books of my life there, yet something remains, a detour, a slight change in direction, a sharp turn that I can share before I leave, he said, as he raised his final drink.

He raised his hand and made a circle in the air. Waiter, he said, just a bit more.

A time after the trip to the south, at age sixteen, I was courting, so to speak, he said, Elena: a beautiful girl, much more sophisticated than myself, with whom I studied in the third year at the National High School of Adrogué. One afternoon, we were coming down a street lined with trees next to a wall painted sky blue, which I can still see clearly, and she asked me what I was reading.

I, who had not read anything significant since the days of the upside-down book, remembered that, in the display of a bookshop, I had seen

Camus's *The Plague*, another book with a blue cover, which had just come out. Camus's *The Plague*, I told her. Can you lend it to me? she asked.

I remember that I bought the book, rumpled it a bit, read it in one night, and brought it with me to school the next day . . . I had discovered literature not for the book itself but for this feverish way of reading avidly with the intention of *saying* something to someone about what I had read. But why? The eternal question. It was a detached reading, directed, intentional, in my schoolboy's room, that night, under the circular light of the lamp . . . Out of Camus's work I'm not much interested in *The Plague*, but I remember the old man who always hit his dog and, when the dog finally escapes, he desolately searches for it throughout the city.

And how many books have I read, borrowed, stolen, loaned, lost since then? How much money have I invested, spent, squandered on books? I don't remember everything I have read, but I can reconstruct my life based on the shelves in my library. Times, places . . . I could organize the volumes chronologically. The oldest book is *The Plague*. Then there is a series of two: *This Business of Living* by Pavese and *Stendhal: par lui-même*. They were the first ones I bought and were followed by hundreds and hundreds of others. I have brought them and carried them with me like talismans or amulets, and I have put them on the shelves of rooms in hostels, apartments, homes, hotels, cells, hospitals.

One can see who one has been over the course of time only by making the rounds past the walls of the library: I heard a lecture by Attilio Dabini about Pavese and bought the book (because I, *too*, was writing a diary). *Stendhal: par lui-même* I found in the Hachette bookshop on Rivadavia Avenue. I remember the train when I returned to Adrogué and the guard who appeared in the corridor and didn't let me finish the sentence I was writing in the back of the book. It remained an incomplete sentence, that trace ("It's difficult to be sincere when you have lost . . . " what?). I don't know if it's a quote or one of *my own* phrases (the ones that don't come to mind when we read them again). I can see changes in the marks, underlinings, reading notes in the same book over the course of the years.

In *This Business of Living*, for example, by Raigal Publishers, translation by Luis Justo. It is signed with my initials, *ER*, with the date July 22, 1957. I annotated it with impressions in the margins or on the last page: "The diary as counter-conquest, or the many ways of losing a woman." I annotated with "see pg. 65." And some quotations: "Youth ends when we perceive that no one wants our gay abandon." And on the first blank page of the book, before the titles, there is one of so many lists that I've made, always with the intention of taking what I've written for granted: "Call Luis, Latin II (Tuesday and Thursday)," and, further down, one of so many superstitious annotations. In that moment, I was writing my first stories; I was *vividly* interested in knowing *how long* a writer takes to write a book, and I reconstructed the chronology of Pavese's work based on his diary:

> November 27, 1936 – April 15, 1937: *Il carcere.*
> June 3 – August 16, 1939: *Paese tuoi.*
> September, 1947 – February, 1948: *La casa en la colina.*
> June – October, 1948: *Il diavolo sulle colline.*
> March – June, 1949: *Tra donne sole.*
> September – November, 1949: *La luna e i falò.*

Back then, a short story only five pages long would take me three months.

The Plague and *This Business of Living* were the first books that were my own, so to speak, and my latest book I got yesterday afternoon, *The Black-Eyed Blonde: A Philip Marlowe Novel* by Benjamin Black, a gift from Giorgio, a friend. You must write something, he tells me, Renzi said, he's like Chandler but missing . . . What's missing? my friend asked. The *touch*, I thought, he's missing the *grit*, as tango dancers say when a tango is played just "*fine* . . . "

Renzi opened the book and read: "*It was one of those Tuesdays in summer when you begin to wonder if the earth has stopped revolving.*" So it begins: it's the same, but not the same (maybe because we *know* that it isn't Chandler . . .).

Too many pastiches, old man, this time of year, he said now; too many parodies, I prefer direct plagiarism . . .

You could lend it to me, Elena said to me. I don't know what became of her afterward, but if she hadn't asked me that question, who knows what would have become of me . . . There is no destiny now, no oracles. *It isn't certain* that everything in life is written in stone, but, I think sometimes, if I had not read that book, or rather, if I had not seen it in the shop window, perhaps I would not be here. Or if she had not asked me, no? Who knows . . . I exaggerate, in retrospect, but I passionately remember that reading—a room at the back, a desk lamp. What to say to a woman about a novel? Retell the whole thing yourself? The book wasn't worth much—too allegorical, a heavy style, deep, overwrought—but, all in all, something happened there, there was a change . . . Nothing special, a trifle, the truth, but that night, speaking figuratively, I was on the threshold once more: knowing nothing of anything, making a show of reading . . .

"Oh fortune, flowers, the girls in bloom . . . I'm seventy-three, an old man, and I go on like this, sitting with a book, waiting . . . "

My father, he said later, was imprisoned for almost a year because he went to defend Perón in '55 and suddenly Argentinian history seemed a conspiracy woven to destroy him. He was cornered, and he decided to escape. In December of 1957 we abandoned Adrogué, half in secret, and went to live in Mar del Plata. It was in those days, mid-escape, in one of the dismantled bedrooms of the house, that I started to write a diary. What was I looking for? To deny reality, to reject what was coming. To this day I still write this diary. Many things have changed since then, but I have remained faithful to this obsession.

There is no evolution, we scarcely move, fixed to our old shameful passions; the only virtue, I believe, is to persist without changing, to go on, faithful to the old books, the ancient readings. My old friends, on the other hand, aspire as they age to be what they once hated; everything they once detested they now admire. Since we cannot change anything, they think, let's change appearances. Entire libraries burned in the incinerator and buried in the backyard . . . It's hard to get rid of books, but what about our way of reading? They go on as always, dogmatic readers, literal, they say different things with the same haughty wisdom of the old days. We live in the error of thinking that our old friends are with us. Impossible! We've read the same books and loved the same women (for example, Junior), and we save some letters that we were not and are not able to send away or to burn in the bonfires of time, and that, then, would be the subject of my autobiography, if someday I decided to write one . . .

My grandfather (since I started with him) died in 1968, almost fifty years after the end of the war he had fought in, and the man missing an arm was with us at the burial, but not Natalia. Who knows what became of that woman? She was as beautiful as a goddess and sang, I remember, when she was happy . . .

It was almost night now. Outside, the asphalt shone under the warm lights of the city. It was time to leave, to return home.

"We ought to go."

We went out to the street and, as we went toward Charcas (no longer called Charcas), walking slowly because Emilio had a little problem with his left leg ("The result of bad habits, the economic crisis, Peronism, rough nights"), we decided to stop for a bit of coffee at the Filippo bar on the corner of Callao and Santa Fe, and at that point Emilio decided to add an epilogue to what he had told me so far, a conclusion, *a visit*, he stressed as he savored the coffee. An encounter that could be understood, with a bit of good will and favorable wind, as the end of his literary education, or something like that. A bridge, he said, a rite of passage.

Once at the student center we organized a lecture series and decided, of course, to begin with old Borges. I called him on the phone to invite him and he accepted at once. He met me at the National Library, friendly, with his indecisive tone, seeming always on the point of losing the thread of what he was saying. Immediately he spoke to me of La Plata, where his friend the poet Paco López Merino lived, whom he visited frequently. One Sunday, at home, Borges tells me, explained Renzi, before leaving after they had lunch, his friend insisted on saying hello to Borges's father, who, as was the custom among the old European *criollo* class, was taking siesta. After some scheming, they decided to accompany him to the bedroom.

Doctor, I'd like to say goodbye to you, said López Merino.

They all felt uncomfortable, but since they liked him they accepted the insistent but friendly request, and Doctor Borges, with a calm smile, gave him a hug . . . Upon leaving, López Merino saw Güiraldes's guitar, which the author of *Don Segundo Sombra* had presented to Borges's mother before leaving for Paris, and López Merino made it sing, softly.

It's out of tune; it never was very good, this guitar, the poet said maliciously, Borges recounted, and Borges added, said Renzi, it sounds hostile, but it was just a joke among friends.

The truth was that López Merino shot himself the next day, and then they understood the imperative and serious manner of his final farewell.

Beautiful, isn't it? said Borges with a tired smile, as if the elegance of the secret goodbye had moved him.

He had an immediate and warm way of creating intimacy, Borges, said Renzi; he was always that way with everyone he talked to: he was blind and did not see them, and he always spoke to them as if they were near, and that closeness is in his writings; he is never patronizing and gives no air of superiority, he addresses everyone as if they were more intelligent than he, with so much intimation that he has no need to explain what is already known. And it is that intimacy that his readers sense.

He loved the prospect of going to La Plata, he was thinking of speaking about Lugones's fantastical stories, what did I think? he said. Perfect, I told him, what's more, Borges, look, we're going to pay you, I don't know quite how much it is right now, let's say about fifteen hundred dollars.

"No," he said, "that's a lot."

I was taken aback. Look, Borges, I'm telling you, it's not our money, it's not the students' money, the University is giving us a fund.

"It doesn't matter, I'll charge you two hundred fifty."

And we went on talking, he went on talking, I don't remember now if it was about Lugones or Chesterton, but the truth is that I felt so comfortable, so close to him, with that feeling of brightness, of clear intelligence and complicity, that a while later, almost without realizing it, while speaking about the endings of Kipling's stories, I said to him, emboldened by the climate of intimacy and grateful for the sensation of talking to someone as an equal: "You know, Borges, I see a problem with the end of 'The Form of the Sword.'"

He raised his face toward me, alert.

"A problem," I said. "Hell, you might call it a defect . . . Something extra."

He looked into the air now, cheerful, expectant.

The story is told with a technique that Borges had already used in "Streetcorner Man" and would use again later: it is told by a traitor and murderer as though he were someone else.

The man who narrates the story has a round and "spiteful scar" across his face. At one point in his tale he faces an informant and marks his face with a curved sword. One realizes then that the man telling the story is the traitor, as the scar identifies him. Borges, however, goes on with the story and closes it with an explanation. "Borges," he says, "I am Vincent Moon. Now despise me." He listened to my summary of the story with signs of agreement and repeated in a soft voice, "Yes . . . now despise me."

"Don't you think that explanation is excessive? It's superfluous, I think."

There was a silence. Borges smiled, compassionate and cruel.

"Ah," he said. "You write stories, too . . . "

I was twenty years old, I was arrogant, I was more of a fool than I am now, but I realized that what Borges had said meant two things. Generally, if someone confronted him in the street to say, "Borges, I am a writer," he would answer "Ah, so am I," and the conversant would sink into the void. There was a subtle wickedness and calm arrogance in that sentence: "This rude kid thinks he writes stories . . . "

The other assertion was more benevolent and might have meant, "You already read as if you were a writer, you understand the way in which texts are constructed and want to see how they are made, to see if you can do something similar or, ideally, something different." Writing, he was telling me, above all changes one's way of reading.

We went on talking a bit longer, and I was distracted and embarrassed and sort of numb. Borges showed me Groussac's circular writing desk, which he passed over with his magnificent pale hand, the hand with which he had written "Tlön, Uqbar, Orbis Tertius" and "The Superstitious Ethics of the Reader."

I realize that Borges has always been a classical story writer: his endings are closed, with everything explained clearly; the sense of amazement is not in the form—always plain and clear—or in the organized and precise endings, but in the incredible density and heterogeneity of the narrative material.

He kindly accompanied me to the door and before saying goodbye added one last thing, as if to stop me from forgetting his lesson on well-closed stories:

"I got quite a good deal, didn't I?" old Borges said, amused with himself.

In short, he buried me, but he recognized me as a writer, didn't he? said Renzi. I had written two or three stories, horrible, poorly ended, but in short, hope must be confirmed once in a while, even if it's by way of humiliation and fright. Therefore, the young—and the not-so-young—go around with their writings, looking for someone to read them and to say, "Ah, you write, too." Of course they put them up on the web now, but they lack qualification in the same way, for someone to say to them—personally—you are on this side, too . . .

I talk too much, I get judgmental and apodictic, as is fitting for a man of my age, he kept thinking. Now we were at the door of the building on Calle Charcas (ex-Charcas) at number eighteen hundred. Maybe he thought he was going to die in that war, my grandfather, but he went all the same. An act of heroism, to go. I would not have driven myself to it, said Emilio as he opened the entry door, held it with his body, and turned around, smiling.

"One of these afternoons I'll finish the story for you . . . We'll see each other, dear," he said, and with an uncertain walk he entered the hall in search of the elevator.

It was already completely dark, and I saw him go up, enveloped in a yellowish light, his eyes beaming and a smile of satisfaction illuminating his face, as if he were still thinking about the girl who had asked him to borrow the book by Albert Camus.

2

First Diary (1957–1958)

Wednesday

We are leaving the day after tomorrow. I decided not to say goodbye to anyone. Saying goodbye to people seems ridiculous to me. Wave to the people coming, not the ones leaving. I won at billiards, made two nine-point shots. I had never played so well. My heart was frozen still, and I shot the cue with perfect precision. I felt like I was constructing the hits with my thoughts. Playing billiards is simple; you have to stay cool and know how to look ahead. Afterward, we went to the pool and stayed until very late. I dove off of the high board. From so high up, the lights from the tennis courts floated on the water. It feels like everything I'm doing is for the last time.

Saturday

The move, in the middle of the night. "We left at dawn, furtive, ashamed." There was a light on in the Yugoslavs' kitchen, on the other side of Calle Bynon. The truck weighed down with furniture, the house dismantled. The stupid docility of the plains; a falcon in the sky, its talons stretched forward like meat hooks, almost sitting in the air, captures, in its low flight, a guinea pig and carries it off with the slow, deep flapping of its wings. We pause at noon in a stand of trees, the dog runs round and round in the field. My father says, "Look, a tramp made a little fire in this well," and he touches the ash with the back of his hand. In the shade, he makes a note in his black notebook, sitting in the weeds, his back against a poplar. He raises his eyes from the notebook, and off in the distance, a dark point amid the immense brightness, I see the far-off figure of the tramp moving on foot through the country toward another stand of trees where he can light a fire and make yerba maté. This tiny event (and my father's words) comes to mind many times over the course of the day, with no relation to anything happening in the present—clear in my memory, unexpected, as if it were a coded message hiding a secret meaning.

Monday

We spend Christmas Eve in Carranza's house; he is a friend of the movement, my father says. All rather cheerless. Mom barely speaks and does nothing but read novels and use unexpected words (as she always does when she's unwell): "This salad's a bit *dilapidated*." At night she gets up two or three times to see if I'm sleeping or if I need anything (she wakes me up!). She is nervous, rarely goes out, suffers but never complains. Her world collapsed (her sisters, her friends), but she traveled with Dad for "solidarity" more than anything else. ("She wasn't going to leave this *good-for-nothing* on his own."). At Christmas Eve dinner she refused to drink at the toast because she said it would "unsettle her."

Tuesday

The house has two floors. The office is downstairs, with the waiting room in front, and to one side is a large room that opens onto the street, two bedrooms, the kitchen, and a patio. My room is upstairs, along with a living room, a little kitchen, and a balcony. I settled in there and brought up the few books I had brought. The window of my room opens over the blue flowers of the Jacaranda tree on the lane. In a tight spot, I could climb out onto the branches.

Thursday

I think I must go back, live with Grandpa Emilio. I write to Elena to cheer myself up, and I announce my plans to her, but she does not believe me. ("If you're going to come, come and I'll be ready, but don't tell me about it every five minutes."). It isn't every five minutes; I write to her every night (not today) with the day's news and my states of mind. At the end of the letter she draws Landrú's cat and writes, "I miss you and miss you. I cry all the time in the corner, like the silly little flower that I am."

Monday
At the beach, yesterday and the day before yesterday and today. It's not the same swimming in the sea as swimming in a pool, the same as the difference between living and reading. "Which do you like more? You, you, which do you *like more*?" (stressed). Elena's questions.

Tuesday
My father, from the office, asks me every time I go out to the street whether I have my papers. Mom, who is on the patio, always reading her novels, raises her eyes: "They're going to arrest you just for being *descended from him.*" *Descended*, I think, in free fall.

Friday
Elena, oh Elena . . . She writes to me: "I dreamed about you twice, a dream the night before last and another last night. We would leave the house to take the San Vicente bus, but something would always happen and we wouldn't end up going (you braided my hair, in the garden). In the end, as we were going out to the street, I woke up. I drank some water, my hair was in my face. Last night I dreamed again, and this time we were together on the bus! Isn't that funny, two dreams, one following the other? Andrea says it's a good omen, but it scared me. This morning I woke up very sick (Emilio, am I pregnant?)."

Thursday
False alarm (Galli Mainini test).

I am reading *The Seven Who Were Hanged* by Andreyev. The condemned in the book are all freethinkers, *nihilists*. They will be executed at dawn; time does not pass, and yet it is always later—or earlier—than they imagine. Impossible to *describe* this waiting. "Death was not there as yet, but life was there no longer." A revolutionary, the heroine, thinks, "I should like to do this—I should like to go out alone before a whole regiment of soldiers and fire upon them with a light revolver. It would not matter that I would be alone, while they would be thousands, or that I might not kill any of them." (Isn't the realism incredible? But "*light* revolver" is perfect.)

Monday
My father still recalls some fragments of the letters that his father would send from the front, when he (my father . . . oh the pronouns) was a boy and his mother would read them aloud to him by the fireplace: "I was crying, General Gialdini was crying, all of the soldiers were crying," which leaves me intrigued as to the content of the letter. It makes sense that a boy would always remember that passage; it is unforgettable to discover in childhood that your father cries, that men cry, and that even a veteran general in the army could cry . . .

The wonderful thing about childhood is that everything is real. The grown man (!) is one who lives a life of fiction, trapped by delusions and dreams that allow him to survive.

For this reason, the shards of past experiences leave the sort of impressions that one remembers without entirely understanding; they are light and sharp, like a foil thrusting forth to pierce the heart. For this reason, these memories are so clear and so incomprehensible, because then, now, in youth, one becomes lost. In my case, I am in the middle of the river, I have lost the sense of total certainty of childhood and have no illusion that it sustains me.

Tuesday
We move a library to the upstairs floor because Mom has set up a loom in the living room. She is going to weave a red and yellow bedspread, with fine wool. "So your father wakes up," she says. She learned how to

weave when she was young, in the nuns' school. "These handicrafts," she likes the word and repeats it, "these handicrafts, *hijito*, you don't forget them, it's like riding a bicycle or making the sign of the cross, they don't leave you . . . "

Sunday
I've written my daily letter to Elena; the postal workers' strike has the effect of a raised drawbridge. So I'm outside of the besieged city . . .

Monday
My mother has a personal witch doctor. She calls him Don José, but I call him Yambó to tease her. I don't like the guy at all. Pale skin, fish eyes—he must be half Umbanda (a *pai do santo*). Mom already saw him in Buenos Aires; the guy warned her back in September that Dad was going to get arrested, but he didn't pay any attention, and she never forgave him for it. Now he comes to Mar de Plata specially. He has clients there and stays in the vacation cottage close to the house, on Calle España, almost at Calle Moreno. The guy speaks and diagnoses. He doesn't use tarot cards, doesn't look in a crystal ball; he says whatever occurs to him. At night, eating dinner, Mom says he told her she was going to go live in a cold place. In Ushuaia, while Dad would be behind bars, I tell her. She laughs. "Don't talk *hogwash*." (Whenever she's acting odd she uses these strange words). Now she's reading Knut Hamsun (the collection bound in blue from Aguilar on bible paper that holds five or six novels per volume). "*Hunger*, they'll have to read it," she says, not addressing anyone in particular, "so that they (she pluralizes) can see what it's like to scrounge." When she isn't reading novels, she looks nervous and argues with Dad ("Can you tell me why we came to this *opprobrious* city?"). Opprobrious city, that's not so bad.

Thursday
There's a postal workers' strike, so I don't get a letter from Elena and can't send the ones I've written to her (I have three). An unsettling interval.

Will she know it is because of the strike? (I'm going to call her tonight.) The strike will accumulate so much delayed correspondence that it's pointless to think the letters I sent will arrive.

Possible careless treatments of loving correspondence: the postman burns them; the messenger is kidnapped violently. The letters that don't reach their destination, how many will there be? Lovers interrupted by the union uprising: it's an interesting subject for a novel. Political history does not permit our love . . .

Monday
The funny thing is that Dad saw one of the delegates for the Internal Commission of Central Post on Calle Luro in his office (the guy signed in as sick and waited his turn in the living room). Surely he parrots Perón's doctrine (now that we're reconciling with Frondizi we have to "tighten things up . . . "). Don't worry, Doctor, we won't deliver a single letter to those turncoats, etc. (And my son's letters, you couldn't take them to his friends? he might have said). The letters don't go out until Wednesday . . .

Thursday
If I'm bored and I spend the day without talking to anyone, I let myself be carried away by murderous impulses. Today I pushed a half-crippled old man I stumbled into on Calle Mitre. "Hey, want to get out of my way?" I said to him, and while he apologized politely I gave him a judo-style elbow and he stood gasping half-bent over on the side of the church. A while ago I threw the kitten against the wall. It bounced like a ball with a terrified meow, all of its hair standing on end and all four feet splayed a meter above the floor, and no sooner did it fall than it dove behind the dresser (and is staying there), and that's my own cat, Fermín, and I like how he spends a long time watching the cloudless sky. I don't answer Mom and she gets really angry. Look, Emilio, don't get funny with me. She says "*Emiiliio*," when she's angry, like scratching a blackboard (*Emiiliio*); otherwise she calls me "son" or "dear" or "M" and speaks formally (and

that infuriates me). In my family, it's very common to speak formally; it always seems like they're messing with you. "You ought to send your regards once in a while," said my Uncle Mario when he said goodbye.

Thursday

Jorge is in Julio's house; we talk for a while. The narrator, should he be unreliable or distant? Unreliable: Dostoevsky, Faulkner; distant: Hemingway, Camus in *The Stranger*. Eduardo G. arrives with his experienced air. "I've got cash," he says, and we put together a game of poker. I lose, I lose (with a full house), I lose all evening and finally win a big pile with a royal flush because Eduardo thinks I'm bluffing (he has a pair of kings and bets everything). He leaves furious because it *seems to him* that I played a trick. I say nothing, he wants me to *believe* he caught me cheating (we go on with this, out in the street and later in the bar on Independencia and Colón with the jukebox, listening to Frankie Laine). When Eduardo—as Dostoevsky would say—believes, he believes that he does not believe, and when he does not believe, he believes that he believes . . . and he loses everything. If only I were a *liar*. A disillusioned young cheater (who knows all the ladies), he travels by train through the provinces, gets off at lost stations, stops in at the plaza hotel, makes a show paying for drinks, with the air of a bored traveler, half-innocent, wakes up all the little widows in town; he accepts a game of poker in the social club the night before moving on . . .

Sunday

In the Ambos Mundos bar, with the members of the film club, is the Englishman—tall, wearing a hat, in a white pilot suit (a costume); he speaks with a strong accent, is working for an American company at the port that exports fish. He set out from Alaska, and they say he is a well-known writer in New York, Steve M. He's always joking. Last night he showed off a six-page letter and said it was from Malcolm Lowry. Apparently he wrote his thesis on *Under the Volcano* at Columbia in '53 (the first thesis in the world about the novel, he said, as if it were a heroic deed). Here, no one knows this book, even though Oscar Garaycochea, who is a genius, remembered *The Lost Weekend*, the Billy Wilder film, because there was a reference to Lowry in *Sight and Sound* magazine. "Yes," said Steve, "Lowry almost went crazy when that film premiered." He knew him personally; he visited him in Canada and Lowry spent a week in Steve's apartment in Brooklyn. He had to hide the whiskey from him, according to Steve, who, at the same time, is getting drunk little by little. Lowry took his bottle of aftershave lotion. Is he lying? It could be. He's brilliant, very entertaining, and he already picked up all the girls from the national school who came there that afternoon.

I wrote down some of the things he said: "Lowry wasn't a novelist, he was a pure autobiographical writer. He wrote many personal diaries, a frenetic writer of letters." He made seven versions of *Under the Volcano*. He said he would give us the novel if we read it in the bar. "I'm renting it," he said. "Illegal to lend it out." The novel takes place in Mexico.

Saturday
Compare Holden Caulfield and Silvio Astier: the two are sixteen years old (*like me*). One complains, has existential problems, wants to go to live alone in a forest; the other has no money, steals books from a school, wants to be a writer and rebel in the city. See the scene in *Mad Toy* of Astier with the boy who wears women's stockings in the one-peso hotel, on Talcahuano and Tucumán, and the scene in *Catcher* of Holden with Carl Bruce in the Wicker Bar at the Seton Hotel. Holden is lyrical, rebellious, sensitive (the little sister); Silvio is desperate, has no exit, and is a whistle-blower. In Salinger the orality is light, lexical, self-pitying; in Arlt it is harsh, antisentimental, syntactical.

According to Steve, Lowry had to change the initial name of the character of the consul, William Erikson, because he found out about the murder of an American with the same name who died in the same way.

Wednesday

News in today's papers (May 21, 1958). Side A: "A submarine of unknown nationality was attacked by the Argentine Navy in Golfo Nuevo. The damaged vessel managed to disappear." Side B: "The British Admiralty announced that the submarine *Avhros* was damaged in waters of the Atlantic Ocean by an unidentified airplane." The only people who believe the news in the papers, says my father, are the journalists. True, says my mother, only the people who wrote it believe what they've read. Lately she is witty, Ida—happier, very clever. The other day she said, "My brain is running cold you know, like it was in the *Frigidaire*."

Sunday

In Mar del Plata the theaters stay active out of season, and to attract the public they show three different movies every day at reduced prices. I take the bus, see one at Gran Mar on Colón Avenue at two in the afternoon, another in Ópera on Calle Independencia at four, another at Ocean on Luro at six, another at Atlantic at eight, and another at ten at the Belgian Theater, on the same corner as our house. I spend all my time at theaters from Monday to Friday, as if I were a madman who had been deprived of movies, a beggar who just wants to sit quietly in the dark rooms, or a nomadic film fanatic. Saturdays and Sundays the program doesn't change, so I stay at home. Theater is faster than life, literature is slower.

Over the course of those weeks I saw: *OSS 117*, based on the spy novel by Jean Bruce; *Barabbas* by Alf Sjöberg, based on the novel by Pär Lagerkvist; *Behind a Long Wall* by Lucas Demare; *A Hole in the Head* by Frank Capra; *The Hidden Fortress* by Kurosawa; *O.K. Corral* by John Sturges; *Ugetsu Monogatari* by Mizoguchi; *The Set-Up* by R. Wise; *I Vitelloni* by Fellini; *The Burmese Harp* by Ichikawa; *Roman Holiday* by W. Wyler; *Rear Window* by Hitchcock; *Citizen Kane* by Welles; *Tiger Bay* by J. Lee Thompson; *Prawdziwy koniec wielkiej wojny* [*The Real End of the Great War*] by Kawalerowicz; *The Quiet Man* by John Ford; *Picnic* by Joshua Logan; *Little Fugitive* by Morris Engel; *Wind Across the Everglades* by Nicholas

Ray; *The Barefoot Contessa* by J. Mankiewicz; *A Man Escaped* by Bresson; *The Nights of Cabiria* by Fellini; *The Informer* by John Ford.

Monday

At the high school we're on strike against the repeal of Article 28, which gives free universities the ability to award degrees of professorship. They're all Catholic. Secular or free.

Tuesday

I discover that the greatest elegance of style depends on the invisible precision of prepositional constructions. According to my mother, Arlt always messes up. Defects are virtues, I tell her. The inverse is true, says my mother, as long as you "drive" at the speed limit and stay consistent. I spend the afternoon at home inventing phrases. The knock made my binoculars fall *to* the floor. The postman had one of those noses, the end *of* which always seems to be *on* the point *of* dripping. Not only did my father find success without knowing it, but it was also useless for his life. Elena was horrified *by* the murky water. She and her sister were horrified *at* the filthiness of the pernicious puddle.

Thursday

The school is still taken over. I spend the night in the chemistry classroom, watching over Calle Hipólito Yrigoyen. No police or Tacuaras of the Catholic right wing can be seen. We sleep in the hallways, some drink yerba maté, there is discussion going on all the time. Weapons I didn't see—slingshots over there, Molotov cocktails. The girls are with us. What do those gorillas believe? asks Elena (another Elena), buxom, with braids, legs like a goddess, wearing a tartan skirt with a large safety pin just at the height of her groin.

Saturday

I went over to Julio's house. We discuss Secular versus Free. What Secular? he says. The Russian shit? I'm a skeptical freethinker, he says.

A contradiction, I say. Well, I'm an anarchist then, and what's more I think there's some higher power in the universe. Ah, well, I say, an esoteric anarchist. We listen to *The Student Prince*, by Mario Lanza. We like operettas. Alejandra Achipenko will lend us *The Threepenny Opera* by Bertolt Brecht and Kurt Weill sung by Lotte Lenya. In the afternoon, at the theater with Julio and Jorge, we saw *The Cranes Are Flying* by M. Kalatozov—Russian, Walt Disney style but with soldiers returning from the war.

Wednesday

I went to school and refused to go up to the flag. In French class, the professor lent me Sartre's *Nausea*. I read it halfway through, all in one go, after classes, in the bar. What stands out is the scene with the door knocker. Roquentin watches it as if it were a creature: it is both alive and inanimate. He can't bring himself to touch it.

Sunday

Steve takes an interest when he learns that my father is a doctor and has been to prison. Only someone who has been in prison can speak of sicknesses, he says. He wants my father to be his personal doctor. They start up a fantastic conversation about alcohol. Incidentally, says my father, everything that has been written about the drink is ridiculous. You have to start at the beginning again. Drinking is a serious activity and has always been associated with philosophy. Someone who drinks, Steve says, is trying to dissolve an obsession. You must first define the extent of the obsession, says my father. There is nothing more beautiful and unsettling than a fixed idea. Motionless, constrained, an axis, a magnetic pole, a psychic field of forces that attracts and devours everything it encounters. Have you ever seen a magnetized light? Steve asks. It swallows up all the insects that approach it, treats them as if they were made of iron. I have seen a butterfly fly ceaselessly in the same place until it dies of exhaustion, my father says. Everyone speaks of obsessions, says Steve, but no one explains them quite as they are.

Obsession builds itself up, says my father. I have seen obsessions build up like castles of sand. One incident alone is enough to alter our lives drastically. An incident or a person, says my father, the kind where we can't distinguish whether our lives have changed for good or bad. The structure of a paradox, Steve says, an incident that is doubled or doubtful in its being. It marks us, but it is morally ambiguous. People move toward the future, my father says, off-center, disoriented, off the road they followed in the past. An amputation, says my father, of the sense of orientation. Obsession makes us lose our sense of time, you confuse the past with remorse.

Prison is a factory for stories, my father says. Time and again, they all tell the same tales. What they have done before, but most of all what they are going to do. They listen to one another, compassionately. What is important is the narration, no matter if the story is impossible or if no one believes it. The opposite of the art of the novel, says Steve, which is founded on the hope of converting its readers into believers.

You would have to be outside of the world of the prison, my father says, to be interested in the prisoners' stories. But those stories are intended precisely for the others who share the prison. They also differ from the art of the novel in that way, Steve says; the personal stories must be told only to strangers and unknown people.

Someone does something that no one understands, an act that exceeds everyone's experiences. That act does not last, has the pure quality of life, is not narrative but is the only thing that it makes sense to narrate.

In the high school, on strike since Wednesday, all are coming and going, furious over Frondizi's (unexpected?) attack on Article 28 against the public school, bastion of the liberal past. A kind of insult to Sarmiento and the other founding fathers, which none of us seem willing to tolerate. Where did this decision come from? From a pretense of "modernization," which has always been the argument of the right wing in Argentina. A way of burying a culture and making another, more "realistic," more "modern," and, above all, more cynical.

Friday

Last night I argued with a communist and Julio until two in the morning. The communist, an industrial student, kindhearted, rejects all art that does not come from or go to the people. And who decides where the people go? I say. Julio dodges the question; it's all the same to him, he's a nihilist. I didn't do anything in particular, just wrote to Elena (the one from back there). The other one, the one from here, is Helena with an *H*.

3

First Love

I fell in love for the first time when I was twelve years old. In the middle of class, a girl with red hair appeared, and the teacher presented her as a new student. She stood at the side of the blackboard and was called (or is called) Clara Schultz. I remember nothing of the following weeks, but I know that we had fallen in love and were trying to hide it because we were children and knew that we wanted something impossible. Some memories still hurt me. The others stared at us in line and she turned redder and redder, and I learned what it was to suffer the complicity of fools. When school got out I would fight with kids from the fifth and sixth grades who followed her to throw thistles in her hair, because she wore it loose, down to her waist. One afternoon I came home so beaten up that my mother thought I'd gone crazy or had been gripped by a suicidal mania. I could tell no one what I was feeling and appeared sullen and humiliated, as though I was always exhausted. We wrote each other letters, even though we barely knew how to write. I remember an unsteady succession of ecstasy and desperation; I remember that she was serious and passionate and that she never smiled, perhaps because she knew the future. I have no photographs, only her memory, but in every woman I've loved there has been something of Clara. She left as she came, unexpectedly, before the end of the year. One afternoon she did something heroic and broke all the rules and came running onto the boys' courtyard to tell me they were taking her away. I carry the image of the two of us in the middle of the black flagstones and the sarcastic circle of eyes that watched us. Her father was a municipal inspector or a bank manager, and they were transferring him to Sierra de la Ventana. I remember the horror caused in me by the image of a mountain range that was also a prison. That was why she had come at the start of the year and that, perhaps, was why she had loved me. The pain was so great that I managed to remember my mother saying that if you loved someone you had to put a mirror on your pillow, because if you saw her sleeping reflection you would marry her. And at night, when everyone in the house had gone to sleep, I walked barefoot to the patio out back and took down the mirror that my dad used to shave in the morning. It was a square mirror, with a frame of brown wood, hung from a nail in the wall by a small chain. I slept in intervals, trying to see her reflection sleeping next to me, and sometimes I imagined I saw her at the edge of the mirror. One night many years later, I dreamed that I dreamed of her in the mirror. I saw her just as she had been as a girl, with her red hair and serious eyes. I was different, but she was the same and came toward me as if she were my daughter.

4

Second Diary (1959–1960)

November 2, 1959

We go to the sea while summer still has yet to begin; there is no time like the end of spring, when the dark days of winter have gone and the beach lies empty. I always go to La Perla, take Independencia straight all the way to the coast. I became friends with Roque, an ex coastguard, a retired lifesaver who keeps coming to the beach and watching to make sure no one is in danger. He has a slight limp and totters a bit when he walks, but when he's in the water he swims like a dolphin, graceful and fast. "We should live in the water," he tells me, and muses on this for a while. "We came from there, and sooner or later we're going to go back to living in the oceans."

He runs an empty hotel, which stands on a hill, facing the park, a great building painted in blue: Hotel del Mar. I went to visit him a couple times; there are rooms upon rooms, unoccupied, down the length of a hallway. He sleeps in different beds—so that the rooms stay aerated, he says. He always keeps a portable Spica radio with him and listens to it all the time. He tells me that he was a singer in his younger days. He shows me a card with him dressed as a gaucho, wearing a sombrero and plucking a guitar; above, in the left corner, there is a little Argentine flag. The inscription reads, "Agustín Peco, National Singer." This was in the forties, when they had "live numbers" in the movie theaters, and artists from a variety of genres entertained the public from the stage in the interval between one showing and another. Roque sang the repertoire of Ignacio Corsini, milonga dances, and folk songs with lyrics by Héctor Blomberg, describing the era of General Rosas. One time at the beach, a little drunk after lunch, he sang, under the sun, unaccompanied, "The Barmaid from Santa Lucía," which is one of my father's favorite songs.

The other day I went far out into the sea, and as I was on the way back I got into a riptide and the current wouldn't let me advance; the high waves before the first breaker threw me out to sea. I wasn't frightened or anything, but my breath failed me and Roque guided me to the shore with shouts and waves. He did not get into the water, but he helped me make it out by motioning for me to swim diagonally, distancing myself from the line of cold, and to keep moving toward the long jetty. Once I was within range, he dove in and pulled me out, swimming with one arm.

November 4
Yesterday a girl, lying on a yellow sailcloth on the empty beach, was watching me. She is from Buenos Aires, came with her mother for a few days. We understood each other immediately. Her name is Lidia; she is beautiful and kind. I kissed her on the staircase leading to the house, where we had sat down together. "Don't worry, *pajarito*," she said to me afterward, as if talking to herself. "No one gets pregnant from a kiss and a hug."

Thursday
I was with Lidia constantly during those days at La Perla; we find each other in the morning and stay together talking until the sun sets and she leaves. She is staying in the Saint James building on Calle Luro. She is intelligent and entertaining. I told her we had come to Mar del Plata to escape from the police because my father was in debt. I could, in that way, speak very openly with her because I was not talking about myself; I am someone else when I am with her (I feel like someone else, a stranger, and that feeling is priceless); I told her I was a writer. That I wanted to

be a writer, anyway. She laughs with a cheerful and contagious laughter, and she made me promise to take her to the alumni dance at the Hotel Provincial.

December

Those final weeks I spent with Lidia; I introduced her to Roque so that we could go to bed in the empty but furnished and mysterious rooms of the hotel. She left at the end of the month and, before leaving, she said that she loved me, that we had spent unforgettable days together. And then, with an enchanting motion, she brushed her hair from her eyes and told me that she was going to Buenos Aires to get married. I was crushed. She was getting married soon and had come to Mar del Plata in search of an adventure for the final days of her single life. You don't know my name or who I am; you told me that your name is Emilio and that you are a writer. One lies while infatuated and living out a fleeting adventure. I was paralyzed. She left on Monday and did not let me go to say goodbye to her in the station. I'm going to miss you, she said, and I'm not going to forget you. She was lying. But it doesn't matter; lies, she told me, make life easier to bear.

Sunday

A rendezvous in a bar with tables on the sidewalk, across from the Hotel Nogaró. She, tender and compassionate, tries to find a way to get rid of my pain, without seeing that for me it is a leap into the void, returning home or going to the beach in the afternoons, hidden behind a novel.

An intense rendezvous with the woman, serious for me and like a game for her. She will be married in March.

Now as always, I wait for her. "I'll come back. I'll call you. Wait for me." Empty words to alleviate the goodbye. She does not know what this has meant to me. If I look at things indifferently, I say: What can you expect? Unexpected summer passion with the first guy to appear on the empty

November beach. Three months before her marriage to an attorney, a friend of her father's.

So as not to put her under pressure, I did not ask for her real name or her address in Buenos Aires. Very gracious, but really I didn't ask because I didn't want to her say she wouldn't tell me.

Wednesday
Roque laughs when I tell him the story of my romance with Lidia. Women are more fearless than men, they are faithful to what they desire and not concerned with the consequences. Nothing of her was left to me, not even a photograph or a memory. I was fond of the way she would brush her hair from her face with a motion that seemed to illuminate her. I gave her my phone number and she hid the paper inside a powder compact. Strange, but, of course, she doesn't want her husband to find proof of her adultery.

"Adultery" is an intriguing word.

Wednesday
Things are becoming clear in my other life. By chance I went with the Mar del Plata students to a talk at La Plata, where I understood immediately that this would be my point of escape. They rent cheap rooms in student hostels, and you can eat in the university dining hall for five pesos per meal. Now it is decided that I will go to live in La Plata, but I still do not know what I will do there.

I bought the three volumes of Sartre's *The Roads to Freedom* for two hundred and sixty pesos at the Erasmo bookshop. I went to the courts with Cabello and Dabrosky to watch the Boca Juniors game. I went to the movie theater: Billy Wilder's *Some Like It Hot*. Marilyn Monroe's body, singing with a tiny banjo in the corridor of the train. Two men disguised as ladies in a band of women.

Helena (with an *H*) gave me an Aktemin, an amphetamine that kept me up all night with extraordinary thoughts that I forgot immediately. I'm studying trigonometry.

I bought new shoes and went out in them to walk down Rivadavia, all self-assured. A half-hour later I started to come to my senses and closed myself up in a theater so as not to think. I saw *High Society*, a musical.

A penchant for positive forecasts, blind confidence in the future. I expect to break expectations, to spend the summer in peace.

Last night I read "The Overcoat" by Gogol ("we all come out of Gogol's overcoat," Dostoevsky said) with his tone of rabid orality: unforgettable. But Kafka comes out of there, too: his comical drama revolves around a coat. It is similar to dreams, where an insignificant object—lost, found, glimpsed—produces devastating effects. The minuscule cause creates brutal consequences. A great narrative strategy: events do not matter; their consequences matter. Here, waiting in a public office takes on the fear and excitement of an epic tale.

I don't believe I'm a paleface or a redskin, but the girls take an interest in me either way. I seduce them with words. A friend in Adrogué, Ribero, who played billiards very well and was an inveterate bachelor, always said that the greatest feat of his life had been getting a woman into bed without once having touched her. "Only with my voice and my words, I seduced her," he would say.

When I reread what I have written of my thesis I want to die. Where did I come up with the idea that I'm a writer?

I called Helena on the phone. I didn't really know what to say to her. I'm a desperate guy. Don't you want to sleep with me? The phone rang several times (eleven times). I was thinking, "If I don't breathe, she'll come." No one answered. I hung up. I went back to my room holding my breath. I can hold my breath for a minute and a half, easy. I've been practicing how long I can go without breathing since I was fifteen. It would be such an elegant thing to be able to commit suicide by holding your breath. I will call her again, tomorrow or the day after.

I just went a minute and forty seconds without breathing. My heart pounds like an eggbeater. If I were with a woman now, I'd tell her to put her hand on my chest to see how it beats. I'm a sensitive type, I'd tell her. Can you feel my heart?

Thursday 7
Inventions to relieve my sorrow, in which I also have faith: Lidia's return, clandestine love, under the sun. It costs me something to recognize reality. I try not to lose my footing.

The writer who writes a masterpiece. According to Steve, in 1930, while he was studying at Cambridge and working on *Ultramarine*, Lowry enlisted as an assistant in the coal room of a ship to Norway in order to meet the writer Nordahl Grieg, because he'd gotten his hands on a novel by the Norwegian author that had a theme that was similar, if not identical, to the one he was writing. From there emerged *In Ballast to the White Sea* and the portrait of Erikson, an alter ego for which he came to feel a special affinity.

Saturday 9
Once again I hid in the sea and the movie theater, so as not to think. Yesterday Welles's *Othello*, today *Compulsion*. I go into the sea and watch the city from afar, flat and calm as if it were a photo. I let it carry me, but to where I don't know.

Tuesday 12
I also saw, in another theater, *Ashes and Diamonds* by A. Wajda. It is sensational. A terrorist of the right, a Nietzschean, kills, "because life

without action, more than lacking meaning, is boring." Why does he always wear black eyeglasses? they ask him. "Because my homeland is in mourning," he answers.

Monday
I spoke to Helena on the phone and attempted to tell her that I was now wearing tinted eyeglasses so that she would ask me why I wore them and I could answer her: "Because my homeland is in mourning." But there was no way, and anyway, it was difficult to explain to her over the phone that I had my dark eyeglasses on. Maybe everything I say to her seems romantic. Helena likes me because she has blue eyes and is rather naïve. She invites me over for tea, and when I'm with her I never get introspective.

Last night, before going to sleep, I reread *The Great Gatsby*, the use of Conrad's technique, a romantic version of *Lord Jim*: men who want to change the past. The best part of the novel is the beginning, where Gatsby is a mystery, all the stories that circulate about him. The weakest part is precisely the denouement; maybe he couldn't drive himself to leave everything in suspense and not clarify whether Gatsby was a gangster or a lucky man.

Fitzgerald was able to realize the fantasy of being a writer better than anyone. One would never be as famous as a film actor, although the notoriety would probably last longer. Neither would one have the same power as a man of action, although he would certainly be more independent. Of course, we are always unsatisfied in the practice of this work, but I, for one, would have chosen no other fate, whatever the reason.

Thursday 21
I saw *The Diary of Anne Frank* in the theater. At the moment of greatest tension (the cat plays with a tin funnel, pushes it with its nose, nearly making it fall from the table while the Nazis are taking over

the apartment, searching for the family hidden in the crawlspace), a fire extinguisher exploded—spontaneously—with a brutal noise and a flash. Panic and cries; the people piled up along the aisle in the darkness, but I stayed calm, ready to observe their figures, as if someone were filming the scene.

Sunday 24
I went to the sea alone, once again to the beach near the port. At noon, there was a confused commotion with the swimmers and lifeguards that ended with the police rushing on horseback at everyone. The fury was shared by women and men in their houses, who also insulted the police, though for other reasons.

Wednesday 27
Every morning, the face in the mirror. I get older, but the image stays cheerful and amused. I should wear a plaster mask.

Yesterday I went to the theater; today I went to the theater. It doesn't matter what I see, I seek only the darkness, the forgetting.

I ran into Rafa. He is totally convinced that he's flawless. He practices gymnastics every morning and gets tens in all the events. We went to Professor Jiménez's house. He started to read Ortega y Gasset to us. He keeps all the yellow books in a separate library, as if he thought that with these books from a Spanish journalist he would become a knowledgeable man. I told him that he was an anarchist. He smiled with his despicable know-it-all smile.

I went to walk along the coast with Helena with an *H*. The wind made the canvas of the awnings vibrate. The empty beach, the fearsome sea; the waves were crashing furiously over the jetty and the water almost made it up to the street. We sat on the steps of the stairway leading to Playa Grande. A terrible wind, the salt air. "The only thing that interests me is writing," I told her. "I know, dear; you don't miss a chance to tell me every two minutes." I didn't say it for you, I told her. "Come on," she said. "Don't play strange. Here," she said, "we're going to take a photo together." There was a street photographer, with a square camera, on a bicycle, his head covered with a black cloth. "Look at the lovers," said the photographer. Helena smiled with a resigned expression. Curiously, I felt a sense that I had offended her. As if, because we had secretly entered close to the Ocean Club, I should have acted differently. I would have, ought to have . . .

Sitting on a metal chair, under the gray light in the office. Dad has gone to Viedma tonight—a political matter, connected to the story of a group of Peronist leaders who escaped from a prison in the south. Among them, Guillermo Patricio Kelly, the nationalist, who was dressed as a woman.

Thursday 28
I went for the first time to a strange rectangular office full of women sitting in front of typewriters, tapping away rhythmically without looking at the keyboards. I had also come to take typing classes, to learn to write using all of my fingers. They put me in front of a big Underwood machine, but I didn't do anything. I don't think I'll go back.

I call Helena. She offers to type up the final draft of my monograph. Poor angel . . . I'm going to go to the house tomorrow. She triggers certain cruel instincts in me, my desires to make her see who I am. It would be a surprise for her to see me as I am. Deep down this is the only thing that worries me. Otherwise, everything would go very well.

It is very early and I don't know what to do.

Monday, January 25
A letter to Elena (without an *H*). Trouble finding something to say, making a "decorous" summary of the time in which I broke with the monopoly

of her friendship to invent new—and ambiguous—partnerships. A presumptuous letter that I wrote in bad faith to prove my "progress." I made a fetish—a totem—for spontaneous feelings, for sincerity. I summarized for her my conditioned (and blind) choice to study in La Plata and not in Buenos Aires. I want to live alone, far from family, even though it is my grandfather Emilio who will pay for my degree because I have broken ties with my father, who threatened me in an absurd way when he discovered I did not mean to study medicine as he had. My grandfather will pay me a salary to help him organize his archive of material from the First World War. Living in La Plata, from what I can tell from these past few weeks of being here, is much cheaper than living in Buenos Aires.

Wednesday 27
I try to isolate myself, try not to think; there is no future, I live in a present without limits. Lidia must disappear from my life.

Saturday, January 30
A subject. An artist who works on a monumental project and dies before completing it. An unexpected end, news of a suicide in the papers. They find his room full of notecards. Inside the typewriter, a page where the only thing written is "A Sentimental History of Humanity. Chapter 1." There was nothing more, and no pages of the announced book were found, only the notecards, which showed a long investigation into a wide variety of sources. Writings in an elegant calligraphy, the numbered cards included quotations, isolated sentences, brief biographies, plans for organizing the chapters, etc. No one knows whether—as it is supposed—he ever even began the work or if he became disillusioned after writing it and made it disappear a day before killing himself.

In the afternoon, with Helena. She is more cynical than I am. She holds back, shows off. As she speaks of trifles, she leans forward so that I can see she is not wearing a bra. I can never be bored with this woman. With her, the best times are always the goodbyes. We are in the kitchen, full of light, floating between the white tiles. On the upstairs floor above, we could feel her mother's coming and going.

Fascinated by a detail: at the end, from some place she brought out a little towel. In such a way she had anticipated everything.

I thought about her. We went up to her room in the middle of the night. Through the half-open door, we saw her parents sleeping. We spoke in a whisper, which I remember now as something very erotic. She was biting the palm of her hand, was so close to me, in the silence and the rough and light breathing.

The difficulty with not having much money is finding a place to be together. A room of one's own to make love. I'd have to write an essay on youth drifting through the city, begging for a place to lock themselves in.

Monday, February 8
For the past several days I have felt restless without knowing why. I don't think about her anymore. I spend the morning on the beach and the afternoon in the public library, looking over old editions of the magazine *Martín Fierro*. I resign myself to thinking that within a month, within a year, all of this that seems insurmountable will be—barely—a memory. Thoughts as compensation, excuses.

Wednesday 24
He keeps going on around here, turning in circles, my mother's personal witch doctor. She is amused, saying that he's much cheaper than an analyst and that he habitually predicts exactly what she wants to happen. Don José, whom I have baptized "Yambó," as though he were an African witch doctor, has very white skin, jewels on his fingers and at his neck, dangerously smooth manners, and a certain hidden insanity that surrounds him like a fine veil. He throws his body forward when he smiles. Today he sat with us at the dining table and, while we talked, he began to preach and

predict my future in La Plata. According to him, I already began very well last year and things would improve this year. He is certain that my central interest is not only my studies but also a hidden river that he sees clearly but cannot name. I must take caution with the political activists and be polite with women. I thanked him for the diagnosis and told him that I would write a note in my journal quickly, this very day, to consult within a few years (which is what I will do). I hope that this subterranean river is a metaphor for literature, but I don't know.

Thursday, February 25
I just recently saw Lidia in the entrance at Sao. You could almost say I left running. Then I returned, but she was no longer there. If what she told me in December is true, it does not make sense for me to approach her now. Every time I go down Avenida Luro toward the sea and cross in front of the Saint James building, I imagine I will find her, but seeing her suddenly in the bar I visit every day surprised me. As though Lidia must always remain in the place where I remember her.

I had gone to the Atenas bookshop to buy Graham Greene's *Brighton Rock* on the corner of Belgrano and 14 de Julio; they did not have it. I went as far as San Martín, passed through the Erasmo bookshop and, as I left, decided to walk to the coast and cross the sidewalk to go to the Salamanca bookshop. I ran into my cousin Celia in the doorway. Mathematical precision: if I'd arrived five minutes before and entered, she'd have passed without seeing me. Celia invited me to have an ice cream; we went and I returned alone. I crossed so as not to pass in front of Salamanca again (because I didn't want to greet the salesman again), searched the book fair in the mall on San Martín and Córdoba, followed the same path, turned around, and there she, Lidia, was, standing in front of Sao, looking forward. I am certain that it was her, especially because of the pants. When I saw her I thought I was falling; I did not know where to go and stood, half-dizzy.

Now I look for meanings hidden within a random series of incidents. I say that a woman called me on the sixteenth. It was her. I was not at home. Trying not to go back to thinking about Lidia, I stopped going to the beach at Luro, where we used to plan to meet. Our story went from the beginning of summer (the end of November, beginning of December) until the festivals. All was well; we spent the afternoons in La Perla Hotel, and one day she turned to me and with all casualness told me that she was going back to Buenos Aires to get married. I could not believe it. She told me, "This way I am not unfaithful, because I am not yet married, and an adventure is nothing too complicated." Of course, I adopted the air of an experienced man and told her that I understood perfectly; she told me that she might return after the marriage and that if I kept going to the same beach I would see her. And that was what happened, but on the other side.

Tomorrow I will go to the beach at Luro. I'm an idiot. I want to live in last year. I'm going to go out and walk . . . And if it wasn't her? What's more, why had she called me again? She doesn't "suit" me, but the women who don't suit me are exactly the ones I like.

Friday, February 26
I'm in a tight spot; I think all the time about the consequences of my most routine and casual actions. The paths I traverse without knowing what might happen to me. Impossible thoughts, without resolution: "If that car had not stopped for me as I crossed the street, if I had not turned the corner . . . " Life is a chain of casual encounters, but we try to explain ourselves to ourselves as if we had decided everything from the beginning. Paths that "seem" casual but are all the result of a way of living. Let's think about what has been going on since November, when I met Lidia, until today, and it will be clear to see that I have rigorously programmed the coincidences myself in order to reach these very results.

Obviously I went looking for her all around the city, a sort of Dostoevskian walk that culminated on the corner where the hotel we always went to is. Then, upon returning to the coast in front of the building with the hanging balconies, I saw her yet again, dressed in white and looking distant. The moral: she existed every moment of the day for me since she left; seeing her was secondary. I had "ceased to be" for her since the moment she left. It made sense that today she would look "through me," without seeing me, as if I were a chair or a tree, because I had sunk away into hypotheticals, considering that she had decided to get married and had a "necessary" relationship with the world. Conversely, for me, of her, what mattered was her presence inside me.

What I can't endure is thinking that Lidia called on the sixteenth and I was reading some nonsense in the library. Of course I could have called her back. But I prefer to think about the opportunities lost by chance. I already said that she does not suit me (after all, she just got married), but who is forcing me to believe it? If I could make her disappear and stop hoping, I wouldn't think about her anymore and would live only in the present. On the other hand, I should not have gone out to look for her today, but I did. I went at four in the afternoon and again at six and finally a little while ago, in order to find her.

What does everything I've read matter to me now? What do reading and knowing matter to me if I am not with her?

Saturday 27
I dreamed about Lidia last night. I found her on the beach, and she seemed bothered that I was there. Then the lifeguard approached us and asked our names. I don't know how and I don't know the reason for this, but she was a prisoner. Then she held onto me, so that I might defend her.

Eisenhower came on a visit to Mar del Plata, along with the ex-nationalist Frondizi. I only saw them from behind, standing in the roofless car; many policemen, people on the sidewalks, little flags. I saw a car with two men standing in the middle and constantly smiling, as if they had just made a joke. I remember the image of General Eisenhower, hero of the Second World War, then the slogan "*I Like Ike*." A walk back with my hands in my pockets and a double game of fantasies. Throwing myself under the hooves of the horses with a bomb hidden on my body. Or also shooting a gun, running to the bus stop, going down Luro, entering Saint James, dying in the elevator that Lidia would take to the fourteenth floor.

Thirty thousand idiots and despicable tourists milling around on Calle San Martín. It's easier to swim across the sea and go down a street with no one around.

Sunday, February 28
My little cousins (once little cousins) Erika and Elisa want to go dancing. We are planning to go out to Gambrinus tomorrow or Tuesday. I ended the afternoon in a sort of jam session at Julio's house, listening to several records of the Hot Club Quintet of France with Django Reinhardt on guitar.

Monday 29
I went to Maxim's with Elisa and Erika; music, dancing, conversations. A while later Jorge arrived; he took Elisa for a dance, and I went to the bar with Erika to drink Manhattans. We remembered the beautiful times past. She studies linguistics at the University of Salvador; she's interested in the original forms of language: metaphors, sayings, riddles, grammatical forms. Afterward, we went to have dinner at the Taberna Baska and finished the night in the casino, where I won fifteen hundred pesos. Unlucky in love, luck in the game, I said to Erika, who immediately turned protective and wanted me to tell her my sorrows. I told her about Lidia with the air of a man who is very accustomed to going out with girls who are getting married the next week. Erika is still single, likes men but not marriage; she is waiting, she told me, to get a doctorate "abroad."

Wednesday, March 2

I went to the beach with Erika. Her sister kept going and went to the Lighthouse with Jorge. We had an unforgettable summer with Erika a long time ago, when we went on vacation in the town of Bolívar. She was from there, and for me she justified leaving my friends behind and spending a season in the country. She was—and goes on being—amusing, intelligent, slightly obscene, and always funny. We talk now as if we were a married couple that has lived together for many years after getting divorced. She takes my decision to study history and dedicate myself to literature very seriously. It seems natural to her and much more intelligent, she tells me, smiling, than to bury myself in one of those "serious" disciplines that aren't good for anything. She said something very sensible: "Disciplines don't matter; what matters is the percentage of intelligence of the person studying. For an intelligent and first-rate historian, things will go much better than a mediocre, second-rate attorney."

March 3, 1960

Abstract desires to go on writing in these notebooks despite the fact that—in essence—there is nothing to say. I spent two months doing nothing and have no desire now to relate what happened. I sustain myself with the delusion of Lidia's return; private fabrications, as if I didn't know that, as I write this, she is living her own life parallel to mine, also hoping for something else. How to continue a diary that has as its object the delusions of the one writing it and not his real life? First possible reflection: How can we define real life?

Friday 4

At the beach today, along with Jorge and my two cousins. When I "think" about Lidia everything is alright; I establish a rationality in which events have an order. If I pause for a moment and cease to be alert, everything falls apart and I miss her. I explained this, more or less, to Erika, the two of us spread face down on a sailcloth, speaking from very close. She sat up then, taking her knees between her joined hands, and said, "You are lost, Emilio; you fell in love with a married woman." Well, not married, I said; when I met her she was single. She smiled with a treacherous air and said she understood me perfectly. After the beach, we spent the late afternoon on the terrace at Maxim's listening to Carnevale, a very good piano player who, when there aren't many people around, plays jazz in the style of Erroll Garner.

Saturday
I think it was lucky that I was not at home when Lidia called: I would have run to see her with the predictable result, since she had surely come here with her husband.

Monday 7
At Alfar yesterday from the morning onward, with Jorge and the cousins. Long walks along the beaches that extend endlessly to the south. Afterward among the trees with Erika, waiting for the bus to return to the city.

Wednesday 17
The greatest pretense is in the very fact of writing these notebooks. Who am I writing them for? I don't think it is for me, and nor would I like anyone else to read them.

Sunday, March 27
I went to vote. Ambiguities of the conscience. I entered the school, determined to cast a blank ballot like the Peronists and my father who follow "Perón's order." When I was alone in the dark room I felt the certainty, or rather, had the conviction that I was a socialist, and then I decided and voted the ticket for the left.

Tuesday 6
The surprises that I set out for myself. Inventing a causality, a destiny made out of fateful encounters, coincidences; choosing the future, inventing the days that must follow this afternoon.

Repeating my "methods," leaving the field open. All because I am caught inside the trap that I knew how to set: inventing a woman, suggesting some history between her and me. Living ambivalently under that illusion, so determined not to let it disappear that I set aside the woman, forget her, determined to watch out for others.

Since I had that realization, I set out to walk in circles around the center. I found Rafael and Raúl C.; we went to visit Professor Jiménez: always so understanding. "You put too much on yourself, Renzi, and afterward you feel you have the right to ask everything of people." He stressed the "everything."

She is clearly the reason why I went back to writing in these notebooks, in February, when I saw her. From those incidents we could extract a poetics. In order to write, it is necessary to feel uncomfortable in the world; writing is a shield to confront life (and to explain it).

It is ten at night, and I am listening to Lester Young with Oscar Peterson. The night is cool and clear, I float in a sort of neutral existence. In the window, the branches of the tree are a refuge.

A familiar story. The sudden flight of my cousin Claudio's wife. She escaped with a toy soldier, a twenty-year-old conscript, and abandoned her two children. Maggie's clan is assembled permanently.

All afternoon walking from one side to another. In Montecarlo I ran into Jorge and Roberto Sanmartino.

Monday
When I want to calm myself down, I take refuge in the future: in ten years I'll laugh at all of this.

Maxim's. I became friends with the piano player who makes his living entertaining tourist couples and shows his talent playing jazz for the group of natives who come to listen to him in the winter, when no one is there. Today, with Jorge and the cousins, we are the only ones to clap for him. His name, this piano player, is Juan Carnevale, and they call him Johnny.

Friday

Unexpectedly, I escape from the city. I went with Morán, the bookseller who leads the film club. We traveled to Buenos Aires together, and the car broke down in a town along the way and we had to wait about six hours until they fixed the radiator for us. Sitting at the hotel bar facing the main square, Morán started to talk about Steve. I will always remember the tedium of waiting in that ridiculous town, the two of us sitting at a table in the bar, in the hotel where school inspectors and cattle auctioneers would stay, lifting the curtain of rough cloth to see the roads of reddish gravel around the square and the monument to some murderer dressed in uniform.

We had set out at seven in the morning with the hope of arriving before noon, but the car started to overheat and we had to leave the main route and get on a side street to enter Hoyos, a town less than a hundred kilometers from Mar del Plata. We found a mechanic's garage where a guy they called El Uruguayo worked; he took a while to come out and, before he examined the car, he went on a tirade about the political situation. It seems he renounced Vítolo, he said, as if we had come to see him to listen to the news. Afterward, he asked Morán to start up the engine and leaned in to listen to the noise, and without touching the car or examining it he said he needed at least four hours of work to get it ready.

We left to walk around the town, which was the same as all the other towns in the province, with roads that get lost among the weeds and little low houses with iron gates. We made some turns and returned to El Uruguayo's shop, but still more than two hours remained before the car would be ready, so we went to the hotel bar facing the main square and started drinking gin. And a while later, without having anything to pass the time, Morán went back to talking about Steve. He didn't tell me how he had found out, simply began telling me the facts and his interpretation. The story was so strange that I believed him at once. Morán raised his voice and recounted the same episodes several times over, and it was all crossed with suspicions and sarcasm.

Monday
In a few days' time I'll be living in La Plata, having new conversations, changing my friends and my address. Today I'll talk on the phone with Jorge S., who is already in the city and tells me news about the University and this year's programs. From time to time, I think I ought to study philosophy.

Monday
At night, a strange scene with Mom. I got a ticket for the bus at one in the morning. We ate dinner together and were alone because Dad is in Buenos Aires. She talked ironically all night about "new life," as she calls it, but in the end, a while before I left, she embraced me, crying, and said I was leaving her all alone. It was as if I was setting off for a distant country, and there is something in that, because she knows that I am not going to return home.

I learn what I want to do from imaginary writers. Stephen Dedalus or Nick Adams, for example. I read their lives as a way to understand what it is all about. I am not interested in inspiring myself with the "real" writers. Dedalus's disdain for family, religion, and homeland will be my own. Silence, exile, and cunning. He wrote a diary (like me). He read philosophy (Aristotle, Saint Augustine, Giordano Bruno, Vico). He had an extraordinary theory about *Hamlet* and discusses it in the library chapter of *Ulysses*. He liked call girls (like me). He went to Paris to escape the world of family (just as I went to La Plata). He wanted to be a writer and wanted his stories and epiphanies to be sent to all the libraries in the world (if he were to die). He admired and went to visit Yeats, a great poet, just as I admire and want to know Borges. That is to say, he saw as his master a writer who could not have been his father but rather his grandfather. Finally, he admired his father's admiration for Parnell just as I admire my father's admiration for Perón, even though neither Dedalus nor I are interested in our fathers' politics.

5

*A Visit**

The government's intelligence services monitored him for months, censored his correspondence, controlled his visitors, and once in a while a nocturnal voice would threaten him over the phone. He would not treat it as a threat; in fact, he kept up a philosophical and theoretical conversation on the meaning of civil duty and moral responsibility with those deceitful voices. Those men were the new intellectuals, the thinkers of the future; any Argentine knows that a mark will be placed on his life if he dissents, which may be invoked at some future moment to track down and incarcerate him. The services had turned into the political version of the Oracle of Delphi; they decided in secret the fate of entire populations. Now they are the witches from *Macbeth* who control the power!

---

* A classmate from the National High School of Mar del Plata, Ezequiel Martínez Estrada's nephew, told me one day that his uncle sometimes came to visit them in the city. I asked him to tell me when, and one afternoon in 1959 the writer received me in a house facing Plaza Dorrego. His frailty and cadaverous air left an impression on me; he entered the living room supporting himself against the walls, but, as soon as he sat down and started to speak, his tone was the same as it was in the extraordinary diatribes that he was writing at the time (*¿Qué es esto?*, his "*catilinarias*," *Las 40*), which I read with persistent fervor. When I returned home I tried to record what I remembered from the interview, and some years later I wrote the story—based on those notes—which I am revealing here for the first time.

They suppress everything that can threaten mediocre and average life; they attack diversity in all of its aspects, control it and surveil it, write our biographies. Conformism is the new religion, and they are its priests.

He had reached a point at which he argued directly with the state, with the spokesmen for the state's *intelligence*. Smash and grab exchanges in the depths of night; the voices came and went, through wireless circuits. They hounded him, cornered him, wanted to turn him into an intellectual outlaw. They know that I know; they want to destroy my thought.

He had made the decision to go into exile. Now he was preparing his Address to the University, in which he would announce this decision. They were planning an homage to his work; he was going to use that event as the stage for his final invective. Would I like to attend? I was invited. He had begun to give shape to his speech: "It would not be untimely nor boastful, ladies and gentlemen, if you permitted me to speak about myself for a moment and employ the first-person pronoun," he would say. He was obliged to take a personal detour; that was what he would say in his Address to the University. He had been very sick, an unknown ailment of the skin, which could be called the white plague. Five years without being able to read or write! Light scabs that gave off ashes like pale butterflies and smelled of death. His body had acquired a gray tonality. The worst of it, however, the most ridiculous and offensive part, had been the continual itching, an unbearable irritation for twenty-four hours each day.

During the years of his illness, he had been unable to devote himself to anything but thought. Stretched out on the bed, in clinics, in hospitals, in convalescent homes, in his own residence, with his skin in a state of sweet putrefaction, minuscule burning spots scattered down the length of his body, he allowed his thoughts to flow. During those years, he had thought everything; no thought could surprise him now. My situation was much like that of Job, and rather than reflecting on good and evil I fell into a meditation on my country. For if I was suffering from a small illness, the nation was suffering from a great illness, and if I could have committed a small error in my life, it had committed an enormous one. Both I and my country were sick. In those years of pure thought, he had refined his intelligence to the farthest point to which a cultured man could. Several times, he had confirmed that his thought could pierce the purest crystal. Because reality was transparent, clear as the air, invisible. He must pierce through that transparent clarity, never pause to contemplate the enigmas around which dozens of thinkers crowded, reclining upon the air. As he advanced, the reclining thinkers dispersed into the walls of glass. New corridors and transparent passageways opened endlessly before the dagger of his intelligence. The first point on which he had to employ his intelligence, during the deepest throes of his weakness, when he was on the verge of being vanquished, was coming up with a strategy to prevent them from treating him like a madman. Ladies and gentlemen, they thought my illness was mental, a schizophrenic episode, the real realization of a lunatic's fragmented body. When, in reality, it was nothing more than exasperation at my connection to my country. My body was the explicit representation of my homeland's general condition, not metaphor or allegory. Economic, geographic, climatic, and historical settings can, under certain circumstances, collude to act upon an individual. He had asserted this and studied it and demonstrated it before his illness. He had dealt with the hypothesis in *Sarmiento*, his book about Sarmiento, written in eleven days, in a fit of inspiration, at a working rhythm of three pages per hour, in his country house on Pedro Goyena, his feet sinking into the dust of the plains; he says that a man can represent a nation. And I do not mean to describe him as an intermediary here; I don't believe in mediation, I believe in the collision of analogous constellations, the direct relationships between irreconcilable elements.

From music, he had learned to think directly. Because he was an eminent performer on the violin. And music is an unmediated art form: tones, rhythms, contrasts, counterpoints. An individual whose life is decided, conditioned, affected—directly and immediately—by the state of a nation. If such a person can crack the cipher to a political destiny in his personal life, he will understand the movement of history. He had said this in many of his books. But he had now decided to treat himself as the object of investigation and in this way to complete his work, begun more than thirty years ago, that Argentinian meditation that the academic community would honor in the final days before his exile.

The book that I announce to you today will deal with my own life, the life of a reclusive poet and thinker who with his existence replicates the deep tendencies of his country. That book will be at once an auto-biography, a treatise on science, a manual of strategy, and the description of a battle. The history of the final anarchist and the final thinker.

During the years of his illness, he had entered a territory of absolute darkness. A territory given over to witch doctors and neuropaths, but a territory also inhabited by living beings, stuck between inert misery and the vastness of the plain. He had not invented this territory out of superstition but rather from a sense of hopelessness. And *coming to be* hopeless can be a lifelong project. There is an extreme lucidity in extreme illness, not for its content but for its form. There are unhealthy thoughts that exist because they are false, and there are wholesome thoughts that nevertheless take the shape of an illness. Ladies and gentlemen, knowledge is like an abstract disease, produced by a body that is not fated to think, he would say in his Address to the University. But this sickness is not a metaphor; it is an ailment of the body, the white plague. Like the oyster and the pearl, if you still insist that I express myself through metaphors.

In order to think, you must stop making decisions. You must strain your intelligence in the useless exercise of pure thought. Indecision is now an illness of thought. And that exercise is the origin of philosophy. Therefore, thought is of the same order as illness and paralysis. I understand this illness as supreme indecision. After thirty years of practicing perfect thinking, my body was won by thought and took on the form of thinking *in place*. My entire body transformed into the pure thought of the homeland.

I am the final Argentine thinker, but still I have not been annihilated; I was on the verge but managed to save myself.

Once he understood the theoretical meaning of his illness, he managed to enter that world populated with material and death with its incredible and varied transformations, clearing away from the materials of civilization the prejudices, the cruelty, the interests that have accumulated like detritus, like white ashes, amid the engineering and bricklaying, and there remained the work of the man interred: earth, water, winds, and dear voices. They survive on a plain of ashes, just enclosed in transparent capsules, a dreaming crystal lost in the great salt mines.

Now he thought about woven patterns. Do you know the criollo weave? Thread, knot, cross and knot, red, green, thread and knot, thread and knot. Sarmiento's mother, under the pear tree, weaving on the loom of sorrows. That phrase from Fierro: "the life of every gaucho you see is woven thick with misfortunes." It is chilling to see the way things are woven into the looms of mysterious spiders. His primary concern was to uncover those secret processes. Just there, in the book he would write in exile, the final book of the final thinker, which he had begun to call *The Book of the Looms*, he would try to sketch out the machine of impersonal events. The mechanical spinning and bookkeeping of fate! Before, it had been believed that it was essential to know something of mechanics, of physics, in order to explain social phenomena; today, biology, cut off from the physical world, is the only thing that can assist us. Can you imagine what the meta-mechanics of colloids could be, for example? Of course you can imagine it. He had discovered the great social embryos that were once called looms. They are weaving somewhere; he must find out where! And our lives are patterns, woven into the plot. It will still cause an institution to take the form of a wasp, another that of a crab, another that of an eagle, and there is no more than a single factory for everything! Ah, if he could break through, even if for an instant, to once more see the workshop where all the looms work. Would he then waste time watching the weave under a magnifying glass? The vision lasts a second. Then I fall into the brutal dream of reality. I have so many terrible things to tell.

I am the last anarchist and the deprived thinker par excellence. No one is more deprived than I (of everything). He worked on his definitive book, which would be a detailed exposition of his discovery, superimposed and woven and intermingled with a musical history of his life.

Out of pure testamentary willpower, he had decided that his book would not be published until a date he would leave in an envelope, which was to be opened twenty-five years after his death. Not before or after. True legibility is always posthumous. We write for the dead, and also for the secret police. Because they read everything, record everything. Deep down, we write for state intelligence. How could we prevent them from reading us? He would like to become an unpublished author. In his Address to the University, he was going to hint that he was thinking of publishing his book under a pseudonym, but not just under a pseudonym, under a name that no one could even remotely associate with his own. Nobody would know what name he was thinking of using. For example, he had thought of publishing it as an anonymous book, but that would draw attention. Wouldn't it be better to publish it as a previously unpublished book by a well-known author, to attribute it to another, allow it be to read as if it came from another? He would like it if any book published after his death could be read as his work. That was his bequest to the stupefied youth of Argentina. That was the enigma that he left to the inquisitive. No better act than to change his name and be lost in the plains like Fierro's children. A book lost amid the sea of future books. A riddle launched into history. A work envisioned in order to pass, so to speak, unperceived. So that one might discover it by chance and understand its message. That was his strategy in the face of the politics of ignorance, isolation, menace, and warfare that the dominant intelligentsia had initiated.

Where all grow rich and shower themselves with honor, I construct a plan to annihilate myself. The decision was symmetrical to one he had made when he got his start: just when he received the highest honors and was recognized as Argentina's greatest poet and the most virtuosic master of the language, he had stopped writing poetry. The willingly unknown masterwork, encoded and concealed among all books.

Sometimes, he said, he would imagine that night, when little time remained before his Address to the University; he was already walking toward the podium and had, resignedly, already listened to the praise from his enemies. He was going to climb the steps with grace and ease. Standing before the multitudes, when the applause quieted down, with the light of the lamps on his face, seeing no one, dazzled and lucid, he would begin by saying:

I have come here tonight, ladies and gentlemen, to speak to you of a unique discovery, and also to bid you farewell. I thought of giving you a little musical performance on my violin. It would have been an excellent means of synthesizing my thought, if I performed before you a discourse made of music. You would be able to see my mastery in the art of violin as a reprise of my mastery in thought. But I have cast that possibility aside, because I would not have been able to make one of the announcements I wish to make tonight—strictly personal announcements. We are at war. My combat strategy can be summarized by two principles. First, I only attack those things that triumph; sometimes I wait until they succeed. Second, I only attack when I find no allies, when I am alone, when I compromise myself alone.

I think, and that changes nothing. I am alone. I am comfortable in this solitude. No light thing weighs upon me. I am robbed by the pain. I am here in gratitude. Would it not be opportune, then, to be so bold as to point out the final part of my nature?

I have lived exposed to the crude light of the Argentine language for too many years not to suffer burns on my skin. Because the light of language is like a chemical ray. That clear light, the purest water of the mother tongue, kills the men that expose themselves to it. The spots on my skin were proof of my alchemical pacts with the national language's secret flame. That light is like gold. The light of language distills gold from poetry. That has been another characteristic of my illness, which many have considered a symptom of madness. Few have known that excessive exposure to the light of the Argentine language, that clarity, and those who have all pay the price with their bodies, because the light of language martyrs everyone who is exposed to its subtle transparency.

If I am going to begin and so on and so forth, he told me, I will humbly expose my thoughts to all who have gathered to listen to me in the Great

Hall of the University, on the edge of Patagonia, within the bounds of austral thought. And I will end thus: I renounce my seat, which I have referred to as Sociology of the Plains. Does such a suggestive title not call your attention? It is plain space, it is the desert, it is the endless outdoors, as the poet said, and it is there, ladies and gentlemen, where I plan to lose myself. Thank you very much.

6

Diary 1960

March 29
Tedium, uncertainty. I write sitting in my car, facing a garage that will fix the engine. We came into this town. Morán gives me some accounts of Steve while we kill time in a café.

March 31
We arrived after noon. Today I declared a major in history at the College. Everything is still very confusing, the streets too wide. The city very calm. As always, a sensation of precariousness, of only passing through. It costs me something to accept that I will live here, alone, for several years. A voluntary lack of any anchor, which turns into a retrospective nostalgia (always: thinking about Adrogué). Close to me, someone is speaking over the phone. Complains about having not been expected and having traveled uselessly. I am empty and neutral—distant, as always. A strange feeling of freedom.

Yesterday, a reunion with Elena. I felt she was more distant now than when I really was far away from her. I have to cut it short to shake off the feeling that, to her, I am the same person I was at the stupid age of sixteen. I keep the relationship going as though deep down I wanted to change that image of myself.

All that comes is new. Imposing a code on myself and following it. Making myself someone other than who I am, beginning at zero, without any burden or anger. The fundamental thing is to endure, to try to live through what comes without thinking, attentive to the present. Fixating on the little things: the minute rituals that save me from the experience of emptiness. Being here, transformed into a student, is only a means for me to write for a few years without too much interference.

April 1960

I went to my first class at the University, "Constitutional History," taught by Silvio Frondizi. He recalled the hypotheses of Max Weber on Protestantism and capitalism. The slogan, according to him, ended up being "*laborare est orare.*" Personal wealth as proof of God's grace.

Yesterday, I spent the night in the boardinghouse—a room over a lattice-work patio, a double door.

Saturday, April 2

All afternoon spent writing letters. It is my most habitual writing activity, even more habitual than this diary. We could imagine a man who stays connected to the world only through correspondence, who writes letters to diverse and unknown addressees with the same enthusiasm as to old friends. For my part: a letter today to my mother, a letter to Julio, a letter to Jorge, a letter to Helena (with an *H*). From a public telephone, I spoke laboriously with Grandfather Emilio, who insists that I come to live with him in Adrogué. I dissuaded him with quips, jokes, and complaints.

Sunday

I went to the game. Boca 2 – Students 1. Soccer brings me back to childhood once again, the world of my father, of my aunt and uncle, who would go to the field with me on Sundays for as far back as I can remember.

Monday 4

At the college, "Introduction to Philosophy." Eugenio Pucciarelli spoke about the pre-Socratics. In the afternoon, I went to the University library to get a library card (I already have one, *querida*, I almost said to the woman at the desk). Afterward, a history assembly at the student center. Young people with leather jackets and serious faces. One of these Papaleos asked me about my politics; I declared myself an anarchist and quickly came into contact with the group identifying as such.

The concept in Socrates. The same as the geometers, who reduce the most complicated modes of existence into the sensible reality of pure forms: polygons, triangles, quadrilaterals, circles. Socrates does the same with the moral world. He applies intellectual intuition to say what constitutes actions, intentions, resolutions, the modes of conduct of mankind, and he reduces them to a certain number of concrete forms—for example, justice, moderation, temperance.

For the Greeks, to ask oneself what something is means to give the reason for it, to find the reason that explains it. They call this reason that explains it "logos" (from there, logic). In his Latin translation, "logos" becomes "verbum," which before, for Socrates, meant conversation. The name that is given to something is what we now call a concept.

April 8

We go to the Archives of the Province of Buenos Aires for the first time. It is in the depths of the Galería Rocha. Enrique Barba conducts us among the infinite and numerous documents that cover the walls.

We learn to copy from the folios, to indicate the turn of a page precisely and to put "illegible" in brackets when a word or a paragraph has deteriorated from moisture or from time or because the handwriting of whoever transcribed or wrote it originally was an incomprehensible graphology. You never know what you will find, Barba told us, by searching randomly, following uncertain clues, guided by instinct, which must be a historian's primary virtue. We search because we have a hypothesis, but we will never write it down until we have documented certainty. And then he said a sentence that I loved: "Any book of history that does not have five footnotes per page," he made a theatrical pause and concluded, "is a novel." (It seemed to me an excellent definition for the genre of the novel).

Barba lives in the archives, spends more time in that subterranean gallery than in his house, and has specialized in Rosas's rise to power; that is to say, he has worked as a deep-sea diver within three years of Argentine history, three years only, which he knows better than his own life. Almost thirty years dedicated to understanding three years. Extraordinary. He knows everything from that period, knows whether it rained on Rosas's camps one day in February of 1829 or how many men formed his personal guard, and also the names of each and how they dressed, what they ate, and how they behaved before the commander.

Friday 15
A friendship with Luis Alonso: he declares himself a poet, a disciple of Luis Franco, and comes from Catamarca. He lives in a hotel on 6th and 50th. Our "affinities" are, in fact, arguments. His aggressive politics question my skepticism (which defines me, according to him).

Monday 18
I have no interest in recording here my everyday life, my activities and the classes I attend. I have always thought that these notebooks must be the story of an ordinary individual's pure spirit. The spirit, because what matters exists beyond immediate materiality, because that is the nature of my choice to become a writer.

In Socrates, logos has morality as its object. Plato extends the field of knowledge, logos, to all of reality, to anything in the world. Plato receives the theory of two worlds from Parmenides. Appearance and essence, falsehood and truth are the two different worlds.

Idea (neologism): a word invented by Plato based on the root of a Greek verb that means "to see." Idea = vision, intuition, defined from the point of view of the subject who sees and intuits. Idea is understood 1. as essence, unity of all of the attributes of a thing; 2. as something that has a real existence. Ideas are the existing essences of things in the sensory world.

Thursday 21
I get onto the tram after waiting at the intersection, let myself be carried through the city while I read. In this way, I have found a way not to remain still and not to lose my will to read several books each week.

The Greeks have two terms for time. The first: the period of life, the time span of life, the duration of (individual) life. The second: the duration of time. Time in its whole amalgam of infinite time. Eternity: the totality of time.

Plato. Time is the moving image of eternity.

The concept of time is bound to the concept of eternity. Eternity: something that cannot be measured by time because it transcends time. Eternity is always. Thus, it cannot be said that eternity is a projection of time to infinity. Time is an everlasting image of eternity because it moves in accord with the number. Eternity does not negate time but rather bisects it, holds it to its breast; time moves within eternity, which is its model.

Sunday 24
Of course, Sundays are ridiculous. On the street, couples pass by with their children; the bars near the College are inhabited by strangers. I

return home and lock myself up in my room to write some letters to my friends.

Wednesday 27

I have, finally, lost my interior life. I thereby realize a dream that I nourished for years. To live without ever thinking, to act in the simple manner of men of action. Meanwhile, I come and go to the University; I individualize certain faces in the multitude and start to be recognized in turn. That is to say, they have already started to ask things of me: to share some class notes, to attend a student-center meeting, etc.

May 5

I place here my established plan of study. I am taking five subjects—in sum, three in history, one in philosophy, and another in literature. I have so many things to do, and I do them with such frivolity and intelligence, that everything seems simple to me. I try to do several things at the same time to keep myself occupied. Here, I once again make a list to provide a record of my real experience.

Finish making a clean copy of the notes for "Argentine History."
Read about culture during the era of Louis XIV.
Summary of *The Essence of Philosophy* by M. Scheler.
Haircut.
Library.
Shave.

I am slowly discovering the city. I cross Plaza Moreno and take Diagonal 74. By crossing the plaza every day in the same place, I begin to leave a trail marked out on the lawn. One might say that I am making a path.

For Kant, space and time are forms of our capacity or faculty to perceive; they are forms of intuition. Time is a priori; it does not come out of experience, it is independent of experience, it is not the concept of something real but is, like intuition, a pure form of all possible things rather than something inside of everything. We can conceive of time without events, but not of an event without time.

Time is not a concept, it is an intuition; one cannot think of it by means of concepts. It is a mode of our awareness, of our lived experiences.

Space and time are modes of thought; they are ideas that exist in our minds prior to all observations of phenomena. Molds into which we pour the results of experience. They are subjective, not independent of the observer. Time is a necessity for thought.

I listen to Marian McPartland, a woman who plays jazz on the piano with an inflection at once lyrical and furious.

Saturday, May 7
Antonio, the brother of the boardinghouse's owner, is a defeated man—celibate, passionate about the Culture (capitalized). He lives complaining about books that he still has not read. He has a girlfriend whom he met when he turned fifty. We have a common interest in Martínez Estrada. He keeps his library in his sister's house to ensure that he will not lose it if, at some point, he ends up getting married and then, as he says, has to divide up the goods when he gets divorced. He collects programs from the Colón Theater, with absurd annotations that try to grasp the gravity of the music heard.

Best so far have been the classes with Silvio Frondizi, Enrique Barba, and especially Boleslao Lewin. He speaks with a gravelly accent, an air of an erudite Jew that, according to him, scandalizes the liberals of the left (and others as well, he adds). Erudite concerning rebellions (he has written a great book about Túpac Amaru), he is an active anticlerical. One of his central themes is the horror of the Spanish Inquisition in America. He is full of manias and tics and demonstrates the qualities of a European intellectual: erudition and self-confidence. He is, by far, the best among the "respectable professors," the only one who manages to ensnare us by being passionate about what he does.

Furthermore, he tells these stories. William Lamport, an Irishman, comes to America in the sixteenth century. Detained by the Inquisition, he succeeds in escaping; it is one of the most storied cases in history of a man who manages to break free from the clerical chains, as he says. He writes a manifesto and posts it in the central plaza of Mexico. He enters the viceroy's bedroom, wakes him, and delivers a copy to him. He leaves to live with the Indians; in the end they find him, arrest him, and burn him at the stake.

Monday, May 9
Aunt Veronica died yesterday. They woke me in the middle of the night, and I traveled on the bus to be present at the wake. People piled up in Lasalle's house; I had my hair very short, everyone seemed delighted to see it that way. Roberto embraced me, crying, too sentimental for me not to be moved as well (despite my new brightly colored silk tie, which I put on without thinking and which made me feel uncomfortable the whole time, as if I were laughing while everyone else was grieving). I remembered the afternoon when my mother carried me in her arms to the fence with rounded pickets and told me that Uncle Eugenio had fallen off of a train. And my mother said to me, "Don't you feel sorry that your uncle is about to die?" I started to cry, of course. I was four years old, I imagine, but that memory came to me like a gust of wind when Roberto embraced me, crying, and said to me in a low voice, "She left us." Then there was a barbecue and we ate on the patio, very cold. Many relatives whom I had not seen in years, arguments in low voices, altered by inheritance. At the burial, I remember a ridiculous succession of figures removing their hats automatically as we pass in procession.

I spent that night at home with Grandfather Emilio; he did not speak of the death of Veronica, whom he loved and admired for making her own way, as he said, when Gerardo, her husband, stopped working in order to devote himself to politics, as he would say. In reality, my grandfather explained, he was a point man for the conservatives, a handsome electioneer, a minor commander in Turdera. My grandfather laughed explaining that Gerardo, always fashionable, in a double-breasted suit and a hat, was a player who was always looking after his fame and would say to his wife, when asking her for money, "Veronica, got any little stuff?" Nono laughed, because the man would act like he had large bills in his pocket and just needed change.

Saturday 14
I often get together with Luis Alonso; he brings me all of the provincial myths. Natural life, lived experience, political conscience, folkloric camp-fires. We went to a lecture by Silvio Frondizi. He predicted the economic crisis, spoke of the impossibility of a real way out for the nation, except along the road of socialism. Alonso, sitting beside me in one of the chairs in the Great Hall that face 6th Street, said to me, "I want to work so that I can raise myself up to the working class. I don't want to be one of the enlightened bourgeois."

When I heard this it seemed so ridiculous to me that I had an attack of laughter and everyone thought I was crazy because Silvio Frondizi was, at that moment, giving a very serious answer to a question about the state of the world.

A while ago I argued with Oscar G., who lives in one of the rooms in the house. Deliberately, and with malice, I destroyed one of his delusions. He is in love with a girl, and with an inflexible logic I made him see that it was stupid to get one's hopes up prematurely. Immediately, I corrected myself; all hope is premature, I told him, you have to live lucidly. I have now succeeded, I told him, in building for myself a disillusioned and cold way of looking. Nothing more.

Sunday 15

I went to the theater to see *That Forward Center Died at Dawn* by Agustín Cuzzani. A kind of allegorical and sometimes entertaining farce about the world of soccer. I left by Calle 44, dark, among the trees, and went back through the city to my single student's room.

Tuesday 17

I am reading *The Rebel* by Camus. Referring to those who place history as a transcendent tribunal that decides the justice of all choices, he writes, "History, as an entirety, could exist only in the eyes of an observer outside it and outside the world. History only exists, in the final analysis, for God."

Wednesday

There is a strike; it began in Medicine and the other colleges gave in. I work on Louis XIV.

The Greek being is a being without time. For Heidegger, the being is with time, where time is not surrounding and almost bathing the thing (as in astronomy). In astronomy, time is there, surrounding the thing, and transforms it, but the thing is what it is, independent of the time that slips away along with it.

In existence, time is inside of the thing itself; the very being of the thing consists of temporal being, or rather anticipation, of wanting to be, of the ability to be, the limit of which is death. That is nonindifference, the anguish that is the inherent and tragic characteristic of life. Anxiety of being and fear of the void.

Saturday, May 21

From reading my journals, some conclusions arise. A certain romanticism, slightly idiotic; an excess of sensitivity and self-justification. At first glance, nothing has happened to me except for the uninterrupted succession of catastrophes. The slogan of the past years has been "I need to change, to become someone else." To truly confront reality. If I were to think again about what I have written about Grandfather Emilio, how he stayed in Adrogué when we left, I could, in fact, see that I have stayed with him, in any case, spiritually. Of course, he is the one who pays for my degree since the conflict with my father . . .

Sunday 22
I ask to speak in a plaza, in an unscheduled political act, and I align myself with the critics of Frondizi's government. Curiously, I do it with great indifference, as though someone else were speaking for me, and it were with someone with whom I didn't entirely agree.

Today I played poker at the University Club and won forty pesos.

National euphoria for the one hundred fifty years since the May Revolution. Frondizi cloaks the nation under the nation's history. We are all Argentinians; why think about the present?
I go on writing from here, from my bed—a refuge and not a battlefield.

Monday, May 30
Once again in La Plata. It rained for the whole trip; I only just found a taxi in Plaza Italia and here I am. A terrible pain in my back, which worries me.

A sharp metaphor for my relation to the body: back pain. I go to sleep in a hard bed. In the boardinghouse, I get a plank in the servant's quarters in the back. I go to bed and sleep; when I get up the pain continues, but I have yellow fingers. An attack of the liver. I stir up the whole house. A while later it is discovered that, in fact, I have stained my fingers with oxide from the plank or possibly with rust; the truth is that I manage to realize that there is no serious problem with my liver and that the pain may all have been caused by the trip on the bus; I recover, the pain leaves me, etc. Myths born from monitoring my body as though it were a stranger, an enemy.

June

To speak of the room in which I live; the space always influences the modes of thought. To speak of the light that isolates me and places me in another reality, again the need to trace limits, to install myself in a sacred zone within which it is possible to watch the world. Then to take refuge in a fragile and luminous space—that is to say, to set aside the darkness. I would have to delineate the regions, to make a personal map of the different places in which I live. There are neutral spaces; they are like a continuation of my body, as if my own figure ended in the border between the light and shadows; here, I write: clarity here, and outside, reality.

Solitude is a kindly moment if there is someone in the periphery; the only unendurable solitude is that of not "mattering" for anyone. For me, the lonely person is not Robinson Crusoe but rather someone no one knows in the middle of the multitude.

A class with Pouza about mythology and about the notion of excess in Greek culture, of overabundance as evil. In contrast, equilibrium and harmony are the beginnings of philosophy.

Thursday 2

I could make an investigation into the inhabitants of this house. To begin with, the landlady's husband, with his Vincent Price air, who has lost his job as an accountant for a cold-storage business in Berisso. He wanders from one place to another, made uncomfortable by the vacant time; he buys some things at the market, sweeps the floors. We all know that he has been fired, and he knows that we all know.

Friday 3

At the College, the philosophy classes are the most intriguing to me. In history, we spend a great deal of time in the archives. As for literature, I have proposed writing my monograph at the end of the seminar on Argentine literature, taking as my subject the stories of Martínez Estrada.

Monday, June 6
I spent a few days in Adrogué with Grandfather Emilio. We went out in the car and drove to Pereyra Iraola Park to get a little air. My grandfather is always in good spirits and makes jokes about himself and the rest of the human race. The experience of the war, so distant, persists within him like a dream dreamt the night before. Equally confusing, equally meaningless: he tries in steps to construct a coherent account. What is vivid for him is divided into two stages: the year he spent at the front, where he was injured and where he saw the horrors up close, and the time when he was in charge of the post office for the Second Army. It was there that he really became aware of what was happening. He was in charge of the letters that were to be sent to the relatives of dead soldiers and also of the classification of personal papers and objects found in the backpacks of the victims, killed in combat. My opinion is that it was this second experience that gave him an all-encompassing view of the war and its cruel and unusual development.

Tuesday 7
I am reading *Socrates* by Rodolfo Mondolfo.

I recall Nietzsche's critical position, regarding Socrates as the culprit behind the death of Greek tragedy. I have to work along this line for my final paper.

Thursday 9
It rained all day; I spent the afternoon in the archives. Afterward I spoke with Elena over the phone and finally went to Fine Arts and infiltrated the film students' group to watch a series of Argentine short films. We saw *Los pequeños seres* by Jorge Michel, *The Binder* by Dino Minitti, *Buenos Aires* by David J. Kohon, *Diary* by J. Berendt, *Lights, Camera, Action* by Rodolfo Kuhn, *Perpetual Motor* by Osías Wilenski. The finest were *The Wall* by Torre Nilsson, a certain expressionism in the lighting and a fragmented and impenetrable story, and Kohon's *Buenos Aires*, a sort of

lyrical documentary on the city. Berendt and Kohon were present, and spoke about the need to rejuvenate Argentine cinema and to promote auteur film.

I come here all the time because the School of Film has opened and they are always showing movies that I want to see. I am friends with Edgar Cozarinsky, a very good critic, and Armando Blanco, who studies editing with Ripoll. Here also I met Eduardo Rollie, who teaches aesthetics and has given several classes on the Russian avant-garde of the twenties. He is a graphic designer very influenced by—or very attentive to the influence of—Malevich, Lissitzky, and Rodchenko. He works at the University with Manolo López Blanco, with whom I have also become friends. Manolo tries to develop an aesthetics based on certain hypotheses from Marxism, or perhaps, put better, Trotskyism.

Friday 10
The days are all the same. Now I sit in an armchair on the patio. This morning I went to the College. It is ill-advised to think. One must try to make everything slide imperceptibly away.

Returning to yesterday's notes about my new friends, they are divided into several categories. The closest is José Sazbón, who studies philosophy and whom I met on the day I first entered the University. I went to the student center to orient myself a little, and one of the people in charge of the center pointed out a young man who looked like a flyweight boxer and told me, "He knows Leibniz." I approached José and said, "They told me you know the work of Leibniz." He smiled and said, "I only know what can be known about Leibniz's work."

Saturday
I am returning to Adrogué; I am on the train. The meetings with Grandfather Emilio are for me the best part of this era. In exchange for the salary he pays me, he has asked that I dedicate myself to organizing his

archives. We have decided that I will spend the weekends with him. What he calls "the archive" is a disorderly collection of folders and boxes that contain a variety of materials dedicated to the Italian campaign during the First World War. When I ask how he acquired them, he answers me: "They were all too preoccupied in the work of surviving in the trenches to occupy themselves with the documents and papers that I took, to stop them from being lost."

I spent the afternoon playing cards in Club Adrogué with my cousins from childhood: Horacio and Oscar. They meet on Friday nights and go on playing poker until sunrise on Sunday. They employ a chef who cooks meals for them during the weekend. The funny and unusual thing is that they call this section of the club El Sóviet. It is a servant's quarters remodeled into a room for chess and billiards, which an accomplice at the club lets them occupy in exchange for some money. I dropped in around ten tonight and they greeted me with a slight gesture, as though I had been playing with them, too. I left around one and they were still going, sitting there with a couple of women from work and some people waiting for their turn to play. They are still there now, going on as I write this note. I forgot to mention that I won one hundred seventy-five pesos.

I go to bed in the back room of the old house in which we have lived since thirteen years ago, a time now distant and strange. My grandfather maintains what I jokingly call "the army routine." He goes to bed at ten at night and gets up at six in the morning. I hear him, half-asleep, doing calisthenics on the patio and singing patriotic Italian songs in his baritone voice.

Sunday
Once again I spend the afternoon playing cards with Horacio and Oscar, who go on as brazenly as ever. The people who play with them sometimes come in from nearby towns, and the poker games have spectators who

often place bets, and they do, too, as though they were watching a cock fight.

Time. Heidegger: temporality as the interior lived experience of man. Temporality as condition. Existence, within its rule, contains time. One must distinguish between the time that is within life and the time that life constitutes. Within life there is the time of physics, which comes from the past. The time that life constitutes comes from the future. A time that begins in the future. The present is the realization of the future. The present is a future that comes into being. And that is the time of life. The time that life constitutes consists of the inversion of the time that is within life. Existence has the property, in particular, that when it has been it ceases to be. When it has passed and is in the preterite, it transforms into a solid material, into something that has the quality of the being within itself, what it already is, that which is identical. Existence is not that: it is anticipation, eagerness to want to be.

Monday, June 20
A patriotic day: there is no class today. A long conversation with my grandfather about the most persistent theme in the letters from dead soldiers. "They all announced the forthcoming end to the war," he told me, and began a sort of litany: "We will be together at Christmas, expect me by next harvest, the war won't go on past the end of summer." They all wanted the war to end, he told me, but no one knew what to do to bring it to an end. The devilish thing about it, he told me, is that we all began to understand that the weapons we used were so deadly that no one among us was prepared to bear them. And the weapons were not, in themselves, going to halt the killing. We dug trenches that flooded and then dug a second line of trenches and a third. But this was useless because, from time to time, we had to go out into the open field. He paused: to die, he said.

Wednesday 22
Excited by Plato's *Dialogues*, which I read fragmentarily in their original versions and in several translations. When I come round, it is already three in the morning.

Thursday, June 23
Conversations with José Antonio, a philosophy student very interested—too much so for me—in Heidegger. We have ironic arguments about his style; he sounds very affected and a little kitsch from what I can tell. Of course he gets angry, and then I open another battlefront and say, "Well, he was a bit of a Nazi." Then he really gets angry; he turns furious and tells me he won't think of arguing over these demagogic positions, outside of philosophy, with me. "All philosophers who are worth the trouble to read, beginning with Plato, were authoritarians, philo-fascists, and also heathens." Usually the conversation would be interrupted there, and we would spend the rest of the time making jokes.

Friday 24
Yesterday I went to see the short films by Resnais—*Night and Fog* and *Toute la mémoire du monde*—at Fine Arts and I ran into Julio A., who had come from Mar del Plata to study film here. I was happy and excited to see him. We went out to eat and talked until late. His intention is to progress as far as he can in his degree but, at the same time, he does not want to leave his mother alone in Mar del Plata. Julio is surrounded by a group of friends here, among them Oscar Garaycochea in particular, who is still publishing his magazine *Contracampo*. Julio speaks to me with great enthusiasm about *Dr. Mabuse*, the film by Fritz Lang, which I still have not seen.

Tuesday 28
I remember Attilio Dabini's lecture on Pavese. It was important to me because he writes a diary called *This Business of Living*. He killed himself, but not before leaving the book ready for publication.

I started going out with the redheaded girl who went to Buenos Aires with us on Saturday in a group in "Philosophy and Letters," on Calle Viamonte, to interview Rubén Benítez, who has written a novel (*Ladrones de luz*), which we discussed in class. Her name is Vicky, and she is very nice. We plan to see each other at the College after the break.

Wednesday 29

I saw Vicky today. We met each other by chance in the bar on the same corner as the College and stayed together. They funny thing is that afterward she wanted to know about the stories I am writing, so I gave her my notebook and told her she could read them, no hurry, and return it to me when we see each other after vacation week.

Thursday 30

I am crushed. By mistake (?) I gave one of those notebooks to that redheaded girl, believing it was the notebook where I was writing my stories. It held my lamentations over Lidia from the year '59. So, do I want her to figure it out? I cannot accept the "coincidence" of such errors. Even the idea that she could be reading them at this moment frightens me.

The trouble came when, searching for the stories that I had written, I flipped over all of my notebooks. I suppose that, without realizing, I put one back in the wrong place and yesterday, in a hurry, I took it with me. The funniest part is that I'm trapped. I cannot say to her, "Give me my diary, I gave it to you by mistake." The best thing would be to tell her that the diary is a novel and make myself indifferent toward her opinion. It is written in the first person, but I don't think I included my name anywhere. I don't think I would have written, "Emilio went here or there."

Neither can I expect her to read it and appear before me at the College and say, "These aren't your notes." I could tell her, "They are my notes, just about something else." I also imagine a situation in which she says,

"No. I don't know how to read. I'm blind. I don't understand Spanish. I forgot it on the bus. I didn't have time to open it. I love you, this notebook shows that you're the man I've been looking for." She sells it; it goes on to be published in installments in La Plata's newspaper, *El Día*.

To top it all, I have no idea what kind of girl she is, enigmatic and beautiful. We only spent one night together. Vicky, send me back the notebook unopened.

Fear of ridicule.

It seems as though I chose that one, the most melodramatic and most idiotic. But am I sure? And what if I had lost it? I mean that they seem impossible to me, not when I am writing, but afterward.

I think of her now, dying of laughter at me.

Every so often I turn over the room, scatter all of my papers and search for it again. I never find it. I am responsible for this almost diabolical bind. Writing the stories, wanting to show them off, messing up everything to search for them, throwing everything on the bed. Getting anxious, putting *that one* away in the wardrobe with my notes from the College. Telling her, "Yes, I'll bring you the notebooks so you can take out the finals." Getting the time wrong and leaving much too early but in a hurry. Flipping through the other notebook (and not that one) on the tram. Not looking it over during Aznar's class. Giving it to her in a hurry, without making sure. Too many coincidences combined.

I also tell myself it's not so bad. Or do I really want to believe that I wrote them for myself alone?

It is nine at night; I have just finished dinner. Earlier I went to the College, saw Vicky. I told her about the diary. Smiling, she told me she had not looked at it (she lied). She asked what it was and I said, "Well, something too personal, not suitable for redheaded girls." Then she burst out laughing and said, "I read it, and it was very amusing."

I killed time in the College library with the windows that open onto Calle 7, sitting alongside the table reading Pirandello's stories. Afterward, I copied citations in the Philosophy Institute for my "Plato and Thought" class. And I ended the night watching *Night Train* by the Polish director Kawalerowicz.

Saturday, July 2
I went to Mar del Plata, taking advantage of the break.

Sunday 3
To be unreal. That is the aspiration of philosophy. It is not right to accept reality as it is. If the appearance of the world and its truth were visible, it would not be necessary to think. It seems to be about leaving out necessities, the body, and gaining access to the world of platonic ideas.

Monday 4
I am a fool, anyway. Tied to the false results of my life, I let myself be swept along, lost in a city, in a nation, in which no one knows me, in which no one would cry for me. I exaggerate as a way of showing my present state.

When I am sitting at the desk against the window, time seems not to pass.

Wednesday 6
If I could come to the end of my ideas, I would have to be able to invent a poetics founded on art being understood as the loss of reality.

I work on my monograph about the stories of Martínez Estrada.

Lately I have started tossing a coin into the air every time I need to make a decision. I don't believe there is anything to regret about a method of thought—or action, at any rate—based upon chance. That must be my way of life: turning my face to the wall so no one can surprise me and tossing a coin in order to know what to do. Letting myself be swept away.

Great difficulty in finding a way to relate what I am experiencing. The only thing that makes me go on noting down the days in these notebooks is the possibility of finding a meaning that breaks the opacity of hours that leave no trace.

I am reading Mallea and Murena—somber thoughts, heavy prose.

Fidel Castro announces new nationalizations. The USA lowered the fees on sugar that it buys from the Cubans. Pressure, difficulties, conflicts.

Saturday, July 9
Yesterday Roberto and Alicia came here—that is, one of my favorite cousins and his wife.

Russia announces that it will support Cuba with its missiles.

Wednesday, July 20
I bathe, I shave. At this altitude, these activities take me all morning. I watch my face in the mirror as I shave; it is the first joke of the day. My own scars entertain me; I make grooves.

I have to write the essay on the Martínez Estrada stories. I am "blocked," I cannot bring myself to begin. For the moment, I do nothing but read Eduardo Mallea. I am reading *Chaves*, an edition by Bartleby; the character says only "No," it is the direct negative, he speaks little and it is—for those who try—indecipherable.

All of Mallea's characters are *serious* people. It actually seems as if they are half-asleep.

I search for intelligent women, because intelligence is the best quality I have. I actually seem like one of Mallea's characters. A slow life that moves through a slow afternoon like this one. I form sentences.

I saw *Pépé le Moko* by Julien Duvivier. He spends it killing Arabs in the narrow and steep streets of the Kasbah. The best part is the death of Pépé (Jean Gabin). The dying man looks at the girl: "Bye bye, honey," he says. "Pray for me."

I had a good day today. I went to the theater. I finished *Simbad* by Mallea. He gave it that name so as not to call it *Ulysses*, but that was the story he wanted to tell. All of the characters are exhausted and speak gravely about their flaws. None of them are rotten or greedy men; they all have great weaknesses. They all want to kill themselves or go off to live in the jungle; they abandon the women in their lives for ethical reasons. They are all introspective.

My face is covered with marks, recent scars, reddish traces. I would like to be black.

I write in bed. Certainty that I spend my life fighting against myself. Something just occurred to me, but I cannot now remember what it was. I would like to return home; we never should have left. My mother did not want to leave my father behind; she came along with him and does not forgive herself for it. Now I am going to turn out the light.

Tuesday, July 26
The anniversary of the Cuban revolution. Castro still endures. Only Mexico and Venezuela support him. We are about to break ties.

I continue my monograph. Yesterday I finished the first part. The only thing remaining is the chapter on "Marta Riquelme." I am going to try to finish it. The best part is working through the ideas: when I write, I let myself be swept away and something else always comes out. I would have to spend my whole life thinking. Rather, I would need to have the magical ability that, when I think of something, I would write only that.

I finished the work. The final sentence reads, "The man who lives in spite of reality is greater than one who lives by virtue of it."

Notes preceding a prologue. A man without personality. The hollow man. He speaks only in set phrases. Readings, quotations, foreign words; a sort of Don Quixote gone off in the tangle of sentences he has read. He lets himself get carried off by books. Otherwise, no one notices this delirium. He has been a professor of literature in a secondary school. He always seems distracted. Single, retired, lives alone.

I spend the morning writing my monograph. The work is almost ready. Remaining is an index of the characters. I could perhaps put it in alphabetical order. I hope to finish tonight.

Saturday
Tired of writing. I worked all morning. I am missing a lot. Rafael V. came—the farewell, the nostalgia. The trip to Tandil at the end of the course. Rafael, his extraordinary intuition for mathematics—he thinks in formulas and geometric figures. I read him ten pages of the essay. Praise, etc. Afterward we talk about suicide. He is leaving for Rosario to study physics.

Monday, August 1
Everything goes on the same here, as though nothing had happened. Nothing ever happens. And what could happen anyway? It is as though I spent the entire month of July underwater. Sitting on the patio before a low, small table, the same feeling as always: great struggles to come. The texts. For the moment, I secretly maintain my resolve to become a writer.

I went to the College. I have been here for months, and now I know more people than I could have imagined. In philosophy, Pucciarelli continues with Socrates and Plato. Pure ideas: essences are material and concrete and atop reality (like a mirror). I am a typical Platonic character (living in the air). In literature, I presented the proposal for my final project on the stories of Martínez Estrada. In this way, I will read Kafka once again.

I went to see Luis; we have great plans for the future. To go to Paris together, to study with Bachelard. I vacillate between declaring myself a Platonist and a Hegelian. Between Ideas and the Absolute Spirit, these are the rivers I will navigate.

In the theater: *Sawdust and Tinsel* by I. Bergman. The scene with a clown who speaks to his wife in the mirror.

An empty, useless day. I did nothing. As though the moment to work had not arrived. Sitting in bars, I watch the girls go by.

Wednesday, August 3
I go to the theater on Calle 7 to see *The Keepers* by Georges Franju. The light was cut off. The film stopped at the best moment. I did not want them to refund my ticket because I want to finish seeing it today. Everything takes place in an asylum, indecipherable faces, all very sensational. I spent two hours in the hall waiting pointlessly with the two or three others, miserable as I was, who had nothing better to do. Finally, I got bored and returned home. I will never know what happened in that movie.

Friday 5
In the afternoon I went to the College, turned in my monograph. I spoke about Martínez Estrada and Kafka.

A lecture by Alfredo Palacios in the Great Hall of the College of Law. So many people. Palacios, with pointed mustaches, hair long and styled with gel, looks like a character from a cartoon, a mix of Colonel Cañones and Doctor Merengue. He made his appearance, accompanied by a spectacular brunette. He spoke about Cuba, where he had been invited by the government and spent three weeks traveling around the island. Agrarian reform, each laborer to receive four hundred hectares, public education, combating illiteracy. "They're not communists, they are humanists." I lean in toward Vicky: "If it's true they're humanists, they'll last three months." She laughs; nothing catches her off guard. She is quick and very clever. "We could use political violence as a form of education," she said in her sweet little voice. "For every ten laborers who learn to read, an oligarch must be executed." "Terrorism," she added after a while, "is the political version of public education."

Saturday
A meeting with Elena and two old friends from secondary school, Lucrecia and Olga. We went to the theater (*Six Characters in Search of an Author* by Pirandello). When it ended, we went to have a coffee in a bar with mirrors and tables against the wall. We discussed Pirandello's imaginary games with identities, and I don't know why but we ended up on clandestine politics and from there moved to the situation in Cuba and the executions of the hit men (of Batista). "Justice," I said, "is the same as power. Whoever has the power is justice. Otherwise, you have to be a believer." We returned at sunrise. Everything has faded with Elena. Now I do not love her, it is true, but I did love her so much. The desire to sleep together persists, but, when we are there, it is as though we were two little siblings bored of being together. We were so young; I was too young to understand that history with her, so we preferred to leave everything in suspense. We took the train together as far as Tempered, and from there she took the train for Adrogué and I went on to La Plata.

Monday, August 8
I am astonished. In class, the professor from "Introduction to Literature" said that my work on Martínez Estrada was the best that she has read in her time at the College. They are going to publish it in the humanities magazine. It was a lot of work for me to write it, and it did not seem so great to me. At the same time, indifferent before praise, I listened to her as though she were talking about someone else. The first public evidence of an ability that I have taken for granted. (First to be a writer and *afterward* to write.) The publications committee for the School of the College of Letters told me to congratulate you, the professor said, and I thought it would improve my relations with the girls in the hallways, especially with Vicky.

I am going to sleep. I would like to wake up within a year (or at least within six months).

Tuesday
In the afternoon and evening at the cinema, I saw *Last Pair Out* by Alf Sjöberg and also *Port of Call* and *Three Strange Loves* by Bergman. The art of cinema has installed itself in Sweden. They make very dramatic films. I was in the theater for six hours.

I said goodbye to José Antonio, the Heidegger fanatic, who left for a semester to study in the United States. Try to bring it to Faulkner, I tell him as the bus pulls up. He gives some answer and makes a gesture, but I cannot hear him anymore.

Thursday 11
An assembly to discuss a student statement in support of Cuba. To accept that the USSR sustains and helps the revolution is to admit that Cuba has turned into a Soviet satellite, but to condemn the help of the Russians is to play the Americans' game. What can be done? We propose a condemnation of the American invasion plans, without

including any observations in the declaration about the Soviet impact, as the anarchists were demanding. The proposal went through, 60 to 40.

Friday 12
I feel so light that I could be a cat. The sky went dark at ten in the morning. A ferocious storm: it rains buckets, as they say.

At the theater: *On the Waterfront* by E. Kazan. Brando tells the girl that he was the one who killed her brother, and at the same time a siren sounds from a ship. Close up of a face and then the rooftops.

Saturday 13
I went to Adrogué, spent the afternoon with Grandfather Emilio. He remains absorbed in his project of organizing the papers that he brought back from the war. A meeting in the old bar. My cousin Horacio, Tagliani, López. They leave for the club. I let them go and I took the train and went to Buenos Aires. A sense of difficulty in "entering" the city.

Sunday
Quickly I began to write a letter to Elena to say that I am not coming to see her. We really no longer have anything to do with each other. I do not say it as directly as that, but that is the theme. Telling her what we have told each other during those months. We are friends, but we live in different worlds. I wrote to her all at once, without thinking. I asked Nono for an envelope, closed it and then tore into several pieces and threw out the remains in the bathroom. You cannot write a letter to say goodbye or break up without making a fool of yourself. From then on I entered the void. I think of nothing; I cannot say anything. Grandfather comes looking for me and takes me to the room where he keeps the letters that were never sent. They keep him awake, never leave him in peace.

Tuesday 16
Zunino, the head of practical work in philosophy, a bit intimidated in the class full of only women (except for me). An analysis of moral impulse in Scheler. Relationships between philosophy and "vulgar consciousness." The distinction lies in the object toward which the judgment is directed. Common sense generalizes; thought is always concrete and directed toward a fact. There is no science of the singular.

Friday 19
Professor Campos once again praises my monograph on Martínez Estrada. "Intensity, refinement, and style." I can barely stop from burying myself under the desks.

I realize that in my discussion of Marxism with Luis I support myself with Camus. And in the anarchist tradition: morally, the reductionism of Marxism is unacceptable, as is its reduction of everything to material interests. The whole argument in Camus consists of reducing Marxism to what is experienced in the USSR.

Thursday, August 25
At the College, they put on a show of New Theater. A performance for the students who can dedicate themselves to the study of theater. Alejandra Boero and Pedro Asquini, *The Farce of the Cashier Who Went to the Corner* by Ferreti. A kind of Kafka mixed with Roberto Mariani.

Saturday, August 27
An assembly at the College yesterday. The anarchist association contended that religious symbols must be removed, especially that of the crucified Christ in the Great Hall. A great discussion, and an appearance at around ten at night by Pacheco, a very well-known anarchist leader who has just arrived by plane from Córdoba. "Down with Christ," he says, "we came to study, not to pray." The humanists whistle and stomp on the floor.

Sunday 28

I feel heavy, distant; I slept fitfully through a siesta. I drank too much alcohol. My mouth is dry, my legs cramped. And what now? The whole day ahead; several options, none very attractive.

I escape to the cinema, watch *Kanał* by A. Wajda. I leave at nine at night, rather lost. I go to the theater: *Time and the Conways*. Interesting—distortions caused by temporality and chronological leaps. The work duplicates the abrupt cuts and switches from the novel; Virginia Woolf is very much present. Killing time—death would be better. As an aside, I wonder: Will I, like the Conways, be a failure in twenty years? 1980, two decades from now: After having lived through those years, will they seem few? Will I think, as I do now, that my life stretches before me? Maybe it does, still, but there can be no doubt that everything will be different. This I know, or believe, but what will it be like? I won't know then either, because in that moment I will want, as I do now, to know my future. (Or will I be dead?)

Wednesday, August 31

Several unexpected meetings with Vicky: I found her in the theater the other night, then, the next day, I saw her on Calle 7 and we went to have a coffee. Tuesday at the College. She is eighteen. Red hair (like all the women I love), subtle, "living"—in every sense. I am blown away; she is blown away as well. In the woods, nothing common. Number 13. The bazaar.

Friday, September 2

Last night, in Plaza Moreno, I thought I had seen Elena. I thought, *She came looking for me.* I started running because the girl was crossing the street toward the tram stop. I reached her at the corner; under the light, I saw that it was not her, and she looked at me, surprised. "Sorry," I said, "you look just like a friend of mine." Then she smiled. "Oh, really?" she said, "it happens a lot . . . but I've seen you somewhere before." It turns out that she studies law and so has seen me at the College. I made an impression on her because I kept looking at her as though I knew her.

Maybe we each have a double, someone the same as us, and also someone who is a replica of one of our friends.

Tuesday 6
The acts and the conflicts continue. The Tacuaras bombarded the University, painted swastikas, ruined the painting of Alfredo Palacios, and wrote, "Jews go to Moscow." Because of this, there was an act of condemnation toward the Catholic right. To this is added the conflict in Medicine. We were marching down Calle 7 when the police attacked us. Gas, Molotov cocktails. "Governments pass and the police remain," as Martínez Estrada says.

A critical situation at the College. An assembly to elect the first-year delegates to the University Federation. Vicky nominates me as a candidate, wants to politicize me, is half a Trotskyist. She makes a little speech about me, praising my oratory ability. In the first vote, a tie. Fifty-two votes for each. My adversary is a girl in Pedagogy with a pizza face, supported by the CP (90 percent of the activists from the CP at the College are in Pedagogy). We move on to the tiebreaker, and when it is my turn I abstain from voting for myself. The other girl votes for herself and wins by one vote. Everyone wanted to kill me. Luis almost curses me out: "Are you crazy?" "I have my principles," I tell him. "You're hopeless."

Vicky comes to console me. We have coffee at Don Julio, the College bar. The students were coming and going; it felt like they were all looking at me and recognizing me as the anarchist who would not vote for himself. A moron, they all think (and so do I, sometimes). Vicky stifling her laughter. "What happened?" she said, and kept looking at me as though I were a Martian. "He was embarrassed to vote for himself," she laughed. I defended myself, saying that I did not want to play their game. To top it all, a girl from the CP said, "He voted first, so you had to see that she made the choice herself." The funny thing was that they all embraced her afterward as though she had won by a mile. "You sure are a gentleman," Vicky laughed.

Why didn't I vote for myself? Though it may seem incredible, I did it to impress Vicky, so that she would say the things she said to me. You're an idealist. It's also true that I didn't vote because I didn't want to get wrapped up in university politics. I have only recently arrived; I don't want to waste my time in meetings. Then why did you agree to be a candidate? Vicky's question, that relentless girl.

Wednesday 7

I received a letter from José Antonio, from New York. Doesn't like the food, is fascinated by the library. The country is at war, or wants to be at war, with whatever it can get its hands on. I would like, he says, to be Robin Hood, but it won't turn out well for me. The Americans demand "force" from their future leaders. The sick demand health as they are dying. Never, he advises me, stop seeing the seven faces of the world, because we can envy lunatics for living in incoherence.

When the class is let out I go to the bar with Vicky. Sentimental confessions. She has a boyfriend in her hometown (in General Belgrano) though she no longer loves him, but if she tells him so, he will suffer. She doesn't want to see him suffer, etc. I calmed her down, told her that keeping up the lie is worse. And I started to move toward her. Emilio, she said, I talk to you like one of my girlfriends and you answer by coming on to me. Of course you already know everything about me, I said; you read my journal, so I don't have to tell you my history, this way is better and much faster. She laughs with a laughter that fills me with happiness. And she has red hair! I tell her the story about the girl I fell in love with in primary school, then I tell her about the first time I was with a woman, at fourteen years old; she had red hair, a neighbor, a married woman, a friend of my mother's. I went after her without really knowing why. I spied on her; if I got up on the roof of my house, I had a perfect view through the transom when she was in bed with her husband and the bedside lamp was turned on. I was above her in this way, with these images, like a lone wolf. Until one afternoon, during siesta, I was sitting on the sidewalk and she called for me, made me come in, and when I crossed the hall I saw her: she was naked in the bathroom with the door open, just having bathed. I told her the story in that way, more or less, and she laughed. She has an unforgettable laugh. So, she said, you want to add me to the series of redheaded women in your life. Come, she said; I'll show you the apartment where I live.

Thursday 8

I spent the morning in the University library; it is the place where I feel best, taking cover. They have everything that I look for, and, even better, José Sazbón works half-days in the periodicals section and gets me whatever I want. Today, for example, *La Torre* magazine, from the University of Puerto Rico. Inside, in the silence, with all of those books at hand, life outside matters little to me. I am reading Jaspers; there are four limit situations: 1. No one can live without struggling against contingency. 2. We are going to die. 3. Our empirical experience is deceptive. 4. Life is a permanent choice. Determination. I felt I must construct a system to evade these four truths. They resist consciousness, and we can only perceive them existentially. To live under limit situations and to exist are the same. Or, to say it another way: I, in existing, do not reach my potential being any more than by confronting—past reason—the limit situations. The consequence: tragic-heroism.

Something strange just happened to me. I see someone signaling to me from the door of the reading room. The sun is glaring at me and it takes a while before I realize it is Vicky. When I get closer, she seems almost distraught and holds out a small package to me. Inside is a Buddha carved from bone (I don't think it could be ivory). At first I think she was pulling my leg and giving me the Buddha because I refused to vote for myself. But no. It's for me, she says, because I need protection and luck. Surprised, I don't really know what to do or say, and when I try to respond, she leaves. I cannot follow her because I have books from the library with me and my notebook is on the table. Now it's been a half hour since I've done anything but think of things I should have said to her. She said, "This is to bring you luck." Could she be a Buddhist?

Friday
I got an A on the philosophy midterm. When we were let out, Vicky was waiting for me. Vicky said, "The Buddha brought you luck." I invited her to the movies, but she said she couldn't go. She had barely seen me and left immediately, as though there was nothing between us.

Saturday 10
In the library once again. I read an article by Martínez Estrada in *Sur* magazine. He speaks of historical invariants. Situations that are repeated through time. For example, he considers the rape of the Indian, the native girl, by the Spaniard, the illiterate conquistador. He finds the recurring image of the rape to be of enduring importance. Could historical invariants be discovered inside one's personal life? For example, I think that I came to the library today in order to see whether Vicky would appear in the entrance and wave and gesture to me. Every time that the door to the room opens, I raise my head.

Monday 11
Women. Yesterday morning, I went to the cinema to see *Smiles of a Summer Night* by Bergman, part of a series the film students put together to make a bit of money and publish a magazine. On the sidewalk I see Vicky with Jorge Becerra standing in a line. Hellos, a slight tension, stray sentences. Jorge is surprised. I thought you had gone to Adrogué. I changed my mind, I said. And Vicky looked straight at me, devious; I knew you were in the city, she said. We go on talking, but the conversation does not prosper. Strangely, I feel euphoric (from being with her, I suppose), with the same

euphoria as someone who has discovered the murderer before the end
of a police novel. She looks at me steadily, I talk to Becerra, he seems to
be off in the clouds. Finally, we enter and sit down in the darkness, with
her in the middle. The movie is a hilarious situational comedy. Someone
describes someone who is in love with love. Then the lights come back on
and we leave and go for a coffee. Vicky gets up and goes to the bathroom.
Time passes, and she does not reappear. She left, says Jorge. What do
you mean, she left? I say. It turns out that Becerra comes from the same
town as Vicky, and soon he is telling me the story of her engagement to
a rich guy in the country.

At the College, as I am leaving, Vicky catches up to me in the hallway
that leads to the patio over Calle 6. You're leaving? she says, and before
I can answer, she adds: When are we going to talk, you and I? We are
talking, I say. When will you get here tomorrow? she persists. I'll wait
for you at the bar, she says. Okay, I say. The silence stretches on as it
does in a poker game. You're changing, I tell her. She smiles. Before, you
would turn red when someone spoke to you, I say. I am red, she said.
See you tomorrow.

Tuesday
When I arrive at the bar, Vicky is waiting for me, sitting at the table by
the window. It is very loud at this hour; everyone is talking at the same
time and you can't hear anything. So, a bit later, I say: We should get out
of here. She follows me, docile, playing the good girl. Out on the street
the air clears my head, I supposed Vicky's, too, because before we make
it to the corner she returns to the confusing story about the boyfriend
waiting in her town. I am bad, she said suddenly. I was always bad. I tried
to explain that she didn't need to worry if it was because of me, but she
went on, talking in general, reprimanding herself but also laughing at
herself in sharp bursts, laughing at the idiot waiting in her town (and
laughing at me, too, I suppose).

Wednesday

I woke up at two in the morning yesterday, an effect of my meeting with Vicky. I went out onto the patio, into the darkness, and sat down in the wicker chair, barefoot, my feet touching the ocher flagstones. I sat there for an hour, thinking about Vicky and our rendezvous in the hotel where we went that afternoon. Now I am caught up in another story, yet still I remain alone, always maintaining two or three sparks to fuel my doubts.

Thursday, October 13

I read what I have written in those notebooks, a disorder of feelings. I search for a personal poetics that is (still) not visible here. A diary records events as they are taking place. It does not recall them, only records them in the present. When I read what I wrote in the past, I find blocks of experience, and only reading allows the reconstruction of a history displaced over the course of time. What takes place is understood afterward. One must not narrate the present as though it has already passed.

Sunday, November 6, 1960

I listen to the soccer game on the radio (Independiente 2 – Boca 0), a narration that, like a distant music, accompanied the Sundays of my childhood. There is a verbal unreality in the telling of actions that we cannot see but must imagine. I am fascinated by the fact that this narration is accompanied by "commentary"—that is to say, the theoretical explanation of what takes place in the game. The story and the concept defining it come together.

7

In El Rayo Bar

I spent all of Saturday reading *The Idiot* because I was writing a story about a jeweler who I liked to imagine as a kind of Prince Myshkin, but after a while I had forgotten all of that and was buried in Dostoevsky's novel. The destructive nature of goodness made the story move with the metallic violence of a train that has gone off the rails. Compassion destroys the Prince and Nastasya Filippovna, who confront each other in scenes of incredible intensity. I remained trapped by the intrigue, and by the time I remembered myself it was after midnight and I had forgotten all about my friends and in particular Vicky, a beautiful redhead I was going out with at the time.

It was Saturday; I was alone and too tired to call anyone. I went out to the street and walked to El Rayo, the bar opposite the train station, and set to watching the world. The city seemed to be a different one altogether, darker and more obscene, with desperate people who left the racetrack and wandered around like cats. In a private booth were the alternators, girls a man would pay with a drink—or two drinks—to talk to until, in the end, he could leave with them and head for the hotels that abounded near the station. At any hour there are men looking for women, crossing furtively toward dance clubs that let a soft music fall over the city at night. In the entrance, a young man, tall, emaciated, dressed in a long black overcoat, had paused with a spectral air and signaled to one of the girls off to the side, who was listening to a bolero by Agustín Lara on the Victrola. He seemed to be a perpetual student who, like me, had come out of his hellhole and was wandering about with the air of a solitary wolf.

I ordered one gin and then another; I felt a strange euphoria, as though I could finally taste the harsh flavor of life. I was eighteen, lived alone, and, the same as every time I had money on me, felt calm and safe touching the bills in my pocket: I could enter the station and buy a ticket to anywhere and travel for days on a long-distance train to the north, I could look for a woman and pay her to be with me tonight. Find a haughty Nastasya Filippovna who would sell her body like in the novel. Myshkin had taken part in the bidding because he wanted to save her, but, in the end, when the villain Rogozhin raises the offer to an inconceivable sum, Nastasya agrees to go off with him. Time seemed to pause in that masterful scene: all are looking at her; she accepts the thick wad of bills, takes a few steps and, with a sweetly wicked smile, throws the money into the fireplace. There were cries, voices, and then a silence that seemed so deeply buried in the plot that I let myself crawl through the madness of the story once more. The men exchange awestruck looks at this deranged act; Rogozhin curses her and tries to recover the money from the flames, while the Prince cries disconsolately. Suddenly the lights went out and then shot back to life; they were going to close the bar, the waiters were placing the chairs on the empty tables, there were no longer any girls in the private booth. It was almost three in the morning; the city was still.

I went out into the cold air of the night and buried myself in my coat to protect myself from the icy wind. Some lights still shone in the station, but I decided to return to my room and crossed the corner toward the diagonal, looking for the taxi stand, and saw one of the girls from the bar taking shelter in a doorway, as if she had been waiting for me.

"Where are you going, *chiche*? Take me with you?" she said.

She was blonde, petite, with lots of eye makeup, about my age, or maybe younger, and was wrapped up in a white sheepskin coat.

"You're one of the ones who works in El Rayo."

"I'm not a *one* and I don't work there, I *stop by* El Rayo. And what's up with you? You look like a ghost," she laughed. "Let's go together."

"I don't feel like it, *nena*."

"Like taking me with you? You're boring . . . "

"Here comes a taxi, take it, come on." She did not move and the taxi kept going, so I stepped into the doorway.

"I don't have any paper," she said, and rubbed the tips of her fingers together. "Gimme a cigarette."

We smoked under the light, refugees from the early-morning air. I sensed the harsh odor of worn hide from her leather jacket and listened to her talk in her childlike voice, never stopping, as though she were frightened. She told me she was from Chivilcoy, that her name was Constanza, but they called her Coti; she lived in Tolosa, said she had lots of inner energy and was a follower of La Virgen del Carmen. She moved under the light, thoughtful, and seemed to be offering herself to whoever would buy her.

She took me by the arm and squeezed herself against me; if I didn't take her with me, I would have to sleep here until the station opened and the first train departed at six. She looked down at the little Mickey Mouse watch that she wore on her wrist.

"I'm used to sleeping here," she said. "Guys do their things and then don't take me back, but it doesn't matter to me. I study theater, and Stanislavski says an actor needs to get accustomed to everything and everything is useful for emotional memory."

Suddenly I realized she was slightly delirious. She seemed younger up close—must have been fifteen, sixteen. Thinking of that aroused me and then, almost without thinking, I moved a step away from her and Coti moved back as though she had seen something dark in my face.

"Don't hit me . . . " She threw herself backward.

"What are you saying . . . You're so beautiful. Here, take this." I slid the roll of bills into her coat pocket. "I need to leave. Keep it. Here's a taxi."

A taxi came down the street and I waved at it.

"What did you give me?" she asked, and took a step to the side, the pile of money in her hand. "Money for nothing, but what are you thinking, you pervert? Are you trying to humiliate me?" she said, and started to throw the cash to the ground. "You think I'm a beggar," she said, and headed for the taxi as I collected the bills from off the sidewalk.

"Take it. Let me help you . . . "

"You're drunk, who do you think you are?"

She got into the taxi, which sat against the curb of the sidewalk with the light inside turned on.

"But you're being crazy . . . Don't you see, I won at the races . . . Put down the window."

She was already inside, as though exhibited in a lit shop window, and she shook her head, though I could see she was laughing.

"Give me a kiss," I said.

I opened the door and the taxi tore off while I sat with her and started to kiss her and feel under her blouse and the driver watched us in the mirror.

"Turn off the light," I said. She had curled up against my chest. "Where are you going?" I asked her.

"To the hotel," she said.

"My place is better."

We spent the night together. She seemed like a little girl. Really she *was* a little girl, but she moved and spoke like she had seen it all before. She stood up, naked, and inspected the room, opened up the Dostoevsky novel.

"What are you reading? *Uy*, you really are boring . . . He doesn't understand emotional motivation. The characters all seem crazy; they do whatever, no emotional memory. I study theater with Gandolfo . . . "

"What? You go to Buenos Aires?"

"No, they come here to Fine Arts; he and Alezzo give a class. I want to do a show in El Rayo. I'm rehearsing—didn't you see me today? If I had the money I'd go to Buenos Aires, I have a friend who works at Bambú . . . She's a contortionist, does stripteases. She's doing really well . . . " She looked at the photo of Faulkner on the wall, examined the wardrobe, and

I heard her rummaging through the first-aid kit in the shared bathroom down the hall.

At noon we went out onto the patio, and she immediately started seducing the *provincianos* who lived with me, including the extremely shy one from Bardi. She stayed with us for a couple of days, passed from one room to another each night. I heard her laughing or crying out in her little doll's voice while I read Dostoevsky. The second part is not as good as the first.

8

Diary of a Story (1961)

Tuesday

I've been in Adrogué since Sunday. My grandfather saw me arrive as though no time had passed.

"*Hijo*, better set yourself up in the back room. We have a lot to do . . . "

Ever since he started losing his memory (he says), he has been worried and wants to get his papers in order. The doctors have prohibited him from going out, and that is what makes him the most nervous.

"I didn't lose myself in the Isonzo. See if I lose myself ['go astray,' he says] here." He pauses, thinking. "I already gave you the money, no?"

He gave me the money. He is afraid of losing his maps, the photos, the letters; he hired me to organize his archive, pays me a salary, etc. I learned from him to say *etcetera* when I want to change the subject, but he pronounces it more emphatically in Italian: *echétera*, he says, and makes a gesture with his hand as if to say, "I don't intend to go on with this." In reality, he is paying for my degree. "I don't want you to become some erudite asshole," my son-of-a-bitch father said.

"He was hoping I'd be an attorney . . . "

"So you could get him out of jail," Nono laughs, with his fox's eyes. He would rather I stay and live with him here, to finish organizing his documents. I suggest that he move to La Plata, but he laughs at the idea.

"I'd have to sell the house, buy there." He paused, thinking. "Moving is always diabolical," he said. It is a quote, but he does not remember whose. He is losing his mind, he says, but he knows a multitude of poems and songs by heart and sometimes sings them, alone, on the patio, with his beautiful baritone voice, now so soft and fragile.

Susy, the woman who takes care of him, prepares us a stew of lentils and we eat on the patio, under the grapevines.

"Colonel," says Susy, "I'm upstairs, call for me if you need anything." The old man drinks wine with seltzer and smokes his smelly, one-peso toscano cigars.

We stayed silent for a while. That night was beautiful.

"Hijo," he says, and reads my thoughts once again, "we are well outside, out in the open . . . Lucky thing that you came, you are in La Plata, no?"

His memory is captured by the war and he doesn't know well what to do with this tumult of images and scenes. Sometimes I put on the recorder and save what he recounts, other times I let him talk; he thinks nothing will be lost so long as I am listening.

"Very close to the German lines, little officer Di Pietro," he says, for example, "was crawling like a Boy Scout to observe and listen to the enemy in the trenches. The white light of the spotlights was like a veil . . . " he remembers suddenly, and pauses, dazzled.

It is always like this that he narrates short fragments, very vivid, but they are cut off, never concluded. I write them down with the hope that he will resume them and they can be finished . . . He participated in the great offensive against the Austrians, fortified at the heights over steep ravines between Monte Nero and Monte Mirzli.

"It was an attempt at mass suicide . . . " He goes on thinking. "Once, in Patagonia, I saw hundreds of white whales that hurled themselves onto the beaches to die; we threw them back into the sea and they returned to swim furiously toward the shore, where they gasped for hours . . . Something like that . . . " (He said it in English: "*Something like that.*")

They hit him in the chest and he was buried in the snow all night long—lucid, frozen. His blood spread out around him, and the mountainside was red in the morning, but the extreme cold saved him. If I ask him about it, he grows confused and does not answer. They are like shards, brilliant flashes, perfect, without elision. I would have to narrate it in that way, I think sometimes.

Thursday
When I wake up, I see my grandfather in the garden, reading in the sunlight. He is sitting in a canvas chair, barefoot, his slim torso naked, dressed in elegant blue-colored linen pants, the scar on his chest is an ugly reddish serpent. The sun helps him to absorb, so he says, the vitamin E preventing oxidation, and on top of that he takes white pills that fortify, it seems, his brain cells and drain, as he says, the lagoons of amnesia, the *mental fatigue*. For that reason, he also drinks large doses of Nervigenol and does constant mental exercises: reciting the recruitment numbers of the soldiers from his platoon or repeating the surnames of the sailors who gave their names to the streets of Adrogué—Bouchard, Norther, Bynnon, Espora, Grandville.

"Who would have thought it—they're all sailors, English, French, European criollos, there were pirates, privateers, they sailed for plunder . . . " He paused, blinded by the sun. "*¿Le trincee dove sono?, domandò el ufficialetto Di Pietro appena arrivato sul San Michele. 'Trincee, trincee . . . ' fu mi resposta. 'Non ci sono mica, trincee: ci sono dei bucci.*" He looked at me as if waking. "Pits, gullies, those were the trenches."

Before I could say anything, he stopped, picked up the canvas chair, and moved through the garden, seeking the heat of the sun, still agile.

First he sits in the open air to gain strength, then Susy helps him with his gymnastic exercises, and afterward he spends the greater part of the day in the rooms inside and I listen to him singing (*Bella ciao, bella ciao, ciao ciao*) or muttering names and dates in a monotone prayer, so as not to think. I am close at hand, in case he needs me, and thus we pass the day, so I write a story at night, while he sleeps or pretends to sleep.

I met Lucía at the beginning of March, although "meeting" is a figure of speech; I had seen her and was approaching her little by little—obliquely, I would say, like someone following an image in the window of an illuminated house. We were in the great hall of the College of Humanities, in Rovel's class, and we were moving closer as his lecture on *The Great Gatsby* progressed.

When Rovel analyzed the [extraordinary] scene of the house open onto the bay, with [the white curtains that waved and] Jordan and Daisy lying on the sofa facing Tom Buchanan's entrance, I saw her appear, dressed also in white because it was the end of summer and the lindens were blooming. She arrived late, the class already begun. Blonde, beautiful, fair in the light afternoon air. She waited, paused in the hallway watching Rovel, who was drawing a blueprint of Gatsby's house at Great Neck on the blackboard.

"Everything is moving, and Tom goes to close the curtains as though he wants to stop the disorder," he said, and turned toward Lucía. "And you, why don't you sit down? Do me a favor."

Confused and hurried, she sat down immediately in one of the rows on the side after making her way between the students. The world paused for an instant, because she was too beautiful [and attracted too much attention] and knew, like no one else, the art of interruption [the art of being out of place], like the heroine of a novel about which we barely know the main points, brought along and carried by the narration's weak movement. Clearly she was not the heroine of any novel because, if she had been, I would have saved her.

Wednesday

Yesterday we worked all day in the room full of letters. He rereads them, classifies them. Before, it had been the dinette, but now it is a room of filing cabinets where he keeps letters in numbered folders. The possessions, sometimes in their envelopes, he has placed in a glass cabinet. When I was a boy, he would let me play with the binoculars of a French cavalry officer. How he got them I never asked. I watched the world through the glasses turned backward and everything, even my grandfather, still young at that time, appeared minute and distant, enclosed in a circle like drawings in a cartoon.

Now my grandfather only wants to talk about his time in charge of the Second Army's post office. They posted him there after he had spent a season in the military hospital of Trieste, recovering from the chest injury that he received during the hallucinatory offensive of the Isonzo (a million deaths), and he did not then return to the front.

He was charged with writing letters to the families of the dead soldiers, announcing the deaths of their beloved, and with sending them the objects found on their bodies. Especially the half-written letters, never sent or interrupted by death.

Mama carissima, I am all wrapped up tonight, writing to you with my hands warmed by the woolen gloves that you knitted for me—I made a little hole with my bayonet in the point of the index finger and thumb to free up my fingers so I can hold a pencil and write to you. I am wearing many layers of clothing, one on top of another, and with my Alpine hat I look like one of the fat dwarves from Snow White. The trench is deep, and I can nearly stretch out my legs to sleep. It is three in the morning. The night is gray because there is a full moon. We are trying out the new watches, a novelty here. They attach with a little leather belt around the wrist. It has an illuminated dial and numbers, so we can see the time without raising our heads and putting ourselves in danger, like I used to have to do with Papo's round covered watch, which I keep well protected in my pack to give back to him when I return. The wristwatch is a new invention. The army is distributing them, and I got one in the first round of deliveries; everyone comes to look at it and admire it. It looks like a woman's watch, but it's beautiful and reliable. Sometimes I bring it up to my ear to listen to the tick-tock or watch the hour, but I barely have to move. I'm going to give it to Giuseppino as a present when I come back home. Right now I am going to . . .

They were written in the laborious handwriting of rural people and in several cases were interrupted—and stained with blood—by the explosion of a grenade or an invisible and lethal bullet. In the folders, Grandfather also had copies of the improvised epitaphs that had been scrawled on the wooden grave markers erected over the bodies or the torn-apart body parts of comrades buried haphazardly under the incessant enemy fire.

In fond memory of this unknown soldier of the Italian infantry.

And in a common grave, wherein lay the defenders who had covered the retreat of the last line of the Second Army in Austrian territory, was written, "*Foreigner, look here and tell the Italians how we have died, fighting until the end, and here we lie.*"

Thursday
From then on I started listening to stories about Lucía; they said that she had abandoned her degree and was now retaking the courses, that she had been hospitalized, that she had gotten married to a cousin of her father's, a wealthy dandy who was twenty years older than her and lived out in the country.

[It was said that she had married and separated from the husband, that the ex-husband lived in the country, that she had been hospitalized—the word "electroshock" was whispered.] Lucía had been married at seventeen to a cousin who was thirty years old.

"It wasn't her cousin. He was her father's cousin . . . "

A man from the country. [She went back to her studies because they had separated. She was a little older than us.] There was something strange in that marriage, a secret detail that no one understood.

She was older than us, had abandoned and resumed her studies several times, had married at seventeen and had a daughter, and now she was nearing thirty and had returned, as she herself would say ("Turned up again like a lost glove"). At that age, she was someone with plenty of experience and everyone walked around her as though she had her own light.

[She was too dazzling and too intelligent for anyone to do anything but imitate her. First of all, her girlfriends, who held their cigarettes like her, with disdain, between index finger and thumb; they dressed like her, spoke in the same way. Despite her complex intelligence, Lucía could show a very convincing unaffectedness, which allowed her to do many things that others are unable to do with impunity. The very speed of her understanding seemed completely natural in light of her intense sincerity.]

Saturday

"An elegant woman," my grandfather said today, "sliding a soft hand under my shirt . . . then I'd get back the memories I've lost." He laughs with his sky-blue eyes. And after a while: "I can only be judged in the context of the idea I have of myself." He speaks as though continuously translating himself from a forgotten language.

Monday

[While Gatsby holds a party and invites Nick, I went with her to the bus station because she was living in City Bell.]

"I'm thinking about coming to live in La Plata," she told me, "at my sister's house." She was separated, she said. Her husband was still living out in the country.

After that, we started seeing each other more frequently. We would meet at El Rayo or Modelo; we avoided the bars downtown, passed the night away with friends, talking about things to come. She felt comfortable and happy in that environment. Lucía was the only one who had been born in La Plata; her family had been there since the foundation of the city. We were people passing through, students who lived in boardinghouses, professors who came in from Buenos Aires to teach.

She came with me at noon and at night to eat in the student dining hall on 1st and 50th, at the Bosque entrance. She got in line and sat at the common table to talk about the Algerian War and Peronism, but her mind always seemed to be elsewhere. Sometimes, when we had to campaign for the elections at the student center, she appeared in her father's car, a red BMW coupé, very expensive, and we would do our errands in that car and then have to go leave it for her father to pick up at the door of the Jockey Club or at the racetrack entrance.

We were together all the time, but it was as though nothing was happening. It was not just that she was reserved (or that she lied). There was something she was hiding (something she hid from herself, of course). [For example, it took me a while to realize that she was going to a doctor or that she had stopped going and stopped taking her medicine, according to the husband.] And I found out what I did from what was said or whispered about her in the hallways of the College and in the bars.

The pills. Equanil. To be impartial, she told me. ("They'll have to invent Whipinol," she joked, "so your friends can suffer deeply and be profound.") Actimin, to stay awake all the time. Antidepressants, antipsychotics . . . (lithium). Her wedding ring with the black stone of insanity . . .

She does not sleep. In bed, she gives herself up as I have never seen anyone give themselves up.

Weak people make visible the weakness of others.

[She took large amounts of pills, several per day. Once I noticed that they were antipsychotics.]

"I don't need to drink alcohol," she said. "I'll stop tomorrow."

She liked to retain information and her means of doing so was to share everything that held no importance. She took me to her house, presented me to her sister, her father. She even took me to meet Patricio, her husband (a fool, dressed in the typical suede jacket that country idiots wear). She told me her story many times; her grandfather had been one of the founders of the city.

"Lucky the streets in La Plata don't have names," she said. "If they did, I would see my last name all over the place, and my father's last name and my mother's. Instead, they have numbers. They were restrained—oligarchs but calm about it, not like the *porteños* who only do things so that their names will be put on a plaza. I have, of course, gone off the deep end. The only part of La Plata I like is the racetrack." It ran in the family; her favorite uncle was a well-known criminal attorney, who had a stud horse and had named him *Mate y Venga* . . .

The symptoms had already started to manifest themselves, in what she herself called the broken cup.

"Without a handle," she said.

One of those little porcelain teacups that has lost its handle and had it glued back on [and you can see the ceramic, white but fit together perfectly, only a groove remaining once you manage to stick it on, though you cannot pick up the cup of tea with that truncated arm].

"I am broken and glued back together. Cracked. I have to conduct myself carefully." She moved an arm, as if it were a little wing. "It could fall apart."

We are at a table facing the window at Modelo, a pub on Calle 59, spacious and calm, reading *The Crack-Up* and there, of course, that the metaphor of the broken china appeared. You have to handle the dishes carefully.

But she had nothing to do with those images of domesticity (silverware, plates, teacups). In those May days, she was always at the student center, buried in discussions, in assemblies. Socialist politics, Peronism, the anarchists from Berisso.

Friday

At some point my grandfather stopped sending the letters, kept them in a maintenance chest and dispatched them surreptitiously to his house in Pinerolo, where my grandmother Rosa lived and where my father was born in September of 1915.

Why? He did not explain it to me; it was a delirium like any other. He had lost his mind but concealed his actions with his brilliant aptitude for keeping up appearances.

"Some soldiers hid money, others saved ration cards . . . " he said. "None think they are going to die."

One day in Turin, where he was working as an engineer for Fiat after the war had ended, he read in the paper that the Italian government was repatriating soldiers who had enlisted as volunteers in the exterior. He sent five chests to Argentina with the documents and objects that he had confiscated in the post office of the Second Army; no one checked him because he was a veteran and was dressed in his elegant artillery colonel's uniform.

[She came with me at noon and at night to eat in the student dining hall on 1st and 50th, at the Bosque entrance. She got in line and sat at the common table to talk about the Algerian War and Peronism, but her mind always seemed to be elsewhere.]

[She was scathing. I felt injured. The frightening instinct women have for penetrating the masculine comedy.]

[Relationship between the cracked dish in *The Crack-Up* and *The Golden Bowl* by Henry James. The material is not broken, it is only weakened "in fine lines and following its own laws." A fracture is a fracture and an omen is an omen, it says in James's novel. "I'm broken, *pichón*," said Lucía. "I'm the one who's cracking . . . The cracked."]

Thursday
Today at midnight they called us on the phone. They had found my grandfather in Plaza Espora, sitting on a bench, disoriented, with a bag of garbage in his hand. He had gone out, dressed in his pajamas and his hat, but barefoot.

"I didn't hear him get up," says Susy.

"He isn't crazy, just really old," I tell the young nurse who takes him.

"Calm down, Colonel," the kid says.

"I am calm," he answers, and he turns toward me. "Look, hijo," he says, "they've called me Nono since I was twenty, because I've always had white hair."

I write about Lucía in the room by the garden, where signs of the past persist: the perfume of jasmines from childhood, a bookcase with the large-format Mister Reeder police novels by Edgar Wallace that I bought in the kiosk at the station, the circular light on the table which comes from my father's old desk lamp with its flexible arm.

Saturday

"Surely my father must have told me once," said Lucía, "'Daughter, you have to finish a degree,' and that's the reason you see me here, Professor, taking your course, so that I can graduate."

This was the way in which, toward the end of the course, Lucía had commented on the beginning of *The Great Gatsby*. We were in the great hall of the College of Humanities at La Plata, one afternoon, in the course on American Literature. The professor was Ernesto Rovel; he was always seducing his most rebellious students, and upon hearing Lucía, I thought that she had entered the game.

Standing on the low stage, to the side of the desk where Rovel sat, Lucía began drawing some diagrams on the chalkboard with the names of characters and arrows showing their relationships.

"Pay attention to what happens with the women in the novel," she continued. "With Daisy, with Myrtle Wilson—they're a disaster, lost, stereotyped, they're killed or they're crazy or they're ridiculous little *chiquilinas*."

Rovel looked at her, smoking, his face heavy, alcoholic, skeptical.

"The women . . . " he interrupted her, and let the ellipsis hang in the air. "You are referring to the use of feminine pronouns in the book. There are no women in a novel, only words."

"Oh, if literature were made of words alone . . . " said Lucía, and could not find the words to continue and chose to smile with a fierce, stunning smile. "The men broadcast those idiotic suggestions to one another and the women are the ones who cut the leash." She paused; now it was Rovel who smiled.

"But Gatsby doesn't follow any advice."

"For that reason, he's a hero."

"Gatsby only tries to change the past. He wants to go back and pick up his life where he left it when he started to go wrong . . . " said Rovel. "Very well, Reynal," he said then. "You can sit down. But tell me," he looked at her ironically, "what other advice from your father you think you've lived out."

She stopped on the stage.

"'Daughter, you need to learn English,' I guess he must have told me. 'You have to study philosophy, you have to be a socialist.' I say that," she said, "because those are the things that I did do . . . "

There was an instant of silence, as though something intimate had crossed into the classroom. Rovel and Lucía looked at each other for a moment, and then she—serene, unhurried—stepped down from the podium and came to sit next to me. Everything had stopped because Lucía was too beautiful and too dazzling, and even Rovel paused as if a light had interfered with the air.

Lucía knew the art of interruption; just by moving her hand, she could produce a shifting of bodies. [She was like the heroine in a novel, brought along and carried by the movement of the plot. She was not, of course, the heroine of any novel, though I would have liked her to be, so as to change her fate.]

She was older than us, had left and returned to the College many times. She had been married at seventeen to a distant relative, older than her, a cousin with lands in Pehuajó. She had had a daughter and lived in City Bell, and all of us walked around her as though she had a music of her own.

"How was I?" she asked me.

"First-class."

She smiled and lit a cigarette. Her hand trembled slightly, and she supported it with the other, as though not caring to hide her nervousness. Rovel had paused on the stage and was looking over some notecards.

"Next time," he said, "we are going to look at 'Absolution,' the short story Fitzgerald wrote as a prologue to *Gatsby*."

The students crowded around, asked him for clarifications. Rovel got down from the podium and approached us.

"Do you want to get a coffee?" he said, speaking for everyone to hear but looking at her. "I have a while before the train."

"Yes, let's go," said Lucía.

There were five or six of us, and Vicky, who was with me at that time, went off ahead. We went down Calle 6 and walked to the París station.

Rovel lived in Buenos Aires and traveled back on the last train of the night. He was one of those men of a certain age who endure until the next generation because they are impervious to experience. He had published articles in *Sur* and was a good translator; his versions of Robert Lowell's poetry are still legendary. "Better than Girri's," he himself would say. I remember how, on that night, he lifted the book I had on the table with disdain.

"They read Gramsci instead of Montale. Are you sociologists?" He repeated the title of the book aloud and added, "There's nothing more melancholic than the national way of living."

"Except the national literature," said Vicky.

The table was covered with cups of coffee, and Rovel had a second whiskey in his hand. Lucía had ordered a gin.

"With ice, querido," she said to the waiter. And then she looked at Rovel. "Excuse me, Professor, you criticize what we're reading now . . . but you're still stuck on what was in fashion when you were a student. Or wasn't all that formalist horseshit of New Criticism a fad?" she finished with a sweet smile.

"You're married to a rancher, no?"

"Doctor."

"Then say, 'formalist disease,'" laughed Rovel.

I turned sour immediately. In that time, I was unable to think about the nature of other people's relationships because I only worried about the attitudes that others had toward me—and it upset me that Rovel knew she was married. How did he know she was married? That distracted me from the theories and jokes mingling around the table.

"The rich are different from you and me," Fitzgerald had written. "Yes, they have more money," Hemingway had answered. According to Rovel, Hemingway's response proved he was not a novelist.

"Without social difference, there are no good novels," he concluded.

"But difference . . . what difference?" said the freckled, neurasthenic girl who studied classical languages.

"Just name-dropping," said Lucía. "Lists of places, clothing brands, jewelry, polo horses, European cars, luxury hotels. Experience as an advertisement."

Conversations at the dusk of a turbulent day. [We spoke like that back then] in the all-night bars, and Rovel entertained himself and provoked us; he was a cynic, the only person who—for the last two years—had been thinking the things that everyone else is starting to think now. And Lucía confronted him; she was a bit out of place herself, but out of place in such a way that she made all of us seem out of place.

She was sitting in front of him and leaned in to ask him for a light. She held the cigarette between index finger and thumb—a certain affectation, which the other girls started to copy as soon as they saw her.

Lucía was playing with Rovel (I then thought), but not playing with me (I think now), and between us was Vicky, a redhead from Entre Ríos, petite and energetic, whom I liked very much and whom I probably would have married if Lucía had not crossed through. Vicky was intelligent, optimistic, serene, direct, and always ready to experiment with any of the sexual fantasies that could have occurred to her (or to me). But one never stays [we never stay] with the person who makes sense for them, or else life would be much easier. Vicky was so bored that night in the bar and so tired of Rovel's affected enthusiasm that she drifted to sleep, and he looked at her, uneasy.

"But that girl fell asleep," he said.

Vicky awoke immediately and smiled, without defending herself or anything like that, simply opened her eyes and said, "I have literary narcolepsy, Professor; I fall asleep when I don't like the style of the conversation."

Vicky was like that; she laughed at herself and at all of us, but after that night she wanted to have nothing to do with me.

We were in the bar until Rovel started putting away his cigarettes and called for the waiter. We went out to the street in a group. The night was crisp, the lights from Plaza Rocha illuminated the trees, and the lindens had already bloomed. Vicky had held back and was lighting a cigarette against the wall, taking care that the wind did not put out the flame. Lucía was beside Rovel.

"Will you come to the station with me?" he said, speaking for all of us to hear but looking at her. "I have some time before the train leaves."

Lucía pulled herself to me, her body warm.

"We have to go," she said, and took my hand. Then she squeezed herself against me; she was a little shorter and had an agile and firm body.

Vicky came closer, and seeing us she turned around and moved away without saying anything, without saying goodbye.

[Through the glass of the lit window of the bookshop in the corner of the post office I saw Vicky leaving, calmly, forcefully, decidedly. Further off, I saw Rovel, surrounded by some students following him to the station.]

And that was the night that Lucía came to bed with me for the first time.

Sunday

My grandfather is sitting in the sunlight once again and in a low voice keeps singing the same song, like a mantra (*"Bella ciao, bella ciao, ciao . . ."*).

"I don't believe I'll go back to living out in the country," he tells me now. "I don't like it here, but I don't want to live in the country any longer. Last night I got lost ['went astray,' he says]. Don't think that I don't realize . . . I have lapses," he says, and touches his forehead. "How is your father doing? I don't talk to him either. I don't like doctors, and I don't like direct children either, you know; I prefer indirect children. Your father spends his time giving me medical advice. Can you believe it? He gives me advice, gives me free samples he carries in his pockets; the medical visitors present them to him, that breed of beggars and servants with their briefcases full of samples, tranquilizers, vials of morphine. We didn't have morphine for injuries; they'd ask you to kill them. These *visitors* are domestic traffickers. They stop in rural hotels. I've seen them in the country, in suits and ties among the farmhouses, traveling salesmen in their rusty cars. He doesn't know what to say when he's with me because of that, your father, but he surely knows what I think, and, since he knows, he can't speak and chooses to give me *recommendations* as if he weren't a doctor, but a *medical visitor* instead," he laughs. "I take it as an insult . . . You realize, the worst part was seeing the horses and mules dead, strewn along the side of the road, and the scavenging dogs that ran between barbed-wire fences eating the dead flesh of animals and Christians . . . "

"*Bella ciao, Bella ciao, ciao,*" sings my grandfather in the sunlight, sitting on the canvas chair in the flowering garden.

Monday

Standing next to the bed, Lucía removed her earrings and began to undress. Blonde, her breasts firm, her nipples dark, the fuzz of pubic hair almost shaved off, as though she were nubile. She had white marks on her skin, a slight pale tattoo that traversed her body. They were signs of childbirth, traces of her past life, which rendered her even more beautiful.

"You want it like that, pichón?" she said, and leaned in toward me.

"I don't need anyone to teach me anything."

"I like men who do what they want."

It felt like she was always laughing at me. I came close and started kissing her. A feeling of intimacy like none I had ever felt.

The next day, the brightness of morning kept us up and we could not fall asleep. We had been awake the whole night; we had foregone dreams to talk, to do it (as Lucía would say). We are going to do it now.

"My daughter has these marks, too, and won't forgive me for it."

Her body had a lunar glimmer, it seemed to disperse when I entered her.

"When I was a girl, I also had a complexion, but I'm proud now. My mother doesn't have it, but my grandmother does."

"Pale-skinned women."

"My grandmother said we had Eskimo ancestry. Imagine, an Eskimo, in the whiteness of the Arctic . . . They paint their skin with whale oil, lines and lines of black and red. They never say their names; they are secrets, only revealed when they sense they are going to die."

"Because, otherwise, their souls are not at peace," I improvised . . .

"Want to smoke?" she asked afterward.

"I am smoking."

"A joint, dummy."

She had it prepared in her purse. Closed on one end and with a very fine cardboard filter on the other, which she had surely made herself with great patience, so that the weed would not get wet when it was smoked.

"Rovel's nice. When Vicky fell asleep he had a face like he was about to die."

"He aspires to being perpetually heard . . . but how does he know you're married?"

"We saw each other a few times in Buenos Aires."

I did not say anything. The air moved the white curtains; the light was soft and warm.

From below, a solemn music reached us; it was Bardi, the nocturnal one who studied engineering and spent his hours listening to music. A perpetual student, very introverted, sending a telegram every now and then to his home in Chaco, saying that he had passed a subject, but after years and years he had never done well in any. [While I was explaining,] Lucía finished dressing. We went down to eat; the house was calm, still. She went out to the patio, looked at the hanging clothes, the flowerpots, the sign for Club Atenas.

I remember she cooked liver with onions. We had no wine, so we ate lunch with gin. She put in soda.

"I don't need to drink alcohol," she said. "I'll stop tomorrow."

Bardi approached very ceremoniously and, after some hesitation and several apologies, he sat down with us to eat because it was already too late for him to go to the dining hall, which closed at two. He spent his time in Fine Arts, sneaking into musical composition classes. He was very systematic and passionate, the first person to make me listen to Olivier Messiaen and the first to talk to me about Charles Ives. He would reconstruct the history of the music by following an order, listening to all of the works of the musicians who interested him from Opus 1 to the last. He played no instrument, but more than once I surprised him by conducting in the air along to the orchestra playing the work he was listening to. Now he had returned to Mahler. He took out discs from the University library's music room, three LPs every week. He wanted to forget everything. He hated his father, a politician in Chaco: "A real bastard," Bardi would say in a soft voice.

Bardi never graduated, and he got work in Casa América the next year, in Buenos Aires, and I remember one night when, getting off the train, I ran into him at the Constitución station in the area near the bathrooms where casual hookups happen, and he was still very inhibited. Two or three months later he locked himself up in his apartment and never left, and they say that he threw some papers from his window into the street that said "Help," but no one paid him any attention or read his cries for assistance, and they found him dead.

But he was calm that day and seemed happy that we were eating with him. He was listening to Mahler's Fifth, very loudly as was his habit. I think that on that day I was advising him to go to Mar del Plata for the season to work in a bar, in a restaurant, in a hotel; during the summer months, one could save money and live on it for the whole year. He was very serious and listened with great attention, and I offered to recommend him a place where he could stay and live for some months. Lucía also gave him advice, and they agreed straight off that one could live with no money, with almost no money, like Trappist monks or tramps. And we were there in the kitchen, talking, drinking coffee, when the telephone rang. Lucía turned pale and stood.

She went out to the patio. I did not pick it up either. Lucía, off to one side, near the staircase, stood with her back turned and smoked. Bardi went to the telephone and did not explain when he came back . . . [It was nobody, he clarified, a man, wrong number.] He was discreet and had understood everything without speaking. She returned to the kitchen and leaned against the wall. How could they have known I was here? I thought. She remained motionless, as though absent.

It was an example of what Lucía called the symptom of the broken cup. [One of those little porcelain cups that has lost its handle and had it glued back on but with you still able to see the white line at the edge.]

"I have to conduct myself carefully," she said, and moved her elbow, as if it were a wing. "It comes apart."

We were in La Modelo, spacious and calm at that hour of the afternoon, and it was there that the metaphor of the broken china arose.

"I was very young when I had my daughter, and she's more attached to her father than to me."

At age five, the daughter was already taking horseback-riding lessons. It seemed elegant to her husband, according to Lucía.

She told me she had a feeling that time was slipping through her fingers, and the lost hours weighed her down. Not that, she said, that's backward. How long had we been together? One night and it seemed to have been weeks. If only we could stop time, she said suddenly.

She took everything seriously, except for her own life. She wanted to do her thesis with Agoglia on Simone Weil. I was thinking of leaving to go live in Buenos Aires; I was working with my grandfather, but I could get a position at *El Mundo*. I am contributing pieces now and have a friend in the editorial office . . .

"What are you writing?"

"Something for the literary supplement . . . "

"Pornography of the middle class," she said.

She always spoke the truth, said what she was thinking. We had already related our personal histories, the summaries of each other's lives, the events one believes to have been decisive. I had started to write stories during that time, and was a bit lost, nearly about to finish my degree without many possibilities except for that work at the paper. The story of that era, which I make for myself now, does not go like that, but that was what I thought of my life in those days.

"I'd like to have been with only one man, so I wouldn't have to go back and tell my life over again," Lucía had said to me. Everything she said made me suffer. And she realized it. She grasped my hand.

"Why don't we go to Punta Lara for a few days?"

"Of course, sure, let's go. Now that summer's starting . . . "

"By the river. I know a place there."

Once again I felt the fires of jealousy.

"No, let's go to Dipi's place. He has a house, he'll lend it to me."

So we went to Dipi's house, near the station, a long corridor and two towering rooms with almost no furniture but with books piled up everywhere. Dipi was in bed, drinking yerba maté and reading with his new girlfriend, a Japanese girl who looked like she was thirteen, same as all of Dipi's girlfriends.

"She isn't Japanese, she's Eurasian," Dipi said. "Her mother is from Kuban, the Tartar desert. Isn't that right, nena?"

The girl smiled and nodded. Dipi, from time to time, between one yerba maté and the next, drank gin but also smoked and caressed the girl.

"Lucía, come, lie down with us," he said, and made room in the bed. One on each side. "You can leave, *nomás* . . . " laughed Dipi.

He gave Lucía a yerba maté.

"Hard to drink maté lying down," she said, and sat down with me in the armchair.

"Trilce is her name—well, not her name. I gave it to her because she's beautiful and mysterious. In the desert—listen to this—in the desert, the Tartars sit around the water's source to talk, like the gauchos sit around a fire."

"What gauchos?" Lucía said.

"The bums are the only gauchos left," said Dipi, who was laughing as though his jokes were coming from someone else.

I remember he made us listen to the first Beatles single that night, with "Love Me Do" and "P.S. I Love You." The Eurasian Lolita had brought it, having spent the summer in London with her father, as Dipi explained excitedly. According to him, all of his girlfriends and friends were exceptional, first-rate sorts of people, who brought him the latest novelties and the latest news and informed him of the movement of the universe without his having to move from his bed or leave his room.

Suddenly, Dipi stood up, naked, turned his back to us, and put on his pants. Ceremonious, an astute gleam in his eyes, he moved close to the Japanese girl and then said to me, looking at Lucía, "I'll trade you for her."

"Even better, I stay with her and lend you Emilio," said Lucía.

"He's very ugly," Dipi said.

"He looks handsome to me," said the Japanese girl. "So handsome I can't look at him."

"*Graziosissime donne*," said Dipi. "We're always in the Decameron," accentuating the first *e*, in the Italian way. "Look what I have here." It was a guide of Rome. "My grandfather was born here, close to Nero's tomb."

"It's handsome, that tomb," said the Japanese girl, and there I realized that "handsome" was one of her expressions, like saying "hello" or "fine."

Lucía seemed happy being there, entertained by the Japanese girl with her stilted expressions and that "handsome" in the middle of her phrases.

"What a tomb, if they'd buried him in the country, in his villa."

"They made it in the third century," said Dipi. "Because Nero's spirit appeared to Pope Ludovico III and wouldn't leave him in peace. Isn't it funny? *Che*, but what a good thing you came to visit us. Do you want something to eat?"

"I've come to ask you for a favor."

"I don't have any cash."

"The house in Punta Lara, can we use it?"

"But of course, *viejo*. I'll give you the key. The motorcycle is here, Ferreyra's motorcycle, with a sidecar and everything. You can split Patagonia apart with that motorcycle."

Lucía sat beside the Japanese girl now, who was still naked in the bed. She spoke to her up close and caressed her hair and brushed it back behind her ear; the girl had very beautiful black hair. "Look what it is," said Dipi, indicating the music coming from his Winco turntable. "Look at what these guys are doing. They're working-class, another Perry Como. The musical middle class is over, dears; now we have Chango Nieto, Alberto Castillo, and the ragtime Beatles from the working neighborhoods of Liverpool."

It was almost six in the evening and had started to grow dark; I wanted us to go directly to Punta Lara, but Lucía insisted that we stop at the boardinghouse.

"I left some things there, some books."

"We can buy everything again."

She looked in her handbag.

"I left the joint and some pills. So let's go."

The house was silent. Bardi seemed to be sleeping with the door closed; there was no movement anywhere. As soon as we entered, Lucía turned strange, seemed nervous; suddenly I could not see her and realized she had gone downstairs and was talking on the phone in the kitchen. [She had called, and I did not want to listen.] It seemed she was arguing with someone.

After a while she came to the room, seeming reserved, almost absent as she searched for her things.

"I have to leave," she said.

"How did he know you were at home?"

"I warned him that I was going to be with you," she said. "I want la nena to always know where I am . . . "

"Weak people make visible the weakness of others," I said.

She answered me with a precise and dry phrase, which I will not repeat.

She had the infallible instinct of intelligent women for penetrating the masculine comedy. That is what I think now. In that moment, I was motionless. I did not want to ask anything of her, did not want her to defend herself.

"A shame," I said.

The terminal was a long platform, with the large buses stationed down the sides, along the street. The Río bus from La Plata to City Bell was leaving shortly. We sat down on a wooden bench. I bought a bottle of beer at a kiosk. She lit a joint and smoked it under the light. Raucous music descended from the loudspeakers, through which the bus departures were also announced. We stood there, motionless, almost without speaking.

"I can never rest . . . "

Did she say that? I am not certain; it was not her style. *The only thing I need now is to start hearing voices,* I thought, I remember.

We seemed like two living dead. What had happened? I was in the past. The present had hardly lasted. She and her husband did their damage and then went back to being together. A gesture is enough and the whole world transforms.

Suddenly, from the void, a beggar appeared—tall, young, dressed in an overcoat, without a shirt, his shoes broken, his skinny legs exposed.

"Have a coin left, mister?" he asked me.

She looked at him. He was blond, his skin pallid, a sort of Raskolnikov looking for money to buy an ax.

"I need some wine to drink."

Lucía opened her purse and took out a roll of bills. She seemed to give him all the cash she had. The beggar stood still for a moment, shifting in his place and muttering incoherent phrases in a sort of soft crooning. Then he searched in his jacket and held out a coin to Lucía, as if he wanted to offer her charity, too.

"I found it on a sunken ship," he said. "It's a drachma. It brings good luck." He looked at her seriously. "I'm always walking around here, if there's anything you need ... "

He moved away, muttering, his two hands in the pockets of his coat, and was lost in the darkness of the night.

At that moment the bus arrived; Lucía stood and approached the conductor, who was standing and taking tickets next to the open door. She waited a moment and, before stepping on, gave me a kiss.

"That's the way things are, pichón," she said.

Then she opened my hand and gave me the Greek coin. The bus pulled out and started moving away and I remained there.

The beggar reentered the station and made a few turns before he approached another pair, sitting at the back, and asked them for something.

I still have the coin with me. The lucky coin, according to Raskolnikov. I toss it into the air, sometimes, even still, when I have to make a difficult decision.

II

9

In the Study

The apartment was vast and luminous, and it was filled with books. There was no artwork on the walls, although on the floor of the corridor, leaning against the wall, there was a painting by their friend Freddy Martínez Howard, a group portrait, composed in the style of a sixteenth-century Dutch painting, in which Emilio, Beba Eguía, León Rozitchner, and his partner Claudia could be identified, and off to one side of the canvas Gerardo Gandini was visible, pale, wearing a half-smile, holding a red rose in his hand. They were all around a table, on the center of which gleamed a cut of red meat—a kind of still life, very Argentine. They had spent some days in the summer at Costa Azul, a Uruguayan resort near the border with Brazil. The surrealist poets, all of whom were friends with Freddy's father, habitually spent their summers in that place, so that Enrique Molina, Edgardo Bayley, and Francisco Madariaga were always around, though by the time they would arrive, Emilio explained, the only one still there was Madariaga. One afternoon, Freddy had painted the piece and presented it to Gerardo in trade for the musician writing him a sonata, the Howard sonata. It was no sooner said than done; Gandini wrote the sonata in one night and exchanged it for the painting, which ultimately ended up in the hands of León, who could not stand the image of his face (a blockhead, as the philosopher said) and resignedly passed it on to Renzi, who put it on the floor of his study.

There were no other decorations save for a framed photo of William Faulkner in which he could be seen walking with a friend past 104 Nassau Street in Princeton, where Faulkner would go, as Renzi clarified. Princeton, because the children of the southern aristocracy had always studied there, or rather their friends, the descendants of their fellow countrymen. While passing through, when he went there, Faulkner would take the opportunity to have his tweed suits made. The books and papers and magazines and folders were scattered in disarray on the tables, on the armchairs, and even on the floor. Emilio would meet me in the bar and sometimes asked me to come up to the study with him because he enjoyed someone's company when he could not write.

We went into the room located at the end of the hall, which was, strictly speaking, the office. There was an order that only Renzi seemed to understand. Several cardboard boxes were piled off to one side and photographs could also be seen, dispersed on the shelves of the library. We sat around the work table and Emilio poured two glasses of white wine and then pointed to the folder that lay open on a wire stand and asked me to copy down what he was going to dictate. He had a bad hand and it pained him to write. He read, in a calm voice, an entry from his diary written fifty years before.

Tuesday, March 7, 1962
There were, as it happened, several times over the years when I would spend entire days reading my grandfather's letters and postcards and notes, and I would even listen to recordings of Nono's voice, sharing his version of events.

I did not write here, in this notebook, Renzi now explains, my files and working notes about the war archive; I wrote them down separately, as

I did back then with the stories that I imagined could help me to write something in the future. I didn't write down everything in my diary; I wasn't crazy. I never thought that everything I experienced had to be recorded; instead I let myself be guided by intuition and wrote what I suspected I would not remember—superfluous details (at first glance), imprecise facts of my life. For example, he said, this moment here, during my second year at the University, in 1961, when I started writing my stories; it was the description of my history with Lucía, which, to tell the truth, was the first story in my life, and which I never published, but have now decided, he said, to include unedited in the version of my diary I intend to publish.

During that year, for "security" reasons, as they say, I recorded almost nothing of my political evolution, as we might call it; I had moved on from the tenuous anarchism of my youth to Marxism, aided by my studies in history and particularly by a modern-history course that I had taken with Nicolás Sánchez-Albornoz, a Spaniard closely affiliated with the Communist Party who had escaped from a Francoist prison along with other activists, among them a woman, Barbara Johnson, an American who had allowed herself to be arrested in order to organize the escape from inside the prison. And Sánchez-Albornoz had ended up in Buenos Aires, where his father, the prominent Hispanicist Claudio Sánchez-Albornoz was, if I am not mistaken, the president or prime minister or chancellor of the Spanish Republican government-in-exile, an imaginary position given that Franco's power was well established and he ruled the country with an iron fist, aided by the Americans. And so, Don Claudio did nothing but get together with the melancholy exiled Spaniards in the bars on Avenida de Mayo, in Buenos Aires, while his son traveled to La Plata every week to teach us modern history in the College of Humanities. He would arrive on Tuesday mornings, give his class in the history department for three or four students, myself among them, and then return to the capital by train in the afternoon. His classes left a permanent mark on me because he decided, in 1962, to

concentrate his course on the passage—or the transition—from feudalism to capitalism and made us read, along with the rest of the syllabus,
the extraordinary chapter in Marx's *Capital* on primitive stockpiling,
that is to say, on the origins of capitalism. A history of epic, legendary
proportions, because the peasants and their feudal counterparts in the
countryside began to be leveled by commercial capital, that is to say, by
money, which was eliminating the power of the rural nobility and causing an ever-growing mass of the peasant population to lose everything
and have nothing to sell other than their labor. Foucault, Emilio said,
Michel Foucault has said that historians are led unavoidably to utilize
the Marxist categories in their analysis. "To say 'Marxist historian,'"
said Foucault, "is a pleonasm, like saying 'American cinema.'" And so,
in that course, while taking notes frantically and reading Marx and
the great English Marxist historians until late at night, I was forgetting
my father's Peronism and the vague family anarchism of my girlfriend
Elena (without an H). University politics also influenced my decision,
and my friendship with Luis Alonso, a provincial who had come to the
University being—or claiming to be—a revolutionary, was another
influence, just as I, like all of my contemporaries, was influenced by
the Cuban Revolution and the figure of Che Guevara, who had given
a stunning performance to the OAS, near us, at the meeting at Punta
del Este, dressed in his olive-green suit, with his thin beard and the
five-pointed star on his beret, which looked like a third eye on his face,
so Argentine. But, as has been the case throughout my life, books were
what really convinced me. One time, not long ago, some friends invited
me to go fishing at El Tigre, and so, to prepare for the occasion, I, who
had never fished or been interested in that private activity of standing
still and silent and waiting, rod in hand, for a fish to bite, I bought
myself a couple of fishing guides (*How to Fish for River Fish* was one),
and the next day, on the island El Tigre, I caught more fish than any of
my friends, who had all practiced the art of fishing since childhood. I
was the absolute champion in that friendly fishing tournament in the
Paraná River. In this same way, I became a Marxist: because of reading

some books in Sánchez-Albornoz's course on the origins of capitalism in England.

We took a break for coffee in the study's kitchen and then returned to the worktable, and Renzi went on recounting the adventures of his second year as a student in the city of La Plata.

He was active in the student union, and his perception of politics soon made him decide, as a Marxist, to oppose the Argentine Communist Party's positions in particular and the politics of the USSR in general. In this way he was naturally getting closer, along with his friend Luis Alonso, to the positions, we might say, of Trotskyism. First, because the Trotskyists categorically opposed the Communist Party, and second because they are very theoretical, ultra-intellectual, and not very practical. So they suited me perfectly, as someone who above all was, and continues to be, an abstract intellectual. The funniest thing is that I came closer to Silvio Frondizi's group, a small Trotskyist sect, very Anti-Peronist and not very practical. For example, the person who "enrolled" me in the movement of the revolutionary left, Praxis, which was the name of the small circle of militants, was Tito Guerra, a perpetual student, very entertaining, who convinced me to join that clandestine and minuscule organization. I can remember our final conversation in the woods at La Plata, in front of the lake, and there, one autumn afternoon, I decided to commit myself to politics and become part of the group. The funny thing was that the day after he convinced me, Tito Guerra renounced his position in the organization and abandoned politics.

Thus began my political experience, organically; my life didn't change too much, I went to some meetings, stayed active in the College, was a candidate for president of the center but, luckily for me, I lost the election by three votes (it would have been by two, if I had voted for myself, something I did not do, of course). Meanwhile, I had started writing the stories for *La invasión*, and with one of the first, "Mi amigo," which was actually the second I had ever written, I won a short-story competition organized by a magazine that carried a fair amount of weight among young writers in those days. The funniest thing is that I discovered I was the winner during a lecture one afternoon by the writer Beatriz Guido, who had come to La Plata to give a talk on Salinger at the College; in the middle of the lecture, she said she had just read a very good story because she a was a judge in the magazine's short-story competition, and she started to talk about a literary epiphany and named me, as I sat in the audience that afternoon in the Great Hall, and praised my story "Mi amigo," and I realized, surprised, that she meant me and felt a contradictory emotion, which has always accompanied me through good and bad: it was not I, sitting there among my companions, who had written that story, it was someone else, different from me, more introverted and more valiant, whereas I was fairly lost in those days, emotionally distanced from everything. I could not bring myself to talk to her; it seemed impossible to me to stand up and tell her, "I am the young writer of that story." A true horror, too real. Literature is much more mysterious and strange than the simple physical presence of the so-called author, and so I stayed in my seat, in the tenth row, I think, which is to say that I was close enough for her to see me but she did not know me, and I preferred to remain sitting, anonymous, though I would later become friends with Beatriz Guido and she was always generous, enthusiastic about me and whatever I was writing. I kept still, and she went on talking, and the people who knew me must have thought that I was not there or else did not realize she was talking about me. The fact is that, with such an acclaimed writer naming me as one of the most serious and promising of young Argentine writers, my stock had quickly risen to a new level. The girls immediately started becoming interested in me—me, who tried to stand at the peak of my brief and stunning fame.

Perhaps as a result, the directors of the Trotskyist group proposed that I act as the editorial secretary for the magazine they were planning to publish. And so, for a couple of years, I was in charge of the magazine

Liberación, a legal publication, at least on the surface, as they would say in the conspiratorial jargon of the time. The director was a Trotskyist laborer, José Speroni, a union leader of great import who belonged to the revolutionary militant group that had followed the instruction of Nahuel Moreno, who, in secret, while a member of the Fourth International, had defined the tactics of "enterism," meaning a militant Trotskyist infiltration of Peronism, undercover agents of the worldwide revolution working inside the unions but never revealing their true political position. The tactic was so effective that ten years later, when he was still close to returning to power, General Perón condemned and denounced the Trotskyists in the Fourth International, those he labeled responsible for controlling the left wing of the Justicialist movement, as Perón called his political force. Speroni had been a "mole" in the Peronist union movement and had reached the level of secretary-general in the textile guild. But he was discovered to be an undercover agent and had to resign from his position and act openly as a militant Trotskyist. He was very intelligent. Very bright, had a great deal of experience, and was a figurehead as director of the magazine. The other editorial member was the great philosopher Carlos Astrada, who had studied with Heidegger in Germany and was one of the favorite disciples of the author of *Being and Time*, but who, being more or less close spiritually, as we might say, to Peronism in his interpretation of the national identity's phenomenological essence, had veered toward Marxism. He wrote a memorable article during that time, explaining how Lukács's book *History and Class Consciousness*, and in particular his chapter on the fetishism of commodities, had a direct influence on the delicate Black Forest philosopher. The magazine was designed by Eduardo Rotllie, a sculptural artist from La Plata who was very interested in the Russian avant-garde of the twenties. In this way, the magazine where I published articles, interviews, and notes really was a school for me and an unforgettable experience. My political activity during those years was limited to the magazine meetings. Meanwhile, the group's activists would go through the working neighborhoods of Berisso and Ensenada, bringing Trotsky's words from house to house, using a system they learned from Evangelist pastors: they rang the bells or knocked on doors (if there was no doorbell) and handed to the surprised refrigeration workers or their wives or their children copies of the group's newspaper, which was called, believe it or not, *The Militant*. The neighborhood people thought it was an army publication because, of course, they confused the word "militant," which they did not know, with "military." They thought "militant" was just another way of saying "military." All except for the Peronist sympathizers, who understood immediately that it signified a Trotskyist daily. In response, following Perón's directive, they insulted them and called them nasty epithets while slamming the door in their faces. I never participated in any evangelical work, and that seemed to create a certain hostile climate toward me in the organization. In fact, one afternoon, during a meeting of "the cell," as they called it, in which my friend Luis Alonso participated, along with his girlfriend Margarita and a Peruvian student who slept in my room at the boardinghouse during the discussions, I remember as if it were today, my friend and comrade Luis Alonso asked to speak and, as though History were speaking through his mouth, contended that the organization should sanction me and sever me from my responsibilities as the magazine's editorial secretary because I did not demonstrate the "mettle" (that was the word he used) of a revolutionary. In short, he wanted to occupy my position at the magazine himself, but he would not say it in that way; rather, he set to describing the differences between a revolutionary intellectual (for example, him) and a petit-bourgeois intellectual (for example, me, who, to my perfect horror, he called "*pequebú*"), so that I saw myself transformed into a sort of animal species, the pequebús, as it were a peccary. Then I asked for it to be put to a vote: Luis and his girlfriend voted against me, the Peruvian either abstained or voted against, and I don't remember if I voted in my favor or abstained. He brought the decision from the tribunal—that's to say, from the cell—to the higher proceedings of the organization, as he called them. They didn't pay him the slightest attention and I stayed in charge of the magazine, but, from that moment onward, I never spoke to him again, treating him as though he were invisible. The case is a minor one, but I realized then that if my comrade Luis had held the power he would have condemned me to the gulag in the name of the interests of the global proletariat. He spoke and was convinced he spoke in the name of truth, the truth of History and socialism as well. That ridiculous situation seemed to me an experience that was replicated elsewhere in the revolutionary groups and in socialist states: someone is accused of failing to obey the laws of History and is condemned to exile or to prison. It was a revealing experience for me and also a way to perceive the stores of depth and anger hiding inside our so-called "Argentine friendships."

Already, in that far-off time, I was living a double life and displaying the schizophrenia that has defined my behavior in the face of reality. On one hand, I engaged in political practice, very theoretical, with a group of advanced intellectuals on the left, and, on the other hand, I traveled every week to Buenos Aires, where I would spend two or three days frequenting the small literary world, a certain juvenilist bohemia, and would meet young writers at the Tortoni bar every Friday; there, on those nights, I became very close friends with Miguel Briante, who, along with me, had won the short-story competition of the most well-known literary magazine in Buenos Aires at the time.

Concurrently, I was tangled up in a typical—for me—triangular relationship with a woman married to a dear friend, who, on top of it all, was a distant uncle. Politics, literature, and toxic love affairs with other men's wives have been the only truly persistent thing in my life. Why, I do not know; many years later, I spent several sessions in analysis with a Lacanian doctor, and the issue of my Oedipal love was so obvious and I was so hooked on that murky cocktail that my analyst said to me, in a somber voice, "Look, Renzi, we'll set this issue aside because it's too obvious not to be hiding or displacing or concealing *something else*." He spoke with a gesture to underline the end of his, shall we say, interpretation. What exactly was that something else? I never found out. I liked redheaded women and I also liked married women and I would fall in love alternately with a redhead and then a married woman, such has been my emotional life. In the case of the *affair* that occupied several pages of my diaries in 1962, I must say that it was actually one of the typical stories of my family: a young man who went wild over a call girl and married her and imposed her on the family. But, in that case, my uncle Toño was expelled, so to speak, from the tribe and, aided by my parents, moved to Mar del Plata, alone and either pursued or disregarded by the tough core of the Maggi family.

And then Renzi opened a notebook and read out some entries in order to show that the story of adultery concealed the germ of one of his most well-known stories, "El joyero," as his uncle was a great goldsmith and Emilio, when he stayed in Mar del Plata, spent the nights talking with him while watching, amazed, as he engraved the extraordinary and very valuable jewelry that he crafted, with great skill, for months in the workshop he had set up on the terrace of his apartment.

February 12
Pained by the disastrous, unforgettable experience with Lucía, I returned to the fold. I am thinking of spending some time in Mar del Plata. I tossed the Greek coin up into the air. Heads or tails. And now here I am, because no one escapes fate. And I have entered a symmetrical position. Repetition is my most faithful muse.

Tuesday
Yesterday at Antonio's house. I spent the afternoon with him in the workshop on the rooftop where he works as an artist, producing his jewelry, watching the vague figures drawn with a compass on Canson paper. He polishes the gold and laminates the diamond, faceting it like a miner in a tiny passage, which he illuminates with a tiny spotlight. We spoke calmly, and I spent the time thinking about her, downstairs. Finally, we went down to the rooms and she came out of the bathroom, her hair

wrapped up in a red towel and her naked body barely covered by a fluffy cloth robe. She was barefoot and, as always, wore a bracelet around her ankle. Then we went to the room that opens onto the garden; I sat in the armchair (individual) and they on the spacious divan with the white pillows. Alcira withdrew (visibly) when he touched her, sometimes only by chance. When I was leaving with Antonio, who wanted to introduce me to the Colombian who had guaranteed him work in New York, she asked me to stay, using a pretense that no one heard. Toño went on alone and, as soon as he closed the door, she burst into tears. "All I want is to be with you," she told me before insisting that we must not hurt Toño. I could not stay, and we said goodbye, promising to go to Buenos Aires together when I returned to La Plata.

Friday

A walk with Toño. A sad role, the young lover of his friend's wife, a friend who is, on top of it all, his mother's first cousin. Advice, vague praise. "Alcira is sure life will be very good to you." The two of us looked indecisively at one another, playing the game. He suddenly began telling me about all of the women he "decided" not to sleep with because he "couldn't have done it, couldn't have done it" (he repeated the phrase twice, trying to seem sincere). Women who would call him over the phone to be met with his iron refusal. At times, we are inside the melodrama. "You know, I left everything for Alcira." We were on the corner of Luro and Hipólito Yrigoyen, and he invited me to have a coffee. We sat down at Ambos Mundos. A tense and murky atmosphere settled around us, the confidences and sincerity "between men" (he, who could be my father). He spoke to me as though he were past the events, was talking about Alcira, about the ways she could help him if I was a friend (to her). "The thing is, she isn't my friend. You know she never believes anything I tell her." I thought I had gone crazy, that Antonio was about to murder me but first wanted to see how far I would go. A double metaphor for that tense reality, in which I entertained myself—as always—by revising my best performances. I said nothing because I had nothing to say that was not an insult, and I left without meeting the Colombian wholesaler who, according to Toño, was going to take him and his wife to live like kings in New York.

Best of all is that, after our deranged walk together, I will write a letter to Alcira asking how far the game will go. We left. He paid (he was ill, but ill from some illness I never knew). "Fine, I'll pay next time," I told him. Everything seemed to hold another meaning; any sentence I said could be interpreted as a slight. I think the problem is too much for me, I write to her; I love this man and respect him, and if it were someone else . . . But if it were someone else, you wouldn't have done anything.

A strange nightmare last night, in which I was struggling to make it on time to a place where they were going to arrest me. At night, I went for a drink with Horacio, my cousin. He is my brother. And he knows about the turmoil and the family epic as well as I do. I told him about everything that was happening with Antonio; he looked at me calmly, unsurprised, as though what I was saying was something commonplace. He simply reminded me that he, Antonio, had to face the entire family because of Alcira, a lady of the night (according to the aunts) who had a son with a man who was in prison. At first, Toño boasted about his conquest, but he later fell in love with her, abandoned everything he had always wanted, and went to live with her and her son in Mar del Plata, protected by my father, who found him a place to set up his jewelry workshop. Seen in that light, my part in the story looked even worse. But that was not what Horacio wanted to say to me; instead, he pointed out that Toño was not exactly a clean character himself. "You know, he always was a womanizer," as though he meant to point out that, in fact, it was Antonio who was controlling the situation. Then we changed topics and remembered the good days of childhood and the bad days of adolescence (so nearby).

Eternal recurrence, in Nietzsche, is an attempt to establish an immanent ethics. You would live each day of your life cautiously if you knew that it would be repeated eternally. He inverts Kant's categorical imperative and says to make each day into a perfect day because you will repeat each day infinitely. It concerns a moral postulate: it does not matter whether Nietzsche does or does not believe in eternal recurrence; what matters is that the risk of repetition would obligate us to be careful in how we live each moment. Freud, following Nietzsche, based the death drive on repetition—the absence of memory. He betrayed Nietzsche, who had based the drive for life—the pure will to power—on eternal recurrence. Apart from that, Nietzsche posits memory as the site of blame and remorse upon which Christian morality is based—a morality of slaves, according to him. Nietzsche's subject has no memory and therefore knows no blame; he lives in the present, convinced that each consummated action will be repeated in the future, circularly.

Wednesday
Alcira called me and we met at Hotel del Bosque. We spent the afternoon together. She assured me that she had never loved Toño and had told him so. She knows I am returning to La Plata in a couple months. "The summer can be endless," she said. She sent her son off to camp, and so, from what she said, she is as free as in her youth.

Thursday
Toño called me on the phone and we met at the Montecarlo. He was calm, told me that she couldn't adjust to living outside Buenos Aires and that she still might decide to return. "Why are you telling me these things?" I asked. He smiled. "Because she fills your mind, you are the only friend she has here." We were silent for a while and then parted. I think about her, and my chest hurts. I have to see her tomorrow and tell her I am leaving.

Tuesday
A frenzy renewed by family invasion, the Maggi clan's plot to rescue Antonio from his difficult situation. None of them say what is actually going on, and if they discuss it in front of me it is because they do not

think I am involved in the problem. The only one who seems informed is my mother. The other night, when I was leaving to go see her, my mother said she was waiting because she wanted to tell me something. I know her style: she never says anything directly, everything is implicit. She talked about the grief that my return to La Plata causes her (as if I had gone off to the Congo), and, after beating about the bush for a while, she said, as though we had been talking about nothing else, "Better if you don't go. You know Antonio is in Buenos Aires . . . " She looked at me in such a discerning way that I stayed with her. She seems to perceive, to read my thoughts. We do not speak any further about the issue. My mother began playing a very difficult solitaire with English cards and I helped her get through it.

The family is supportive as long as you share the common space. Very good management of the presence and operation of the tribe's subjects, which always paints the absent one as guilty. Constant tribunals, summary judgments, conclusive truths. But my mother has a moral guideline that I admire. She never judges anyone who is a member of the family, or rather, she always absolves and understands anyone, provided they belong to the clan. For example, if there were a serial killer in my family, my mother would say, "Well, he always was an anxious boy." I learned from her that narrators must never judge the characters in their stories. And for my mother, and for her brothers and sisters, it is essential to go back, again and again, to telling the family stories. It is impossible for me to synthesize all of the stories accumulated from the tribe's many witnesses. But perhaps it is from there, deep down—the clear water—that all of my books issue forth. For example, Marcelo, who fell in love with a woman he met as a dance partner, a way also to forget the specter of his first wife, a fragile and neurotic woman who died without seeing darkness because she slept for her whole life with the light on the nightstand lit. A woman whom death canonized with a motion symmetrical to the rejection of the intruder, to whom all of the women in the clan—except for my mother—have given the cold shoulder. Or I myself, for example, had begun a triangular relationship with the wife of my heroic distant uncle, Antonio, who left everything for the call girl who immediately betrayed him with his closest friend. So that I, too, have come to be a (minor) figure in the family saga.

Therefore, the story of Alcira, a girl of the night, as Toño called her, who married her nevertheless (maybe because of that) and who has been condemned by the furies, including his own sweet mother, and who received help from Ida and my father and moved to the city so that she might, as they say, initiate a secret relationship with her husband's nephew (who is the one writing the story).

Tuesday
I went out with Toño, and we walked around the city until sunrise among unsteady tourists dreaming of winning big at the casino. We sat down at a table in the Montecarlo, where Antonio seems like the owner, and gradually an assorted and fascinating ensemble of men and women of the night approached his table. Of course, Toño plays games by initiating me into life's truths without ever mentioning the detail that I have been sleeping with his wife for almost a month. Last night, along with one of the casino's croupiers, they invented an infallible trick. It was almost two in the morning, so there were only two hours left to play in the casino, but all of us in the bar with Antonio followed him. He paid the admission from his cut, waited for the bellhop to get me a rental suit and tie so that I could go in "dressed like the people." (I had to show my national identification papers so they could see that I was older than eighteen.) We went to a heavy table at the back where they were playing baccarat. Antonio gave someone cash to get a seat and then sat at the table and started playing hard, following both his intuition and "scientific" plays, as he would say. By four in the morning he had won four hundred thousand pesos. He gave tips to all the employees at the casino and left like a king, accompanied by his procession, and we went to wait for morning in the bars along the boulevard, sitting under

the parasols of tables in the open air to watch the sun rise over the sea, drinking champagne.

He was writing down these slightly imaginary versions of his life, Renzi told me, and at the same time reflecting in the notebooks, or rather, trying to think about the experience of being captive to passion. And so his history with Alcira began, from what he had recorded in his notes.

January 8, 1962
A great meeting at home to celebrate the holidays and also the arrival of Antonio and his wife Alcira, who came to live in Mar del Plata, along with her little son Camilo, escaping from Buenos Aires and the condemnation of the family; my father helped them, supportive as he always was toward expelled members of the Maggi clan. We were there at the party, at home, and I went up to my room for a brief escape and was still there when Alcira, who must be thirty and is beautiful, with very black hair and white skin, appeared at the edge of the stairway and looked at me with moist eyes and a smile on her lips, as though she had something to tell me. Her smile was incredible, a little suggestive I think, looking back, but in that moment I thought she had come up to look out on the night from the terrace. As I stood there next to her, she took my hand and pressed it to her chest, my hand between her breasts, and said, referring to her heart, "See how it beats."

We kissed, and I was excited and slightly confused because there were always people on the terrace on this night, watching the fireworks burst in the sky. We had seen each other very rarely. I had come to Mar del Plata a month before and went to their house and spent several days with Antonio, who is devastated and has not adapted to the change of place. He had lost everything, his contacts in the jewelry stores of Buenos Aires, his place as head craftsman in the Ricciardi workshop, and had moved here with her to start over. "You're just like Dante when he was young." Dante is her ex-husband, a prisoner in Sierra Chica, and that was why, she said, she "fancied" me. Because I was like him (I always seem to be like someone else).

We began an affair that lasted the whole summer, Emilio summarized, and was important for me because she was a very worldly woman, with a slightly cynical and cruel side that fascinated me. We would get together anywhere—in the bathroom at their house, say, while Antonio polished his jewelry and listened to music on the radio in the attic where he had set up his workbench. It excited her, I realized, the sensation of danger, the imminence and risk, because we could have been discovered at any time. She would touch me with her bare feet under the table, with Antonio right beside her. He had given up everything for her, met her while she was a working girl and for months had paid her to sleep with him. And he had fallen in love and brought her to his friends and family but had been condemned, and now she, placing her life in jeopardy, was sleeping with her husband's nephew. I was always astonished at women's audacity in gambling everything for passion or a whim, without taking into account the consequences of their actions. And I realized, with her, that it was precisely this risking of everything for a clandestine relationship that made her feel alive (as she would tell me), because, for her, to live was to be in danger.

In that time, apart from my parallel lives, I also found a friend with whom I would undergo many decisive trials during those years of learning and (emotional) education. I was advancing smoothly in my degree, and in the following year, 1963, I found work as teaching assistant in two subjects and, for the first time, began earning my own living and even—maybe as the result of having a job—lived with a Uruguayan woman, Inés, which I have called my "first marriage," although of course not because we married or anything of the kind, only because I established a stable relationship for several years with a woman.

10

Diary 1963

July 10

I am worried about my tendency to speak about myself as though I were divided, were two people. An internal voice that soliloquizes and digresses, a sort of soundtrack that always accompanies me and sometimes filters into what I am reading or what I write here. Yesterday, I thought I would have to keep two separate notebooks, A and B. A would contain the events, the incidents, and B the secret thoughts, the silent voice. For example, today on the tram I started thinking that I had to get off and escape, far from here; I have the wages from my grandfather in my pocket, could go to Uruguay on the ship *Vapor de la Carrera*, rent a room in a cheap hotel on 18 de Julio, and get lost forever, never having to be held accountable to anyone for the things I do or stop doing. None of it was as coherent as what I have just written; in the thought, there was no syntax, only blocks of words. For example, run away, a few days, Hotel Artigas, a girl from Uruguay, low class, an Asian girl, Calle 18 de Julio, CX8 Sarandí, Montevideo, from the press box at Centenario stadium. Would it mean I'm crazy?

Instead, I attend the "Argentine History 101" class. Advancement without an exam, nothing to miss, and I'll have to write a monograph at the end.

July 12

With her, the girl with the dark hair, Graciela Suárez—very Joycean. I started seducing her, or trying to seduce her, never remembering, never realizing that she was going out with my friend Yosho, and when we had our first date and I took her to Adrogué to meet my grandfather and to sleep together, she asked me, "How are we going to tell Yosho now?" And only then did I realize that I had snatched away a friend's woman. I call that the suicidal act; I see nothing, see only the object of my desire.

Maybe there is a time when one does not retreat but grows stronger, lives with back turned to the exterior world. As though we were on a train traveling to La Pampa—I say La Pampa because there is nothing to see on the plains; I have sometimes thought that I must write a novel without descriptions, and that would suffice to create the velocity that I rarely achieve in my stories.

Saturday, August 3
I am going to a meeting for the magazine. These days I have forgotten to record anything, or maybe it was a precaution or a way to continue my clandestine politics: in the movement, I am editorial secretary for Liberación magazine. Led by José Speroni, a unionist who attempted "enterism" within Peronism and reached the level of secretary-general. There is also Carlos Astrada, the greatest Argentine philosopher, a disciple of Heidegger.

August 6
It is worth noting the experience of temporality that arises from any history book you stop to analyze. The classic problems of all narration appear: the preambles required to explain events taking place in the present and to reconstruct their conditions. On the other hand, the need to describe events that transpire in the same time but in different places. Finally, the decision to pause the reconstruction of events in order to develop some hypotheses. Analytical interpolations form a part of the story. A book of history is always pure. These ideas derive from my experience of narrating some events that took place in Banda Oriental based on certain documents presented by the historian Pivel Devoto. Even a history as

abstract as that of the transition from feudalism to capitalism can be seen as the epic tale of a cosmic catastrophe.

Thursday, August 8
A beautiful sentence written by Sartre in *Being and Nothingness*, p. 630: "Thus death is not my possibility of no longer realizing a presence in the world but rather an always possible nihilation of my possibles which is outside my possibilities."

Friday 9
In a bar on Calle Suipacha.

My best writing so far has arisen from a minor autobiographical reality transformed into a different story, wherein the lived experience only persists in the form of the feelings and emotions expressed in the story.

Monday 12
In the days when men—and sometimes women as well—were armed, social relationships were friendlier because the risk of conflict was excessive. In nineteenth-century Argentina, duels were common events. A bad mood or misunderstanding would transform suddenly into drama.

A beautiful poem from the popular tradition: "Dispossessed of dagger by the badges, he remained confined to dance the milonga, and was sad." The way of telling how the man was disarmed by the police is based on a prison language and an almost inscrutable slang (although the verb that opens the poem is a wise and perfectly fitting choice: "dispossessed" is perhaps the best verb that could be employed to remove any subjectivity from the event being narrated). From then on, the poem adopts a classical form: the malefactor does not enter the dance but is confined ("remained confined"); the scene is described with a word that condenses multiple meanings ("milonga") and then closes with a melancholy and beautiful conclusion. Constructed with a suspended verb ("remained"), which seems to sustain the man's sorrow through the night (because he is no longer armed).

Monday 19

On Saturday night, after the magazine and I gave a collective lecture at MAPAM, in a garden near La Plata, we returned, walking along the edge of the road, and suddenly a body grazed my legs and there was a muffled sound. A car had hit Vicente Battista, who lay strewn across the ground as if dead.

A visit to Vicente at the hospital where he is confined.

Wednesday, August 28

Last Saturday, they debuted an event at the New Theater called Festival de Buenos Aires, which included several short sketches by Enrique Wernicke and also my story "Mi amigo," adapted into a terrific dramatic monologue by Héctor Alterio. It is strange to see something you have written performed on a stage; there is also the curious sensation of seeing the public, out in high numbers on the night of the premiere, responding with laughter, excited silences, and applause at the words of a fiction you have written. Graciela and I went together, but indifference always claims me and I never manage sufficient happiness from what I have received.

September 2

I spend the afternoon with Dipi Di Paola, a very good time. He, like Miguel Briante, has a powerful command of style and writes with great elegance. We form a kind of tercet, opposing everything that we see in contemporary literature. At the magazine, Briante and I form a sort of anti-conservative front. Essentially, we dislike the imposition of anti-avant-garde poetics.

Other discrepancies. What does it mean to be in the present? In any event, it is not something a writer needs to define. I do not like the emphasis with which people at the magazine self-define and shield themselves inside a sense of generational membership. It ends up being rather comical to me, the way in which they all cultivate a juvenile and anti-intellectual brilliance.

September 17
Ludovico il Moro: "He took leave of himself with a bar to his beloved servants, so that they had to scream to make him hear them."

In Machiavelli, virtue is the affirmation of man's autonomy in the face of natural forces (or human nature . . . much of the time) and chaos. Therefore, we must understand it, this virtue—but as necessity or as possibility?

September 21
We went to Mar del Plata to read stories from the magazine. Always strange, the experience of reading a text aloud. There is a certain false eloquence in the act. True reading, on the other hand, is silent, personal, requires isolation and a secret passion. Reading aloud in front of a crowd is different from the literary experience.

I meet Alcira in the hotel on the coast. Everything goes on in the same way, yet everything is different. On this trip, I did not go to visit Antonio.

October 3
Elsewhere I have already written the reasons for ending things with Vicky (I crossed paths with her today at the College). I have tried to tell that story some other way, considering that it started (by mistake) with her reading one of my notebooks. For that reason, I have tried to keep her separate from these notes.

A difficult and lethargic meeting at the student center.

October 19

An unexpected definition by Ezequiel Martínez Estrada: "The socialist system is, of all political and economic models, the most rational and equitable and concordant with the advancement of technological civilization and humanist culture." *Marcha* magazine, May 1963.

December 10

Maybe, in the end, it is about telling the family history. Cholo, whose wife left him for a conscripted soldier of twenty, also abandoning her son, just a few months old. And before that, Marcelo. And then Antonio. Each one of these an individual world. The clan pushes them into a bad lifestyle, through women. The men rebel and break with convention, dragged along by a passion (vile, as they say).

Someone, a superior man, may choose a life outside the law. He is not an artist and therefore does not employ creation as an alibi to justify his vice. The damned poet is already a consumer good, allowing his readers, vicariously, to have an exceptional and dangerous experience. In this instance, by contrast, the point is to remain anonymous. No one, save for his intimate circle of friends and accomplices, knows of his perilous adventures, that man aspiring to sainthood. One may decide to become a thief and potential murderer, just as someone chooses a degree or a profession to which to dedicate his life. I met Cacho Carpatos when the two of us were high-school students in Mar del Plata. He was in trade school and I was in my fifth year at the national school. We thus belonged to two different planets, separated by galactic distances, but our orbits collided by chance in Ambos Mundos bar. We had friends in common, and he was exactly the same as me and my friends. He was interested in everything and had a brilliant intelligence, but he had placed all of his energy in high-powered motorcycles. He would go down Boulevard Marítimo like a maniac, trying to break I don't remember what speed record or what suicidal personal best. He was the same as us: arrogant, ambitious, avidly living life, never paying attention to the limits. I stopped seeing him when I came to La Plata, but I ran into him again this year. He still goes to that bar, but his interests have changed. Walking around the small streets of Playa Grande together, crossing through the tunnel, he told me that he had decided, after completing high school, to become a professional thief. He thought he was a superior man—intellectually superior and even, he added, morally superior. Laws and the protection of personal property did not, he told me, form part of his experience. He had no intention to work and wanted to live well; therefore, thirteen years ago, as soon as he finished secondary school, he had dedicated himself to studying and delving into the means of appropriating the fortunes of men and women who, in turn, had taken hold of the riches and land and the fields and the fruits of society over the course of decades. I thought he was hoping to impress me, but with a gesture he showed me his hands and forced me to see the truth of his condition. He is a young man—blond, skinny, with pale eyes, dressed with blasé handsomeness—but his hands could belong to a laborer. Broken, deformed, with a rather brutal appearance because, as he told me, he enters the houses of the rich to steal from them by forcing open the bars and the windows, and that effort has left its trace on each of his hands. Some exceptional men, he concluded, and some very beautiful women, could live outside the law because their qualities surpassed the social norms. We had made it all the way to Torreón and there, unexpectedly, he called a taxi with a wave, smiled at me, told me he was late for a date, said goodbye, and was gone. He was living in Buenos Aires, and we might meet in the city or even in La Plata. And we made plans to see each other. He is staying in Mar del Plata through the summer because everyone comes here for the season, he told me. He seemed like a hunter, following his prey when they migrated, and was therefore doing his work now in the chalets and the residential houses of La Loma, the wealthiest neighborhood in the area.

December 11

I make a phone call, from Adrogué, from the public phone in López Market and run into Inés, the girl from Uruguay who came to Buenos

Aires to study philosophy. We went out together, the beginning of something.

Thursday 12
We went together to see Visconti's *La terra trema* in an experimental theater—few people invited, an intimate space. Inés is from Piriápolis, on the other side, as she says. We went out to eat at El Dorá and then spent the night together. Strange woman, so similar to me, so over-the-top. "You're a foreigner, *uruguaya*. You're the kind of woman who gets a thrill from finding out something," I told her. She smiled, malicious. "So you can write a story about it," she said. The truth is we immediately created a shared language, an idiolect, a private language that only two people can speak, which, for me, has always been the nature of love.

Friday 13
I have a fear, stemming from my past, of all rhetorical excesses. For me, it is the greatest of virtue to use language with precision and clarity.

Saturday 14
Inés is possessed—according to her—by the past. A past that she always imagines differently. She is always smiling in my memories. We met at Tortoni; she was waiting for me. "I didn't know if you were really going to come," she said.

Friday
Inés and I have been together for days in La Plata. For her, this geometric and calm city is a sanctuary. Buenos Aires bothers her and she constantly misses the sea, which is not a sea, she says, but rather a river of giant waves and salty water. She wants to write a thesis in philosophy about the province. She constantly wants to return to Uruguay but never gives in because she respects her convictions, which are, for her, as she says, unstable.

Tuesday
I should work on the relationship between Pavese's diary and *The Seducer's Diary* by Kierkegaard. Suffering eludes understanding as long as one is living through it, in spite of knowledge, which cannot transform it or prevent it from taking place. A quote from Sartre may be tied to what I am saying: "Knowing the cause of a passion is not enough to overcome it; one must live it, one must oppose other passions to it, one must combat it tenaciously . . . Knowing is not a knowing of ideas but a practical knowing of things."

Thursday
Perhaps I should create a summary of my situation, as I have been ignoring these notebooks for several months. This year, for the first time, I have come to realize, as they say, that I am no longer unpublished. I published an essay in the magazine on Pavese's diary and also a story ("Desagravio") dedicated to my friend José Sazbón; the subject is the bombardment of Plaza de Mayo, mixed together with a private story (a man who kills a woman).

These changes have ultimately been the realization, minor perhaps, of my projects or of the fantasies I have carried with me since I was sixteen. This year I even started to earn my living with the two courses in which I work as hired assistant.

All synopses are sad, and so I will do nothing but leave behind a summary from which, for now, all of the facts and circumstances are missing.

11

Pavese's Diaries

To earn fame, it has been said, it is not essential for a writer to show sentimentality, but it is essential that his or her works, or some biographical circumstances, stimulate pathos. This epigram serves, no doubt, to explain the presence of Cesare Pavese in contemporary literature. None of his books has added to his ambiguous fame as much as the incidents on August 25, 1950, when a man with glasses and a distant expression rents an anonymous room in an anonymous hotel in Turin (the Albergo Roma, on Piazza Carlo Felice). He reserves a room over the phone—his biographer Davide Lajolo explains it in *Il vizio assurdo*—and they put him on the third floor. Pavese locks himself in his room. During the day, he makes several phone calls. He speaks with three, four women. He asks them to go out, to have dinner. They all refuse him. Last of all, he calls a girl he met a few days before, a cabaret dancer. Little is known about this conversation between a writer of forty-two, recently consecrated with the greatest distinction in Italian literature (the Premio Strega), and a woman who earns her living entertaining men: it is the last conversation of Pavese's life and the hotel operator records the end: "I don't want to go out with you, you're a boring old man," the dancer says. Pavese hangs up the phone. He does not go down to dinner. The next day (Sunday, August 27), at nightfall, a waiter, worried about his patron who has not shown himself all day, calls at the door. When no one responds, he decides to force entry. Pavese is stretched out across the bed, dead, dressed immaculately; he has only taken off his shoes. On the nightstand, there are several bottles of sleeping pills, all empty, and a copy of his most beloved book, *Dialogues with Leucò*. In his spidery handwriting, Pavese has written his last words on the first page: "I forgive everyone and ask everyone's forgiveness. OK? Don't gossip too much."

The authority of failure

There is a beauty at once trivial and tragic in that end—a "turn of the century" quality that has seduced, and still seduces, those who cultivate Pavese's legend. Solitude, anonymity, the impossible search for a woman, the tedium of a summer weekend and that man, seeking salvation in a dancer who does not wanted be bored—the theatrical dignity of that suicide has everything needed to turn Pavese into a symbol of what someone describing him once called (not metaphorically) "the sickness of the century." Today, people listen to Pavese, no longer reading him, because he is one of the people who speak (and the phrase comes from Fitzgerald) with "the authority of failure." His life has become a model because it proves that all writing holds a secret and is the site of some revenge. The secret is always a wound (impotence, alcohol, self-destruction); the revenge is the penance that life makes the writer pay. The poet consumes his life up until the final judgment and, in suffering, pays the price for the beauty he produces. A strange chemistry, requiring pain to purify the words; the writer is the hero who discovers how to use suffering in the economy of expression, in the same way that saints discovered the utility of pain in the religious economy.

A society that successfully upholds the reasons behind its economy is able to recognize the "aesthetic" qualities of failure. Perfection in death, as we know, constitutes an aristocratic myth; beauty is fed by all forms of erosion and destruction and particularly by the suffering of that priest the consecrated artist becomes. If he suffers as a man, as a writer he is capable of transforming his suffering into art. In this compensatory sublimation, failure is always necessary for the "profound" success of a work.

Pavese is a martyr for this superstition, and the circumstances of his biography renew the legend of the poet's loneliness and inability to adapt to the world. Ultimately, his suicide is symbolic because it comes to confirm an ideology (one that has been in fashion, furthermore, since the days of fascism) of the intellectual's impotence, of his uselessness in face of the simple truths of "life." Pavese himself, it must be said, made this cliché his own. It is no coincidence that, in his diary, he merges the writer with a woman: a paradoxical affinity originating from a certain misogyny but supported on the idea of the writer's feminine, passive sensitivity and in the opposition between an active life and a contemplative life. Pavese's biography really holds little meaning unless his will to failure, his "mania for self-destruction," is projected onto it, nor if you do not take into account the (romantic) hero who grabs hold of literature, the writer as "man of letters" in a literal sense, like the *raté*, the frustrated, always failing in the business of living, opposed in everything to the "simple man," the man of action, possessor of a direct and triumphant knowledge of life.

This Business of Living

"In my work, then, I am king. In fifteen years I have done it all," Pavese writes at the end of his diary. "If I think of the hesitations of former times . . . In my life I am more hopeless, more lost than then . . . What remains is that now I know what will be my greatest triumph—and this triumph lacks flesh and blood, life itself. I have nothing left to wish for on this earth—except the thing that fifteen years of failure bars from me. This is the balance sheet of an unfinished year, that I won't finish." It is about the balance of a life, clearly: the success that he always sought, and which he celebrates, is worth nothing. There is a metaphor here as well: at the very moment in which literature is recognized, the gratuity and emptiness of that useless work is also discovered. "Which do you like best," Stendhal noted in a copy of *The Charterhouse of Parma*, "to have had three women or to have written this novel?" There is no need to say what Pavese's answer would have been. He knows well that it is those "fifteen years of failure" that have made his triumph: that "one thing missing" is the wound that the writing uselessly tries to cover.

Pavese condenses his life into the gap from 1935 to 1950; these two dates form the border, the limits within which his life is reflected as in a mirror. In 1935, Pavese is imprisoned in the south of Italy, condemned by Mussolini's government as a result of the antifascist intellectual circles in Turin. That year, he finishes his first book (the poems of *Hard Labor*), starts writing his diary, and a woman ("the woman with the hoarse voice" in the poems) abandons him to marry another man. In 1950, he writes a novel that establishes his status (*The Moon and the Bonfires*), thus reaching the peak of a dense and varied body of work, within which an ensemble of four short novels stands out (*The Fine Summer*, *The House on the Hill*, *Women on Their Own*, *The Devil in the Hills*), novels that, as Italo Calvino points out, constitute "the most complex, dramatic, and homogeneous narrative cycle in Italy today." Affiliated with the CP since 1945, he is actively involved in Italian intellectual life. Director of collections for the Einaudi publishing house, he undertakes intense work as translator, critic, and essayist. That year, another woman abandons him, Constance Dowling, a young American actress to whom the best poems in *Death Will Come and She'll Have Your Eyes*, his final book, are dedicated.

An almost perfect symmetry governs the events. At the beginning and end, a woman is lost, there is confinement and loneliness, writing, failure in life. "The thing most feared in secret always happens," Pavese wrote at the beginning and on the final page of his diary. This sentence written twice is an oracle, it is the writing of destiny. During those fifteen years, Pavese tries to catch a glimpse of the secret confined in that oracle; he wants to know the thing it most secretly feared in order to be able, then, to accomplish it.

The Temptation to Commit Suicide
Deciphering that enigma has produced one of the most beautiful books of contemporary literature, *This Business of Living*. Hieroglyphics, full of silence and darkness ... You could say that in that diary, beginning with

his term of imprisonment and ending with his term in a hotel room, all of Pavese can be found. A moral novel, a monologue that proceeds without naming the events, attentive only to the perverse logic of repetition, this admirable book is charged with a tension at once lucid and tragic. "When a man is in such a state as I am," he writes in the first pages, "there is nothing left for him to do but examine his conscience. I have no grounds for discarding my own firm conviction that whatever happens to a man is conditioned by his whole past. In short, it is deserved. Evidently, I must have been an utter fool to find myself at this point . . . Only so can I explain my actual suicidal urge in life. I know that I am forever condemned to think of suicide when faced with no matter what difficulty or grief. It terrifies me. My basic principle is suicide, never committed, never to be committed, but the thought of it caresses my sensibility." There is a dogma and a fatality in that sentence; the emphasis is placed, visibly, on the *idea* of suicide, and therein lie temptation and terror, what Pavese called his "secret vice." You only need to review his correspondence to find that same obsession from the start: "I'm thinking about suicide," he writes on October 22, 1926, and in September 1927, "for the past year I have been thinking about suicide constantly." A secret obsession, a solitary passion, suicide is a vice of thought, an obsession of the intellectual who thinks too much, who is condemned to thinking.

The trajectory leading from those letters, written at the age of eighteen, to the hotel room where he will lock himself up to die, is narrated in his diary. *This Business of Living* (which someone called, with no malice intended, "the business of dying") is, deep down, nothing more than a slow construction of that journey, a stubborn labor to transform thought into action.

The purpose of the diary is to make suicide possible; in fact, (Stendhal wrote) "a diary is always a kind of suicide." This motion explains the technique underlying his writing; Pavese often splits into two, speaks of himself in the second person. He plays with the double; the text is a mirror, and in it there is an attempt to persuade the "other." From there that frozen passion is derived, that quality like a manual detailing the perfect suicide, which made an optimistic man like Davide Lajolo, in *L'Unità*, say that *This Business of Living* "is not a book for reading."

It is an empty story, a story in which only the thought (of death) is recorded; yet, at the same time, Pavese is writing the diary in order to postpone suicide. In this sense, his work with the double is, as always, a means of conjuring death. Textual limitation . . . The desire running through it is one of being dead and, concurrently, being able to write about that death. That contradiction resolves, in the imagination, the myth of the double, fascinated with the idea of suicide. The final sentence of the text, relentless, demonstrates that writing was his only (and last) defense: "Not words. Action. I shall write no more." Death lies in the future tense of that verb: what shall come when he can write no more.

A book in which death and writing intertwine, Pavese's diary is one of those rare documents (like Kafka's *Diary*, Scott Fitzgerald's *The Crack-Up*, Cyril Connolly's *The Unquiet Grave*, or Michel Leiris's *The Age of Man*) of the kind that continues to find a place in literature. Thirteen years after his end, reading that almost perfect book assures the only interesting memory of Pavese. He is that book, and when, in coming years, forgetting erases the biographical circumstances that enabled his writing, or when memory distorts his biography so that even his suicide is transformed into a happy circumstance, Pavese will have to be viewed, surely, as the man who, in *This Business of Living*, has written some of the most memorable pages of contemporary literature.

12

Diary 1964

January

A year that began with a walk down La Diagonal, cool under the shadow of the trees, with a few policemen drinking gin from a jug behind a roadblock, and the image of a man with crutches, in the sunlight, and beside him a beggar on the corner watching the little flame of the lighter he held in his left hand, because he was left-handed, and finally two old men, two meters apart from one another, trying to sell the same sweets, carried on trays hanging from their necks, to a group of indifferent people waiting for the bus. I imagined that neither of the two wanted to give up the location and would therefore spend hours observing one another.

"Language is the immediate actuality of thought," Marx.

Sunday, January 5

Cacho and Bimba come to see me, and he tells me about his clash with the police: he escaped in a stolen car. She is blonde, very beautiful and provocative, but, behind her femme-fatale act, she is a simple girl, says everything that passes through her mind. She has no filter. One of her preferred ways is the expression "I feel like." What it feels like to her is always rather indecent and unexpected. For example, today while we were chatting at La Boston, she opened up and said suddenly, "That man there in the flowered shirt was a client of mine. I don't feel like

173

I need to say hello." She is a prostitute, or rather, as she says, "I work on the street." She did not say, "I worked"; to her, the business seems like an activity and a way of life that can never be left behind. She did not work out on the street; she was in a fine house, as she says. She was a call girl; the madame received calls from the clients and referred them to the girl, whom the man already knew or would chose based on a folder of photographs. Bimba did not have direct contact; the madame would get her on the phone and tell her that a very discreet man would visit her in her apartment at five in the afternoon, etc. The most boring part of the work, she would say, is that you have to sit and wait for a call. She met Cacho in a bar on Córdoba and San Martín and left with him. I imagine Cacho thinks that his vocation requires that his wife be a whore. To make that life more believable (for Cacho himself).

Sentences must be able to create situations. A sentence condenses an act. The image must be narrative. The narrative image. Wittgenstein's example, describing discernment from a room: we see a man through the window, walking with difficulty, moving his arms as though rowing. The image changes if we know there is a storm outside and a strong wind is coming in from the sea.

Cosmic pessimism is a comforting doctrine (see Martínez Estrada).

The outsider, arriving at some place, incites thoughts beyond what is visible.

There is no maturity, he said, other than awareness of one's own limits.

What is learned in life, what can be taught, is so limited that a sentence of ten words would suffice. The rest is pure darkness, probing in a hallway at night.

Monday, July 1

Too often I have preferred the present, a fleeting pleasure, so as not to doubt my project. It may be paradoxical, but improvising things, thinking at the last moment, is a way to reach calm and tranquility.

Strange, but I discover a certain naturalism in Cortázar; he secures the fantastical effect within the local color and the everyday. I recalled a quote from Aragon: "Only I can know the sacrifice and what I abandon in creating realist literature."

Tuesday 2

Sarmiento: "If you kill people, shut your mouth. They are bipedal animals of such perverse nature that I don't know what can be gained from treating them better." In 1863, he decreed that those who destroyed the state's weapons would be punished with the lash. The constitution had abolished that barbarous punishment, but Sarmiento supported his assertion with some old Spanish ordinances that were still in effect in the army. The measure was directed against the urban guerillas, who cut down guns to adapt them to their style of combat (Sommariva, *Historia de las intervenciones federales en las provincias*, p. 210).

"And, in fact, this is the secret of happiness; to adopt a pattern of behavior, a style, a mold into which all our impressions and expressions must fall and be remodeled," C. Pavese.

Fundamentally, to narrate means to take charge of the distance between the narrator and the story being told. That distance defines the tone of the prose and also its point of view. A simple example is (the narration's) abrupt step into the present, leaving behind the incidents occurring in the past.

Without thinking, I have decided I will go to the College, to see her. What matters to me is just the present and not the consequences. "I cannot be

175

if I don't go," I thought, and saw the sentence written in the air with its dislocated syntax.

Friday, July 3
Yet again, no one but me understands what happened. I will know how to proceed next time. That was what I thought last night at the party in the Villarreal house. Because I went. It suggests a methodology, not an isolated error. I was there from ten at night until three in the morning. Clarity came in the end, once everyone had assumed the necessary positions. Gin takes care of that. A blonde and broad girl, lying across the floor, trying to seduce a very affected young man, talking about politics. The failure of avant-garde socialism was employed as a means of erotic conquest. As for her, Celia H., inscrutable, the empty gaze. And, in the end, I was the one who left with her because the other one, my friend, took too long in understanding the coded messages.

Sunday, July 5
Captain Ahab is not a character (like Madame Bovary, for example), but rather a verbal force that cannot exist without the white whale. More than an individual, he is a composite of energies, eclipsing all of the other protagonists revolving around him, without free will, tied to Ahab's obsession. The ship, the harpoons, are also parts of his body. Only Ishmael, the one who narrates the story once it has already ended, has a life of his own.

Monday, July 6
The divergence between the Past and Present people in the CP is perfectly understandable through the differences between the Italian and the Argentine CP.

She only asks to spend one week together. I always repeat the same thing: circumstances change—people, events—but the syntax is always the same. I postpone and wait for life to decide for me. My relationship with V. is just an example. I cling to her, without thinking, or rather I cling to her so that I don't have to think.

Wednesday 8
Everything I do has "public status"; there are no secrets and no reason that there should be.

December 3, 1964
In a way, for me, this year has not ended. A strange and fertile year. Perhaps the most important one I can remember.

Faulkner does not now distance himself from memories, but from a new vision held by someone who remembers. He places a second point of view in the interior of memory. I have lived through something. Then I recall it. But when I return to recall it years later, I modify it. In that sense, Faulkner places two time lines in the same act of remembering. He establishes an intermediate time that has made the memory change and perhaps even the event itself.

Friday 4
I am reading *Intruder in the Dust*, perhaps the most baroque and intricate novel that Faulkner has written. He does not only conceal what has taken place, but what is going to be described: "That smell which if it were not for something that was going to happen to him within a space of time measurable now in minutes he would have gone to his grave never once pondering." A form of annunciation. The style collages commonplace gestures, dragging them out with the magnificence of an epic poem and making them crash and burn like objects made of lead.

I will try to narrate what I did yesterday. Since I know that what is important is the thing that defines the day, and that this act will only appear afterward, I have to concentrate on the events. My meeting with Germán García, my conversations about Cortázar in the bar on Callao, my wandering down Corrientes. Briante's tiresome insistence on his own literature. I must, then, assess what took place or what I thought about the things that had taken place.

Monday 7
A great heat, yesterday and beginning Saturday, making turns through places near the river. I spent the night on the Tigre. And yet it was only from the train, while I was returning, that I had a complete panorama of the river's image, because while I was there I only saw fragments and unsettled remains of something that could only be seen in their totality later, from outside, through the window of the train.

Last night, I again ran into Casco (but that is not his name), who a few years ago I saw every day in La Plata. Always lucid, always very radicalized. This time he appeared with Francisco Herrera and told me I was right to insist on the need for specific work on the Cultural Front. The differences are present. On all sides.

In *The Fire and the Vespers*, Beatriz Guido tries to narrate Peronism but in reality narrates the history of opposition to Peronism and, in that opposition, a conflict between the traditional sectors on the right and what we might call the liberal intelligentsia. With that as the subject of the book, Peronism appears like a sinister phantom setting fire to churches and hatefully repressing any expression of liberty. In a sense, Peronism invades all of reality and transforms it into the reign of evil. It is narrated well, with a clean and restrained prose, sometimes approaching "objectivism." Then, when we met in the Falbo bookshop to discuss the book, it was obvious that she, like Pedro Orgambide, operated with many biases that she would not consider as such. Syria Poletti and other writers were also there, and I exerted myself defending Beatriz, insisting that her novel had nothing to do with Peronism because it was viewed exclusively from the opposition, which was actually the subject of the book.

Writers like Beatriz Guido, Sabato, and Viñas himself view Peronism as a continuous and daily apocalypse; it would seem the nation has reached a point at which there is nothing but theatrics and falsehood. They cannot understand the reasons for which Peronism was widely supported, and they regard corruption and calumny as the explanation for its backing. The Peronist masses are viewed as naïve and wickedly gullible, deceived by power. At one point, they replicate the model that Mármol used in *Amalia* to narrate the Rosas period; it seems that the model of the romantic and melodramatic novel has been maintained until today.

I went out with Cacho and when we crossed San Fernando I could not stop thinking about Inés taking in the sun with her friends at the river, which bears the overflow from the sea. It does not concern the past, but something taking place where I am not present and that I cannot control.

Faulkner's system of comparison tends to be narrative—that is to say, the relationship is not established with a concept or a static image but rather with an action. For example, "as if he had been lying on an unswept floor a long time in one position without being able to change it." The simile is a minor action, a micro-story that could be isolated and then joined with others to construct a net of microscopic narrations. For example, as when someone feels around on a table in the dark, knowing that there is a dangerous jumble of broken glass. Often the event one intends to narrate is eclipsed by the power of the comparison.

Tuesday 8
A meeting with Szpunberg and Herrera, which may result in a project. Nevertheless, I am skeptical of associations and leagues of intellectuals. It implies the belief that a specific field of study, in and of itself, gives common interests. It would be more logical to organize writers according to their literary poetics and thereby view their political positions.

Curiously, Faulkner notices a certain aristocracy in the black population of the south that is at odds with the new blacks. In *Intruder*, Lucas
says, "I don't belong to these new folks. I belongs to the old lot." And he
never takes off his hat in front of the whites. In short, Lucas is punished
by society because of this, because he does not comply with the rules
that govern black behavior; he is half-black and is actually punished for
thinking that he is not the same as the rest of his race.

Temporality in Rulfo and in Faulkner is not psychological but epic.

Wednesday 9
Buried in apathy and the heat. It has been several days since I have done
anything more than change my project and subject. Things only take
place in my head; I neither read nor write. As always, my basic action is
to postpone, to leave things "for later," so that everything stays half-done,
as though reality were a meter away from me.

I meet Professor Caldwell, from the University of California, who is
working on new Argentine fiction. He said two interesting things, that
Faulkner is a narrator who creates myths and that he is therefore close
to the oral tradition. And then he said that Borges is a seventeenth-
century English poet (a definition which would have pleased the subject
of that quote).

Thursday 10
The excess, avarice, and violent desperation of Cacho Carpatos make
him appealing to me, make me attempt to help him. He is an outsider,
like me, or like the writers and heroes I admire. He is outside of social
matters, does not want to be involved there, keeps himself apart, but
the fact that he makes his living with theft places him in a strange
situation, and he is always uneasy, not only because of the risks he
runs every time he goes out to do "his work" (in general he only "goes
out" on Saturdays), but also because of the free time, the tedium that

leads him to act impulsively. He is an "alien" (with all of the meanings that the word carries—among others, that of living on theft), and I am attracted most of all to his capacity for gambling his life. That same capacity is what destroys him. I saw him go into curve at top speed on a motorcycle to test if it was possible to make it at more than a hundred kilometers per hour. The same thing when, on Saturday nights, he dresses with style, takes an amphetamine to get himself ready and awake, says goodbye to his band of friends, leaving them with three or four locations where he can be found if everything goes well, and then goes off alone to steal from the large suburban houses in Olivos or San Fernando. The other day, he escaped in a pinch and was able to climb a tree and from there surveil the police, who were searching for him on the opposite corner and lighting up the gardens and parks with their flashlights. The routine danger in which he lives makes him so sensitive that that he can barely sleep at night, constantly remains vigilant, like a man to whom everyone is a potential enemy. He is the quintessential man on the run; at any moment, he could be discovered or killed.

Someday I will write a (fantastical) short story in which an engineer (or a nurse?) meets with an immortal, and when he wants to reveal him, they both suffer an accident and only the engineer survives. That event attracts me; he is the only person who knows who the immortal was and his testimony is unique, but he tries to tell the story and no one believes him. The good part of the story lies in thinking how immortals, under circumstances we do not know, can also die in an accident. In one sense, it feels like a ghost story, and, in another sense, it is the story of my relationship with Cacho and the truthful account of that early morning when we nearly killed ourselves entering Bosques de Palermo at top speed, when the car spun out and for an infinite moment we hung on the point of killing ourselves. I remember the things I thought: not only that we were going to kill ourselves but also that I might survive and would then face the problem of explaining why I was with Cacho in a stolen car. The dedication of the story would be "To Enrique Gaona, who decided on that night to come down."

We left the College with Professor Edwards, who brought us to meet his lover, an attractive blonde; he has set her up in a house and with her lives a life parallel to the one he maintains with his wife and children. The funny thing is that, in his social-history classes, he describes the double life or, as he calls it, the class schizophrenia in which men of the dominant class lived in nineteenth-century Argentina. Or rather, he experiences the things he explains to us, as though it were a practical work.

We will see if I slowly manage to overcome this heat and the clumsiness I feel and so double back over the story and finish it. Only one scene remains: at the end of the party, she approaches as he is crossing the garden, and they leave together. I need a violent scene, with action, in which he repeats his flight from the city. He needs to lose his false liberty, his availability.

Sartre's *Baudelaire* is an execution—that is to say, a process in which the poet, in drawing upon his biography, is condemned. It seems that Sartre wants to demonstrate that the choice to be a poet (or to live as such) is condemnable because it involves a choice of the imaginary.

Saturday

In literature, I believe, the fundamental thing is to possess a personal world. In my case, the material is secretly autobiographical and depends upon the multitude of family stories that I have heard over the course of my life. In this way, the novel works to diverge from a reality that has already been told, and the narrator tries to recall and reconstruct the lives, the catastrophes, the experiences that he has lived through and the things he has been told (for me, things lived through and told about are the same).

Sunday 13

Taking part in the daily experience of someone who, like Cacho, lives in constant risk is a revealing experience. I understand that decisive acts or heroic moments do not exist until after they have taken place, when they are recounted. Before that, they are a confusing succession of small gestures, of chances and emotions. For example, putting on the holster, sheathing the pistol, hiding a screwdriver and a crowbar in the folds of a very handsome white bomber jacket. Going out in a stolen car, which runs because the cables under the wheel have been hot-wired, advancing though the city, knowing that the police are also searching for this car. Heading north down Libertador, letting yourself be led by intuition and suddenly turning down a side street to pause and see if they are following. Staying there for a while with the lights turned off in the darkness. Then continuing ahead at the pace of someone watching the houses, trying to guess which of their owners have left and will not return for a couple hours. Breaking off the bars, searching for the alarms, deactivating them, forcing open a window, and entering the house.

The funny thing is that danger has now become routine for Cacho; he complains because it is Saturday and "he has to go to work" (the same, for example, as Puchi Francia, who grumbles every time she has to go to her job at *La Prensa* newspaper). For this reason, I think, Cacho takes greater risks each time, searching for something, though he does not know what it is—"to save himself" perhaps, to pull off the job, to learn some information that will let him get rich in one shot, and then to retire (although I doubt he ever will). Courage is a way of being, something that also appears afterward, when he is describing the events or when he has already lived through them, but it changes the gestures, making decisions, without thinking, guided by instinct and a passion for danger. That, in short, is what defines him.

At times, I live in another time, not concerning a memory but rather reliving emotions from the past. For example, that night with Elena in front of the high school, or with Vicky in the plaza among the trees and with Amanda at the radio-station exit. It may be delirium, but I see myself inside the scene, and then I see that I remain sane by imagining that I am narrating the things I have lived through. The strange part is that I do not remember—or cannot see—the contents of the situation, do not hear the conversations, do not really know what is taking place, although sometimes I do have a vague recollection. In short, I would like to establish a distinction between remembering and living—or seeing yourself living—in the past. The only true certainties are the feelings and emotions, which in the present seem to correspond to what I felt back then.

Wednesday 16
Yesterday, a long tour of the bars. With Beatriz Guido, experiencing the strange phenomenon of a person more lucid in writing than in speech. (But is it so strange? The same thing happens to me in reverse with David Viñas; he is far better than his texts.) I mean to say that the coherence of Beatriz's novel is greater than what she demonstrates when talking about politics. On the other hand, she always develops her novels to the point of journalism—and, in that, is the same as Viñas. She has the ability to "situate herself" and is completing a novel about the "historical event" of the Pinedo case and the fictitious rise of the dollar. Cambaceres or Martel must have been doing something similar when they "selected" their subjects.

Together with Oscar Garaycochea, I prepared a script on "Las actas del juicio" in three parts. 1. My story, with the soldier narrating; 2. A vision of the daughter; 3. López Jordán. We were thinking about a kind of semi-historical "Rashomon"; the story passes from one version to another without taking a side on the events.

Afterward, at Inés's house, she was relating what Isabel had told her about Rosario, that she has a certain provincial skepticism accompanied by a political stance always bound to personal interests. In Uruguay, Inés said, things aren't like that. She did not say what they are like, simply distanced herself from the state of things, which is her way of defining reality. The state of the world, she says sometimes, is conceivable, unstable, and at the pinnacle of its existence. Only negativity, according to her, allows her access to the truth.

The sensation of completeness as you begin an essay, when you enumerate what you are going to write. The blueprint has the same charm that arises in the discovery of the anecdotal core of a story, which seems as though it has already been written. That is the only full happiness of literature.

You can always imagine that you are helping to correct social injustice without putting your literary philistinism in danger. Literature, on the other hand, must be able to critique the dominant uses of language. In this way, literature might be an alternative to the machinations of language and to the state's uses of fiction. At the moment, a writer in Argentina is a harmless individual. We write our books, publish them. We are left to live, we have our circles, our audience. How, then, can we accomplish utility with the only thing we know how to do? To say it another way, everything must be centered around the use of language. In this way, the content will have different effects. The subject does not matter so much as the particular type of structure and circulation of our works.

One example is the thing that happened in the congress of Paraná in Entre Ríos. It was, in a certain sense, a congress of the others. Then someone, Saer, spoke out for all of us. His action was transformed immediately into a scandal and, therefore, was seen as an individual posturing intended to make himself known. Everything seems to be a spectacle from which no one can escape.

A dream. I am in the middle of a multitude on a street in an unknown city and am speaking another language, a language no one understands.

Today is a summary, an abstract of the times. We are without money, without food, and tomorrow Inés will pass an exam and I make turns around the essay I want to write.

It is fair to consider us a generation, that is to say, a group of people with common experiences (Peronism, for example), who have read the same books and chosen the same authors, because age—or youth—is also a cultural problem. In our case, we are outsiders to the established and dominant forms of cultural development. We break from reading Roberto Arlt, who for us is a contemporary. They want to represent us as petulant young people who rebel and attempt yet again to turn the problem of a new literature into a matter of sociology and the zeitgeist. They presume or imagine a particular "madness" in some young people, in this case Saer; the same method was used with Arlt. Saer is placed into the category of the petulant youth, someone strange, raving, declaring falsehoods. Saer knows, better than anyone, that what took place in Paraná is an anecdote, a detail within a wider reality. We are, stated ironically, a group of writers who toil for a new culture in Argentina. A new culture that rebuilds tradition and chooses its own point of reference; Saer cited and defended Juan L. Ortiz, and he could just as well have talked about Macedonio Fernández because they, those great old men, are our contemporaries.

Thursday 17
Last night, with Edmundo Rivero, I went to listen to Horacio Salgán at Caño 14. You hear the tango now in clubs where no one dances to it. The same happens in New York with jazz: rock has swept away all previous traditions of popular music.

Juan Goytisolo, like Pío Baroja, believes that, in the novel, "the most complex psyche fits inside a rolling paper." We are close to Hemingway and a kind of narration that develops emotions based on actions.

One of the paradoxes of this era—and not of the younger ones—lies in the fact that, as artists, we fight for a world that may be uninhabitable for us.

Wednesday 23
I am in Mar del Plata, I go to the beach. A dazzling time in the sun and sea, where it is not necessary to think.

Thursday 24
I finished reworking and typing up "Las dos muertes." A good story, well narrated, with a great deal of action. I will give it to Jorge Álvarez. Maybe "Las actas del juicio" would be a more accurate title.

Friday 25
In Hemingway's memoir and in Henry Miller's *Tropic*, I am bothered by the attempt to show life as it is, to search for veracity in the hope of telling it without artifice, as though the grammar were not already an artifice in itself. It is like walking in on an intimate conversation between two people and knowing that they are talking about their private matters, knowing that someone is listening to them.

Saturday 26
Suddenly, I recall Inés's words, spoken on the edge of the bed; the things she said return like a blessing but also like something already lost, belonging to the past.

Method. Someone narrates a story in a confused, almost unintelligible manner; before he can finish, someone walks into the room. The person who had been listening to the story, told confusedly by the other, summarizes it for the newly arrived man who has just come into the room. The method is typical of Dashiell Hammett.

Monday 28
Dashiell Hammett narrates action from the outside; he needs to detail the actions and objects, and that meticulousness, that care for transcription, is the only thing he wants. The implicit question is that of why it is narrated in this way. Because everything in that world is in danger; they all feel they are being watched and violence could explode at any moment. The narrative proceedings make this understood without ever stating it. The technique comes from Hemingway: everything is told on the same level without creating a hierarchy among the actions or the events. A murder and a pleasant afternoon in the countryside (which could be more dangerous) are narrated with the same tone. In this way, it is narrated without selection, and it is only afterward, when the action rises up like a gust of wind, that the order of events can be recomposed. Narrating physical action (fights, etc.) is a very useful way to proceed, but it poses problems for showing the relationships between characters, making them dull and similar. Clearly, dialogue is a primary means of representing the people in those novels. They are what they say (but no one believes them).

Thursday 31
I am reading Sartre's *The Words*. It possesses a pure style, in the best sense, a constantly open syntax that pushes the language forward. The style is made apparent because the ideas too are malignant and are therefore surprising but clear. The book is written against literature, considering it a false representation, something a subject makes of his or her place in the world. For Sartre, a writer chooses the imaginary and dismisses reality. As proof, something he has already used against Baudelaire and against Flaubert, he takes himself during childhood and adolescence, during the years of *Nausea*, as a sort of sentimental clown trying to please others. In the end, Sartre says that he has saved himself from that sickness

(literature). The book is so well written that it does not matter if he says that literature is useless, because his prose refutes it. In any case, and with all due respect, two pages by Borges in his story "Borges and I" say the same thing better and more laconically. I admire Sartre but do not share his moralism and his good sentiments.

Whenever I am in love with a woman, her past interests me, like a way to see how she and I have ended up meeting each other at a definite and unstable point in time. As if we had traversed a road full of curves and turns from birth to the present, which led us nevertheless to a place where we would inevitably meet. Love tends toward mystical thoughts; you believe you were destined to see and seduce the other because there was no other option.

I have no interest in making a balance for this year, because I am not a storyteller in the economic sense of the word, but rather a narrator (that is to say, of course, a storyteller who analyzes his story without fixating on dates or changes in the calendar). What has come to an end during this time? I am about to finish being a student to become something I am still unable to decide. In that sense, qualitatively, 1964 is more valuable than previous years and will not, therefore, end today.

In the story that I am revising, "En noviembre," a problem has surfaced. The story begins with this sentence: "There is nothing like the start of spring, when the dark days of winter have gone and one may return to the sea." That is, the narrator is recalling a day on which he went to swim on the empty beach; he is narrating, in the present, something that took place before. However, in the version that I am working on now, the narrator relates the events as they are taking place. He is on the beach and is speaking about the sunken ship that he wants to reach, by swimming, to see if he can find something in the submerged cabins. I will rewrite it, will perhaps include it in the book. It is based on a man I met at the beach who wanted only to live in the water. I changed the title; it is now called "The Swimmer," and the narrator does not know what is going to happen, that is, what he is going to find on the ship. A narrator who adheres to the present and relates the events as they take place without imposing onto them the meanings they will have in the future. It is the technique Hemingway uses in his first stories: the narrator does not want to remember, so he tells everything in the present as though he has no memory, as though he does not know what is going to happen. The same technique that Camus uses in *The Stranger*. The narrator has no opinion about the acts he commits. Narrating is like swimming, Pavese would say.

13

The Swimmer

They call me the Polack because I have blue eyes and blond, almost white hair; I sleep anyplace I can and live on what I find in the sea. I come to the beach very early and search for a calm area, between the dunes, on the other side of the long jetty, on the side of the port. From here I can survey the whole coast and see the sunken ship in the mouth of the bay. It lies some three kilometers offshore, near the last breakers, capsized on a shoal. When the wind comes in from the south, you believe you can hear the soft creaking of the rigging, the rusty noise of irons shaken up by the tides. There is nothing more mysterious than the remains of a sunken ship silhouetted on the horizon, like an apparition.

They say that there is a spell on the ship and that those few who reach it discover something unforgettable. It seems impossible to think about that beneath the sun and brightness of this spring morning, the air transparent and tranquil.

Everything is suspended and I lie in wait. First came the divers, then the tourists will come and nothing will be left. If I manage to reach it, maybe I will still find something.

Sometimes I think that the ship has been there since far distant times, that it sank three hundred years ago, and then I imagine the ancient settlers who saw it struggle against the waves and capsize. I see the loneliness of the plain, ending at the sea, and someone who approaches the shore on horseback and, impassive, looks out at the immensity of the ocean. A Pampa Indian perhaps, scrawny, sallow, sitting on the back of the horse, which, like me, breathes the salty wind coming in from the south.

In the distance, there are gulls turning lightly in the wind; there is an abyss below, which has survived since before the land existed. We have a memory of that immensity and so are happy on the sea and wretched on land. When we enter the ocean, we lose our language. Only the body exists, the rhythm of the oar's strokes and the resplendence of day on the water's surface. While swimming, we do not think about anything, only the brightness of the sun against the transparency of the water.

The sea here is dangerous and deep, but not treacherous. You have to know the subterranean movements of the tides and avoid the frozen currents towing in the sea. It seems calm today, but the current, dark and heavy, is visible like some submerged creature in the clarity of the water. It means that the tides are low, and I will be able to swim, dodging the cold edges of the undertow until I cross the final breaker and reach the calm sea.

I pause at the water's edge. The sun is at its zenith and there are no shadows on the sand. Nevertheless, in the background, far off, you can see rain falling on the remains of the sunken ship. A damp fog seems to shroud the desolate edges of the deck. The ship, under the rain, looks like a ghost ship, and I enter the sea and, determined, start to swim toward the center of the storm. The waves are slow and form in the distance, rising and rising until they violently break. I face the first breaker, some fifty meters from the coast. I sink a few meters and swim beneath the water, calm in the transparent stillness, and feel the waves above, breaking forcefully and buffeting me along as though someone were pushing me from behind.

I head for the open sea as soon as I have left the protection of the breakwater. The waterway is off to my left and I skirt its somber darkness and, for a moment, when I come too close, I can feel the water's frozen depths. I move away toward the left, swimming almost diagonally. I advance calmly, rhythmically, my mind blank.

I face the second breaker and the waves push me toward the waterway, which reappears at the end of a line of foam. The current tows me away from shore, but I manage to float without much effort and without trying to fight the tide that gently tows me. The sea has changed color and is dark and temperate and tosses toward the horizon, in a line parallel to the coast. Little by little, I move myself away from the undertow, swimming on and off, skirting it, until again I feel the water growing more transparent and calm.

I am far away from everything, some two kilometers from shore. The city is no longer visible; the sheen of tall buildings is confused with the resplendence of the sun on the water's surface. There is a clean and clear light, but further off, in front of me, the sea changes color, the sky is dark, and rain is falling like a gray cloth. There, amid the storm, sinking in fog, the ship is visible, tossing and creaking, beaten about by the tides.

All of the stern is underwater, but half of the deck projects upward from the surface. From below it appears impressive and motionless, like a building run aground. The gulls screech and circle above the red-painted chimneys.

I swim toward the rear and climb up along the anchor's chain until I can clamber onto the keel, and I manage to gain footing on the deck. The ship is tilted slightly, but I can walk toward the prow. At first, the water covers my feet, but the end of the deck is dry, the white excrement of gulls scattered over the metal plating.

I am alone in this silent vastness, standing before the horizon. The water makes a slight noise as it shakes against the upperworks. I feel like a castaway on an island in the middle of the ocean. I wave my hand, but, of course, no one sees me. The storm is over the city now, and from here you can see the dark mass of the rain like a liquid light. Here, however, the sun is out in full and the sky is clean. The stillness is complete. It takes me a while to realize that the ship is barely moving.

Off to one side, there is an open hatch with an iron staircase descending toward the machine room and the hold. The water reaches up to the second step. I start to descend and sink under; I keep my head out of the water at first, but, in the end, I plunge and submerge myself into the depths of the ship.

I dive for a narrow passage. Along the sides, doors are open, leading to the cabins. Everything is ravaged and the water renders the objects and furniture distant and unreal. A table is floating near the window. I submerge myself once again and pass through one of the doors and enter a room full of water. There are strange sounds, like lost voices or whispers.

I am out of air and turn back toward the staircase and try to recover my breath. Afterward, I dive again and once again cross the passage to enter the main cabin. On the floor, there are metal objects, screws and clasps and the remains of broken bottles. I try to open drawers and cupboards, but the pressure prevents me from moving them. When I leave for the surface once again, I notice that I am bleeding from my nose. I can breathe because the water does not fill the room completely and there is a kind of layer of air. I lie on my back, the ceiling close by, and breathe calmly. There is a light in the corner, off to the side—a lit lightbulb. I fear there may be some short-circuited cable and the water may be electrified. Could there be a generator? A dynamo? I am hallucinating. But I immediately calm myself and sink again into the flooded cabin.

Behind an open door, off to one side, close to the passage that leads to the hold, I see a shadow and approach slowly. I touch and do not understand; it seems to be a dead body. Once I come near, I see that it is a fabric: it looks like a sack or maybe a flag. I am out of air and turn upward again but am slow in finding the brightness that guides me, and for a moment I am seized by the panic of remaining trapped there. Finally, I manage to ascend, and, when I stop at the staircase, I see that my nose is bleeding once again. I wash myself and start to breathe calmly again. I dive and swim directly toward the door and, after struggling with it for a while, get the fabric to break free. Above, I realize it is a jacket made of waxed cloth. The sun is on my right, so it must be close to four. I throw myself down to rest on one side of the deck and think that I drift off to sleep for a while. Then I examine the jacket, wet and oily. It's missing a sleeve, but I manage to put it on all the same. It clings to my body, looks like a snakeskin. It has a pocket with a zipper. I discover a handkerchief and a map of Bahía Blanca that breaks apart as soon as I open it. At first, I think there is nothing more, but in the lining, underneath, I discover an object—flat, metallic, maybe a broken key, a stone. When I finally manage to get it out, I see that it is a coin. I take it in the palm of my hand. It seems to be made of silver; it is Greek. I do not know its value; it has a date I cannot decipher. I watch the sun shining. How many hands it must have held it before the sailor put it away in his pocket, in Athens or Thebes, and then sank with it. A Greek coin. It may yet bring me luck. I could use a bit of luck. It could do me no harm.

14

Diary 1965

I should explain what has happened these days, all very dizzying and strange. As always, the events enact themselves; a chain of contingencies decides things for me. I realized, some time ago, that my stay in La Plata had come to an end. My life is always divided, split into two, between Buenos Aires and this city. The issue lies in seeing which part will prevail.

Coti started coming over to the house again after a few months during which we knew nothing of her. She had bought a Vespa scooter and would travel around between the boardinghouses, spending three or four days in each. The boys put their money together and paid for her to stay. She would comment, amused, "I have my own harem of men." One afternoon, she turned up here once again and stayed with us. Everyone called her "the girl with the Vespa." Always entertaining and anti-dramatic. According to her, the experience—a rather promiscuous one—serves to enrich her vocation as an actress. She is still studying acting with Gandolfo but makes her living as a "working girl," which is how she defines herself.

She was with us on the day that Bardi had an accident and injured his hands: he had gone up a staircase to look for his summer clothes in the attic and fell into the window glass. Coti started taking care of him; both of his hands were bandaged and she helped him eat, bathe, and stayed with him all the time. Bardi fell in love with the girl and would, in fact, have preferred to stay with his hands bandaged so that she would look after him. At the end of the following week, Coti came, stayed with him for a while, and then started going from one room to the next, doing "her tricks," as she says. Late at night, Bardi, who is a very purposeful and calm person, had a euphoric attack, entered the room of the man from Corrientes who was in bed with her, and made a mess, broke a lamp. He had an attack of jealousy, and Coti never understood what had happened to him. She stopped coming around for a week, but then everything went on the same as before, with the routine and habits of seeing her walk around the house. Sometimes she would cook for everyone, and on one of those days, a Saturday that rained without stopping, she showed us her talent as an actress. She dressed up in men's clothing—she put on my leather jacket—and acted out Chekhov's monologue "On the Harmful Effects of Tobacco" for us. She even slipped up in announcing the work that she was going to interpret, saying, "On the Harmful Effects of Work." It was a joke, of course; she had a natural innocence and joy that is charming.

Coti was in my room, one afternoon, the two of us in bed, studying the declinations and morphology of Indo-European languages for one of the subjects I was thinking of taking in March. She was very interested in the idea of a language that was the common basis for all existing tongues and in the hypothesis that the group, or tribe, who spoke that language once existed but had been erased from the map by various barbarian invasions. She was very delighted with that rather unearthly history. And, standing naked in the middle of the room, she recited the Indo-European roots of Spanish verbs; she took the matter seriously and repeated the grammatical forms as though they belonged to a work of theater, written in a versified and incomprehensible prose.

I was half-asleep that afternoon but was awoken by the voice of Inés, talking to someone at the foot of the wooden staircase that leads to my attic room. Suddenly, I realized that Inés was coming toward me, accompanied by my father. No nightmare had never been as uncomfortable as this situation. There was no way to slow them down before they entered. And so, my father, Inés, and Coti crowed together in the room and greeted each other with a strange tone. The only one who did not lose her calm was Constanza (that was the name she gave my father when she shook his hand, formal and naked), who dressed at top speed; in a flash, she was ready and left.

My father had called Inés on the phone to ask for me; they had met in a bar near the building where she lives in Buenos Aires, and the situation became so strange, according to Inés, that, to lighten it, she proposed that they come to La Plata to look for me.

I can't quite remember the details of what happened that night. I know that the three of us returned on the omnibus and that I made the decision to move to Buenos Aires and live with Inés. That was what I did. As always, the important decisions come along with circumstances that survive in my memory, stronger than the reasoning that has moved me toward great changes. I don't even remember how I managed to get dressed that night.

Then we found a place to live; Cacho helped me move, and we went to La Plata together to look for my things. He had gotten—or "lifted," as he would say—a rural Mercedes-Benz pickup truck, spacious enough to hold the books, albums, and few other possessions I brought with me. The conversation that afternoon, while traveling, was unforgettable. Cacho seemed to live on an unstable surface, and I realized he had lost all notion of personal identity. And so, on the route returning from La Plata, he started to talk about politics. I gave him a history of the left and a view of the general dead-end situation, caused by the military strike against Perón and the prohibition of Peronism. I discussed that because it seemed to be the logical framework that he could assume as his own. He is very intelligent and listened to what I was saying with great attention, asking precise questions about details or about situations that he wanted to better understand.

January 2
We will see how my life progresses. Maybe this will be a decisive year, though there are no decisive years.

Clear beginnings, murky endings.

I saw Antonioni's *Red Desert*, a great film. He narrates it from the perspective of a disturbed woman, to whom reality seems threatening and hostile. Somehow, it seems similar to the story of Rosetta (from *Le Amiche*), as though she had not committed suicide and was married, yet still enthralled by the phantoms. (A subject. What happens after a failed suicide? How does life go on?)

Friday 8
The young student, after his attempt to "calm himself down." He is settled and wants to "save himself." Bardi, for example: his world is music, he is paused, motionless. He does nothing.

Thursday 14
Ever since I can remember, I have thought of myself as though I were immortal and had all of time available to me. Not immortality understood in a mystical sense (the denial of death), but rather the incomprehensible certainty of having time at your disposal that you do not need to use until some point in the future, one that you will never overtake. It is true that I have not thought seriously about my death (in this matter, my thinking, if it exists, is not at all philosophical, but rather a kind of thinking that, on the surface, seems to get me

"to safety," as though nothing but what I seek and what I want to do could matter to me now).

As for Inés, I accept her without reservation, like a presence here with me, and I watch her living with a mixture of detachment and confusion.

It's absurd, this need for the endless days to pass, to lie in wait. I suppose I never stopped to think about how these days are really all I have and that in the future I would give anything for them. They are days, the same as the others, but for me they are like an empty syllogism or hypothesis. I am immortal as long as I have memory and can bear witness. Now it is raining and raining.

Saturday 16
A *situation*. Someone is stuck in an elevator on the upper floors of a building. We can go on about the setting (the lights cut out, for example, and it's impossible to know that he is there), and then we would have a story in which the protagonist would be secondary. But if the person going up in the elevator is, for example, an assassin coming to kill someone on the top floor, a situation naturally starts to develop. In one case, the story sets off from the stopped elevator; in the other case, we set off from the character who has just murdered and is fleeing. I need to think about this situation further.

I was with Cacho until sunrise; we went to the casino, spent part of the night playing there, as Cacho says, with stolen cash. The feeling that money is just an object, taken without much effort, gives him a strange hint of lightness and emptiness that is clearly visible in his style of play. He would bet on red and, if he lost, he would double the bet, and, if he lost, he would redouble the bet and keep it raised in the air until the ball favored him. Then we sat at a baccarat table and lost fifty thousand pesos. We were forced to keep betting on banco because Cacho had the cards, but we went down a bad streak and it went to punto seven times in a row. Leaving, a silent walk in the sunrise with the clarity that sometimes comes when you think you understand everything.

Encounter with Cacho. I think I have already spoken about the way he caught my attention, but his story comes back to me again and again. We were going to secondary school, at different high schools; he was a year ahead, was a friend of a friend. He started coming to the bar where we spent time in those days; he was particularly interested in motorcycles. He would go down Boulevard Marítimo, beating his own speed records. He was one of ours and, like us, did not really know what to do with his life. I saw him again in Buenos Aires because he was hanging around near my cousin Horacio. By then he had turned into a sneak thief. He went out on Saturday nights and broke into houses in Olivos and San Isidro. He is blond, with sky-blue eyes, and dresses in very fashionable suits when he goes out to steal. He had been taking amphetamines that night to be more lucid and conquer the internal barrier that was a greater obstacle than the barred windows. He chose that form of life the same way someone decides to be a daredevil. "The first time, it seems impossible to make up your mind and enter a house, jumping the fences and moving stealthily, with a hunch that the owners are out for the night." That first night, it took several hours before he made up his mind; when he finally entered, he left again without taking anything more than a silver trophy. Later, he said, everything became easier; he would study the place and make his move, certain that the owners had left and wouldn't be back until sunrise. Sometimes he would see them leaving and listen to their conversations from the sidewalk, hidden in the shadows. You don't have to think once you're in, he would say, you have to make up your mind and go with the flow.

Now I am in the kitchen of the house, full of light. I prepare myself coffee as it goes on raining. I am tired and content with being alone.

Monday, January 25

I went to Buenos Aires and then to Piriápolis to meet Inés at her house. We ended the night at the club with ships anchored on the dock; strangely, all the people there know everything about everyone else, and they see me as someone whose story still needs to be told. Inés's friends and old classmates came up to the table where we were to investigate who she was with and who I was. The past arose and then she became, to me, a stranger; many of the people there knew secrets about her, of which I was still unaware. Inés laughed happily when I tried to explain something about being jealous of the past. "The past doesn't exist now," she said, but I didn't believe her.

Wednesday 27

"Herzen's moral bankruptcy . . . " and the whole discussion about those years in Russia correspond with our situation here since 1958 (I am reading Lenin). The notion of moral bankruptcy is a political category that must be taken up again.

Telling the story of an old-fashioned commander. My uncle Gerardo, who kept proud and serene even though he was already broke and lived off his wife's money.

Saturday 30

As always, an aggression arises suddenly within me, rising up from some unknown place. Today I got in a fight with an employee at the library who was talking back to me, and I was about to hit him, but Inés put her hand on my back and that calmed me down instantly.

I have thought a great deal about my assumptions concerning Inés's past; they have to do with the fact that she is from Uruguay. It makes no sense to think in this way, but I am not really thinking so much as expressing what she means to me. In the end, I can only conclude that I am experiencing the loss as if she were a stranger, about whom I only know the present. Nevertheless, there is only one "solution" (if there is a solution): I have to understand that only my literature matters, and that I must set aside and abandon whatever opposes it (in my mind or in my imagination), as I have always done since the beginning. That is my only moral lesson. The rest belongs to a world that is not mine. I am a man who has gambled his life on a single hand.

Two disputing tendencies exist with respect to the avant-garde and politics. On one side, the Lenin-Gramsci version: they revive everything from the cultural tradition that seems useful and productive to them (Tolstoy for Lenin, Pirandello for Gramsci); on the other side are Fanon and Sartre, who propose direct opposition to and destruction of the other culture (see, for example, Sartre's writings against Flaubert). One, the former, speaks from inside of tradition, while the latter acts from the outside and stems from the scorched earth of antagonistic cultures.

Sunday 31
A story narrated in the future tense as though the narrator knows the events before they take place, through some unexplained mechanism that transforms the story into a science-fiction text. "I can guarantee that he will die within five seconds. Within five seconds he will collapse down the escalator with a bullet in his head. He is crossing the hallway now, and death is already beside him, etc."

Tuesday, February 2
The worst part of last night's dream was the possibility of that woman I did not know staying with me. She was insecure, and so any gesture on my part was decisive. And I was so trapped by the situation that I could do nothing but make hollow and meaningless gestures.

In *Los albañiles*, Vicente Leñero's novel, technique is such a perfect clockwork mechanism that it becomes affected, too visible, and it detracts from the action. But his ruptured way of telling the story of Jesús C. (in which he tells how he was murdered) is remarkable and works very well.

Wednesday 3
Once again, as always, I can't make my mind up to break through what is overwhelming me, to take off the weight of this constant sensation of failure. It will be something that Inés does, one day or another, something I do not yet know, that will bring us to the end. What we fear most secretly always comes to pass.

Monday 8
In the library. Leñero has attempted, in *Los albañiles*, to "distill" Faulkner's technique; it is the characters who narrate the story, mixing together the time lines. He writes with an ascetic prose, not at all baroque. For that very reason, his technique is too "noticeable."

Friday 12
Losey's *The Servant*, with a script by Harold Pinter. Menace and things unsaid create a claustrophobic atmosphere. A cinema of the absurd (that is, with strange motives and reversed causality), a Kafkaesque allegory.

Saturday 18
A short story. Connecting the story of the immortal with the subject of a man five minutes ahead of his time. The state of the universe at any instant is a consequence of its state in the previous instant. That is the reflection of the man ahead of time, who once studied physics but has abandoned the profession.

"The moment of repentance is the moment of initiation. More than that: it is the means by which one alters one's past," Oscar Wilde.

I have to think about whether that character—the man who has broken through time and lives outside of it, displaced ahead by five minutes—is able to know his fate or whether he has been sentenced only to exist ahead of reality. Either of the two alternatives is cruel; one condemns him to the lucid state of knowing what is to come, the other demands that he live in the void, in a life not yet his own.

Monday 15
A subject. (This story suddenly came to me yesterday). An old man in a hospice watches a wall being built, cutting him off from the street, which he used to watch with a mixture of surprise and interest. In the end, he remains sitting alone, facing the barrier.

Tuesday 16
I finished the short story; it is called "La pared." The first character in my book, who is a silent and secret hero. I have to find that form again, the form of the story based on the history of a heroic character (even though he fails, or rather, is heroic in failure).

The immortal. "Many people let themselves be tricked by typographical and syntactical artifice and think that an event has happened because it is printed in big bold letters." I received this assertion from a man I met by chance while traveling on a train to the south.

Wednesday 17
Last night Inés was talking, like so many others before her, about my distance, about my separation from things, about my indifference toward her. She is right, but there is nothing deliberate about defining a way of being. As a result, she insists on imagining immediate changes. "There's no pleasure in your life now," she told me.

Balzac, at the start of the nineteenth century, already knew how to write by changing the point of view. In "A Passion in the Desert," the narrator directs his account to someone conversing with him. But the story has been narrated to him in the first person by the protagonist of the events; that is, he achieves several levels. Someone lives through an incident. Then he meets an individual and recounts it. That individual in turn tells it to a woman.

The immortal. He had been in combat with Güemes, ridden against Urquiza, had told bedroom anecdotes, archaic and outmoded, which he attributed to his friend Lucio Mansilla. He said he was Alem's man but not Yrigoyen's, claimed that he had suffered prison during Peronism. In that way, using incidents known to everyone, he told the long years of his life, making himself the protagonist in numerous successive events in time. In the end, he sat in a bar on Las Heras and Lafinur, showing that he knew a lot about the interlinings of Frondizi's government and that, therefore, he was living in the present.

"The world is changed... not by what is said, or what is blamed or praised, but by what is done. The world never recovers from what is done," G. K. Chesterton.

Last night, close to here, a fire. Above all, the image of a man throwing furniture, suitcases, clothing from the window.

Inés talked about the scar on my ankle. She stopped to think but refused to tell me what she was thinking about. Another scar on the leg of someone she knew in the past, I thought.

A police story. A lucid murderer "scientifically" constructs a crime that no one will be able to solve. The story consists of an account of the event and the successive narration of a series of chance incidents, unexpected pieces of information, footprints that do not belong to him, which end up constructing, unexpectedly and for the wrong reasons, his guilt. The issue is that the crime is perfect, but chance creates a series of false proofs that send him to prison.

As always, there is something like a mandate (from no one) for me, a mandate I have built for myself (writing and being a writer). I don't know if that makes sense either. But, just the same, always, it comes back and persists.

Saturday 20

A short story. A Peronist laborer is hospitalized in the intensive care ward while, outside, the 1955 revolution breaks out. Convalescent, he is partially aware of the events that have been percolating while he was in a semiconscious state. His dreams and his ideas and convictions have made him think that the revolution was defeated. When he goes out into the street and sees a demonstration, he believes it is a march in support of Perón, who has fled from the city several days before.

Someone does something but recounts it as though it were something else, and it is the reader who must replace the missing meaning. It's as though the narrator were ignorant of the names of the things that must be named, so that his tone is one of stupefaction toward what he narrates, but his stupefaction is connected to the difficulty he has in naming the events, rather than toward the events themselves. He is not able to hierarchize the incidents, and describes a crime and the act of drinking a glass of water at a bar with the same distance. In the police genre, all characters are despicable and efficient.

Sometimes I have visions of Inés as though anticipating her actions, which are always reproachable and take the form of betrayal in my fantasies. Should I think that this way of seeing is a necessary consequence of love, or its opposite?

Friday, February 26

This summer ends as well and, like all summers, leaves me with the feeling of a light and luminous time, lasting as long as the span of the sun's journey toward the end of afternoon.

For me, 1964 has only just ended.

Monday, March 1
In the end, I will always be an outsider to things. Last night in the middle of the dance at the club near the river, surrounded by unknown people belonging to Inés's past.

Tuesday 2
The town once again, the port of Piriápolis, with dive bars and the great bridge over the river, the café as metaphor for the town because it mixes together everything that is separated in the place. Someone has come there with his woman, to the place where she was born and became who she is; he is there as an observer of a far-off time, which survives in the middle of the coast by the sea. He knows that the people there share a common history and that everyone is watching the outsider with interest. That figure, the outsider, is a hallmark of fiction, someone who comes in from elsewhere, someone unknown; the passing traveler brings with him a gaze that no one knows. Ulysses was the first outsider, and tonight I imagine that I am the last.

Before, on Saturday, a long and tranquil walk through Buenos Aires with Inés, the bars (that bar on Maipú that is deserted at this time of day). We continue as far as Bajo, then walk down the covered walks of Alem to Retiro and then to the port with the muddy river, the color of the desert, which is always motionless. We went to Adam, the beautiful pub that opens onto the park and Torre de los Ingleses. We drank beer and remembered other times and other people in this very bar. Finally, we ate dinner at Pippo and went to the festival on 9 de Julio, and Aníbal Troilo was playing on a stage.

Wednesday
Iguazú Bar. Escaping from that town, we returned to the tiny and very tall room, happy once again in the city. In a hiding place between

the books, I found four thousand pesos that I had forgotten there a while ago.

Now I go back to reading Proust, the long paragraphs, his magnificent cadence: "Remembering again all the places and people that I had known, what I had actually seen of them, and what others had told me," M. Proust.

Another comparison, or rather, another kinship: in Proust as in Kafka, power is thoughtless and irrational and is always paternal and has a nonhuman character. "My father's conduct towards me was still somewhat arbitrary, and regardless of my deserts, as was characteristic of him," M. Proust.

Friday, March 5
I am in Las Violetas, I want to write a short story: they spend the summer in her town, and the woman stays there; during the journey, on the way toward the town, there were already hints of their breakup. Spaces have an emotional value that goes beyond the landscape and experiences. The story of the woman who does not leave seems to me the inverse of Briante's story "Dijo que iba a volver" and Rozenmacher's "Raíces." The town as a passing place. The outsider as the modern hero. He has no birthplace, is always passing through, and, in the end, perhaps without anyone foreseeing it, he discovers the place where he was born. As though Ulysses didn't know that he wanted or needed to return to Ithaca.

Sunday, March 7
Yesterday on the train, on the way to San Isidro, a surprising and novel fear about the immediate future. I was on the point of getting off anywhere I could. I had money in my pocket and this notebook in my bag. And that's that. Later, at Haroldo Conti's house in the country, many writers, too many writers. Miguel Briante was there, and so was Enrique Wernicke, with whom I had some verbal skirmish, in the routine tone of cultural machismo and hooliganism. (The two of us went to piss in the

garden and competition and comparison immediately arose, then we saw that, while we were there, everyone was watching us from the living room through the glass of the large picture windows.) Marta Lynch applauded, I was already fairly drunk, and everything had that intellectual-party atmosphere—atrocious.

In the morning, Alberto Szpunberg and Jorge Herrera trying to put together an intellectual front, wanting to organize a writers' liaison with the MIR.

Tuesday
Last night, with Pancho Aricó and others, it becomes clear that the leftist front does not work without considering the issue of Peronism. He has proposed several times that I become involved with the magazine *Pasado y Presente*.

When speaking about new writers (Rozenmacher, Briante, I myself), it is important to remember that they are not made so because of a generational issue, but rather because they have a different idea of art than that of the writers who preceded them.

Is it about studying Argentine culture in the wake of Peronism? Yes, with the Pavesean concept of "lived history."

Thursday
I take the train to El Tigre, the carriage packed. Near me, a fat and disproportionate man, of a certain age, drinking beer "so he wouldn't go to bed cold," after having spent fourteen years in Alcoholics Anonymous and becoming a teetotaler, "never drinking anything, not even Coca-Cola." He has gone back to drinking and is "afraid of death" but sure that he won't die like a dog, because he keeps dynamite under his bed and sleeps with a lit fuse, even if it's cold and there are no mosquitoes, because he says that keeping the fire close is enough "to make everything fly."

Tuesday 16
I go in loops through the bars in the city even though I know that this journey makes no sense. In the end, it is an ill-devised existence, which I only came to understand a short time ago. "Ill-devised" means you have accepted the risk of gambling everything on one card without knowing if that playing card was really there in the deck.

Thursday 18
For the first time in my life I am afraid of failure, yet I go on, static, not doing anything, as though searching for the end. On top of that, we have no money, and I escape the room and go into the city to stop thinking.

Monday 22
Miguel Briante reads me *Habrá que matar los perros*, a very good *nouvelle*—brilliant, lush, Faulknerian. In the bars on Corrientes with him, drinking until sunrise.

Today, the experience of listening to Oscar Masotta in Arts and Sciences presenting his book on Roberto Arlt. A notable autobiographical text following Sartre's technique and, as in *The Words*, the speaker takes himself as the object of analysis and then speaks about himself but refers to who he was before—that is, another person who was him—without the clarity he has in the present. He recalled his misfortunes, his strange relationship with his father, his insanity and his neglect.

Tuesday
Tata Cedrón debuted a tango, "Trocha angosta," and another with lyrics by Paco Urondo. In Chacarita, I wait for Casco, my old political contact from the days in La Plata. Now I am waiting for him in this place, full of flowers for the dead, a populated cemetery, strange, like an old fair.

Monday 29
I don't want to start another notebook because I don't have the money to buy one. This one serves to clear my mind of these days, in which I have lived adrift, without tying myself down to anything and without expecting anything but the passing of days.

April 5
In Florida bar. The waiter had a black stone ring on his left hand, which moved as he opened the bottle of beer and tilted it against the glass so the foam would go where he wanted. Then he said that it had been a while since he'd seen me there, his friend; on the other hand, he said, referring to Júnior, he always comes. Curious, a waiter's knowledge. He knows the regulars only through what they do or say while they are in the bar. Maybe someone (not me) confides in him or tells him episodes from their lives. But most commonly they know the remnants of experiences arising from conversations exchanged at the tables, because each waiter has a section of the place assigned to him and because—if I take myself as an example—those of us who frequent a café occupy the same tables almost unconsciously. And so, the waiter has a variable ensemble of individuals at his fingertips, who come to the place habitually and let him know unexpected areas of their lives, which he always accesses by chance.

I live frugally off the money earned from the classes I give at the University. I travel to La Plata once a week and stay for three days, sometimes two. Anyway, I always spend a night in the city, always in the same hotel. The money I make from my two positions is enough for me to live on if I don't have unusual expenses. But, like everyone else, I am only interested in unusual expenses, so I habitually have no money.

Through the window, I just saw Inés arriving with the black handbag she always uses, her way of walking hurried but elegant, her hair tied with a black ribbon.

I suddenly recalled that large theater, with a long corridor down the side leading to the bathrooms, the sounds from the street that filtered in despite the heavy curtains of the entrance, the matinées where I watched the *Tarzan* series, one film after another. It was the Brown theater, and I was seven or eight years old then and swelled with pride at going to the cinema alone.

What I have kept from that far-off time is the delusion that each day is valuable in itself and is justified as though it were the only one. Childhood is a timeless time in which only momentary happiness matters, and you try to replicate it amid the inconceivable series of obligations to which a boy is subjected (school primarily, the daily rhythms at home forming an undeniable cohesion). Formally, nothing changes as you mature: it is always a combination of personal moments and imposed obligations.

Wednesday 7
Writing Pavese's story: bound to the life of a cabaret pianist who plays tangos and milongas every night until, unexpectedly, he kills himself one morning.

Recently, on the corner, while walking down the stairs to the subway at Medrano station to go downtown and lose myself among the people, I decided to come back, without wanting to, like someone who has forgotten something and goes back to look for it. And now I am in my room again, at the table, and can vaguely imagine what would have happened if I actually had taken the subway and gotten off at Callao and Corrientes.

Once again in a lethargic state, the world is darkened and moves away from me. I lose my notion of space (first issue); what is far is near, and what is near is dangerous and almost becomes intimate (second issue). Now, for example, the cup of coffee, which, almost at the instant when I feel its proximity, falls to the floor of the bar and breaks. Sometimes I have to invent a reason to justify my hypnotic state, Inés's slight lateness, for example. I saw her come in, greet me, and go over to a public phone; immediately I thought, among all the possible alternatives, that she's calling someone else and making a date with him. In this way, though it may seem strange, I calm myself down by finding an explanation for my chaotic state. Then Inés comes over, sits down with me, laughs at the story of the broken cup on the floor, and says she was talking to Alicia on the phone, so we can go have dinner with her. Of course, I think these are the alibis that girls create with their friends. She agreed on that explanation with Alicia beforehand and was actually talking to a man. Alicia, on the other hand, is perfect in this area given that she is married to a musician but has been having a clandestine relationship with a surrealist poet for years. Of course, I don't reveal my thoughts to Inés so that she will not suspect I have become aware of her adventures.

Thursday 8
I am on the train to La Plata, much better than yesterday; I can look out the window without danger and listen to the conversations of passengers traveling behind me without thinking that they are talking about me.

Friday 9
I won the competitions for my two fellowships because no opponent came forward. Anyway, it is a position that opens up every two years, and therefore my economic situation is resolved.

Yesterday with fat Ferrero, long conversations about some Spanish poets he and I both admire. Poems by Jorge Guillén and Luis Cernuda. Then we discuss the draft of the story I'm writing and Ferrero immediately picks up on the pretentiousness of the prose. When someone reads one of my texts and immediately mentions an aspect I'm certain about, I look past it; on the other hand, if they mention, in a confused but critical way, an aspect that I feel insecure about or doubt, it is clear that I have to go back to working on it. Giving an unfinished text to someone else is a way for you to read it with their eyes, meaning that you can separate yourself from what you're writing and see it with a certain distance.

Theme, a variation. A Peronist laborer or employee is confined in a hospital during the days in September when the military coup against Perón took place. He becomes aware of the events confusedly, amid the stupor of the painkillers and medical treatments that constitute the everyday routine. On the radio, he hears differing and confusing versions and dies without knowing the conclusion of the historical events, which he was interested in but could not decipher.

Saturday 10
Vietnam is, for us, what the Spanish Civil War was for my father. A conflict in which something more than the immediate result is in play. According to the newspapers, tactics are being tested in all of the (western) armies to suppress guerrilla warfare.

Sunday 11
I am in Las Violetas; I come here every day to write in the morning hours when the bar is almost empty. Around five in the afternoon the women from the neighborhood start coming here, to meet with their friends and drink tea. Today it is raining and the city behind the large windows looks like a gigantic fish tank populated by curious individuals who pass running through the street, holding up some circular cloth objects with canes that rise from their hands to a swarm of metal ribs, flipping around easily when the wind meets them head-on.

I should connect the notion of "destiny" in Pavese with the "past" in Faulkner. They are crystallized ways of defining motivations that the characters act out without understanding. Faulkner writes as though the reader belongs to the story he narrates, never explaining anything that the characters already know. Therefore the air of abstract incomprehension and magic that events in his books possess.

215

Monday

I am reading Faulkner's "The Bear," a story of learning that, for me, has slight secret echoes of Melville's *Moby Dick*. Stories with wild animals are the only ones worth telling, even though you sometimes come across peaceful and familiar stories with cats or dogs as protagonists. The best animals in literature are those of Kafka: "Investigations of a Dog," "Josephine the Singer," "A Report to an Academy." In fact, in Kafka the animals are intellectuals or artists. Whereas Faulkner's bear and Melville's whale are forms of untamed nature. Having said that, what can be said about the horses that abound in Argentine literature?

Monday, April 12

A few days ago, one of Inés's friends, who is coming to live in Buenos Aires, came in from Rosario. We go around the city, from one end to the other, through Bajo as far as Palermo. We saw Alberto Szpunberg and Daniel Moyano. Inés's friend writes some conceptual poems, which I enjoy. When we went to wait for her at the terminal in Once, she was reading a novel by Osamu Dazai.

Thursday

Yesterday with Daniel Moyano and Augusto Roa Bastos, looking for certain places we had read about in some books. For example, Plaza Vicente López, where you can see the shadow of the ghosts in Bianco's story, or the cupola of the building on Talcahuano and Lavalle, where the hotel from *Mad Toy* was located, where Astier meets the boy who wears women's stockings. For them, the landscape has a power superimposed onto the story; Roa in *Son of Man*, and Moyano in his Kafkaesque stories, find the space of fiction in the wasteland.

Friday

Last night, a round table in the College of Philosophy and Letters to present *La lombriz*, the book by Daniel Moyano that we published in Nueve 64. In the discussion, I faced off against everyone. While they defended so-called inland literature, I stood as the sole representative of Buenos Aires. Saer cracked a few jokes in bad taste, but then we went on arguing in several bars and ended up eating at El Dorá.

Monday
Many projects are in my hands—the book of stories, the magazine, which I'm publishing by myself. It's important to hurry, to choose a direction; I must make up my mind. What am I doing here? Everything is ridiculous. I have found myself in the middle of a task that I didn't choose. I can neither work nor stop working. It's as if there are some problems—or traps—that I don't want to escape from. But we are coming to the end now, slowly.

Tuesday 27
I return to dreaming the same dream: someone lights the room in La Plata on fire, all of the books and my stories burn. That dream repeats, as though I had assimilated my old myths, the fire in a library, the image of burnt books; of course, it doesn't concern the other fable: the writer who destroys his old papers or manuscripts so that they will not be published. Although, perhaps, a careful interpretation of this recurring dream unites the two traditions: my books are burning, but I am also burning them myself.

I have to go back—since I am in the tunnel of introspection—to the breakup that, I suppose, was the end of childhood for me, a paradise lost. Of course, all paradises are imaginary.

Thursday 29
I won ten thousand pesos in the Instituto del Libro's short-story competition for "Una luz que se iba." You can live for a month with that kind of money.

Interesting, in current literature, the opposition between the artist and the intellectual, seen as incompatible. Each carries his own shortcomings:

the artist, always inspired, is customarily a bastard who thinks he has privileges and others must be at his service. On the other hand, the intellectual manipulates others with his rational excuses and his historical blackmail, explains everything and everything serves to justify him. In short, it is another embodiment of the tension between art and life.

Monday, May 3
An American invasion of Santo Domingo. Several protests in Buenos Aires condemning it. The American paratroopers occupied the city within an hour and eliminated Caamaño's supporters' center of resistance. Immediately, my friends on the left saw clearly the difficulty of establishing a revolutionary strategy in urban insurrection (Lenin's model). Today, it seems impossible to resist in a city that has been conquered; therefore, the discussion has veered toward rural guerrilla warfare with liberated regions in the mountains. But that strategy is madness in Argentina.

Look at L. Johnson's justification: "The American nations cannot, must not, and will not permit the establishment of another Communist government in the Western Hemisphere. This was the unanimous view of all the American nations when, in January 1962, they declared, and I quote: 'The principles of communism are incompatible with the principles of the inter-American system.' This is what our beloved President John F. Kennedy meant when, less than a week before his death, he told us: 'We in this hemisphere must also use every resource at our command to prevent the establishment of another Cuba in this hemisphere.' . . . But revolution in any country is a matter for that country to deal with. It becomes a matter calling for hemispheric action only—repeat—only when the object is the establishment of a communistic dictatorship."

Thursday 6
Last night, shooting and gas from the police at the protest for Santo Domingo. We assembled in front of the Congress and the mounted policemen charged the crowd, which dissolved into small groups and

reassembled again and again. For my part, I have a confused version of the events. I remember Alfredo Palacios speaking against the American intervention from the stairway of the Congress, and then I see myself sitting at a table in La Ópera bar on Corrientes and Callao, but I don't remember what happened in between.

I watch *Chronicle of a Boy Alone* by Leonardo Favio. A notable first film of great quality. An intuitive artist who knows how to tell stories and has seen very good cinema. The film reminded me of S. Ray.

I am in London on Florida and Avenida de Mayo. I make a circuit through the bars, obliged to feel a certain detachment, as though traveling through. Very unfocused, no capacity for work.

Monday 10
I am in Las Violetas now. I work in this brightly lit bar, just in front of the hotel where I live. I prepare the introduction for the magazine. I don't hope for much from this either. I also think, as has happened to me in other magazines I have worked on, that it is very productive and enjoyable to work in a group, creating a composition, but at the same time I know intimately that true work is always solitary. Yesterday, I spent the afternoon in Martínez with Sergio, translating the work of A. Wesker. Everything is ready now; the index is set and I can start preparing the introduction. I don't want it to be an editorial, but simply an essay that deals with some issues discussed in the magazine. I still have reservation concerning the title of the publication. It could be *Letras/65*.

Rereading my notebooks is a narrative lesson: everything is organized chronologically according to the cuts of days of the week. That continuity is exterior to the events, so that the form these notes take depends in some sense on the time I take to write them. But, in reading them, things change and I start to discover connections, repetitions, the persistence of certain motifs that reappear and define the tone of these pages. In short, the events, the characters, the places, and the states of the soul are combined here; the distinctive feature is that all of that is present while at the same time the days are narrated, one after another. In that sense, a diary seems akin to dreams.

One of the lessons—if there really are lessons, because deep down it is idiotic to think you can learn from the experience—is the fluctuation between what can be done or said and what can be neither said nor done. A diary should be written about the second part of the sentence; that is, you should ultimately write about the limits or the frontiers that make certain words or actions impossible. But where do those obstacles come from, the feeling that there is something—a space, a person, a series of actions—"that cannot be done?" It wouldn't mean a "real" impossibility but rather a place it is prohibited to enter. Then we ask whom it is prohibited for and start again . . . It's also true that my past (what Pavese calls personal destiny) allows me to see or define what I can do; the rest of the alternatives and options I could never see nor conceive of directly. Literature could be, among other things, helpful as a way of discovering or describing these blind spots.

Tuesday, May 11
In the bar on Rivadavia and Gascón. A sensation of being clean, shaven, tranquil, up in the air. Maybe take a trip to the south, to Banfield.

The introduction to the magazine becomes clear as soon as I frame it as an attempt to treat culture as a politically specific field. Politics has its own registers and modes, which cannot be applied directly to literature or culture. It doesn't mean they are autonomous, it only means that they have their own ways to discuss and "do" what we call politics, or rather that they have their own power relationships. But we cannot forget that literature is a society without a state. No one, no institution or form of coercion, can obligate someone to accept or enact a certain artistic poetics. The material decisions of art belong to their own sphere; in fact, more than talking about politics in general, it is necessary to talk about the dynamic between the museum and the market. The museum as site and metaphor for consecration or legitimacy, and the market as the sphere of circulation for the works, always mediated by money. In that frame, the problem of "creation" becomes at once more clear and more complex. That must be the crux explaining the meaning of a new publication.

Wednesday 12

It is not by chance that now—as I work on the article for *Literatura y Sociedad*, which is what the magazine will be called—the tranquility of my best times returns. For me, the essay must center around the letter *y*: it is about investigating the difference that this letter establishes and also the connection that it defines.

Thursday 13

In Florida bar. Last night in front of Congress, another protest against the American invasion of Santo Domingo. In the middle of the action, a confrontation between the Tacuaras, the nationalist group of the right, and the Communist Party. The gunfire lasted more than a half hour. I took refuge in the entryway of El Molino and could only see the confusion and the commotion and a young man in a suit with black glasses shooting a pistol toward a target I wasn't able to identify. He was crouching behind one of the benches in the plaza and would appear here and there, supporting his arm on the back and firing, and then, without losing calm—or at least it seemed so to me—and without hurrying, he would go back and hide behind the wooden bench. In the end, there was one death, one casualty, and five wounded. At midnight, the protest returned to the city center, listlessly. In the end, on the corner by El Obelisco, a group started shaking a Coca-Cola poster on top of a lamppost. They threw it down and everyone celebrated as though it were a triumph . . . Then a Neptune water cannon appeared (the police also have their irony and know the classics) and started shooting water at everyone there. There was also tear gas, dogs, etc. For my part, I left running not very heroically down Diagonal Sur. I was with Inés, Raúl E., and Sergio.

Sunday

I see Roberto Jacoby, who tells me about some of his experiences in New York. Especially the spectacle in the street of groups fighting against the Vietnam War. Surprisingly, on a very crowded corner of the city, three or four actors hidden among the people feign a violent argument about the facts of the war, almost come to blows, but a third actor intervenes, and then an actress, who adds to the verbal violence. Quickly, the passersby join in the argument and the city erupts in a debate about the political situation. By that point, the actors have already withdrawn from the place; they enter the subway and get off in another populous part of the city. According to Roberto, it is a theater of violence that does not speak about it but rather acts it out. Connected in particular to *The Living Theatre*.

Monday

We are always without money. I hope the magazine—in which we have invested our reserves—works out well. I always have the article half-done. The truth is that the project is underway and it is impossible to turn back and there is nothing left but to undertake it. I hope to finish writing it this week so that the magazine can go to print before the end of the month.

Last night we went to listen to Osvaldo Pugliese at Solís Theater; it was all of the friends from the magazine, and we took photos of ourselves and with the musicians. Very extraordinary, the first bandoneon player Ruggiero. He is unique, they call him "lead bandoneon" because he pushes on all the rows of bandoneons, like the lead horse drives the team pulling the cart. Pugliese's bandoneons sound like a train moving forward while he plays the melodies on the piano. They finished by playing "La Yumba," in which, if you listen closely, is all of Piazzolla.

A proposal from Alberto Cedrón, who offers me a place in the tenement house on Calle Olavarría where all of the brothers live, including Tata. Very possibly I will accept the offer. The house is typical of the buildings in Boca, made of tin. When you enter, there is a patio with the sinks and bathrooms, and stairs lead from there to the second floor, where there is a line of rooms with more or less the same layout. It opens out into a hallway that goes to the kitchen and living room. At the end, on either side, there are two large rooms and a smaller place at the back of the living room. I would be in one of the ones that open onto the street, very spacious and well lit.

Wednesday
In Florida bar, eight p.m. A certain anxiety in the face of everything I don't control, what others do without me. As though, in this moment (confronting the objective decisions that others make), I could recognize the opacity of the world, the exteriority I have always denied and avoided as though it did not exist. Though it may seem strange, I have acted for years as though I were alone in the world.

La Paz, eight p.m. Strange, Cortázar praises my short story "Desagravio," which I published a while ago, in a letter to a friend (A. C.) at the magazine where I no longer write.

Subject. The *morochito* wrapped himself up in the blanket, looking like a pile of gray rags fluttering in the cold air that filtered in through the slits of the cell. A soldier had brought in the mattress less than an hour before. (Describing it in this way, dry, without making it clear what is taking place. Or if not, only through dialogue.)

Thursday 20
I am rediscovering the advantages of detachment. Anyway, I spent the afternoon with Sergio Camarda. He is trying to create a structure: bookshop + publishing house + distributor + magazine. Short twenty

thousand pesos to buy the paper. Three thousand copies with one hundred sixty pages are sixty thousand pesos (paid ten thousand per month).

The amusing part of the afternoon was the discovery that Sergio keeps several weapons in his house. We opened a chest looking for some photographs, but in fact found only weapons. "They're a friend's," Sergio said, but I didn't believe him. It's not hard to see a relationship between these weapons and the magazine's funding. Something distantly connected to money from some Cubans (I think).

Thursday 27
In Boca, at Tata's house, I feel good here, working by night. The article is almost ready. Very humid and hot. I have several days ahead of me; I am alone, Inés in Tandil, I have one hundred pesos.

Tuesday, June 8
You are inside the world you narrate. What I mean is that you must never say anything that is external to the universe of the action. The narrator must know less than the protagonists.

Monday, June 14
I escape constantly. I hope to find an anchor in Boca. A fact I am fleeing from is that I barely write in this notebook. Always the same distance with Inés, as though a sheet of glass separated us.

Friday
I live here in this hospitable house, through which many friends circulate. Our place opens onto a calm street.

Tuesday
Last night at home, Gelman, Urondo, and Tata. After recording "Madrugada," while we were talking I told him he could put music to

Juan or Paco's poems. They were working on that as we slowly got drunk. Then, after midnight, Tito Cossa and Germán Rozenmacher arrived, working on a collaborative project about the myth of Perón's return: *The Black Airplane*, they call it.

Sunday 27
Things are resolving themselves slowly.

Monday 28
I quite like Cortázar's story "Instructions for John Howell." A spectator is kindly invited to enter the interior of the theater; he thinks it has to do with some type of questionnaire, but he suddenly sees that they have brought him onto the stage and he must participate in a work that is underway. It has something of Onetti's "A Dream Come True," with the woman who has a recurring dream and looks for a theater director to stage the oneiric scene: on a corner in the city, she crosses toward a man she knows and, on the way, a car runs her over and she dies "inside the reality" of the theatrical representation.

Cacho comes to visit me, he enjoys the place, we go down to eat nearby and then leave to take a turn in a Chevrolet that he has stolen hours before. Of course, the beauty of the matter lies in the risk of being stopped for any small traffic incident.

Going out with Cacho made me abandon my intention to travel to La Plata. Sergio calls us, maybe I have to go to the bookshop, to hurry up the delayed release of the magazine. But I remain shut in, waiting. Outside it is raining and the summer ending.

Tuesday 29
The point could be the following: to destroy—to attempt to destroy—personal fate as manifested in the repetition of events. We know that we repeat actions but do not remember. In this case, the point would be

to deliberately remember some incidents from the past, over and over again. It might be a single event—for example, an afternoon playing chess at the club—remembered with the intention of reconstructing everything surrounding the scene. Another alternative would be to reread these notebooks, to choose something recorded there that you no longer remember and try to do the same thing again—that is, to try to reconstruct everything around that event. Of course, there is no assurance that you can overcome the repetition of events by remembering (for example, in my case, by remembering my tendency toward isolation, which has persisted since childhood), but, in any case, it would give a new dimension to the events. It's like the reaction of a cat, scratching or biting when it is stepped on by accident. Memory works in this way: you step on the toe of a memory and then the scratch and the blood come. Nevertheless, there doesn't appear to be a solution; it's impossible to rectify the past. And there in the past is the event, one which you have forgotten but which is repeated in other ways—yet always the same, again and again.

Friday, July 2
Yesterday, all day organizing the house. As always, all I need is a table by the window and a lamp. I pass the night working.

We watched *King and Country*, Losey's film about the First World War. Sometimes a bit annoying, the pretension of "proving a thesis." Excellent for the last ten minutes, after the soldier's sentence of death.

Sunday 4
I am reading Céline's *Journey to the End of the Night* once again. The rhythm of the prose constructs the story. Later, in Suárez bar on Maipú and Corrientes, too much whiskey to be lucid with Inés.

"I have entered the literature when I have been able to replace the 'he' with the 'I,'" Kafka. In my case, I could say: I have entered my autobiography when I have been able to live in the third person.

Subject. Narrating the war from the perspective of someone who did not go. It is achieved through "notices of war." I talk about it with my grandfather Emilio, who comes to see me. He has been to war but never speaks of it, only keeps the papers, documents, letters, maps, and photographs, and always tells me that one day he will take on the work of organizing his archive. In the meantime, he has actually paid for the first years of my degree with the sole condition that I come see him at the house in Adrogué and listen to him telling his fragmented stories. It was delightful, as always, to see him once again. I accompanied him to the station and watched him walking away down the platform, very upright and elegant, illuminated by the white light of the locomotive.

Tuesday

I spend the day reading Céline. Several pending things have resolved at the magazine (the cover, the majority of the articles). In Céline, I am excited by the confessional tone in which "evil" is narrated. In one sense, it is the limit of the first person: you have to explain why this individual is able to accuse himself of acts that society considers heinous. Céline consciously constructs horrible scenes, never self-incriminates, never complains, only narrates the events with a slightly cynical tone in order to show that, in the moment of writing, he can only remember the wicked events he is narrating. He is another who seems to have purified himself only by telling the truth.

Subject. Told to the man going alone to where she was born. He waits for the train and now, on the journey, finds someone in the train car who knows the woman and starts telling shady stories about her. When he arrives in the town, in an almost fantastical manner, he starts receiving fragments of his wife's secret life by chance from the strangers he encounters in different places. He returns, gets off at Retiro, and is lost among the people. (He had gone to the town to "recognize" the place.)

You could construct an almost fantastical story based on past events in the present. The protagonist could begin the day with a small memory, which arises unexpectedly and lasts barely seconds, and as the morning advances the memories grow more extensive; now he has to stop, for example, and sit on a bench in the park to resist the emotions of what the memory brings. When night comes, toward the end of the story, the man lives in the present for a minute—in the moment he turns off the lamp before going to sleep, for example—but, except for that instant, the rest of the time is completely taken over by his past.

Another subject. The only person who did not see the luminous phenomenon that appeared suddenly in the starry night was the director of the meteorological observatory, who was facing the wall at that moment, talking to one of his colleagues on the phone. When he returned home, everyone told him about the strange experience of seeing a pale and wicked light in the sky, which seemed to pause over each one of them. The observer started to think that everyone in the town except for him was having visions, given that his mission in the place was precisely that of observing cosmic phenomena.

Friday 9
I spent the afternoon with the sculptor Mario Loza, then we went out together and ended up at a club close to the Boca stadium, eating pizza and drinking wine. Now I'm trapped in a sort of exaltation that could easily be confused with happiness. Meanwhile it is raining outside and you can hear the archaic sound of water falling on tin roofs. What is the meaning of this meeting, in a bar and then in a restaurant, drinking wine with someone I barely know?

Earlier, at the College, I run into Vicky, huddled, always fragile, beautiful, with her slightly childish aggression. (I no longer love her, it is clear, but I did love her so.)

Sunday

I spend the day with Miguel in his house. Conversations that flow up from the past, as though we had never stopped seeing each other. He is married these days to a blonde girl, a kind of giantess, who will make him suffer.

Monday

Letter to Daniel Moyano.
Telephone. Call Eduardo.
Perspectives. F. Herrera. A. Szpunberg. Ramón.
Clothing to the laundromat.
Buying oranges.
A shirt.

At night, in London, the Porteña Jazz Band.

Tuesday 13

In La Plata, the fellowships are renewed. I sign a contract for "Introduction to History" and "History of Argentina I." I will give classes two days in a row, possibly Monday and Tuesday. (I am going to spend one night in a hotel close to the train station.)

Wednesday 14

At some point Freud made an important discovery: there seemed to be a tendency to repeat past situations even when they had been painful. "This compulsion to repeat also recalls from the past experiences which include no possibility of pleasure, and which can never, even long ago, have brought satisfaction even to instinctual impulses which have since been repressed." Freud thinks that the tendency toward repetition is an attempt to repair the trauma (often—and this is very curious—the repetition goes back to the time when the trauma still had not taken place). In short, for Freud, repetition is an attempt to dominate and control experience.

I have forty-five pesos to finish off the day and Alberto is calling me every other day to reclaim the alleged debt of twenty thousand pesos that he claims I owe him.

Thursday 15
A ridiculous cold. Mornings need not exist. We have to get up in the afternoon or at nightfall, whatever time allows us to elude the diluted, frozen light when the day is still ahead and we do not know what to do.

Wise words: *del dicho al hecho hay mucho trecho*, the thing is easier said than done. The phrase has been coming to me ever since, a few weeks ago, I announced the plan of things that I am going to do and yet never do. Of course, the sentence depends on alliteration, the sound of the "ch."

I went to the bank. I couldn't collect the wire transfer that my grandfather sent me (it was three thousand pesos). We'll make it through the day with ten pesos. For maté, etc.

Friday 16
I remember one summer in Bolívar, the image of myself at the edge of the pool, about to dive. We walked on dirt roads under the sun from the country house by the train station to the forest; the swimming pool was beside the trees and, at the end, you would pass slowly from the shadows to the light, the summer on the water.

In the bar on Olavarría and Almirante Brown. A long conversation with Inés about ending things. Everything breaks down, sooner or later. Ever since I stopped living in La Plata as a student and came here to conquer the city, I have felt slightly restless and static. It seems like everything I do is for the last time.

July 17 (1:15)

"A great means of consolation: make the heartbroken man analyze his pain; it will diminish at once; pride always triumphs, wherever it intervenes," Stendhal.

Now, after that almost unreal afternoon with Inés in a club confirming the disaster, I understand that these notebooks (their deformations, their silences) are justified by Stendhal's sentence.

Recently, listening to the Beatles, an aggressive style, lyrical, asexual, full of rhythm. Neurotic. I don't know why, but I was reminded of Céline's prose.

"Betrayal is something akin to opening the window of a prison cell: everyone wants to do it, but it's the rare person who actually succeeds," Louis Céline.

There is a single thing that I do not want to understand: in order to do what you want to do, you have to be capable of rejecting and losing other things. To be alone in the moment of writing, to not rely on anyone. That can serve as an example for me today; I worked while I was alone. Later, now, I turned circles around myself and around Inés and entered the room, closed off from stupid states of mind. I did nothing that served any purpose. Except for taking an Equanil.

It is obvious that this restlessness immobilizes me, impedes me even from reading. I turn over the same thing, become distracted, look through books, articles, kill time before sinking down and sleeping.

Saturday 17

You leave those brilliant times when everything seems to belong to you, where nothing is beyond us or alien to us. But, slowly, you learn of others' gravity, learn of the foolish resistance of things; becoming aware can take all of a lifetime, and you can never know how much there is to learn. The presence of others is a limitation that you must understand as well. Now, here in this house on Calle Olavarría, Alberto Cedrón and Raúl Escari persist in their way of being; they read, silent, and yet I feel myself being observed, as though everything I did had something to do with them.

Chaos is maintained. I took an amphetamine but cannot drive myself to work and waver between the article for the magazine and the *nouvelle*. I go from one side to the other, doing nothing.

What matters? Everything has the same end. Exerting yourself to prove to yourself and others that you have talent. Why? What is it for?

I am more intrigued than "arrested." I search for an escape like someone on a sinking ship who imagines an exit. I try to understand what is happening to me. In this way, I turn, submerged, looking for the window that will take me to the open air.

What to do? What single, definitive act can cut this circuit? There is nothing—that is, no one ever knows what is really happening. We can only invent reasons and motives for ourselves. Now, Inés is here and she bothers me too.

Sunday, July 18
It is four in the morning. I spent the night *thinking*. Everything I think is useless. I go around in circles in the void. How to leave here? Where to begin?

You have to begin from below, not with humility, but with pride.

Tuesday
"It was academic at first. I wrote of silences, nights, I expressed the inexpressible. I defined vertigos," Rimbaud.

Inés that night on the sofa. Then we went out to walk and drink beer in the open air.

Thursday

Getting up at noon, going out to the street and seeing the other people like sleepwalkers. The things that must be done (pay the phone bill, shave, write letters) are a superficial organization of personal experience. Today, I want to finish the article for the magazine. Then I have to think about the publishing house. Writing the notes to intersperse between the short stories and articles. I make a note of this here to indicate the constancy of my dedication to wasting time.

Friday

The police took Cacho. They were playing dice in Acapulco, in Maipú and Lavalle—Horacio, Adolfo, Costa, and him. A robbery-and-theft commission came; it only took them away. Someone betrayed them. I spent the day with Bimba looking for an attorney to bring a habeas corpus appeal. We don't know the police precinct where he is detained and expect the worst.

Saturday

The truth of a story depends on the circumstantial details that seem to serve no purpose. The dull sound of a falling body. Then the blurry image of a pile of rags moving in the darkness.

Sunday, August 1

I write the whole night through. I complete *"El calabozo"* and then, for the excitement and drive of my own writing, I write another short story, *"Vértigo."* It is nine thirty in the morning and I was able to write two stories in a night.

Monday

If I analyze the night between Saturday and Sunday, referring to the two stories written almost at the same time, I am able to discover the means by which they were made. On the one hand, the natural facility for breaking narrative time and avoiding dead points and situations that have no meaning; on the other hand, narrating what is taking place, allowing the prose to be defined as the plot.

Saturday, August 7
Cacho got out of jail today. We waited for him at the door of the police station here in La Plata. He appeared at the end of the hallway, in a suit and tie, made a couple of imperceptible gestures of mutual understanding. I saw him signing the release papers, then, suddenly, an arrest warrant came through from Córdoba. They took him in again, he turned around, and once more spent the night alone in a cell. Meanwhile, I ate with Bimba in a restaurant on Calle 7. She told me her life story, always changing some of the details. How they had met, where she was when she saw him for the same time, etc, etc.

Sunday 8
In La Paz, Inés not understanding the three days I spent in La Plata handling Cacho's release, jealous of Bimba.

Monday
Two thirty in the morning. I've just started working. Earlier I went down Corrientes with Inés, stopping at all of the bars, and we finally sat to eat in Bajo. Now I have to prepare a class on Spengler for the next topic, historical problems of methodology (progress, morphology, causality, etc.).

Tuesday 10
At Fausto, I ran into Constantini, who was secretly buying Mario Benedetti's book *Gracias por el fuego* [*Thank You for the Fire*]. Distrustful, he apologized, as though it were a crime to read contemporary writers.

I got up at three in the afternoon, walked along the edge of the river to the bridge; from here the city always seems to be the same.

Wednesday 11

Last night Cacho finally out once again. Nervous, aggressive. He, a man walking down Lavalle after having been tortured, tells me about "marking people" with a policeman who guards him. In the jail, a prisoner with no reputation who puffs himself up until the guard decides to shut him down with a beating. The letter that Cacho writes for one man's woman, which all of the others copy. Speaking about women under a blanket of remembrances in the nighttime.

Sunday

"There are strange friendships. The two friends are always ready to fly at one another, and go on like that all their lives, and yet they cannot separate. Parting, in fact, is utterly impossible," Dostoevsky.

Wednesday

I gave my first class of the year in front of more than eighty students at the College. I spoke for forty-five minutes about Spengler, said certain unexpected things, and left quickly at the end, not wanting to hear any comments while the students were leaving through the hallways at the same time. I came to Modelo to have a beer and write these notes.

Wednesday, September 1

Yesterday the magazine finally went to the printer. In the afternoon, I gave a good class about Toynbee.

At the end of the afternoon with Antonio Mónaco. We continued with the idea of the apartment. Everything happens during the party, not taking the actors out of there.

Friday

I am working on an article about Alejo Carpentier.

235

"We do not go to a country funeral to take picturesque notes of everyday life; what leads us to such a place is the desire to know what concept of death is held there," Alejo Carpentier.

Sunday
All night on Friday, imprisoned in the police station on Calle Maipú. A cell much like a freezing-cold bathroom. With Tata, Jorge, Osvaldo, and old Cedrón. Really, everything is too absurd. We were at El Hormiguero, went to listen to Mercedes Sosa, a folk singer who has recently started and has a voice with a tone like Joan Baez. Tata sang some tangos, we were a bit drunk, and suddenly, while leaving, we started to fight with a group of guys from the country, for some reason that we've all forgotten. Suddenly the police arrived and we were arrested. Very unfair because they stayed free. We spent the night talking, and in the morning, Albert Szpunberg, who didn't really understand what had happened either, also turned up arrested. In the end Bimba, Cacho's woman, who has a lot of experience springing people from jail, got us out.

Delighted with the albums that Cacho gave me. He found them, as usual, on one of his adventures and made off with them and brought them for me. Also, Cacho telling me about his passion for going to the airport at sunrise to watch the planes taking off.

I have a feeling like being trapped amid objects that shoot past me and must be stopped.

Sunday 11
Unbelievably, I was working on Hegel so I could give a couple of classes at the College on his philosophy of history. The professor learns what he has to teach two days before the students find it out.

"Understanding the real, making it plainly intelligible, is the ultimate objective of philosophy; everything must be recognized to be rational, that is, sufficiently knowable through reason," Hegel.

"To him who looks upon the world rationally, the world in its turn presents a rational aspect," Hegel. For Hegel, the categories of thought are, at the same time, the categories of being.

Sunday
Nights like this now seem like the nights of another age. I go out to walk down Vuelta de Rocha as I used to do in the area around the train station in La Plata. I try to calm my "abstract rages," and walking becomes a form of thinking.

Monday
The imaginary. The dream disperses, the fantasy acts like a star—directed at a center, from which it launches new rays. Fantasy is always centered around an object. Remembering the fixed idea.

What can I do to improve this diary? Maybe the time has come to type out a copy of these ten years and find its repeating motifs and tones.

If I think about what I have done over the years besides feeling the euphoria of writing freely and finding a tone, I see few variations. The best is "Las actas del juicio," an archaic orality, nothing realist, based on rhythm and a collection of little scenes strung together by a narrator who tells them as though he does not understand them. The same technique in "Tierna es la noche," in which I also recount many situations, in a more personal tone, a written confession that comes from Kerouac's *The Subterraneans.* The same happens in "Una luz que se iba" and "La pared": several plots within a single story told in the first person. The key lies in finding that personal tone but in the third person. The rest of the stories in the book have the same structure, telling one event as it is taking place but secretly telling another. (Best is "En el calabozo.")

Formally and in its style, *La invasión* has nothing to do with Borges—or it is a rejection of his way of understanding literature. In that, I differ from all of the other writers, who generally copy him down to the way he spits. Nothing to do with Cortázar either, the other plague. Thematically, the influence is Arlt—too many betrayals.

Analyzing the novels written in the same period: Nabokov's *Sebastian Knight*, Gombrowicz's *Trans-Atlantyk*, and Beckett's *Malone Dies*. In all three there is double narration, a low, degraded first person, and a prose born out of people forgetting their mother tongues, no longer exercised (exile and language). They are the highest level of writing without homeland, without novel. The first value of the narration is the comical—for example, Nabokov's sentence that "the heroes of the book are what can be loosely called 'methods of composition.'" I read *Trans-Atlantyk* in Italian a couple years ago; Dipi lent it to me in La Plata.

Meeting with Borges. The feeling of standing in front of literature, or rather, seeing the workings of a marvelous literature-making machine. He speaks slowly, with strange cutoffs in the middle of sentences. Absurdly, I felt tempted to give him the words, as though he paused because he couldn't come up with them. In the end, he always brought out a different word from the one I had imagined, more beautiful and more precise than mine. He touched his head to indicate the scar from the accident that gave rise to "The South." It was impossible to perceive any mark, but I felt that the act was, in some sense, a ritual for him. The same thing when I left: he held my hand for a while and I feared that I was the one holding him prisoner, but finally he gave it a soft squeeze and smiled again. He is not as tall as I remembered and more handsome: gray eyes, smooth smile. Impossible to make him say anything different from what he always says, which doesn't change the magic he creates by speaking, saying the same thing you have read. I was moved every time I heard him use a sententious and intense tone to recite his and other's texts. (Small and ugly hands, absurdly old shoes, and an unforgettable tone of voice.)

October

I pick up *Eloy* by Carlos Droguett from Temple bookshop. A while ago on Radio Municial with Rubi Montserrat, reading some passages from Borges's *Personal Anthology*. Tata Cedrón was also on the program.

Bimba talks about Cacho the way someone remembers a dead man. She is amazed at his perfect and delirious logic, which leaves her confused, but she is also able to describe how she caught him masturbating in the bed, right next to her.

I am in Boca, bothered by Alberto Cedrón's *affaire*; according to him, I owe him fifteen thousand pesos. He has the ability to always seem to be the victim of circumstances or of the world itself, and so can make demands and berate others for not helping him.

Saturday, October 2

A beautiful line from Marx: "Death, that revenge of the species over the individual."

Sunday 3

The difficult part of living in a house with others lies in the different concept of order that each person holds. The result is the fluctuation between the happiness of social life and the desire to be alone and isolated, here in this house where there are always people.

Interesting, Ismael Viñas's idea that, under Peronism, the army fulfills the role of the hierarchical intellectual.

I am reading *Where the Air Is Clear* by Carlos Fuentes. He works with a structure similar to that of John Dos Passos, where individual lives and social histories are mixed. He has trouble escaping from a certain superficial schematism. The characters are explained and not narrated. On the other hand, he only describes, or rather, tends to describe exclusively the extraordinary (wars, revolutions, catastrophes). He has trouble finding the short, brief dimension, the meaningful moment, the detail that lends reality. The most attractive thing is the breadth of possibility in Fuentes's prose, which ranges from the essay ("For the first time in Mexican history a stable middle class exists, the surest protection against tyranny and unrest . . . ") to poetic, almost surrealistic illustration ("City of motionless pain . . . city of the violated outrage . . . ").

Monday

Yesterday I went out with Inés to walk around in the area, calm, unhurried. We sat down to have beer at a bar, watching the people passing as though they were outlandish beings.

Now I have the day in front of me and am ready to write a short story, for which I already have the entire plot. A man has been—or believes he has been—abandoned by a woman; he travels to some city in order to forget her. Calls her on the phone. Settles into a hotel. At a certain point, he sees her at the station in town. He believes she has come looking for him, but when he moves closer he realizes that it is a stranger who doesn't even look like the women he loves. After that he keeps seeing her—in a bar, in the plaza, in the hall of the hotel. The loss of love has driven him insane, well, not quite insane, it has only changed his way of seeing. Worried about himself, he returns to his hotel room and tries to devise a theory about this resemblance and the "as if." The story ends at sunrise, when, as he is leaving, he actually does find his wife, who has come to the town looking for him.

Tuesday 12

We woke up with Cacho in Olivos, in front of the river. The country houses on the ravine. We saw a man stealing some railroad ties on the bank, close to the tracks. Bimba left. To walk around.

These days I am working until seven in the morning every night on a story called "Bajo la luz," which I haven't been able to resolve.

Thursday
The magazine is assembled, almost ready. Accepting the risk that it will be published in November, on the brink of summer, does not concern me, leaves me indifferent.

Tuesday 19
In Florida bar at noon. For the first time, the book has a harmonic form and a certain structure. In *Fichas*, a notice appeared announcing the magazine.

I shouldn't have to think like this, but my friendship with Cacho also has the quality of a novel I would like to write. He knows it and jokes with me about the matter. Those of us close to him (Bimba, Costa, Horacio) are never sure how he can endure that feeling of constant risk. But I am not surprised when he makes unexpected decisions and suggests unbelievable trips or impossible expeditions. A while ago, returning from Olivos, we almost killed ourselves because he started accelerating and we entered the woods of Palermo at great speed, far above the speed allowed on such a winding road. Of course, I never told him to slow down, because I felt that he wanted to test me, or at least show me that his relationship with danger and death was very different from mine. The truth is that I barely remember how things went after we passed the tanks of the sanitation works, except that the car spun out on a curve in the middle of the woods and almost went up on two wheels, and for a stretch we could have rolled over, but mysteriously it landed upright and Cacho, without slowing down, looked at me in the rearview mirror and winked.

Wednesday 20
I am in París, in La Plata. I only earned twelve thousand pesos and not the twenty thousand that I expected. I have to give a class in a while, and

my attention is always drawn to the fact that the students are my age. I enter the packed Great Hall, get up onto the platform and say to them, "So, in 'Introduction to History' we are looking at Hegel's hypotheses," and from there I go onward as though walking along the edge of a precipice.

Friday 22
Today there is a general strike decreed by the CGT. I am in Florida bar and wonder, once again, why I feel this need to record what happens. I stopped at the publishing house and Álvarez confirmed that my story about Urquiza is going to be published in the Features series. For the first time, then, my literature is moving outside the familiar spheres. I remember the early days, now some years ago, when I hoped that the whole city would be talking about me so that my name would ring out everywhere, spoken by a vast ensemble of strangers. I spent the night with Horacio, with Cacho and Júnior, each of us with his own fantasy and his own realizations as it begins to take shape. It's impossible to live without hopes, but you have to know that the hopes are just stories you tell yourself.

It is necessary to isolate the two essential characteristics of Hegel's conception of history: on one side, the unbroken continuum of time and, on another side, the gravitational pull toward "now" in the historical present. "Custom is activity without opposition, for which there remains only a formal duration; in which the fullness and zest that originally characterized the aim of life are out of the question," Hegel.

Sunday 24
With Julia Constella tonight, a roundtable about violence. About a woman who was thrown from the fifth floor by her husband (or was it her father?). Maybe my better side appears on days like today, when I walk alone though the city, then have lunch in a restaurant with tables outside along Cerrito. The strange feeling of being a passing traveler or tourist in an unknown city.

A good method for reflection in a narrative is the procedure of the police novel, which consists of the detective's meditation on events that have already been told; the key, in that situation, is that the character announces what he thinks will happen. In summary, the ideas in a story always have to be directed at what lies ahead, and not at explaining what has already been told.

Thursday, November 4
I am on the train to La Plata. Last night the final corrections for the magazine. The cost rose from 110,000 to 190,000 pesos. We'll see how we make up the debt.

Tuesday
Topics for the "Introduction to History" midterm:

1. Relationships between the progression of the absolute spirit and the concept of progress in history according to Hegel.
2. Relationships between Hegel's system of history and the political history of the period in which he taught his classes.

Subject. Maybe the ending of my novel about Cacho will be in the apartment in Montevideo with those three gangsters trapped there, lasting sixteen hours and resisting four hundred policemen and enduring gas, fire, bullets, water, bombs until in the end they burn the money and yell, "Come get us, *guanacos.*"

In García Márquez (*Leaf Storm*), as in Rulfo before him, I discover the technical possibilities of naïve vision. The narrator is outside of the literate culture and watches the world with amazement. It allows the discovery of almost absurd and fantastical levels within reality. Facts are given without synthesis, events connected by the partial (and magical) understanding of things that naïvety seems to impart. In the novel about Cacho, Bimba must be at that level.

243

Wednesday 10

At the College, taking the midterm exam for "Introduction to History." Twenty students are writing because I dictated a subject, because I taught some subjects. And they have studied and they have worried, etc. There is no need to state the strange quality that this situation holds for me.

Saturday 13

I run into Dipi Di Paola, neurotically sick, always concentrated on the invisible symptoms of an illness that is never manifested. Sympathetic, seductive, he read me a beautiful story, but he speaks about himself and about his writing with an insistence that is excessive, even for him.

Monday

After three hours, I went back to writing "La Pared," a clean, loose story with a smooth Beckettian quality, invisible to anyone: the old man in a hospice laments that they have built a wall and he can no longer see the street.

Saturday 20

Cacho just called on the phone, informing me that he is coming to see me and get dinner in Costanera.

Sunday 21

In Ramos bar over Corrientes. I see Miguel, who is still mulling over his half-finished book of stories. Very good, from what I understand.

November 25

They cut off the lights, the gas, and the phone for lack of payment.

November 26

The magazine is ready, wrapped up at the press. I spoke with Sergio; he will go pick it up this Monday.

December
Wednesday, 6 p.m. A strange time, very productive (four stories, the magazine), very conflicted (the house, money, misfortune). It will be hard for me to forget it.

Friday
Sometimes I can't forget the image, that image. Yet I still look for it myself, invent it. I need it. It attracts me, in some way, like the low railings that enclose a terrace. How else can I understand this chronic temptation; I am searching for something, and so many different associations summon it, that familiar quality.

Saturday 4
Sometimes, after the denouement (with García, Tata, etc.), when things start to happen, there is no time or place to write. That rift has marked my life. Definitions, decisions, should matter but must be reconfigured, historicized, told as though they had happened to others. The delusion of living in the third person.

Monday 6
In Florida bar. It's raining in the city; the sun filters between the clouds, lights up the street, the pavement acquires a yellow color, very pale.

I try to keep the competition at the College at a distance in order to renew my assistantships in two courses. For now, my economy depends on those appointments. I have had two positions since 1963 and live on that (and on the work in Nono's archive). I earn my living as a historian but live like a potential writer; in recent months, I have tried to unite the two trajectories, writing stories that have the form of an investigation and working in the archives of Buenos Aires province. The point is not to thematize the things that take place in the bowels of the post office in Galería Rocha, but to bring modes of being into the narrative that draw from other places (alien to the literary tradition).

Finally, issue I of *Literatura y Sociedad* is coming out. The editorial that I wrote is an attempt to critique the left's stereotypes. The inadequacy of these stereotypes represents a particular world view. Peronism seems to be the blind spot of the historic gaze. The second point consists of opposing the notion of "committed literature" because it has an individualist posture; instead, my idea is to think about literature as a social practice and see what function it has in society. For example, what is the purpose of fiction, etc. The Sartrean idea that each individual work must be answerable to the responsibility of art is ridiculous and paralyzes any action. Sartre's question of what Nausea could do for a child dying of hunger is moralistic and a sophism. Nothing that an isolated individual does for himself, in solitude, can do anything for a child dying of hunger. It is the same logic that the right uses when it mandates more repression and justifies it with the question "What would you do to a delinquent who wants to kill your child?" If the answer were individual, there would be nothing more than surprise and "personal" attitudes (which do nothing but change the subject). What can a man do in the face of the world's injustice? Unite with others seeking nonindividual means of action. Leaving behind the I and the subjective consciousness, that is the path of Marx and Wittgenstein. In one case, it is about class, and in another, it is about the linguistic games that condition political action. The impact—the answer—cannot be individual.

The happiness of events: it means both the irony contained in events and the happiness that survives in the face of what has been done.

If, as Cassirer says, reality can only be experienced by means of symbolic forms, which are always variable, and by means of the innumerable linguistic plays within which we act, culture is the sum of the learned and integrated norms of conduct (like a second nature), which are fundamentally inherited: these norms are transmitted by means of language (law, contracts, and pacts) and learning ("domestication," as Sartre calls the education that children suffer), on the margins of instinct.

Wednesday 8

Always the feeling of neglect and the "toughness" of the reality ahead. Writing now, alone, in this empty house, with the microscopic series of small decisions that are constantly made in order to survive. One word after another, a word and then another and another, phrasing: that is everything (a music).

At the same time, culture—civilization—depends "simply" on the unusual breadth and size of the brain. It simply depends on the bone structure that has given rise to the "encephalic mass," or rather the enlargement of the cranial cavity that developed millions of years ago when prehumans started walking upright in the savannah (the jungles where they had lived had been wiped out by various natural calamities). They learned how to walk and defend themselves with the high gaze of the predators. That posture caused the jaw to have the necessary weight to open and give rise to a new use of the tongue, which allowed the articulation of language. I have, I fear, become a kind of Darwinian positivist in reaction to my abstract idealist tendency. I pass from materialism to material as such, and lose myself there.

And so, one of two: either everything depends on the formation of the brain (absolute contingency), or everything depends on the spiritual or immaterial reality of learned norms of conduct and codes of comportment (law, prohibition, what cannot be done).

Thursday 9

A certain inexplicable happiness, absurdly. It must be left hanging. What can fail is the ending, with the joke of death. It must be left unsolved. Searching for a story of old age (or of a particular old man, for example, old Socrates or old Borges). And nothing more.

In December

Writing "El hermano de Luisa." Who is he? etc. Correcting the whole book. With Haroldo Conti, a conversation about the book's title. *La invasión.* Drier, less "stated" (the invasion is one thing and the wars are another).

December 10

In Florida bar. I have a headache, it is hot. Today in La Plata, did I make twenty-seven thousand pesos? Incredible. Always the same unreality in relation to material life. In any case, things are a rush between December 21 and 31. The competitions of the College (end on the 24th). A trip to Uruguay? And the magazine? What's more, my family's phantom presence continues. Hamlet's father and Lady Macbeth ("*Al lecho,* to bed, to bed," says Lady Macbeth).

Saturday 11

In Florida bar. 6:30. I don't need to look or hope for anything beyond work. A unique moment of fullness; reality is suspended. There are no other "satisfactions." It is absurd to invent them or ask for them. If I don't learn this, I will never be able to avoid distraction and insanity. I am seeking equilibrium; without it, I cannot live (suicide). Everything else (except for love) is illusory. But love would be illusory without the bodies we love.

Considering the concept (very much in use lately) of a "new generation" as information to analyze. What new quality can each generation have if they all have the same desire to erase the others? And yet, there is a visible aspiration to fit in with the direction of the dominant culture. Meanwhile, the motto has to be "Stay on the margin." But what is the margin? What characterizes us is a greater education outside of literature; we seek to innovate by means of techniques that come from elsewhere; for example, in my case, the unexpected use of material made available through research. The story is constructed based on a nonliterary experience. The artist's movement toward "intellectual" artifice, talking about what he does (and not about what he is). The role of the magazine in this process.

To speak about a generation is to make a cultural judgment, Gamsci said; discovering your age is a way to determine what you must have read and learned in your youth. The concept of generations ceases to have a purpose: the artist is no longer analyzed in terms of the cultural horizon of his age (that is, of his epoch). More than his opinions or declarations, a writer's age is a fact of the epoch to which he belongs. Age, in terms of literature, is a symptom. Each generation reads its own pared-down series of books, and that is what identifies it and becomes visible in its writing.

Sunday 12

5:30 in El Castelar. Tense, waiting for Sergio Camarda. Ready to redesign the magazine. I need to control myself and dominate the situation. It is essential that I let him talk and let him start with his critiques and then refute him, calmly, because this is not the time to break things up. A valuable meeting last night, especially due to the presence—and ideas—of José Sazbón.

Anxious tension (the future invading the present) is one of the few emotions that I can recall over the course of my life. It appears suddenly, without exterior changes, in different situations: loneliness, strong emotion, nostalgia, hopefulness (like now).

Copying and recopying the book of short stories on my keyboard seems, at this stage, to be my delirious and routine occupation. Not writing it, or correcting it, or critiquing it, but only copying each one of its pages over and over again, making mistakes (like I just did), and leaving it half-done. The man who copies himself. Nothing changes or improves; only the same repeats. Searching for what?

Monday

Every so often, a sudden confidence in the book—for example, just now, walking in the rain, after drinking a glass of milk and speaking with Briante. We go around in circles and circles about the state of literature.

He and I are free from the Cortázar fever that has invaded the majority of current writing. Of course, Miguel is contaminated by Borges (by some idea of "European" style) and by a certain affected use of adjectives that prevents him from finding his own voice. For my part, I advance blindly, through the bushes, without a guide. On the other hand, the work that lies ahead (the magazine, the book, certain ideas or conceits I would like to write about someday) does not give me any time for introspection. On the other hand, the carrying out an action, a series of actions, takes me outside of myself ("gets me out of my head," an enigmatic expression). Publishing the magazine, for example, demands that I pay attention to external appearances. I have to check my defenses along the ramparts. I can't accept any weakness; I have my back covered (I am edging along the wall), but I see the traitors in my own troop (Osvaldo denounced me to the Italian), the defectors (Camarda "splitting off," blaming me for the "flaws" of the magazine, which he "accepts"). My determination must not waver; I have to regain my fortitude, never allow myself to be trapped by despair. No one understands the criterion underlying the first issue: an aggressive conceptual intervention, shaking off the lethargy of culture on the left, which reconciles with the "progressive" prejudices we have broken away from (that is, the culture of the CP). I am referring to the cultural effects of Peronism and its sympathetic myths, but it is clear that I am not a Peronist and will not allow myself to be blinded by pragmatism.

We have to change the state of things, which seem very chaotic these days. What are the problems? *The house*, I have to get away from here. Complications with the furniture and books. A possibility of staying in Cacho's apartment in Ugarteche. But Cacho fled to Mar del Plata and I can't see him to confirm. I can straighten it out with him at Christmas. I will need to make sure in January; there is also the house in Boca. I have the summer to sort out the move.

Suddenly, I found the room on Calle Medrano, in the boardinghouse, and saw the image of that barbecue with Haroldo Conti, behind Retiro, crossing the tracks and the avenue that separates the port from the city. I accepted the invitation because I had no money for lunch.

Tuesday 14
I sleep too much, as though in these times of conflict I could only aspire to silence and darkness. Sleep is a refuge for the prisoner, Cacho told me one day.

It is striking to experience the clash between my awareness of myself and the way others see me (Sergio, Alberto Cedrón). The adversarial gaze is only between friends. Striking, this relativism. Because there is a sideways, uncertain, third awareness (the third eye, as they joke), in which I see myself as though I were another (as though I were the other). Furthermore, almost always with amazement, I gain everything that I want for myself, deep down. The certainty I have about my "virtues" and of the existence of "occult forces" that oppose their development. Because I place too much value on these "forces" (or because I disguise my fragility with them), I actually practice misfortune, as though convinced of failure. You have to establish an ethics and a poetics of the No, of the impossibilities that make life possible.

The tightrope walker. "It is essential to invent an order. To believe in it, in its value, in its meaning, in its utility. Then, in a leap, to enter it." Then he (the tightrope walker, on the wire, at the height of the circus tent) said: "I must undergo the change that always occurs in the face of this event. First, an attraction that forces me to lean forward and listen. Then the certainty that as I watch what is happening down there—which is happening to someone else in a different place—I am looking down upon the person I was in another time."

Writing for enemies, not for social reasons, searching for concealment. Ensuring the survival of the Argentine writer. The pageantry of this class (and not of this generation). Graduating class: advancing, groups that appear on the same date.

Thursday

In Florida, 6:30.

I am waiting for Szpunberg, about an open letter in support of the guerrillas of the EGP, who are on a hunger and prisoners strike. Are they or are they not political prisoners? They cannot be treated as common delinquents. An afternoon with several meetings. Néstor García Canclini is going to Paris to study with Ricœur. A possible interview with the philosopher about the act of storytelling. Then, Héctor Alterio will possibly record his performance of my story ("Mi amigo"), and I add to it "La pared" (the monologue of the Beckettian old man). Afterward, I meet with David Viñas about a possible collaboration in the magazine.

Friday

We are interested in American literature because it allows us to see how great artists (Salinger, F. O'Connor, Truman Capote, Carson McCullers) are also popular. A unique case in contemporary literature. There are three reasons, I think. The breadth of the educational system, which places works on the obligatory reading list, and a very developed literary industry. The third reason is the great narrative tradition, which incorporates formal experimentation into the novelistic tradition.

The impossibility of accepting convention, the sharp feeling of embarrassment that forces me to listen to myself when I speak "intentionally," throwing my possibility of adopting stylistic nuance into disarray. Calling a woman on the phone represents an action founded on certain standards that cannot be named and are implicitly understood. Recently, H. said, "Sleep well," and I waited for her laughter, but she was serious . . . As at the same time, I said to Elena, "The princess is sad," in my best ironic and antiromantic style, and she took it seriously and asked, "How did you know?"

Note. A language is an arbitrary system through which members of a community interact with each other and thereby learn a particular way of living. Reality as we know it is conditioned by the grammar and syntax we use (they decide the order, the continuity, the verbal tenses—that is, our awareness of the distinction between present, past, and future). Grammar organizes the organization of the world and proposes a morphology (which is responsible for the structure of the words) and a syntax (which responsible for the ways in which the words are combined into clauses and sentences).

Friday
Last night I got drunk, without realizing it. I found out this morning when I woke up with an unknown woman in my bed. *"Hola, precioso,"* she said, and I looked at her (she was blonde, with pale eyes and large breasts) and asked her, "Where did you come from?" She was offended and left, so I never figured out what her name was. I have fleeting memories, the taxi or the elevator, the pillow. The rest is silence. The memories were erased as though they had been written in tears.

A while ago, walking down the arcade in Bajo from Plaza de Mayo to Viamonte, talking by myself, I became sure of everything again, convinced about my future once again and the star watching over me, and I was happy and blind.

There is no narrative method that is not artificial—that is, that is not imposed onto everyday language as an unusual usage. Because of this, I was surprised by Germán Rozenmacher's statement that narrating in the present tense was artificial, by which he meant affected, and yet the people you hear on the street use the present as the basis for conversation. "So he tells me . . . and I say to him . . . and he says"; a fairly "natural" way of recounting one's own life.

(On the same subject.) A man who, in order to overcome his wife's past, leaves her and thus becomes the past for her. A past more novel or more valuable than her previous one (which had made him jealous). In love

253

only the present, the time of pure passion, is truly important. In certain cases, however, the ardor of the imagined past can be as interesting as the present (as in *Othello*, for example). We must occasionally make the leap, leave the present behind, and reenter the past in order to exist on equal footing with our lover upon our return to the present. This regression is akin to finally seeing the faces of unseen enemies that have been hurling insults at us from afar. That is the point at which Othello smothers Desdemona with a white pillow, so that he does not have to hear the cries coming in from the room next door (all in his head).

We must insist: escapism (in escapist literature, for example) is neither a defect nor a virtue in itself. Everything depends on how we return from the escape: whether our attitude facing the world is strengthened or we deteriorate and our life is diminished.

Now, with the book almost ready, I see the approach of my real encounter with literature, almost ten years after having made the all-or-nothing bet. Will I be able to overcome a failure?

The competitions at the College are also telling, and they define the real possibility of a concrete job.

The chances for the magazine. Is there a team? How long can I deal with the matter and how long will it interest me?

The negation of the real as a way of life . . .

"I don't read the reactionaries, to avoid becoming embittered," said Perón.

Wednesday 29
I have an incredible amount of papers on the table, which constitute the book; I am trying, as they say, to make a clean copy. Last night Inés left to visit, according to what she said, her mother. I am at home alone,

with two clean and empty days ahead of me. It feels like being in this city again, but in 1958 and 1959. I see the same panorama from this window.

The difference now is that I have finally written a book. Perhaps more defined and more personal than any of the best books of stories that have come out in recent years (*Las otras puertas, Las hamacas voladoras, Cabecita negra*), which are close to other books also unitary in their poetics and their narrative world (*Los oficios terrestres, Palo y hueso*), but I do not compare myself to anyone: I compare the written book to the book that I imagined I was writing or meant to write.

Friday, December 31
Rereading my "notebooks" is a novel experience; perhaps a story can be extracted from that reading. It astonishes me, all of the time, as though I were someone else (and that is what I am).

It is incredible to realize that I blindly decided my destiny in those two years (1958–1959), here in this room, with a window opening onto the branches of the jacaranda tree, planted on the path, before I was born. Incredible to remember—speaking of destiny—the importance of chance.

15

Hotel Almagro

When I came to live in Buenos Aires, I rented a place at the Hotel Almagro on Rivadavia and Castro Barros. I was finishing writing the stories for my first book, and Jorge Álvarez offered me a contract to publish it and gave me some work at the publishing house. I prepared an anthology of American prose for him, which went from Poe to Purdy, and with what he paid me and with what had I earned at the University, I made enough to settle down and live in Buenos Aires. During that time, I was working on the "Introduction to History" lectures at the College of Humanities and traveled to La Plata every week. I had rented a place in a boardinghouse near the bus terminal and spent three days a week in La Plata dictating classes. My life was divided: I lived two lives in two cities as though I were two different men, with different friends and different routines in each place. What was the same, however, was life in a hotel. The empty corridors, the transitory rooms, the anonymous atmospheres of those places where one is always in passing. Living in a hotel is the best way not to develop the delusion of a "personal life"; I mean, not to have anything personal to tell of but the traces left by others. The boardinghouse in La Plata was an endless mansion, converted into a kind of cheap hotel, managed by a perpetual student who made his living by subletting the rooms. The owner of the house was hospitalized, and every month this guy would wire a little money for her to a mailbox at Las Mercedes hospice. The place I was renting was comfortable, with a balcony that opened over the street and a very high ceiling. The place in the Hotel Almagro also had a very high ceiling and a picture window that overlooked the back of the Argentina Boxing Federation. The two places had very similar wardrobes, with two doors and shelves lined with newspaper. One afternoon, in La Plata, I found a woman's letters in a corner of the wardrobe. When you live in a hotel, you can always find traces of those who have been there before. The letters were concealed in a gap, hidden like a bag of drugs. They were written in nervous handwriting, and barely anything could be understood; as always happens when you read a stranger's letter, the allusions and subtexts are such that the words may be deciphered but not the meaning or the emotion. The woman was named Angelita and was not ready to be taken off to live in Trenque Lauquen. She had escaped from the house and seemed desperate, and I got the sense she was saying goodbye. On the last page, in another hand, someone had written down a telephone number. When I called, security at the City Bell hospital answered. Of course, I forgot about the matter, but some time later, in Buenos Aires, stretched out in the bed in the hotel room, it occurred to me to get up and examine the wardrobe. Off to one side, in a gap, there were two letters: they were a man's responses to Angelita's letters. I have no rational explanation. The only explanation I can invent is that I have been drawn into a decoupled world, that two other people had also been drawn into a decoupled world and had, like me, left their own behind, so that, by those strange permutations produced by chance, the letters had coincided with me. It is not unusual to run into a stranger twice in two cities; it seems to me more unusual to find, in two different places, two letters from two connected people whom one does not know. The boardinghouse in La Plata is still there, and the perpetual student is still there, now an old man still subletting the rooms to students and business travelers passing through La Plata along the route from the south of Buenos Aires province. The Hotel Almagro also goes on in the same way, and when I walk through

Rivadavia toward the College of Philosophy and Letters on Calle Puán, I always pass through the door and remember that time. Las Violetas café is across the street. Of course, you need a calm and well-lit bar nearby if you live in a hotel room.

16

Diary 1966

Saturday, January 1
The first thought of the year was a memory of Inés's childhood, on the beach, playing with a dog that would run into the sea when she threw a ball for it to fetch. Maybe she turns to her past because I lack my own memory. In fact, I am fighting against a confusing series of alien memories. Instead, I have in the present what others have lived through.

You are only what you are, but how are you seen from the outside by others? There is a piece of evidence that counteracts solipsism: you perceive that you are not alone through the sensation of discomfort that others cause you.

You have to pay attention to the perceptions of the narrator who is personal but alien to the plot, who is dedicated only to telling a story, appearing in the third person but still only a shadow amid the intrigue. There is a difference between the voice that narrates in Dostoevsky ("But we will not give an account of his thoughts, and this is not the place to look into that soul—its turn will come.") and the voice that narrates—and writes—in Saul Bellow: "I don't know why I should write to you at all." There is greater freedom in Dostoevsky because he breaks the narrative convention of the narrator as invisible figure. D. quickly makes him appear as a witness to the events: we do not know who he is or what his name is, but he is there to show us the conventional quality of the story (someone narrating). In contrast, B. works with a more predictable method: the man writing the story speaks to the unknown reader as though writing a letter to a friend. B. uses the first person, while what is notable in D. is the use of a third-person narrator who quickly transforms into an individualized figure. Arlt uses the technique in *The Seven Madmen*, but he identifies that third-person narrator, made present in the action, with the name of Commentator (which mainly appears in the footnotes).

In my case, I work narratively in reverse: imagining, building theories for and versions of a microscopic incident. For example, I found a photo of one of Inés's childhood boyfriends, by chance, in one of her books. A young boy playing basketball at the Peñarol club. Immediately, I transformed the photo into an event in the present (it became present, the seven-year-old photo, because I found it yesterday). In this way, her past was between us, not far from here, since the photo was now a presence, a third person. That is the logic of delirium. Everything happens in the present, and some people kill to escape that absolute time and recover a normalized temporality; crime is a logical consequence of the nightmare of the present, of the weight of passion. That is the time of tragedy, not the time of narrative. What we want is for this trace of the past to fall back, for the photo to lose its absolute immediacy, for the creation of a story that has a tiny place within a vast succession of lived events. I already said that it is not the quantity (a detail is enough: a young boy on a basketball court), it is not the past, it is a single incident from yesterday preserved in the present as a photo, it is a single moment that persists and cannot be erased. And so—apart from crime—there are two paths: avoidance, removing the images, and losing my mind, or, on the other hand, delving into the figure, not leaving, persisting with the fixed idea. I try, as you can see, to convert my experience into a lesson of narrative ethics. Absorbed in the photo, the narrator constructs a circular story that does nothing more than revolve precisely around a fixed image (it is a photograph, not a film), terrible because it is fixed in place and cannot be narrated, that is, cannot be advanced toward another situation.

As Dostoevsky writes in *The Brothers Karamazov*, "I may add here, for myself personally, that I feel it almost repulsive to recall that event which caused such frivolous agitation and was such a stumbling-block to many, though in reality it was the most natural and trivial matter. I should, of course, have omitted all mention of it in my story, if it had not exerted a very strong influence on the heart and soul of the chief, though future, hero of my story."

I feel what I feel because a woman's past is unbearable to me at certain times. Or I feel that a tiny thing (a photo of a young idiot playing basketball) is unbearable because I am reading Dostoevsky and I observe everything I experience through the exaggerated and delirious lens of his novels . . .

A start to the year that I hope will not be repeated. Inventing the tragedies and misfortunes myself. Alone, in this empty house (the *family* house), with no one to visit. I go to the movie theater every day and read Dostoevsky at night, searching for the exit, the escape. Now, at three in the morning, tired, unable to go on reading, unable to sleep, lacking a focal point.

Tuesday, January 4
At the beach with Cacho. He tells me his plans, he came to the coast as sneak thieves do, following the people with money. I have some information about one of my father's patients, a rancher from the area; he has a stud farm and keeps too much money in the bottom of a tall green china vase, the dollars hidden there, he told my father about it one night over drinks and my father repeated it as a joke at home, talking on the phone with his sister Gina. And I heard it. Cacho made a mental note of the house, the layout of the rooms and the vase on the landing of the staircase. In return (but it was not in return, it was not an exchange), I arranged the possibility of staying in his apartment until April.

I am twenty-four years old, Raskolnikov's age.

"I will only tell you one thing: that I will describe everything about this character through his actions and rather than appealing with disquisitions, so that you wait for a personality to result from a piece," D. letter from October 9, 1870.

Monday 10
Facing the trees, above, sitting on the terrace of Cacho's apartment in Palermo where I may stay this year, in peace. After going in circles around the city, earning seventeen thousand pesos and spending two thousand on *Cantar de ciegos* by Carlos Fuentes and *Herzog* by Bellow. I walked through the city, practicing the tourist's gaze. I walked to Florida, then down Viamonte, entering the bookshops, the temples of used books on Avenida de Mayo.

Tuesday 11
A rare happiness, almost unknown, one afternoon in Mar del Plata. I was going down Calle España toward the sea. A window that opens onto two trees, in the terrible forty-story buildings, at the back. I was walking alone. I wanted to be lying down on the sofa reading Carlos Fuentes's stories, without thinking, clean, eating peaches, listening to the dull noise of an engine nearby.

The point is not to foment self-control, but to control chaos.

"All of those whom we have loved, hated, or known, or only glimpsed, speak through our voice," M. Merleau-Ponty.

I have to reread all of Merleau-Ponty this year. But there are too many things I would like to do this year.

"The purpose of the subject's years of study consists of him nodding his head and adapting his desires to existing relationships and the relationality of the same, so that he joins the world's interconnected chain in order to acquire an adequate point of view," Hegel.

This is an age of quotations.

We are on the left not because of generosity, not because of insidious piety, not because of the exercise of compassion, but because—as Engels says—"in any event, what is certain is that before taking sides in a cause we have to make it into our own cause, and in that sense, forgoing possible material expectations, we are communists."

Wednesday 26
I am reading Stendhal and Melville to discover what part of us was already present in the nineteenth century.

The solemnity in Sabato's prose leads it—without reprieve—again and again, to ridicule.

Thursday 27
I want to erase my tendency to hold others responsible for the weaknesses and shortcomings that I suffer. Since it pains me to recognize "my virtues," which I do not attribute to others, I will do the same with my avarice and my mean streak.

"Born to die, nothing can restore the immortality of youth; after the golden age has ended, only degradation remains," M. Merleau-Ponty (although the sentence could come from Pavese). Some people desperately yearn for childhood because—I now realize—they were, or felt themselves to be, immortal.

"Our past acts," he thought, "come to us from the end of years to come, unrecognizable, but our own." He had seen that sentence written in the air, in front of him, like a psychotic motto—or a quotation. He was hallucinating but could imagine only written sentences. He saw them in the air, in the hospital corridors or up in the trees, on the faces of his companions in captivity. Sentences and sentences and sentences, unforgettable. He asked the nurse for the favor or permission to replace his phantasma-gorical writings with murky or terrible images, but abstract, devoid of all language. He was confined in a detox clinic, only accompanied by his "assistant" or double; perhaps she was his daughter, unadopted, who stayed with him day and night and would say that she was Mexican.

Yesterday with Edwards, the professor of social history, and his lover (an attractive blonde) and the classmates from the course (only three of them), at Ricardito, listening to Piazzolla's quintet.

Rodolfo Kuhn and Germán Rozenmacher propose that I write the script for one of the *Historias de jóvenes* that they and other writers are making for television. Maybe I could write Lucía's story.

I was thinking about *Herzog*, the novel by Bellow, admirable for its abil-ity to capture a period of crisis, the crisis—personal, political, moral, philosophical, and intimate, but also current—of a liberal intellectual, a distinguished professor who has lost his hopes (and also his women), ambiguous, alone, hanging in the air. It is differentiated in this way from *Rabbit, Run* by J. Updike, which recounts the escape of a common man, an ex-basketball player famous at the college, a physical man in fact, an anti-intellectual, formed by popular culture, who is trapped in the middle of his flight, who is desperate because he has become a loser, living off his past—and mediocre—glory.

Memories shared with a woman loved populate sleepless nights (when it is always three in the morning in the dark night of the soul), for the survivor who finds in them only dry leaves, words, I mean dead leaves.

Despite everything, he said in the future, looking from there, this must be a happy time because the future is—potentially—in my hands. Economically, there is no unease (I have these three months of life until April guaranteed). For the moment, in spite of repeated dreams in which

I wander through "alien houses," I have Cacho's apartment ("since where the wild cat makes its den, a man can live as well"), because he will have enough money to buy another house after the summer. But if he can't, where will I go? But nothing depends on me, directly, and this waiting is my Beatrice (my muse). In any case, I must struggle against this "restless-ness," which does not let me live.

Perhaps, in the novel, I can base Cacho on my own adolescence, give him my life experience from those years, extract it from my diaries. I must also find an almost political anecdote (which everyone will already know so that it will not have to be explained, as is the case with events in Greek tragedy: everyone knew the myths and the plots around which the works were based). For example, the theft of the bank truck and the criminals' flight to Uruguay. In this way, using the pretext of nonfiction to escape from verisimilitude and costumbrism. To write, so to speak, an epic drama, or rather, a tragedy.

Saturday, January 29
The days pass by empty, as they do in allegories. Nothing I might have "created," and yet, nevertheless, are these useless days not the basis, the cement that makes other "moments" possible, fleeting and perfect?

Once again—once again, as happened that week in 1961—I find my body hostile: it is here, I am me (who?), but it is alien to me and has laws of its own, imposes itself, inexorably, and marks the passage of time in a way that I always saw in others (they grew older around me). Like that day in the Adrogué station with Elio Spinelli when, in a fight, I first discovered the fragility of my body, which did not measure up to my courage. These are surprising discoveries, short-lived, because later I disregard them, let them live their lives. But, in the end, the body (a skeleton, a shell, a frame, an empty skin, without a soul) is right, and I cannot ignore it.

Something of that happens here, in this house where order is alien to me, and my friends want to impose it upon me, want me to be "molded" (to enter the mold) and accept it. Of course, it is impossible to live without others, without the body. And solitude is false, an illusion, like magic, as it was for Plato and the Platonists, for the mystics who cast off and condemn the body, not as an austere sacrifice, but for the great pride of being able to surpass physical "limitations." Living life outside of the world, being hermit in the desert—these are sealed exits. What then? To understand that you are—if you can be—the shape of the face, the ineptitude, the restlessness.

You think, say, *Within thirty years . . . Such a phrase is the only possible awareness of temporality. Looking back from the future (as though that were possible) is one of the qualities of fiction, like parallel lives, pure bodies: one goes onward, toward what is to come, in order to endure the present. This reflection is way to destroy* the images we have of ourselves, to understand that hope is impossible, that no one has the inhuman resilience that would permit living in the pure present; destruction lurks in everything, and none of us have certain dominion over ourselves (none of us have our own dominions assured). Yet, in spite of everything, there are objects, entities that appear secure, to which we must subject our absolute spirit.

Cantar de ciegos by Carlos Fuentes, a brilliant book, ingenious, almost superficial but very intelligent, with an astute perception of the relationships between people. "A Pure Soul" is the best story.

The virtue of Sartre's autobiographical prose (*The Words, Nausea*, the portraits of Merleau-Ponty and Nizan) consists of his ability to transform reality into concepts, in the reverse of Borges, who turns concepts into realities.

Monday, January 31, 1966
The collapse begins. Cacho (and Bimba and Victor) in prison. I was the only one who understood the emptiness of his life. Robbing, being in

danger, being pursued, taking risks was his way of feeling alive. The rest of the time he was bored; he perceived the senselessness of life better than anyone. He went to the casino to regain something of that intense time of transgression and danger. He started to lose in a fiendish way; he bet against himself and always lost, only seeking to sustain the feeling. The other night he left the roulette table, crossed the street, and, in one of those buying-and-selling caves, there to prey on hardened players who sell their clothes to keep playing, he sold a stolen Rolex watch and wrote his real name in the check book, the address of the house and his mother's, and his identification number. The police followed him for three days and finally arrested him and all of his friends. While interrogating him, they told him that they had proven during their surveillance that Bimba was sleeping with Victor and that no one was loyal to him. They broke into his mother's house and took away all of the electronics he had stolen and even the money he had hidden in one of his shoes.

Meanwhile, Cacho was inside. Everything fell apart for him in a moment, as in a dream. The police came to the house at two in the morning. They took three revolvers, two suitcases of jewelry. He must have imagined that someone had betrayed him, but it was he who set the trap for himself.

I began this notebook with the crisis at the house in Boca and now continue with Cacho's arrest and the end of a golden age, a dangerous time for him although I have remained safe (since he, under torture, did not name me or implicate me in his doings, even though, according to Bimba, the police questioned him about me).

The first thing I thought was that I had lost my typewriter. I left it in Cacho's apartment in Buenos Aires, which the police have surely searched or will search.

Sometime I will leave a notebook only half-finished (as I am now doing with this one).

February

I am reading *I'm Not Stiller* by Max Frisch. I like the outrageous reasoning of the plot: one man who is taken to be another—or confused with him—writes the book as a defense and testimony of his true identity. "Today they brought me this notebook of empty pages. I'm supposed to write down my life story." Technique becomes the theme; the same happens with Beckett's *Malone Dies*, where he receives some pages of paper every night and writes the novel we are reading, there in his mother's room, in the bed, with a pencil. Nevertheless, there is an appreciable difference between those tricks and the way in which Pavese, for example, writes his diary. In his case, the artifice is reduced to a minimum—someone is writing out his life—and it is legitimized, implicitly, with the author's suicide.

We must avoid the canonization of literature made into an absolute (example, Sabato) and therefore meaningless triviality, or, inversely, doing the same as Henry Miller, who tells us that his novels are written based on life itself—and without form (another fraud). Sabato first creates his figure of the tormented writer, and Miller has first read Thomas Wolfe. Diaries avoid these two delusions and set out on an uncertain and fragile path.

I'm Not Stiller is the reverse of Pirandello's *The Late Mattia Pascal*. In both cases, there is a play on the unfolding of identity and possible lives. Everything comes down to the name, which is the condition of confusion and changing place; that is why there are those titles, where a personal name shines (how many other novels have the male surname on the cover?). Frisch advances into a Kafkaesque atmosphere (Joseph K. seems to have been confused with another man); the individual is interrogated and imprisoned by the authorities, who treat him as guilty from the first.

268

I walked along the old covered walk, dappled with water. I crossed it from side to side, made my way among passersby who had taken refuge there and were piled up escaping from the rain. The business, a kind of glass kiosk, was almost at the exit, over Rivadavia. I knew he hung out around there. Last night, no further than this, he almost crashed into me in the middle of the street and I had to jump off to a side to avoid him and escape. I moved quickly and mixed into the crowd and then started to walk slowly so that he would not notice me as he left. Perhaps because of this, today, I spied through the glass before entering. I turned my back to him, trying not to make sudden movements, not to break the rhythm of the pedestrians who moved between the shop windows and passageways. He was behind me. I started to walk and distance myself, not knowing if he had managed to see me. I imagined that icy touch at the back of my neck and at my waist, close to my spine, expected to feel it with the contact of his soft and tired voice.

Wednesday 2

I woke up slowly, at seven in the morning, as though frightened, covered in sweat. Nothing but complaints with the attorney since last night. Cacho is in jail in Buenos Aires; they took him for forced entry in the apartment in Ugarteche. There is nothing I can do for him. There is nothing I can do for him? Impossible to go to the place on the eighth day as we planned. What's more, after beating him, the police figured out everything, and they told Cacho that they knew about his impotence, that they had discovered Bimba's relations with Ernesto and Victor. They had been following them for days and told him the details of his woman's secret rendezvous with his friends. "All to bring him down," the attorney told me with a mournful air. They even went to Ernesto's apartment and took away everything hidden there. After the night when Cacho sold the stolen Rolex and gave his own address, the attorney told me, they had started following him and all of his friends, including me. He recommended that I "make myself scarce." What I did was to go to Adrogué, to my grandfather's house, which used to be mine. I always go there when I am in trouble. My grandfather always welcomes me with the same knowing smile.

The difficulty is remaining calm. The "changes" (emotional or material) impede me from thinking and acting effectively. But I already knew that. The essential thing now is to insure my footing, get money, look for a place (with de Brasi, in another boardinghouse, etc.) that hasn't been compromised. From there, I will be able to start everything again and help Cacho.

I just walked alone, in the sun, down the empty street. I found a certain peace. But now I am centered in myself again, like back in '59, as lost as I was then. I feel—with news of the events—that all of my certainty has broken down, that nothing is stable, and then I turn circles and circles around myself.

Thursday 3
"The truly strong man in any sphere is the one who most clearly realizes that nothing is given, that all must be made and paid for; who is uneasy when he fails to find obstacles, and so invents them . . . For such a man, form is grounded in reason," Paul Valéry.

"Great music consists of fulfilling the *obligations* the composer incurs with virtually the first note," Arnold Schoenberg. He worked based on conventions. In literature, they are grammatical, syntactical forms, implicit in genres, methods and techniques already used by others, themes, motifs, and plots already written and stereotypical characters (the hero, the miser, the dumb girl, the femme fatale), for those of us who try to relive by writing.

Friday 4
The character is "the indifferent man," but socialized. You have to pay attention to his sick characteristics, how he stains everything he touches

and everyone he knows. He lives outside of society, in the void, but through his actions he contaminates others with his vitriolic presence. Everyone falls down on him; the method is denunciation—as with Cacho, betrayed by those who were the closest.

Saturday 5
Cacho turns up in the newspapers, caught, arrested. The papers have the power to stupefy us, especially when we are implicated in the news we read. The sinister thing is that they seem to be written by no one, as though they were just information, stripped of prejudices or subtexts. They want you—by reading the name, seeing the photo, reading about the "misdemeanors"—to accept everything as though it were irrevocable.

For a history of literature, the only valuable criterion must be the present, meaning that what justifies a writer historically is not his or her permanence in the zeitgeist; instead, his or her reality is a kind of continuous present, becoming contemporary in some times and obscure in others. Because for no one, at any time, are there absolute values.

Sunday, February 6
Every morning this uncertainty, like hanging in the air. Maybe I haven't learned to go backward, but I am afraid of returning to the hotel room on Calle Medrano.

Yesterday, almost without realizing it, but displaying my discomfort through some nervous jostling and a kind of persecution complex that lasted a while, I accepted—in his mother's house—the five thousand pesos that Cacho had left me before falling prisoner.

The only thing I need to save is the work. I lock myself in to write as though creating a replica of Cacho's incarceration. I work neurotically, in spite of everything.

Yesterday in the theater, a film with James Bond, an essential contemporary figure who combines the adventurer, the dandy, and the
romantic conqueror. "A *gentleman* of the night," as he says about himself
(girls, passion for gambling, fine food), forgetting—and letting you
forget—that he is a spy, 007, with a license to kill, who lives a double
life. He seems to be a reincarnation of Superman, but updated for
the modern consumer world. The hero is an expert consumer and a
secret warrior who not only defends his style of life, but also a form
of social life.

Monday 7
Yesterday at the sea, on Sorensen's beach, and then in Barrilito and then
in Beruti's melancholy and Kafkaesque hotel, where she and I tried to
create an absolute. Escape the uneasiness of this time and the worry over
Cacho's incarceration. Withdraw for a closed-off and perfect time. But
it was pointless.

Today, tonight, the journey; at the end of the respite that was already
growing worse on its own, I am returning to Buenos Aires. There I will
find the situation as such: the apartment on Calle Ugartecho searched
by the police (my typewriter was there). I doubt that the hotel on Calle
Medrano is a good idea. So I have to change residence, look for money
and some calm to resume my pending work.

To what extent do the best American "hard-boiled" narrators (Hammett,
Cain, Chase, and Chandler) destroy, trivialize, or in fact improve on
Hemingway's narrative technique?

Wednesday 9
I am in Buenos Aires, I rented a place in Hotel Callao, near Corrientes. I
installed myself here alone, and we will see how things go. I am writing
this in the Ramos bar. As always, I begin by rediscovering the familiar
places, the bars empty at midmorning, where you can sit down almost

on the sidewalk and watch life go by. I read Pavese (*American Literature: Essays and Opinions*).

At night in the hotel once again, on the balcony. The avenue below. The people walking on the sidewalk seem little rubber dolls at that distance. I used the day today to check how far the water had risen, from the flood that sank Cacho.

Some news: Jorge Álvarez asked me for my book of stories. Francisco Urondo wants a note for the magazine *Adán* (in exchange for two thousand pesos). F. Khun and Germán Rozenmacher went on about a television script; they make the series *Historia de jóvenes*, and the writers take it in turns. In this way, I can say that I more or less have the money I need for the coming six months guaranteed, and I've never thought about my future beyond that limit.

Thursday 10
I am in La Paz. In the paper, a note from Félix Luna about the anthology makes a reference to my story "Las actas del juicio." I copy the text of the first review of my writing, done by a stranger: "E. R.'s debut work is an excellent conjecture into the spiritual conflict of one of Urquiza's soldiers under the trance of murdering his old leader, disillusioned about him: a fascinating subject that surprisingly had never been undertaken by an Argentine writer until now."

I go to see Viñas in his apartment at the end of Calle Viamonte, almost in Bajo. He is grumbling about Carlos Peralta, who had promised him the text for the back cover of his novel, which, according to David, is now ready. In a bar, we talk a while about the difficulties of earning a living in Buenos Aires. A summary of the topics we covered. Novel-film. Possible impact on Latin America. Historical guidelines.

The generation of post-Peronism. How some see others. Europe as mirror, market, and home.

For my part, as always when I'm in danger, I would like to write about myself in the third person. To avoid the illusion of an "interior life."

Monday 14

I am in Piriápolis, at Inés's parents' house. Very hot, too much beer. I have the impression of being stuck inside of a world I have always wanted to deny in order to live. As though all of the dikes crumbled down and the water flooded over everything.

These days, I remember the lessons of other times: work, literature—sadly—is not detached from reality. There cannot be a "cure," or a cutoff, or a parallel reality.

In some way, the central mistake of Argentine writers can be detected in their "tremendous" and falsely literary metaphors. They always give a definition for each situation—that is, they always define and give a meaning to characters' actions as they occur.

Tuesday 15

The world of Kafka—whom I have come back to reading with the same passion as always—is one of infinite mediations. Therein lies his greatness. What is postponed, what is always interrupted and diverted is, for him, reality itself. In fact, the extraordinary thing is that we do not "arrive" at the meaning either; everything is postponed and also interrupted in his texts.

A subject. Maybe the story of the man who gives his woman to a friend ("I'll lend her to you," I told him), isn't she the same as she always was?

Thursday 17

Last night, drunk, I really laid into Inés. The rage was coming from somewhere else. Sometimes you can actually "lose your head" (because you wagered it first).

A rainy day. As always, I have no desire to go out when there is no sun. I went to meet with Rodolfo Khun about his proposal of writing one of the episodes of *Historia de jóvenes* for television. Afterward, I went to the theater and saw *Odds Against Tomorrow*, a very well-written police movie by Robert Wise. I left the theater and took a bus, which passed in front of the hotel on Medrano where we lived, and I felt a certain nostalgia; as always, the memory matters more to me than the experience itself. At night I saw Noé Jitrik; we went back to discussing the possibilities for courses and the institute that could replace the University, now seized by the military.

"Consensus is the most important foundation for constitutional order; it is not material force, it is a reserve force for exceptional moments of crisis," A. Gramsci.

Friday 18
Too many things to do. Search for a place to live. Get the furniture from Boca, collect the issues of the magazine that are now "out," put together Issue 2, write the main article, correct the book of stories, prepare a script for *Historia de jóvenes*.

"The only way of expressing emotion in the form of art is by finding an 'objective correlative'; in other words, a set of objects, a situation, a chain of events which shall be the formula of that particular emotion," T. S. Eliot.

Saturday 19
All I have left now is staying away, escaping, as though everything were going to fall apart at the same time. And it is logical that everything should fall apart at the same time. Yet, slowly, mysteriously, happiness returns, as though for an instant everything were held outside, separate, lasting as long as happiness can ever last.

Sunday 20
I want to live in this delicate mist forever, my head slow and eyes tired, without thinking about anything, without a future.

Reading Bioy Casares, *The Dream of Heroes*. The intention behind the style, a colloquial prose, is to satirize and show the weaknesses of language from areas outside of literature. At the same time, the precaution of writing in an "Argentine" style (as seen in Cambaceres or in Cancela and Cortázar) takes these writers away from personal expression and moves them toward parody. By contrast, others, like Arlt or Viñas, show the "foreign" mark of their translated works and thus lose the local color (for the better), but also lose what they are seeking, a writing that is "free from literature."

A slow and empty day. I am unable to clearly see the aim of my essay for Issue 2 of the magazine. Then, my notes on Bioy and my rereadings of Mansilla. Maybe I am hoping to place the concept of "Argentine literature" in question. Or, anyway, to bring that adjective into discussion (what, in the end, is the meaning of an Argentine quality in literature?).

I am reading the stories of Henry James. I would like to overcome the temptation of letting myself be carried away by the episodes, the flowing of events when I read stories, in spite of my resolve, and to pay attention to their composition, how they are put together. James is essentially a narrator of uncertainty. And in this story of vengeance ("The Abasement of the Northmores") we encounter that constant duplicity again, with excessive interpretation of the protagonists' actions and intentions. What is ambiguous, of course, is not the reality but rather the motivation; the distortion seems, in that way, to form part of the plot. A story half-heard or misheard, broken, fragmented, never fully understood. The same as when you unintentionally hear a phone conversation in a bar and must recreate the speakers' lives based on it. On the one hand, you hear a single part of the conversation and must therefore imagine the responses. But even if you get it right and manage to "follow" the talk well, you would still understand almost nothing. Incredibly, Henry James writes in this way. Within the story, we cannot decide whether the vengeance will be realized or not.

In the case of *Daisy Miller*, James's technique is more descriptive and goes from large to small; an observer narrating in the first person describes the tourist section and then "descends" or goes to the hotel area, and then he descends further and goes to one hotel in particular, and then descends again and goes to a room in that hotel, and then concentrates on two people next to each other, having a conversation. A dramatic way of narrating, that is, of showing rather than telling the events, situated in the place of an observer who witnesses the fragmented conversation but does not synthesize it the way a traditional narrator would. James knows that in order to tell the story effectively you have to respect the opacity of reality. You have to present the facts and leave their (possible) meaning open.

Monday 21
Here I am, sitting in a plush armchair by a window that opens onto the rooftops and terraces of Buenos Aires, reading Henry James, and at the same time the most varied thoughts pass before me, as though I could see them, as though my mind were connected to a personal television channel. A channel that works parallel to reading, as I have sometimes seen happen with friends, when I visit them at home and find them reading with the television turned on, sometimes no sound, only images, while they listen to music on a record player.

Tuesday 22
Unconcerned, I postpone the visits, the letters, the phone calls, the meetings with friends, I keep myself hanging, like a trapeze artist who jumps, imagining that there is a net below to catch him if he falls.

A short story begins. I was the first man who slept with her, long ago now, almost ten years; I saw her at Antonio's party last night and did not recognize her. She came toward me, smiling.

Wednesday 23
I have spent several afternoons visiting hotels and boardinghouses in the city, looking for a room for myself. It's a very strange exercise because you have to choose a place to live without much information. I walked and walked and walked. There is a special section in the classifieds, where offers of rooms for rent appear. You are guided by the very concise information detailed in the ad: basically, the neighborhood, the street where the place is located and the offering price for rent. Finally, with no doubts, I let myself be guided by intuition and chose a room on the third floor in a petit hotel over Riobamba, almost at Paraguay. The room, with a balcony, opens onto the street, has a mini bath with a shower and a kitchen with two burners built in between two doors. Price, 220 pesos per day, which is close to 7,000 per month. I will bring my things tomorrow.

Thursday 24
Settled in now, I placed a table by the window, hung my clothing, left two suitcases on the side covered with a blanket. I enjoy changing to a new neighborhood and starting to walk around and scope out the place. This time, I am very close to the city center but also far enough removed for it to be more tranquil. I return to the circumstances of my arrival in Buenos Aires a year ago: in a boardinghouse, without money, placing my hopes on a half-finished book.

I am reading James Purdy. All of the stories are a long conversation between two people who are building—in the moment, so to speak— rather than a story, an atmosphere.

Recently, my cousin Horacio called with news about Cacho; the option materialized for me to go back to his searched apartment and live there, until he gets out. Staying in the discovered hideout would be a means of staying in danger, always vigilant to the movements outside. What better training for a writer? Installing yourself in an imprisoned friend's foxhole and, while there, writing his story. So many ideas would cross through my mind if I were there. That night when Cacho called us together, Bimba led us in and we saw the bed covered with thousand-peso bills and him, sitting there. He had stealthily entered a two-story house in Martínez one Saturday night when, according to his calculations, the residents would be at the cinema or the theater or out visiting friends. He had fifty minutes, he thought, to get in, pick up whatever he found, and then leave under cover of darkness. He forced open the bars with the crowbar he carried on his belt, under his double-breasted suit, and leapt into a room on the second floor. He found a safe behind a painting. "I thought," he told me, "the husband has one key. The wife has another. Where does the wife keep her key? I was cool, calm but aware of noises from the street. Where does the wife keep her key? *In the kitchen*, I thought, *in a coffee tin.*" He went to the kitchen, opened the tin, found the key, and went back to his apartment on Calle Ugarteche with two million pesos in American dollars and Argentine bills. But living there would be impossible for me, not only out of fear for being disrupted by the police, but rather because nothing would be the same now as back in the days when Cacho and I would swerve around the city together, certain we could conquer it, between the two of us, each in his own way.

Suddenly I recall the days in Cacho's apartment, not long ago, in January, alone there, reading *Cantar de ciegos* by Carlos Fuentes and also, from time to time, writing the stories I had imagined long ago in the same place. The summer had begun and everything was possible.

Now, on the other hand, amid the desolation, I create passageways for myself to escape the storm. The way someone might build up ever more precarious barrier walls, absurdly, to halt the swelling of the river that threatens him, having diverged from its course, flooded the defenses one after another, and laid waste to everything.

I live in the present, attentive to brief pauses of calm, unable to plan anything, imagine the days to come, or work in the long range, because doing so always means coming back the image of Cacho in prison.

February 26
Rereading my notebooks from last year, I recognize that the technique I have used for my stories—antisentimental, hard and objective—works well for short-form writing in which everything is resolved in the narrative situation. It is ineffective, I believe, for showing the temporal evolution of relationships—that is, for writing a novel.

Last night I saw *Breathless* by Godard again for the fourth time. I enjoy his approach to genre: open, tangential, but simple in the construction of the plot. And I particularly enjoy his use of quotations, allusions, discussions, and cuts connected to a diverse store of knowledge, which act as context for the action. In this sense, Godard is, for me, the finest contemporary storyteller.

Once again I have a thousand pesos to live on for a week. Pending matters: introduce Orson Welles, finish the script for R. Kuhn.

February 28
I hung up a photo of Roberto Arlt in this place where I have settled, hoping to finish the book of stories. I write beside the second-floor window that opens over Riobamba while the sun burns on the asphalt, wet from fleeting summer rains.

Last night, after leaving the movie theater and still in the atmosphere of the film, I made a furtive visit to Cacho's apartment to look for my papers and books. Not wanting to turn on the light, I went in with a lantern and saw the deliberate destruction the police had caused while searching the place: clothing strewn, the mattress ripped up and open, the floor covered with boxes, tins . . . At once, I imagined Cacho with his hands tied, beaten, present for the disaster, humiliated, watching as the police broke everything (after they had forced him, under torture, to reveal the address of his house in Buenos Aires).

Dubliners. In his short stories, Joyce deliberately avoids all events; they have almost no plot, except for an oblique vision that shows a fragment of a broader theme. He does not seek adventures or dramatic incidents, is interested in the routine of the everyday, and attempts to present the greatest possible amount of otherwise implicit material so that, in the stories, there is always a glimmer, a light that fleetingly but clearly illuminates the whole world. The measure of success for such an open form resides, of course, in its level of concentration. Even if Joyce—in bad faith, from what I understand—claimed not to know Chekhov, his stories are connected to those of the Russian writer in terms of his effort to write stories without endings, which signified the first important transformation of the genre after Poe.

I catch myself counting the pages of this notebook, in which the notes tend to be too long and too varied (because it really is the only thing I'm writing these days), since I don't want it to end. Filling up a notebook in a month proves to me that something in my life has accelerated, a need to be on top, as though I meant to write, without naming it, about the vanishing point that has led me to change many things in my life, including where I live.

"Now, Marat, you are talking like an aristocrat. Compassion is the property of the privileged classes," says Sade in the theater piece by Peter Weiss.

The indifferent man. The protagonist lives locked up in a room. In the afternoon, between two and ten after three, the sun filters in through the little window. Even though it is summer, the man and the room are freezing cold most of the time. The character fears and hopes for the moment when he will be able to abandon the bedroom. He envisions himself, pale, almost gray, walking between passersby, whom he imagines are happy. One afternoon, in a bar, they interrogate him violently to find out where he comes from. He is afraid that they have confused him for a convict . . .

The indifferent man II. One afternoon, he situates himself under the sun's rays, which filter into his room for an hour every afternoon. He acts methodically, putting in both of his hands first, then his left arm, later his right arm, one day the side of his face, the next day yet another part of his body is warmed and allowed to take in the heat. One morning he turns up dead, and his body appears tattooed, with white expanses between the areas that have acquired a natural hue.

Tuesday, March 1
I went to La Plata and came back, spent the night there in a hotel facing the station. I taught my classes, saw my friends again, José Sazbón, Alejandro Ferrero, Néstor García Canclini, the ones who always seem the same to me, as though only I have changed, but that is an illusion. What happens is that they persist in their being, and while talking with them I hear words and phrases, ideas and schemes that I have heard before. As for me, I am multiple, and I imagine myself as a man capable of change.

Because Joyce's *Ulysses* is written in present and indicative (Buck undresses, the milkwoman serves them milk, etc.), the internal monologue marks out the passage of time.

Wednesday 2
I am in the Botanical Garden, at noon. I have always felt the need to capture the moment, now on this bench in shadow, under a tree, circles of

sun on the grass and on the mud caused by last night's rain. Meanwhile, I am reading Bernard Malamud.

Thursday
The hardest part of morning is finding a reason to get out of bed.

Friday 4
I go back to that image. These days and these places seem akin to the swelling of the Paraná, laying waste to everything it finds. I cannot stop building up the levees though they are already in ruins from the swelling current. Last night, Horacio informed me that Alberto C. stole the refrigerator I had left in the house in Boca. You should never be close to an "artist," a low-class one even less. I hope he didn't also make off with the three suitcases of books and papers that I left there. Thieves don't bother me, but friends who steal from me do.

In the end, what really worries me are the diversions in the path: tests, formalities, meetings, etc. For better or for worse, I have only five thousand pesos to make it to the end of month.

Monday, March 7
Later, sitting at the table beside the window, he thought it would be best to cut off from all of his hopes once and for all and leave things as they were. But the thing he had to do at three in the afternoon stood in the way, a kind of curtain, and there was no way to do anything, as though all internal order had collapsed.

I spoke with Alberto C. today and the situation improved. I did nothing in February and the magazine is on hold, despite Camarda's excitement; he says that the first issue has already run out and wants me to prepare the second. I don't know what to do with my stories either. Maybe I should publish them this year.

Translating Joyce. Regarding the difficulty of certain translations and the need (in general) to maintain the music and tone of the text, this passage from *Ulysses* is a valuable example: "On the doorstep he felt in his hip pocket for the latchkey. Not there. In the trousers I left off. Must get it. *Potato I have.* Creaky wardrobe." The enigma is that emphasized sentence, which Salas Subirat translates as "I am a carrot; *soy un zanahoria,*" which isn't bad, because it's his way of solving an unsolvable problem, unless he had already read the entire novel under a magnifying glass. If he had, he would have seen the potato appear in the scene in the public bathroom, when Bloom puts it to the side as he looks for the soap in his pocket before getting undressed. Finally, the potato appears once more in the scene at the brothel, when the mother's ghost asks if he carries the potato with him to fight his rheumatism. This is proof of two things: Joyce's way of writing, never explaining what the character already knows, and, on the other hand, the need for the translator to know the general sense of the work. The motifs in the book work like musical themes, reappearing without explanation.

In *Writing Degree Zero,* Barthes establishes the distinction between language, style, and writing, which is useful—although a bit mechanical. For me, the issue that Joyce poses has to do with the limitations of language. As though language were a territory, after which there is a void, which results in literature. If the desired effect in Joyce is often one of incomprehension and impenetrability, Barthes defines the opposite—clear, sharp, transparent language—as "degree zero," an example of which would be Hemingway's prose. But Barthes seems not to have noticed what Hemingway said, that following Joyce he had to start over from zero and work with a few simple words, with a disjointed and oral syntax. Beckett also took the same path, noting that, after Joyce, it was better to abandon English, and, as we know, he started writing in French because he could write badly in that language—that is, without style. In both cases, always an esoteric quality: in the example of Joyce, there is an esoteric quality in *Finnegans,* namely a rupture of the lexicon; in his turn, Hemingway worked with extreme subtraction, and his best stories are also esoteric because their allusions are not explicit.

Tuesday 8
I went to see Viñas in his apartment at the end of Viamonte, and then I went through the bookshops that abound in that area, five on each block, though they have started to diminish since the College of Philosophy and Letters relocated to Calle Independencia.

These sudden outbursts of happiness—this one has already fled, now that I want to record it—are like epiphanies, unexpected and brilliant, which I find are connected to the sheer presentness of writing: quickly, everything seems to open up and become simple, everything is possible in language, and that happy feeling lasts as long as you stay in that volatile state of writing, thoughtless.

Friday
I am writing this at noon, in Florida bar. Searching for a narrative that does not distinguish between feelings and reasons, that works with plots—in both senses, that is, with stories but also with schemes.

Sunday 12
If it is true, as is the case in quantum physics, that experimenters form part of the experiments they undertake and their presence alters the material, we might say that literary experimentation essentially implies a renewal for the writer himself. The writer experiments—for example, by abandoning a previous style that has become commonplace and taking the risk of attempting a new way of writing—whether or not the result is a traditional work.

The potential of a terrorist is hidden in every writer. Example: Roberto Arlt. A terrorist because he can never get away from the feeling of illegitimacy, of illicit life, of being a man pursued.

Monday 14

I was hungry and the hunger was distracting me, so I went down to the street; the icy wind seemed to cut at my skin. I bought two rolls, cracked them in half and topped them off with ham and tomato. I ate slowly, trying not to get my papers dirty. Then I made a pile of the remains and the crumbs and cleaned the table so that there would be no traces.

"A great work is impossible today, in view of the fact that the writer is involved in his writing as though trapped on a dead-end road," Roland Barthes.

A soft breeze with the distant perfume of watered soil and jasmines just came in through the window, taking me off to the country house in Bolívar at the siesta hour while a workman watered the patio with a tin can. The silver color that came along with that memory instantly made me "see" the tin-plated jars where priests poured the *dulce de leche* they made at the monastery in Del Valle, a nearby village full of cottages and milking stables. And so we could say that this perfume now was like the scent of wet soil from my childhood, making me see the tin watering can that the gardener Don José used at the siesta hour, and its silver shine immediately led me to the memory of the priests making the candy, pouring it into large jars, they, too, colored silver.

Tuesday 15

Yesterday in Florida bar, a discussion with Eduardo Romano and Alberto Szpunberg, once again about the question of the second issue of the magazine. I left there and ended up in Plaza Rodríguez Peña, sitting alone on a bench facing Palacio Pizzurno, wavering between going to the library in front of me or returning home. Once again an instant of epiphany, a moment suspended in the pure present, but this time the effect was negative, a perverse miracle.

I have three projects in my hands. I hope to continue with the book of stories until October, rewriting, correcting. I have to go ahead with the second issue of *Literatura y Sociedad*. Finally, I have to prepare exams for "Introduction to History"and "Argentine History" so that I can keep my positions. I may have lost the draft of my story "Entre hombres." I abandoned it among my things—the papers, the magazines that I kept in two suitcases, which I left in the house on Olavarría in Boca. Maybe it is scattered on the patio, among the flowerpots and the washing basins.

"The novel has always taken the conflict between living men, and petrified human relationships, as its true object. The same absurd situation, for the novel, becomes an artistic medium," T. W. Adorno. It seems that he means to say that telling stories always deals with ghosts and memories of the dead, as though the story were always the pause after the ghost of Hamlet's father appears and the prince delivers his monologue.

I turned out the light so that I could be present for the fierce storm that shakes the city and hastens summer resolutely away.

"The author did not then know (1919) what his working path in life would be. If he would be a businessman, a thief, an employee at some commercial firm or a writer. Above all things he desired to be a writer," Roberto Arlt (note to the second edition of *Mad Toy*).

"There is not a single critic of *The Seven Madmen* who has not written: The greatest quality of this book is Erdosain's pain. They think that great pain is not invented, think that I myself could be Erdosain," Roberto Arlt (letter to his mother).

"This stage in Argentine civilization, spanning between the years 1900 and 1930, presents curious phenomena. The children of shopkeepers study fantastical literature in the College of Philosophy and Letters; they are ashamed of their parents and in the morning tell off the maid if they find a discrepancy of a few cents in the bill from the market," Roberto Arlt, *Love the Enchanter*.

Wednesday

In Florida bar. I meet with my father, always dull tensions. Looking at him, I try to find signs of things that I see as virtues when I notice them in others.

Friday

Last night I ate dinner with Dad at El Dorá in Bajo. After talking a while about politics and Perón, suddenly—as though he were a stranger to me—he started confiding in me and telling me about his relationships with other women, with a false naturalness that made me more uncomfortable than the content of his stories. We have been fairly distant since the days when I went to the University (years ago now); little by little, we had reestablished some cordiality and some confidence, but today everything fell down once again. A man who tells another about his romantic adventures is a fool, and if he's his father on top of that, that childish stupidity transforms into something sinister.

I am in the bar on Lavalle and Rodríguez Peña. Inés rented an apartment on Uriburu and Santa Fe, a clean and bright place to live. For my part, I am going to look for a room in a boardinghouse nearby, where I can lock myself up and write.

Monday

I went to Boca and came back, gathering the rest—mattresses, chairs— in the Cedróns' apartment, and I left everything, like after a storm, not knowing what to do.

It is four in the afternoon. I haven't had anything but a coffee since I got up. A few things are left to do: finish the move, get the refrigerator, and, most of all, prepare myself for the exams at the College. Deal with the magazine. And then, only then, begin to write.

Tuesday 22

All morning transporting papers, dealing with a Kafkaesque mattress (there is nowhere to grab hold of it, like in the story "The Judgment"). Things are decided little by little. Now all I have left to do is prepare for the exams and succeed. Money and the future depend on it. I have a room in the boardinghouse on Riobamba and Paraguay. I took my things out of the house in Boca and out of Cacho's apartment. Now I am tired, my hands are dirty from going through so many ink-covered papers.

Wednesday 23

Amazing, Stephen Dedalus's system; he had 500 pesos to make it through the month, I stopped at a kiosk, spent 250 pesos on Mansilla's *Memorias*, and, the trap already set, forgot it on the subway.

Thursday

After my delirium on the subway yesterday, today I am paying for the consequences. I only have eighty pesos for the day and then comes the void. I have no way to make money until the tenth. I will see what I can do.

It was almost noon when I got up today. I read a few articles in French magazines about Brecht. I met Sergio Camarda; our differences regarding the magazine grew worse. I bought bread and a Suchard chocolate to ease my hunger; I decided to eat the bread first and then the chocolate, and while I was eating I saw this in *La Razón* newspaper: A woman committed suicide by lying down across the train tracks "with her arms spread open," she was forty-five years of age, had on a black dress, and wore black shoes and brown leggings. A change purse was found next to her remains, in which she had a fifty-peso bill, a sky-blue handkerchief, and a small piece of paper on which she had written with a fountain pen, "I have no family, throw me away wherever you like, I am alone and I come from the country." For my part, I have forty pesos. Now I'm going to make a copy of the story "La honda" to give it to Horacio, who is coming to visit me.

A short story. On that Saturday afternoon, the two of them were playing chess on the patio. Tell the whole story in the third person. Do not immediately reveal that the key is Pelliza. It was there: I had discovered it quickly. Using the description of the game in order to describe the secret.

Friday 25
An hour on Corrientes and Montevideo with twenty pesos in my pocket, loaded down with books, after walking around the city waiting for Raúl to follow him to his house. I sold two volumes of *Historia* by Vicente F. López for one hundred pesos each.

I take an amphetamine and sit down to work. Immediately a feeling of fullness comes, lasts one night, and then is abruptly extinguished.

"We suffer not only from the living, but from the dead. The dead holds the living in his grasp," Karl Marx (preface to *Capital*).

Sunday
Yesterday I walked down Callao to Corrientes. I took the subway. Ate dinner in Bajo, alone. Came back slowly on the same route.

The building opposite is a dark square. Every now and then the metallic noise of a window opening can be heard. Suddenly, along with the noise, a rectangle of light appears, seeming to float in the void, suggestive of abstract paintings.

Thursday, March 31
I write letters: to Daniel Moyano, to José Aricó. They took Cacho away in February, I moved into this place in March. The competitions at the College are next week. I hope to win at least one of them and live off of

that. I spend the afternoon locked up in this room, alone, going around in circles, and nothing matters much to me.

April 1
Last night, Norman Briski at the Di Tella. *El niño envuelto.* Very fine performance with a poor text.

Subject for a short story. The lunatic escapes with clothing given to him by the laborers who work in the asylum, and he goes to the police station to report that they have kidnapped him. The ones who saw him coming glimpsed the insane glimmer in his eyes. He was dressed in blue work overalls, lent to him a moment before by one of the laborers whom he had been badgering for days.

Sometimes I would like to go back to certain periods of my life and live through them with the consciousness I have now. For example, to start history over in 1956. It's a strange hope because if it weren't for the way I lived at the time, I would be nothing; that notion is one of the effects of literature, wherein you can always start a story over again. At the same time, it is one the great novelistic themes: Conrad's Lord Jim, who tries to change the past, go back to the day when he acted like a bastard and change it. Borges has a similar story called "The Other Death": a soldier who acted like a coward in battle makes a Faustian pact, and he returns to combat to die as a hero. It is also the subject of Fitzgerald's *The Great Gatsby*: a poor man, rejected by a woman in the past, doggedly becomes rich in order to find the girl again, now a man of fortune, and thus change destiny. Ultimately, it concerns thinking about the past with the categories that we use to imagine the future. The hypothetical past.

Monday 4
With fifty pesos in my pocket and without having eaten, I travel to La Plata by train, worried about the competitions and the magazine, unable to find the calm I need in order to write. A calm that, for me, is defined

as the absence of thoughts. Not thinking as a way to write, or rather, writing as a way to achieve the not-fully-conceived thoughts that always define a writer's style. At least, that is the Río de la Plata tradition, that of Macedonio, Felisberto, Borges: the writer vacillates, does not quite understand the story he is telling, the opposite of the despotic figure of the classical Latin American writer who has everything clear before he starts to write.

The competitions were postponed again. I have spent a couple of weeks studying the bibliographies from the syllabi, preparing for the exam classes. We'll see what happens.

I meet Dipi Di Paola and we go out for a coffee. Always entertaining and emphatic, he creates beautiful retrospectives about himself and his friends. He reminds me of Miguel Briante, who, like Dipi, settles into the self-defined space of an artist. We are great friends, but we see things differently; I am not interested in posing as a "creator," which is what gives him all of his magic, but what interests me most is creating a figure that is separate from the Argentine stereotypes of the "writer." All writers are self-designated, but the ones who really interest me are those who do not believe in self-indulgence. Dipi would walk around with Heidegger's *Being and Time* under his arm because he's no fool and puts his faith in culture and intellect, but underneath that, the light of a genius illuminates him.

I go back to reading Pavese's "Wedding Trip," which I read for the first time in 1960. The recently married man leaves his wife in the hotel room on their wedding night, goes down to the street with some trivial pretense, lets himself be swept away by the enchantment of a summer night in the city, and returns at dawn, surprised to find his wife desperate and weeping. In it, you can see the excision of conscience transformed into a story: the man who stays with the woman is also the man who fantasizes about having the freedom to lose himself down some street at night. There are always modern and weak or inoffensive versions of *Dr. Jekyll and Mr. Hyde* (although there is now no shortage of magic potions in contemporary literature).

Philosophy. The authentic being is the being that cannot be broken up or reduced into other beings, it is the being in itself. In this way, "to be" means:

1. To exist, to be there, in essence.
2. Conceivable as being one or being another.

Ontology responds to the question of who exists, or rather who is the being in essence. The being founded upon itself.

What is contingency? The self, for others.

Asking what the self is, in essence, is the same as asking who exists.

The next step is given by the distinction between things that merely appear to exist and those that exist in actuality. The distinction between essence and appearance. Contingency, the being of that existence, is unnecessary. Here, the difference is contingent, necessary.

Friday 15

In Don Julio bar. The competitions begin within the hour; I hope everything turns out well.

I won both competitions (head of Practical Work in "Introduction to History" and top assistant in "Argentine History II"), which means economic security for a whole year and the tranquility to write. On the other hand, just like every time that I return to La Plata, I find myself surrounded by people and friends asking me to stay.

Saturday

Juncal and Suipacha: John Ford's *Stagecoach* at 9:45 at the Núcleo film club.

See: Roa, Romano, David V., Szpunberg, Murmis.

See: Library of the Goethe Institute (Walter Benjamin).

Saturday, April 16, 1966
Literature is the experience and not the knowledge of the world.

It is four in the morning and, as always, I understand my own conception of literature better while writing. It is the result and not the condition of a writer's work. Ideas are not the condition, but rather the result of the writing. The meaning of literature is not to communicate a defined exterior objective, but rather to create the conditions for understanding the experience of reality.

Sunday 17
I wake up at five in the afternoon. Last night, before I went to bed in the room on Riobamba, I finished reading Vasco Pratolini's *Bruno Santini*, which made me strangely uneasy with its melodramatic ending. What constitutes the emotional effects of reading a book—or how are they constructed?

I went out to the street and walked down Corrientes as far as Florida, watching the profiles of buildings being erased as night fell.

Monday 18
It is raining. I got up in the afternoon. By reversing my sleeping hours, I have managed to turn myself into a lone wolf, leaving my lair when night has already begun to envelop the fields of the mind. The day passes by and is lost, me sleeping until nightfall and living with the city in shadow.

With the habitual changes, facing the window now, indecisive, I understand that experience is always lying in wait and does not depend on our decisions.

Tuesday
I left Inés's apartment for a few days and settled back into my room on Calle Riobamba. I brought my things, my books, and feel safe once again in a place no one knows.

Wednesday 19
I fell asleep at noon and awoke at night, as though the day had been erased. I took a short walk a while ago, the light luminous and clear, the men passing hurriedly, and for a while I followed a beautiful girl with long legs who walked slightly bent, as though sailing into the wind. I went with her down Paraguay, until Callao, and when I approached her she answered perfectly naturally that she had already seen me several times at the bar on the corner. She is studying philosophy at the University of Salvador and her name is Flora. She is interested in theology, but not men, she told me with a smile.

Sunday 24
Diverse readings (Barthes, Sartre, Edmund Wilson), preparatory notes for a discussion on the issue of realism. Yesterday, I traveled to La Plata to give my classes and returned that night, without sleeping, so as not to delay my return to this room where I always feel sheltered. Powerful, the impression of the bus terminal on Constitución in the first light of morning, the men and women going down into the subway as though someone were pursuing them. At the bar in the station, as I ate breakfast, two young men were drinking gin, surely trying to find the spirits needed to go on living.

A father. The father commits suicide, or rather attempts suicide but is saved; he goes several months without speaking, and they have to watch him so that he doesn't try again. They call on the son, who lives in another city, to come look after him. They live together for a week, and the son criticizes him or asks him about certain things that he alone seems to know. The father remains motionless in his silence. The son finally leaves him alone.

Monday 25
Dazed in the face of the uncertain reality I have created for myself by superposing the nights and days in abstract and dark circles, casting me outside of the world as though I lived in a society where no one can see

me. The lone man, inhabiting a hotel room in the center of the city and making little rounds, searching only for what he needs from one day to the next.

A telephone call, just a short time ago. I am frozen, paralyzed by horror. Sometimes everything is too irrational. Alejandra, Celia's daughter, has died, crushed under a car, and she was six years old. She had left the house to go to the bakery and buy the bread for breakfast. I have no image, can imagine nothing, see only the wall in front of me. What is there to say?

A while later. These are the things that reveal the sinister, unexpected logic of reality. Things can always be worse.

Tuesday
It is three in the morning, I lay down to sleep. I talked on the phone with Celia, who, as she told me, was still not even crying.

In any event, I worked on the article for the magazine all night and left it almost ready; in short, there is nothing new, and Sabato's complaints sometimes seem excessive to me.

It is six in the morning, and it becomes clear that notions of personal time disappear when you go several nights without sleeping. Occasionally I want to follow the criteria of this notebook and mark the dates, but I never know quite what day I'm living.

I write several versions of "Tierna es la noche"; piece by piece, I am finding the tone and sense of the story.

April 29
I continue with my routine of sleeping through the day. I got up at ten at night today; this system of flight from reality is more dangerous than even I had supposed.

Monday, May 2

Things in my life gradually become distorted, and I persist with a stunned indifference. Today I begin the day at four in the morning. Yesterday I woke up at six in the afternoon. We might say that I'm experimenting with time and duration, a bit lost; I have dedicated this sleepless night to gathering some remnants of the reflections I know about time.

Tuesday 3

I get up at six in the afternoon after dreaming that I was in a hotel on the coast. My notes continue, written in order to understand the days I am living through.

I have reached an impasse, strewn out on the bed, inactive, wanting to escape, living by night, insecure in myself, amazed at the power of a man who lives next door and has survived many catastrophes. From what he tells me. I used to see him on the staircase and he stopped me one afternoon, saying he knew it was me because I lived by night. We made plans the next day to meet at the bar on the corner, and he told me about his life. He was a factory worker but had, from what he said, "several contretemps." He never explained it to me with any word other than that. His name was Agustín Doncelar.

At present, what has stayed with me from this conversation is astonishment at the word "contretemps." All the philosophy I have been able to extract, while dutifully reading the great philosophers in order to save myself, is that none of them has said anything new about contretemps.

Space and time are forms of thought; they are ideas that exist in our minds prior to all observation of phenomena. Molds into which we pour the results of our experience. They are subjective, not independent of the observer. Time is a necessity of thought.

Wednesday 4
Three in the morning. Duration is not time. I can't sleep.

Saturday 7
I can't understand what it is I'm fighting against; I imagine numerous enemies and confront them one by one, as though dueling. It is impossible to fight them all at once because I must also fight against myself. Everything is simple, he said, if you understand that you must never lower your defenses. You have to be on guard, he said; the rest is illusory.

Sunday 8
It was intolerable that he turned back to inner climates; as though my body were a landscape, he said, or rather a building with extreme temperatures within. For three months, he said, I felt reality's pressure so much of the time that I am not able, now, to seek solace in my inner life or in more or less abstract states of mind. What's more, I have been trying to resume my "normal" sleeping hours for ten days. And so the nights go by, him lying prone on the bed, not sleeping until morning comes and he arises like a zombie, trying to turn the day around and reach a new morning.

Tuesday 10
It is six thirty in the afternoon. I am sick, am I sick? I have shivers, sleep badly, turn over in bed until noon, wide awake—wide awake?—and everything slips away in an exhausting—exhausting?—light sleep.

Yesterday, I stupidly entered the Self-Defined Man's game. And I stupidly asked for tickets to see his work of theater. Tickets that he reluctantly offered, offended because I had not gone to the premiere, etc, etc. When I arrived at the theater, of course, there were no tickets reserved. And so I bought one even though I was on the verge of leaving, but Inés insisted, etc. I know the jungle where I live, yet I insist on acting as though I were in an amusement park. What was I thinking, asking the Self-Defined Man for something in this atmosphere?

Wednesday 11

My neighbor from the room next door left the hotel sometime this week. I had grown accustomed to eating breakfast with him at any hour of the day and listening to him enumerate his complaints as though they were philosophy lectures. Last night I did no work, just let time pass, looking out from the balcony as in the distance the lights of the city went out. In the end, the only ones left alight were the streetlights and the old lamps of the Palacio de Obras Sanitarias, on the corner of Riobamba and Córdoba. In the bar, as I ate breakfast alone, the waiter informed me that "my friend" had come to say goodbye. "He came in with his suitcase and seemed ready to go, from what he said."

Today I discover serious defects in the article I wrote for Issue 2 of *Literatura y Sociedad*; it's hard for me to draw it out from the well where it has fallen. On top of that, I have to go to La Plata, and I'm going to lose two days and a night there, teaching the morphological hypothesis on the history of Spengler and working in the archive for the "Argentine History I" course, in which I am an "assistant" (Kafkaesque).

Meanwhile, in the midst of this unease, I have managed to resolve the story about Lucía, which I have decided will be called "Tierna es la noche." She is walking in the rain. At the end, Lucía, covering her eyes.

Saturday 14

I have three options: 1. Go to Inés's apartment for the second time, accept it. 2. Stay here, read, and wait for her. 3. Leave, go and have dinner alone, walk around the city.

Monday 16

The crisis is confirmed. I haven't done any work in a month, and I have trouble finding the rhythm. In this age, I let myself be, sleep, try to escape.

I travel to La Plata. Travel around the city, an ambulatory obsession. Travel to Adrogué. Better put it like this: He understood that some of the decisions he had made blindly at the age of sixteen were the only light amid the darkness, choices he had made in order to be faithful to what he thought he wanted to be. You can have doubts about everything, he thought, but you can't have doubts about the choices made without motive, without meaning, but with the certainty and conviction that everything that came was a way for him to come closer to the place his guiding light had shown him.

Thursday 19
"The concept of genius as akin to madness has been carefully cultivated by the inferiority complex of the public," Ezra Pound.

Waiting for Sergio, we are finishing Issue 2 of the magazine today. It is better than the previous one. We'll see if Camarda got the thirty thousand pesos.

Monday 23
The tone of these days only becomes apparent in rereading this notebook. The sleepless nights, the story about Lucía is almost ready. But everything here in these pages sounds laborious because I only write about myself (in the third person, I expect) and about reality, which seems ever more hostile and indecipherable.

Anyway, this notebook will be reread in the future as well, and then some sense will be restored, in a few months or, perhaps, even tomorrow. Lived time grows beautiful precisely because it is in the past. These dark days will seem luminous when distance allows me to observe them as though they were landscapes. The landscape of the soul, he said, you understand?

Tarde de amor. But she had crossed the hallway, as always, proud and beautiful, never imagining that when she saw them again she would be naked and unconscious, lying in the bed.

Friday, May 27
I wrote the story "Tarde de amor" in one night. Let's look at the beginning and end of "Tierna es la noche." But Lucía is dead now, and everything is pointless. I am halfway through the year and things are not well. Economically, literarily, and emotionally.

Saturday, June 4
I am in the professors' lounge at the College, waiting to give a makeup exam for "Introduction to History," in a while, at one. The students appear in the door and make gestures after they see me here. I try to convey "I'm with you" by only moving my hands and putting on an expression of solidarity. Malicious weekend, without money. Now I am more tired than hungry.

Tuesday 7
The relationship with Inés is finished; both of us go on, anxious, trusting in the power of miracles. The aggression grows frantically. I am always just visiting and then lock myself up in the room over Riobamba, the only place where I feel safe.

I saw Beatriz Guido. She gave me an envelope with pictures and a thousand pesos inside; it is payment for the summary of the possible film or script for Torre Nilsson's film about the old house that still survives on Calle Lavalle, near Maipú. Beatriz says that the book stand Arlt talked about in *Mad Toy* was at that house or in its surroundings.

"Nigh to the plain a battle they pitched both stiff and strong. But the lord Cid long-bearded hath overthrown that throng. And even unto Jativa in a long rout they poured. You might have seen all bedlam on the Jucar by the ford, for there the Moors drank water but sore against their will," *Cantar de mio Cid.*

Friday, June 10

At the College. Will I get paid? The secretary is late. A narrative situation: at first I thought would get paid, but it turns out I get paid in July, and I don't know how I'll live through the month. And so the real problems appear, which may draw out my relationship with Inés ever further.

A while later, at the College library. Maybe these absurd months had to end up this way. Few options: asking for borrowed money, asking for a place in the boardinghouse with rent overdue, living without money. I have learned to observe my own life from a distance. Everything consists of assessing those pure instants, at times when life no longer makes sense. Thinking "in perspective," which is the advice of people with nothing to lose.

Now that the motto of "write for the people" has been dispelled, many have decided to "write for the critics at the paper." Given that the hegemonic critics are *Primera Plana* idiots, all of them write in the style of Cortázar: torrential autobiographical stories, without form, without style, but "sincere," conforming with the poetics imposed by ex-surrealists who now earn their livings in executive seminars. As a result, they all seem the same (Néstor Sánchez, Mario Espósito . . .).

Sunday

His relationship with Inés had ended. He had thought often about the beauty and creation of meaning that comes with endings, and so he wanted only to avoid the rhetoric of stories that stretch pointlessly onward.

Nevertheless, the sadness did not abate and would not leave, he felt.

End of June

Ultimately, you never notice catastrophes. Separating with Inés seems like a commonplace event, but there is something more; I still expect her to come up the stairs, which means I am in a phase of transition. It also means that this is a time to open up and not allow myself to be surprised; everything is ready now, and I am the one seeking another path to follow. What you have tried to salvage is now lost and what you get, at best, is hopes that makes the past come forcefully back. You have to learn to avoid, to let it pass; heroism and courage are nothing more than clumsy sliding, breaking free gradually until only your fingers touch, and then the void, and you already know that you have started to forget that woman. I always lived like this and that is my life. This room is cold, of course, but I have few other solutions or places to go.

These days are like the bridges that sometimes appear in dreams. A suspension bridge on which I advance slowly while the noise of the river below distracts and frightens me. What I mean, he said, is that my decisions have already been made. Deep down, it is the events that choose for him.

Even the most absurd goal has some meaning and becomes connected once you discover its axis; it's like learning a new language, forgetting the language you created with a woman, a private language that only lasts as long as love. Then it falls away like a dead language—that is, a language no one now inhabits. I have also found this in certain tics that I was not aware of, which alienated me at once.

I always knew that the best way to live life was to invent a character and live according to him. If you have chosen well, there is a response ready for every situation. As though you could speak a foreign tongue that no one else knows and were waiting to meet a fellow countryman with whom to speak. You have to choose love according to some imaginary way of living life (and not the other way around). And isn't that happiness?

Meanwhile, just like those schematic dramas, reality follows its course. Real world, coup d'état. Illia's end. For a moment, I imagine that the political catastrophe is duplicating my personal drama: the end of love experienced as a coup d'état. In short, there is a turn to the right, the end of an open cultural climate. Hard years are surely coming, when we will need to work alone and in secret.

In the meantime, I am working on the short stories for the book. "Tarde de amor" went from twenty pages to twelve. The best thing I have written these days is "Tierna es la noche"; I wrote it in a strange way, drawing from a life experience that dwindled until it was only an image.

The worst thing is when I encounter traces of the past—today it was a ring—when a memory is imposed and then it feels like you are living outside of time. You can't change the past. You can't change the past? Throw out the ring.

My resistance to telling the story of our conflict and breakup comes from my theory, adopted many years before, that what happens in moments of great pain must never be told directly. You must find an object that allows you to half-state what you must never state directly: the ring I gave Inés, for example, a pure aquamarine that she returned to me because she didn't want to become emotional whenever she noticed that she still carried it with her. I have it here, on the table, like the trace of something that has died, and so it becomes an amulet that keeps its emotion. (I didn't throw it away.)

Sitting at Ramos on the sidewalk of Corrientes, after eating dinner, that strange atmosphere in which you seem to float amid the night. Listening to two regulars talking about horses and discussing the odds of guessing right at the races: study *The Hot Tip*, says a very frail, skinny man with fervent eyes, or go with chance and your intuition, responds a heavy and fat man, who gives off the sense that he has seen it all before. "You wouldn't believe me if I told you," the skinny one says, "that every time they threw me a hot tip or I followed the signals from the chair, I won. It wasn't many times, but they taught me a lesson." Then the conversation takes on a technical quality, and they start talking in a kind of idiolect that I can hardly decipher. And in this way, I can confirm that it is not only lovers who build up a personal language; wherever passion is at play, language is also forced to conform to the peculiarities of the people using it. At this point, the waiter comes up to serve me a coffee and reads my mind and asks, "What, the brunette didn't come?" I looked at him like he was pulling my leg and said, "No, she's traveling."

My relationship with reality, defined by loss, has only one sense: opacity and detachment. My stories, the place where I live, Inés, the books I read, my friends, everything that is exterior, seems—to me—to lie behind a dark glass, distant, alien.

Suddenly, as though it came from some distant place, I find myself with the image of my first meeting with Borges: I remember how he smiled with bad timing, how his hand caressed the air before changing the subject, his deceptive and persuasive humility.

I am in a bar over Lavalle, in the late beginning of night, and I think about going to see *The Knack* with Inés and whether she remembers, as I do, our last date. In front of me, a conspicuous stutterer clumsily tries to seduce a plump blonde girl. He said, slowly and laboriously, that she's a bad girl, then claimed several times that it's only one step from hate to love. A phrase the girl doesn't mind repeating ironically when she says she does not have another boyfriend. Inés arrives at the bar, hurried and beautiful, and leans in to give me a kiss as soon as she sits down; I realize that she is already someone else (she has become affected and snobbish).

If I could replicate—and determine—the secret rhythm of what is happening, up close, I could live life with some style.

Making love to her again that night, in the furnished apartment on Calle Tres Sargentos, was the end of an era that I was beginning to forget.

Friday, July 1

I should go back to *Hamlet* to escape the photographic realism of current Argentine theater. I should search there for the aggressive and criminal structure of family relationships and thus avoid the benign tone those works possess. In Argentine theater, families grow bored, melancholy, and nothing ever happens. Whereas, of course, the aggression and hate in Hamlet's family are transformed to devise a theatrical game. The characters revolve in their own orbits, always opposed to one another.

I am in La Plata, in the old Don Julio bar, and everything seems to copy the atmosphere I encountered when I first came in 1959. Back then, everything was amazing to me; I was living alone for the first time, far from the family novel (not at all naturalistic, very epic), and maybe I can now imagine that I have accomplished everything I hoped for in those days.

Saturday 2

Sometimes I think suddenly, like a flash, about Cacho in jail. Every time I visit him, he's the one comforting me. I bring him a grilled chicken, a carton of cigarettes, a can of peaches in syrup. We remember the old times, and I tell him what things are like on the outside.

Of course—to go back to the subject of tragedy—the hardest things, strangely, are not the great catastrophes that leave us cold and cut off from everything and confront us with critical decisions, but instead these slow, ambiguous moments when a tiny, contingent gesture—waving a hand in the air—can change reality abruptly, and events seem to depend on us and not on destiny. The matter, then, lies in living alert, passionate about the simple passage of time because, sometimes, your whole life falls into jeopardy from a single glance or a badly used word. Tragedies are caused not only by evil omens, but also by the misunderstandings that occur in life, and there's no need to go seeking the sphinx's riddle. I try to build a reality in the same way that Robinson built his life, without any hope, so lonely that he had to speak out into the night even if no one could hear him. The man who seeks salvation does so because he is already lost.

It also seems that you must learn to forget your notions about what you are for others. To learn, in this way, how to cast aside all attempts to be understood. Great wisdom comes from Nijinsky; when his friends came to see him in the asylum and comforted him with the hope that they would see him in the theater again, he answered, "No, I cannot dance, because I am mad."

Monday 4
In the monologue from *Hamlet* at the end of the second act, there is a theory of the imaginary close to *bovarysme*—that is, a theory of illusion, or at least a way of thinking about the ways that fictions participate in reality. The prince remembers having heard that criminals witnessing theater have felt so profoundly moved by the spell of the scene that, then and there, they have revealed their crimes. From there, the sentence I quote here from memory and translate as follows: "The play's the thing wherein I'll catch the conscience of the king; *el drama es el lazo en el que atraparé la conciencia del rey.*" If I go back to my note from a few days ago about the ways in which we are seen by others, we could say not only that the theatrical stage is the site of performance—that is, of identification—but also that all of life in some secret sense is a performance (for others), which does not mean that it isn't true.

In Scene ii of Act III, Hamlet thinks that the purpose of the dramatic art, from its origins up to the present—he says—has been, and is, to hold up a mirror, so to speak—according to the prince—so that men may see their true faces. The weight of delusions upon reality. What we call real is, for the individual, a fabric of delusions.

Therefore, it makes sense that it pains me to remember Saturday night. I saw Roberto Jacoby and Eduardo Costa. An entertaining and "modern"

307

conversation. Then Inés came in, a bit irritable, and as things became clear, she was less secure. In brief, the story of the party in the horrible ramshackle house on Calle Olleros. Afterward, in Patricia Peralta Ramos's exotic apartment, where Antonio Gasalla and Carlos Perciavalle recited *Romeo and Juliet*, taking turns playing the role of the woman. I ended the night in Gotán, listening to Rovira at a table with Pirí Lugones.

As for the magazine, the political situation caused by Onganía's coup will surely make the publication of the next issue impossible. The University is also affected by the coup d'état. Once again, everything must be started over from the beginning.

Wednesday 6
The difficulty does not lie in losing someone (for example Inés) but rather in choosing the moment of the loss. It is always a slow retreat, the same as when you start visiting a friend less and less, reading a poet less and less, going to a bar less and less, gently retracing the path of return to avoid injury. Like walking backward down a dark corridor, feeling around and moving back: you always look them in the face and smile, not saying goodbye, as you see them grow distant.

Women loved and admired him at first, but then something made them perceive the emptiness and they backed out—he thought—and he aided in their retreat, opened the door so they could leave unhindered.

Sunday 10
They always leave in the end; who knows where they go. The most persistent thing is sadness, an exhaustion that falls over him as he awakens and surprises him. In any case, in the middle of that void came Julia, a student in my history class. Her or anyone else—it didn't matter, but it was her. Her incredible face, her past, which she told me about quickly, as though afraid of forgetting, the two of us sitting in that bar, by the window over Calle Alem, in Bajo. Now, as always, I think I must hide or

to flee, but yesterday was very pleasant, going around between the bars we found open, each speaking in an intricate individual language that the other will have to learn.

Now, best if I steep some maté, looking out at the light from the street. Sometimes I start wondering if I just need a place, need to stop going in circles, stop going out, but then suddenly I think that the best thing would be to sleep for a few months, wake up in October, for example. But for now I will try to sleep, more moderately, until noon.

Monday
There is always a moment when things become clear; recently, stretched out on the bed, not long ago, while translating a story by Hemingway, I understood that I hopelessly fall in love with tempestuous women (with intense pasts, that is what attracts me). Julia runs away with a musician at age eighteen, he abandons her in Bahía Blanca, she returns to her house defeated, so to speak, and immediately gets married to the family doctor, and they have a daughter, whom Julia abandons when the child is six months old. Ever since then, she tells me, she has heard a baby crying without seeing her daughter. She left her there, like a sacrifice, so that she could live her own life, alone. What makes her story circular is the fact that her mother had had a fling with the man who was her father. She never told her who he was, never gave her the name. Her mother got married again, had two other children, and Julia was always the illegitimate daughter that her mother's husband—and her siblings—watched with distrust. You can see how hard it can be to describe the fluctuations of a family history. Julia told it to me in broken fragments, with irony and some cynicism (although she cried at one point, but much later, once we were already out in the street and had already forgotten her family novel).

"Yes, I fly, I fly ceaselessly. I cannot avoid it . . . I know very well what I fly from, but not what I seek," Montaigne.

When I think about characters, I remember Michael Craig, the husband of Claudia Cardinale in Visconti's *Sandra*—a measured man, never crossing the line in the midst of all the chaos.

At this point, the best thing would be for me to go back and start correcting the short stories. Wrap up the book once and for all. As it were, I am going to take advantage of the vacation to paint my apartment. But what happens is that, these days, I am also afraid of choosing a color to paint my walls.

I cook two soft-boiled eggs, keep an eye on my wristwatch for the three minutes needed to achieve a perfect soft-boiled egg. I imagine the egg losing its whiteness, somewhere between milky and yellowish, and beginning to harden, but not too much, not enough to become a hard-boiled egg.

Wednesday
An ambiguous meeting with Jorge Álvarez about publishing the classics in the collection that I am going to direct. We will begin with *Notes from Underground* by Dostoevsky (prologue by George Steiner), then *Robinson Crusoe* with a prologue by Joyce, then *Bouvard and Pécuchet* by Flaubert with a prologue by Raymond Queneau. Then I went to La Paz and was surprised to read Beatriz Guido's generous opinions: "I prefer reading the young ones, Emilio Renzi, author of some magnificent stories, because they are not emotionally implicated in the past."

Thursday 14
Will I finally get paid? Several things depend on it. I must also learn techniques for survival.

"I'll return with iron limbs; dark skin, a furious look: from my mask I'll be judged as of mighty race," Rimbaud.

Wednesday 20

I am approaching a time of silence; the introspection will suddenly come to an end. Indifference once more.

"All of my novels began as short stories. I never started by saying, well, I am writing a novel," Hemingway.

Saturday

For me, finding a tone is always the way to resolve unclear moments. My best stories always depend on the tone of the prose and not on the incidents.

Wednesday

How can you know which is the best, among all the possible stories that present themselves while you are writing? It is always about making decisions; writing is making decisions. I never know what the story will be like until I write it. And as I write it, I let myself be led by intuition and the rhythm of the prose.

Joyce: "The task I set myself technically in writing a book from eighteen different points of view and in as many styles, all apparently unknown or undiscovered by my fellow tradesmen."

Sunday

Sometimes, to amuse myself, it occurs to me to walk down the street, talking alone. I speak out loud, gesticulating; bystanders turn around to look at me, and I find that amusing, honestly.

Tuesday 2

This spacious bar with glass walls near the station, these days that are all the same to me and pass, imperceptible, without prior ideas of what is going to happen. Restless, as in other times, I sometimes ask myself how I will break out of this fallow time, filled with tedium and a monotonous inner monologue.

Saturday 13

I arrive at the house; she is with another man. I am with Julia now. After everything, I no longer even have the memories left to me. What was the point of the three long years I spent with her? Loving her. Finishing a book, coming to live in Buenos Aires, making my living.

We are saved by our inability to imagine the consequences that the events we live through must have. The only thing I can do is try to avoid the memories. Brush off the images the way you take off a suit.

Tuesday 16

I spend the night mired in Librium, made sluggish by dreams that do nothing more that remind me of things I want to forget. I try with effort to "get used to the idea" that Inés no longer exists and is moving further away from me, as though going backwards in time until becoming a stranger. Days and days will pass, diverse experiences will turn her into another person, different from the one I have loved.

Wednesday 17

A slight pain, imperceptible, made up of images, as though I were standing before a cataclysm that has already taken place and, covered in dust, thinking about how laborious the reconstruction will be. Perhaps inside—to put it that way—of three months or four months or six months, these days that drag along slowly, that are so painful to endure, will produce nothing but a melancholic nostalgia. A person in love surrenders to the relief of passing time, the only consolation in the face of loss.

The only comfort left to me is knowing that everything was foreseen and that, even as I began writing in this notebook, the dice were cast but I didn't know how to make myself receptive in time. Who knows, however, whether I could have held back and not gone looking for her. You need great courage to retreat before the fire alarms sound. To decide, beforehand, that it will be impossible.

I am going to finish this notebook tomorrow and, as always, magically, my life will change as soon as I start to write on blank pages. Anyway, I will go to Gotán tomorrow, I will sit down at a table with Julia and reveal the social "experience" of the ending with Inés.

Thursday
Our last meeting was a somber one at El Foro. Inés, in white, flustered and sad. Both feeling some desire to cry and not speaking. We exchanged cherished objects as though they were words. Then I watched her go and set out on the street to walk the opposite way.

Cacho's address. Dolores Prison, Calle 3, number 526, side entrance.

I go to Gotán with Julia; my friends are used to these changes and don't ask for any explanation or reasons.

Saturday 20
The imbalance of "The Pit and the Pendulum" comes out of an error in perspective; this story, told in the third person, requires (like almost all of Poe's short stories) the first person in order to reify the horror of the experience. Poe's best stories are always confessions.

Wednesday 24
Deep down it is always about the same thing, rebuilding the collapsed structures so that we can live in them. The only thing that matters is the strength of the buildings and not the means used to raise them. And yet, it is also true that the methods determine the durability of the structure.

Poe's cruel stories are grounded on this sentence from "The Premature Burial": "What I have now to tell is of my own actual knowledge—of my own positive and personal experience." The other technique lies in the scientific, nonliterary quality, which legitimized the events (the plots seem extracted from publications or are prefaced with meticulous theories).

Thursday, October 6

An unexpected period of happiness, which has lingered since the start of spring. On one hand, a great physical, intellectual, musical closeness with Julia. And also the irresistible, ecstatic way in which I wrote "Mata-Hari 55" in two days. In that story, I microscopically employed the method of storytelling truth that I am thinking of using in the novel. Perhaps some news from outer space adds to the good humor. Recently, Samuel Amaral told me that in an issue of *Análisis* magazine dedicated to Argentine literature I appear as the most read among young people aged eighteen to twenty-two. They are readers of my own generation, barely younger than myself.

I have to recall the way in which I left the universe of Inés and entered the world of Julia, coldly and without regrets. Everything changed; love is also a language that you must learn again each time, to forget breakups and separations. As though the language of passion were a single one, which transforms along with each person, so that you forget the words of the past and learn the words of the future. A single language, whose syntax and verbal content changes according to the circumstances of love.

Monday, October 10

In the middle of the afternoon I see Inés by chance in El Ramos, the same table on the sidewalk where we were talking in February, in the middle of summer, she with her hair very short and some yellow earrings, very beautiful. I had forgotten the words to speak to her with, so that today's conversation was interrupted several times by misunderstandings. An unhappy meeting for both of us. Each one now starting to be forgotten.

I resist correcting the stories, am certain that they are well written in the first draft. As though style were decided in one go and any (conventional) "improvement" would destroy the effect of the whole. Either way, I have to close the book and forget about it so that I can begin writing the story

314

of the criminals who flee to Uruguay. So close to me that I have to write it as though it were taking place now.

Wednesday 12
Why doesn't anyone talk about the reactionary and archaic meaning of Columbus Day, the so-called "día de la raza?" I imagine it derives from the Hispanicist tradition: when they lost the last colonies with the war in Cuba in 1898, the Spaniards invented the myth of a common culture between the mother country and what they called Hispanic America.

When, by chance—like someone finding attractive and slightly perverse photos in a forgotten drawer of the family house—I reread some of these notebooks, in which days of intense happiness run across intense spells of sorrow. I perceive, in an unexpected lesson from life, an emotional relativism, a fluctuation of emotions that obeys no visible logic. When they are set down in writing, states of mind turn into physical spaces that are repeated here and there, the same way that someone in his childhood home—where he found some disturbing photos of his mother in a chest of drawers—happens by chance to pass once more through the bedrooms of the house, some dark and dismal, others illuminated in the full light of the morning sun. We could describe a landscape, modeling it on the rooms where we were happy (or wretched) in far-off childhood.

Within the same day, I see *Diary of a Chambermaid* by Buñuel, in the early afternoon, at Normandie, and *Pierrot le fou* by Godard, close to sunset, at Loire.

Thursday 13
There is a lack of gravity in these days of waiting; nothing significant seems to happen, and yet something I cannot imagine makes itself known.

Why does everything always come from so far away? For example, yesterday Inés leaving the theater with G. at the end of Godard amid the drizzle, a stranger, as I got into the car with Julia, with Nene and Alberto, already in another territory, speaking another language, abroad. Am I not an image as well, and don't I, too, have strength and sense? So, why should I think about my importance from a single hostile place, where I am invisible?

Friday 14
I continue my resistance to correcting the stories; I am afraid of breaking an unstable equilibrium upon which, imperceptibly, the plots are supported.

I witness an insulting situation. Two German professors speak to a professor who has been condemned by her colleagues. She makes them sit at the table, get comfortable, "break the ice" (they have come to deliver terrible news, and she knows it).

Sunday 16
Like someone testing his own courage or the scope of his chance decisions or using himself as an object of experimentation, I left, walking slowly and disdainfully, not looking at anyone, walked out of the overpriced restaurant with glass walls without paying.

What is valuable in Faulkner is the constant presence of someone telling the story; the narrators circulate, but they all have the same plaintive and furious tone.

Monday 17
A month ago we were living in Dipi Di Paola's house. I have always felt an attraction to places that do not belong to me, where someone has lived before me and left a mark through the furniture, the paintings, the books. We stayed there, Julia and I, like two furtive lovers secretly inhabiting the house of the friend they are betraying.

I have gone back to the heavy days in which I struggle to come back to life, as though I did not want to wake. How much was I upset by my encounter—that's what I will call this crossing of two strangers—with Inés last Wednesday, leaving the theater? It seems like I can't stand her going on, living her life without me there.

Tuesday 18

Now she even appears to me in dreams. Strangely, I have a date with Inés, who shows up with G. I think I made a mistake. What's more, they have to go somewhere and I don't want to go with them.

Wednesday 19

I pass the night without sleeping, returning, it seems, to insomnia: I have been prone to sleep loss all of my life. I can't remember any other night like last night. I thought I was traveling in a long-distance train, I had settled into the upper bunk of the personal cabin in which I was prepared to spend a week. The feeling of forward motion, the sound of the tracks, and the light of the deserted towns that we swiftly crossed made me fall asleep near sunrise. Light sleep, the stage immediately preceding sleep, has an oneiric quality, and yet we are the ones imagining what we see.

Part of the night I was also scheming about inscriptions for the book I still have not published or finished writing. In these images, when you personally give a book you have written to a friend—or someone—and sign a copy after writing a phrase, isn't there a distant sense of literature? We always write for particular people, and you could write an essay on the meaning of inscriptions.

The insane lucid state of five in the morning, after the long meeting with Ramón T., drinking gin. He wants to convince me to continue with *Literatura y Sociedad* magazine. He has a clear notion of what must be done, since it is dedicated to building on what he calls "the revolutionary situation." A literary magazine or an attack on the headquarters have the same purpose, to him, as long as someone is able to connect one truth with the other. In a sense, it is classic paranoid thought. Like lunatics, professional revolutionaries are convinced that "everything has to do with everything."

I make a note of one of the inscriptions that occurred to me in the night. *To Lucía, guilty of 87 percent of this book.* (I like to include a number in an inscription.)

I came out of insomnia with bleary eyes and one certainty: I cannot accept that I decided to lose Inés.

But today, she told me, you can free yourself mechanically from this divided body. In an era, she said, when there are stimulants and sedatives, it's inconceivable to have love pangs that last more than six hours. She was smiling, young and beautiful, when she went on, cynically announcing the truths of the world, and said, "In an era with cosmetic surgery and beauty schools, it is senseless for you to prefer one woman over another. In an era," she added, "when there are birth-control pills and artificial insemination, it's impossible to still pass on our flaws, our angst, and our ugliness to our or others' children." She leaned in over the table and asked if I agreed.

Saturday 22
A special time in my life, I can say, without introspection, only facts. I spend the days with Julia in this city where I lived years ago, where no one now knows me. I drink gin with her after we make love so I can sleep. And I have nightmares about Inés every night. A man of habits, a man who does not want to lose anything, not even things he himself abandons.

Sunday 23
The story that has given me the most work is "Tarde de amor." I keep revising it over and over again. It seems a clockwork mechanism with

pendulums that must be balanced. In this rough and final version, there are two possible endings. I don't know if that is a merit or a fault.

Tuesday 25
The cat died. It was called The Consul (because it always seemed drunk). Yesterday afternoon it was staring at me from a bench where it lay. I thought, *This cat is strange, something is wrong with this cat,* and it was already dead (with its eyes wide open).

Wednesday 26
An era of underground happiness. Days and days without leaving this vast and luminous room, witnessing the new trials of a passionate love with Julia. For now, we each exchange words in our personal language and the encounters are, more than anything, physical.

I am content with this new history, despite my nostalgia. I understand that other woman, who was the first I truly loved. Reality or cosmic guidance always helps with our burden, and I force myself, so to speak, to follow the path after breaking up with Inés and finding a new intense passion, etc.

Running away is an end in itself, Cacho would say. The speed sensitizes, sharpens, intensifies everything. Landscape, woman, ordinary life, friends. Everything takes on a new dimension while you are running and then, once the door of the car is closed, you and the car are the same thing. Man assimilates the motors, feels alone, free, at two hundred kilometers per hour life is purer. He said this after having ridden on motorcycles since a young age, later riding in "prepared" cars (which he takes the precaution of stealing first).

Thursday 27
I have memories of the origins behind the stories in this book.

"En el calabozo": The first thing I remember is an afternoon in 1961 at the Tiro Federal in Mar del Plata. A soldier, I remember his shaven head; he told me the story.

"Mi amigo" strangely arose when I went to visit Helena with a friend and he amended my high opinion on Bioy Casares. Well, what if you told me you didn't like it?, he said, making it clear to me.

"En el terraplén": Lina Flores told me the anecdote in El Bosque in La Plata and I liked the double ending.

"La honda": Walking down a dirt road one Sunday, I saw some laborers working and suddenly discovered the story.

"Mata-Hari 55": Manolo Comesaña told me the story, last year. The protagonist's successive changes in name were suggested to me by Inés, unintentionally, when I discovered her speaking on the phone and saying that her name was Enriqueta.

"Las actas del juicio": The plot arose in the "Argentine History" class that Beatriz Bosch taught in 1963. There were several versions. A discussion with Julio Bogado made me clean up the excess; a conversation with Inés (who didn't like that the story was told in plural by a "we") led me to invent a narrator for it and justify his tone, making him the man responsible for Urquiza's death.

Monday, October 31
Novel. (The characters make the technique visible, which has some effect on the truth of what they tell.) "Much of what Costa narrated was made known in the presence of his voice on the recording and could therefore contain distortions."

The purpose of including "ideas" or thoughts in a story is to complicate the motivations. The distorted reflection, slightly arbitrary, is justified in that it is valuable not only as a theory, but also as part of the story's plot (when it is uttered or thought by characters or narrators implicated in another world—that is, in the relationships that weave together in the interior of the novel).

For me, it is about reproducing—as though I were recording it—the perception of reality in the midst of the action and danger, which define Cacho's life "philosophy" (it is antagonistic to reality and will therefore "crash" against the stone wall of the real).

Wednesday, November 2
For a while I have lived precariously, with a hundred pesos per day, very little cash. I always feel a slight restlessness caused by hunger, but I never think about the future; economy doesn't matter to me if I know that I'm going to work all night (one economy against another, necessity and desire, as they say, Laurel and Hardy—the Thin One and the Fat One).

I found a more fluid beginning for my story "La honda": "I don't let myself be deceived by boys. I know that they lie, that they are always putting on innocent faces and laughing at everyone underneath."

Thursday 3
I remembered a goodbye and a meeting. Suddenly came the image in which I myself was present. At first I didn't see her in that bar facing the station, but later we talked agitatedly about "various things" (a crime the day before in that same place). In the end, the train arrived and we parted, comfortable. Earlier, I had received a letter.

Facing the path of the novel that makes conventions visible and says "this is a novel" and puts belief in its fiction in crisis—for example, Günter Grass, Néstor Sánchez (they say, for example, "It is raining now, or maybe it would be better to say that the sun is high in the novel . . . "). There is a less obvious but very experimental tradition (Conrad, Faulkner) that justifies the narrator by explaining the reasons why he is telling the story and implicitly signaling the possible distortions. (In Faulkner, there is no narrator who orders and hierarchizes the material; the characters take the floor and tell their own versions.)

Reading Conrad, with his multiple narrators in the same story, with a high and literary prose, Faulkner's admiration is understandable. In Conrad, the fiction—or rather, the already storied quality of the account that is going to be told ("the legendary tale" in *The Duel*)—is always present, and then there are the interruptions and commentaries of the second-ary narrator (Marlow), which underline the presence of someone who is relating the story, which has already taken place, to a group of listeners. The cutoffs and interruptions and explanations allow jumps in time, lend the story the tone of a lived experience. In *The Duel*, the established narrator narrates a story that is already partially known, which suffers deformations as a result of being interpreted from the outside by some-one who doesn't know it well (but tells it, fascinated by the mystery of what he does not know about the characters' motives, although he does record the events that have transpired).

Thursday 17
Certain stories can't be corrected because the structure and the tone set out directly toward a mistaken denouement. Correcting them involves the risk of juxtaposing several "meanings" that, in any case, don't enrich the story. I do not believe in "committed" subjects as justification for a story. Because of this, I am not going to include "Desagravio" in the book, despite the fact that its subject is the bombing of Plaza de Mayo by the Naval Aviation in 1955 and it has political resonance. In order to create the tone of Peronism I have to narrate my own experience, or rather, my father's experience.

Paul Valéry recommends, in a letter to André Gide, *Discourse on the Method* as a model for the modern novel. It relates the life on an idea and not, as is customary, the life of a person.

Monday 21
Yesterday with Beatriz Guido, always outlandish and entertaining. Dizzy-ing in her baroque house, antique furniture and circular conversations.

Edgardo Cozarinsky was there, and he gave me the first edition of a Manuel Puig novel.

I prepare seven copies of the book of short stories to send to the Casa de las Américas competition. An insane project, with carbon paper that the portable machine only admits in small doses. I have to go over the whole book three times. I decide on *Jaulario* as the title for the volume (it bothers me that it sounds like Cortázar's *Bestiario* and Neruda's *Crepusculario*, but I can't come up with a better name and do not want to use the title of one story for the entire book [but why not?]).

Tuesday 29
I left the book with Jorge Álvarez last night. Now I understand the void that follows the moment when you have managed to finish something after months. How long will I withstand the uncertainty of living from day to day? But maybe that is where the merit lies, not thinking about the future or thinking that I won't make it to the month of March alive.

There is a scrap merchant, a junkman, who passes every morning at this hour calling at the top of his lungs that he buys disused materials. "I buy old beds, I buy mattresses, I buy broken chairs, I buy heaters, boilers." He is a buyer who announces his intention to find objects that have remained outside the market; he seems like a collector and reminds me, through an audible likeness, of the voice of another second-hand dealer a year ago in Boca, who talked to himself, every morning at eight, when I was about to go to bed after working all night. And I was just going to bed after I heard him crossing Calle Olavarría.

December 4
Ramón Torres Molina tells me, as a friend, that my book is the best book of short stories of the decade. It is the first reading I have had. I gave the book to Celina Lacay, José Sazbón, Jorge Álvarez, and Beatriz Guido to read.

323

Fact. Between 1875 and 1907 Argentina imported enough wire to surround the perimeter of the Republic 140 times with a weave of seven strands. As I sometimes say—to frighten those who practice determinism outright in literature—when they fenced in the fields with wire, the gaucho was finished . . .

Wednesday 7
Last night, José Sazbón talks to me about the book. Critiques of "Mi amigo," "En el terraplén," and "La honda." He finds issues with the ending of "En el calabozo." He likes the tone of the book very much, the quality of the style, the temperance in narration. According to him, the best stories are "Tarde de amor," "Tierna es la noche," and "Las actas del juicio."

Saturday 10
Once again I run into a woman I have lived with while delivering books to the library. Now with Inés, I let her take whatever she wants because it doesn't matter to me. It isn't even valuable as a metaphor for the things you carry and leave behind when love ends. Finally, drinking beer on the sidewalk, stupidly.

I went down Diagonal Sur and sent the book to the competition in Cuba by plane, or rather, in copies with airmail paper. Praise for the book from Jorge Álvarez and Beatriz Guido.

Sunday 11
I see myself, sitting on the hallway floor of the dismantled house, days before leaving Adrogué behind to live in Mar del Plata. I have a notebook and am writing the first entry of this diary.

Several concurrences among the readers of the book. The best, "Tierna es la noche," "Mata-Hari 55," and "Las actas del juicio." Everyone rejects the story "Mi amigo." What worries me is the criticisms of "En el calabozo," which for José Sazbón are formal problems and for others (Álvarez, Frontini) are at root "gratuitous violence." I don't share that critique, but I have to revise the story.

In Cortázar, the brand names that accompany objects in the stories have a fetishistic connotation, in the sense that they are the magical illusion of advertising (which is based on the brand). The clash between an object and its designation produces an imbalance in style; the "sign of knowledge," that he is an expert in the privileged objects of the market, becomes too evident. The same thing happens with jazz and with books. Objects that gleam and illuminate the consumer in his novels.

Last night—as Cortázar would say, in order to gain a reputation for knowledge—I went to listen to Piazzolla at Nonino with several friends (who don't much matter to me): Frontini, Mae, Humberto Riva.

Another function of objects: in a Dickens story, the narrator has, as proof that he has entered an imaginary universe, a pair of eyeglasses (which he brought back from there).

Mae, a woman who has a nomadic literary knowledge and ties up her surroundings with the provincial snobbery of La Plata. She makes me think of Hilda Edward from *Point Counter Point* by A. Huxley, and Mrs. Headway from *The Siege of London*, and old Miss Bordereau, with her flashes of irony, in *The Aspern Papers* by Henry James.

A decision. The driver Juan Gálvez refuses to put on his safety belt because he is afraid of burning to death if there is an accident, but he is killed in a race because the car crashes into the concrete.

In *Acto y ceniza*, M. Peyrou commits the same stupid schematizations of any social novelist "on the left," but with the measured cynicism of an author on the right. He is a kind of writer who doesn't know what he is doing and confuses his novels with the editorials in political newspapers. It is a problem of false poetics. Or can good novels really be written along these lines, with an explicit (and trivial) political thesis? It isn't about a character's being politically defined, but about a book whose a priori bias is to prove an existing thesis (in most cases, political).

It is curious that *Under the Volcano*, behind its immense jumble of words, manages to maintain ambiguity. The dialogue is fluid and easy despite the fact that it is explicit and constantly transmits thoughts and ideas; the novel survives like a great ambiguous fresco, full of nuances and overtones, recreated laboriously in the raging sea of his drunken and Faulknerian language. The virtue of the book is that it moves forward in a narrative present (not in terms of the verb) of pure action—even if the action is minimal and blurred—which lasts for an entire day, and closes with the death of the Consul, clearly announced in the first chapter. He is going to die and it is known.

Friday 16
After the separation some time ago, I took refuge in La Plata. First in Dipi's house and then in friends' houses, until I finally rented this enormous and brightly lit room with a balcony that opens over Diagonal 80. I make a note of this to summarize my situation and indicate that I have spent all day today and yesterday transporting two heavy suitcases of papers, journals, and books from Buenos Aires. The man who carries with him everything of value in his life—a value that, like all true values, only he understands. If something sets me apart and supports my conception of literature, my personal brand, it's that I've never had—or tried to have—a place of my own (or private); I live in hotels, in boardinghouses, in friends' houses, always in passing, because for me that is the state of literature: there is no personal place, nor is there private property. I write to you, I joke, from there. A man from no place.

Sunday

Recently, dodging cars on 1st and 60th. Under the drizzle, heavy thoughts about my economic future. What to do after March?

One of the most surprising social games is trying to guess what others think about the things that wait for them, what they have to do.

December 29

I have come to Mar del Plata to visit my mother. I spend the mornings on the sea and the afternoons at the Municipal Library. The clock with giant Roman numerals is still there, the static happiness of this sphere, which sustained me in the delirious search for a world where I could settle down by my own choice. You "decide" to be a writer and then clear things up only so as to become what you said you were. This library, very good, founded by socialists who loved culture—people laughed at them—in which I can find everything I look for, that is, I can find everything I needed when I was seventeen or eighteen years old and would read two or three books per day.

Friday 30

I enjoy returning to La Plata, where I effectively began my life, I would say if I were telling my own history. Alone, without anyone, with passing and fleeting loves, living in anonymous boardinghouse rooms, I created the space I had imagined and lived there, intensely, and then began writing my first stories. Suddenly I remembered the end of last year, in Cacho's apartment in Ugarteche, while he made his secret life on the coast, where the police arrested him in the end: all of the future was available to me. Now, by contrast, I have come back to this place as though I had never been here.

A Novel. Involuntary memory. A race of cars and motorcycles, the "masculine" world of fast turns through the night with Cacho, by the river: paradise lost.

Bimba: at first the naïve girl, a figure he used in his work (a lady of the night); then, gradually, her true character becomes visible. Some time later, Inés tells me that Bimba seduced her and got her into bed. Why didn't you invite me? I asked. Now, with Cacho in prison, no one knows who betrayed him. Bimba is possessive, malicious. A very brave and aggressive woman, but she does love him (she describes her history in front of him, which makes her more perverse).

I have to stress the significance of this year, to which I ascribe a special transcendence. I remember the room on Hotel Callao, Inés stretched out on the bed reading, while from the balcony I watched the beloved streets of the city where I was finally living. Now I'm looking for a place where I can live (Cacho's apartment, a boardinghouse, whatever it may be, but outside of the suicidal sprawl).

I will end the year with a quote from the book that I am reading once again. "'I understand nothing,' Ivan went on, as though in delirium. 'I don't want to understand anything now. I want to stick to the fact. I made up my mind long ago not to understand. If I try to understand anything, I shall be false to the fact, and I have determined to stick to the fact,'" F. Dostoevsky, *The Brothers Karamazov*.

17

The Greek Coin

I have been told many times of the man who, in a house in the neighborhood of Flores, is hiding a replica of the city that he has been working on for years. He has constructed it with tiny materials and at such a reduced scale that we can see it all at once, up close and manifold and seemingly distant in the soft dawn light.

The city is always far away and that sensation of distance from so close up is unforgettable. You can see the buildings and plazas and avenues and see the suburbs trailing off into the west until they are lost to the countryside.

It is not a map or a miniature, but a synoptic machine; all of the city is there, concentrated, reduced to its essence. The city is Buenos Aires, but modified and altered by the madness and microscopic vision of its creator.

The man says his name is Russell and he is a photographer, or earns his living as a photographer, and he has a darkroom on Calle Bacacay and will go for months without leaving his house, periodically reconstructing the southern neighborhoods that the swelling river floods and destroys every time autumn arrives.

Russell believes that the real city depends on his replica, and is therefore insane. Rather, he is therefore not a simple photographer. He has altered the relationships of representation in such a way that the real city is the one he hides in his house and the other is only an illusion or memory.

The floor plan follows the sketch of the geometric city imagined by Juan de Garay, with the expansions and modifications that history has imposed onto the distant rectangular structure. Between the ravines that are visible from the river and the tall buildings forming a rampart on the north frontier, some traces of the old Buenos Aires survive—its calm wooded neighborhoods and pastures of dry grass.

The man has imagined a city lost in memory and has replicated it precisely as he remembers it. Reality is not the object being represented, but rather the space where a fantastical world takes place.

The construction can only be visited by one spectator at a time. That approach, incomprehensible to everyone, is nevertheless clear to me: the photographer reproduces, in the contemplation of the city, the act of reading. The person who contemplates it is like a reader and must therefore be alone. That aspiration to privacy and isolation explains the secret that, until now, has surrounded his project.

I always thought that the secret blueprint by the photographer from Flores was the diagram for a future city. It is easy to imagine the photographer, lit up by the red light of his darkroom, who, in the empty night, believes that his synoptic machine is a secret cipher of destiny, and the changes he makes in his city are then reproduced in the neighborhoods and streets of Buenos Aires, but blown-up and sinister.

The alterations and erosions that the replica suffers—the little collapses and the rains that flood the low neighborhoods—become real in Buenos Aires in the form of brief catastrophes and inexplicable accidents.

The photographer acts as an archaeologist unearthing the remains of a forgotten civilization. He does not discover or determine reality except for when it is a series of ruins (and in this sense, of course, he has, in an elusive and subtle fashion, created political art). He is married to those obstinate inventors who keep alive what has ceased to exist. We know that the Egyptian definition of the sculptor was precisely that: "One who keeps alive."

The city is thus concerned with replicas and representations, with reading and solitary perception, with the presence of what has been lost.

In short, it is concerned with the ways of rendering visible the invisible and anchoring the clear images that we no longer see but that still survive like phantoms living among us.

This private and clandestine work, constructed patiently in the attic of a house in Buenos Aires, is linked, in secret, to certain traditions of the art of reading on La Plata River: for the photographer from Flores, as for Pierre Menard or the anonymous editor of Marta Riquelme's memoirs by Martínez Estrada, for Xul Solar or Torres-García, the tension between real object and the imaginary object does not exist: everything is real, everything is there, and you pass among the parks and streets, dazzled by an ever-distant presence.

The diminutive city is like a Greek coin, sunk down into the bed of a river, that shines under the last light of afternoon. It does not represent anything except for what has been lost. It is there, dated but outside of time, and possesses the characteristic of art; it is worn away, does not age, has been created as a useless object that exists only for itself.

In this time, I recall the pages Claude Lévi-Strauss wrote in *The Savage Mind* on the work of art as a miniature model. Reality works on the real scale, "*tandis que l'art travaille à échelle réduite.*" Art is a synthetic form of the universe, a microcosm that reproduces the specificity of the world without passing for mimesis. The Greek coin is a scale model of an entire economy and an entire civilization and, at the same time, is no more than a lost object shining at sunset in the transparency of the water.

A few days ago, I finally decided to visit the studio of the photographer from Flores. It was a clear spring afternoon and the magnolias were starting to bloom. I paused in front of the tall inner door and rang the bell, which sounded off in the distance, in the depths of the corridor that could be glimpsed from the other side.

After a while, a gaunt and tranquil man, with gray eyes and gray beard, dressed in a leather apron, opened the door. With extreme friendliness and in a low voice, almost a whisper, in which you could perceive the harsh tone of a foreign language, he greeted me and made me enter.

331

The house had an entryway that led to a patio, and at the end of the patio was the study. It was a wide, one-story house with a pitched roof and tables, maps, machines, and strange metal and glass instruments were piled up within it. Photographs of the city and drawings of ambiguous forms abounded on the walls. Russell lit the lamps and invited me to sit. In his eyes under thick brows burned a malicious spark. He smiled and then I gave him the old coin that I had brought for him.

He looked at it up close with great attention and then moved it away from his sight and moved his hand around to feel the light weight of the metal.

"A drachma," he said. "For the Greeks, it was an object both trivial and magical . . . *Ousía*, the word that conveyed being, substance, likewise meant wealth, money." He paused. "A coin was a tiny private oracle, and, at life's crossroads, they would toss it into the air to know what to do." He stood and pointed to one side. In a plan of Buenos Aires, the city stood out among the drawings and machines. "A map," he said, "is a synthesis of reality, a synoptic mirror that guides us through life's confusion. You must know how to read between the lines to find the path. Pay attention. If someone studies the map of the place where he lives, he first has to find the place where he stands, looking at the map. Here, for example," he said, "is my house. This is Calle Puán, this is Avenida Rivadavia. You are here now." He drew a cross. "This is you." He smiled. "Our grammar has no synoptic sight. Synoptic representation generates comprehension, and comprehension consists of seeing connections. Therein lies the importance of discovering and inventing intermediate case studies." He opened a book. "Reading teaches us to see synoptically. The concept of synoptic representation defines our form of representation, the way in which we see things. There are representations that are connected to the things that they signify through a visible relationship. But, in that visibility, they make the original fade away. When you look at an object as though it were the image of something else, it produces what I have decided to call synoptic substitution. Such is reality. We live in a world of maps and replicas. The concept of synoptic representation is of fundamental importance. It defines our means of representation, the way in which we see things. This synoptic representation is the medium for comprehension, which consists of seeing connections. Wait and see. "That was," he said, "the passion that inspired the readers."

Serial killers murder replicas, a series of replicas that repeat and must be eliminated, one after another, because they reappear unexpectedly, perfect, on a dark street, in the center of an abandoned plaza, like nocturnal mirages. For example, Jack the Ripper was searching the interior of his victims to discover the mechanical elements of their construction. These English girls, beautiful and fragile, were mechanical dolls, surrogates.

He, on the other hand—in contrast to Jack the Ripper—wanted to set aside human beings and only to build reproductions of the spaces the replicas inhabited.

He spoke faster and faster, in a low voice, and I could only capture the murmur of his words, resounding like static hallucinations.

"We are attracted to the idea of one thing that becomes another, which is exactly the same, and is substituted for its double, and therefore we produce images. But while the division in representation concerns an unfolding relationship, assembled around a replacement, the synoptic substitution, what I call the synoptic substitution, signifies an immediate suppression of the replacement. The replica is an object transformed into the pure idea of the absent object."

Then he said that his true name was a secret from which the city was suspended. That it was the innermost center of the construction.

"The southern cross . . . " he added, with a smile.

There was a silence. Through the window, the distant shriek of a bird reached us.

Russell seemed to awaken and remember that I had brought him the Greek coin, and he held it once again in the palm of his open hand.

"Did you make it?" He watched me with a knowing look. "If it's fake, then it's perfect," he said, and then studied the subtle lines and metal ribbing through the magnifying glass. "It isn't fake, you see?" You could see slight marks, made by someone with a knife or stone. A woman perhaps, from the contour of the stroke. "And look," he said, "someone has bitten the coin here to test if it was authentic. A peasant, maybe, or a slave."

He put the coin on a glass plate and observed it under the raw light of a blue lamp and then set up an old camera on a tripod and started to photograph it. He changed the lens and the exposure speed several times to reproduce the images engraved on the coin with greater clarity.

As he worked, he forgot about me.

I walked around the room, observing the drawings and machines and the galleries that opened along one side until, at the end, I saw the staircase leading to the attic. It was spiral and made of iron and ascended, disappearing above. I rose, feeling around in the semidarkness, never looking down. I supported myself on the dark railing and felt the steps, uneven and uncertain.

When I reached the top, the light blinded me. The attic was circular and the roof was made of glass. A clear light flooded the place.

I saw a door and a cot, saw a Christ on the back wall, and, in the center of the room, distant and yet near, I saw the city, and what I saw was more real than reality, more indefinite and pure.

The structure was there, as though outside of time. It had a center but no end. In certain areas of the outskirts, almost on the border, the ruins began. At the boundaries, from the other side, the river flowed, leading to the delta. On one of those islands, one afternoon, someone had imagined an islet infected with swamps where the tides periodically set the mechanism of memory in motion. To the east, near the central avenues, rose the hospital, with white-tile walls, in which a woman was about to die. To the west, close to Parque Rivadavia, the neighborhood of Flores extended, calm, with its gardens and windowed walls, and, at the end of a street of uneven cobblestones, clear in the stillness of the suburb, the house on Calle Bacacay could be seen, and, at the top, barely visible amid the extreme visibility of the world, the red light of the photographer's darkroom twinkling in the night.

I was there a while, how long I cannot remember. I observed, as though hallucinating or dreaming, the imperceptible movement pulsing through the diminutive city. Finally, I looked at it one last time. It was a remote and unique image that replicated the shape of an obsession. I remember descending the circular staircase, feeling around toward the darkness of the living room.

Russell, from the table where he manipulated his instruments, saw me enter as though he did not expect to see me, and, after a slight hesitation, he approached and placed a hand on my shoulder.

"Have you seen?" he asked.

I nodded, without speaking.

"Take it," he said, and returned the Greek coin to me.

That was all.

"Now, then," he said, "you can leave, and you can say what you have seen." In the half-light of sunset, Russell accompanied me to the entryway that led out to the street. When he opened the door, the gentle air of spring came in from the motionless fences and jasmines of neighboring houses.

I walked through the wooded lanes until I reached Avenida Rivadavia, and then I entered the subway and traveled, addled by the muffled rumbling of the train, watching the faltering image of my face reflected in the glass of the window. Piece by piece, the microscopic circular city was sketched out in the half-light of the tunnel with the fixity and intensity of an unforgettable memory.

Then I understood what I had already known: everything you can imagine always exists, on another scale, in another time, clear and distant, just like a dream.

Russell always refused to let his work be revealed, and that decision transformed his efforts into the obsession of an eccentric inventor. And there was something of that in him. But I knew (and others knew) that this fanatical work, carried out over decades, is an example of the revolution that art has maintained since its origin.

Russell belongs to that lineage of stubborn inventors, dreamers of impossible worlds, secret philosophers, and conspirators who have been kept apart from money and common language and who have ended up inventing their own economy and their own reality. "Normally," wrote Osip Mandelstam, "when a man has something to say, he goes toward the people, searches for someone who might understand him. But with the artist, the opposite occurs. He escapes, hides himself, flees toward the edge of the sea where the land ends, or goes toward the vast rumbling of empty spaces where only the cracked desert earth lets him hide himself. Is his walking obviously atypical? The suspicion of madness always falls back on the artist."

Until the end, Russell kept that spirit of neighborhood inventor and amateur alive: he spent the days in his darkroom in the neighborhood of Flores, experimenting with the quiet rumblings of the city. His work seemed to be the message of a traveler who has arrived at a lost city: that this city might be the city where we all live, and that this feeling of strangeness has been achieved with the greatest simplicity, is another example of the originality and the lyricism that characterize his work.

The project in the artist's studio was individually visited by eighty-seven people, mostly women, over the course of twenty years.

Some have recorded their testimonies of his vision, and for a while it has been possible to consult those stories and descriptions in the book *The Close City*, edited by Margo Ligetti and published in March of 1965, along with a series of twelve original photographs by the artist.

Many Argentine words are secret tributes to that enigmatic city and reproduce its spirit without ever naming it because they respect the desire for anonymity and simplicity held by the man who dedicated his life to that infinite, impossible construction.

Art lives on memory and what is to come. But also on forgetting and destruction.

The city—as we know—burned down in February of this year and immediately gained notoriety because only catastrophes and scandals interest the proprietors of information.

The photographer had died two years before in darkness and poverty.

Of the city, only its scorched remains now survive, the skeleton of some buildings and several houses in the southern neighborhood that

336

have held up amid the destruction. The filmmaker Luisa Marker filmed the ruins and the last conflagrations, and the images we see prompt thoughts about a documentary that records and traverses a city burning in a nuclear holocaust.

In the reddish half-light, the construction survives in ruins, spectral, flooded by water and partway submerged in the mud. Certain signs of life have started to suggest themselves among the scorched remains (houses where lights still shine, live shadows amid the rubble, music in automated bars, the siren of an abandoned factory ringing at daybreak). They seem like the nervous images of a newsreel about Buenos Aires in the remote future and what we see is the flash of the catastrophe we have all expected, which surely draws near.

A few days ago, I saw those images again and discovered something I had not noticed before. I saw Plaza de Mayo. And in Plaza de Mayo I saw the cracked open cement and off to one side—beside a wooden bench—I saw the Greek coin, the Greek drachma: a point, I saw it, scorched and almost driven into the ground, blackened, clear.

Sometimes, during insomniac nights, I get up and through the window observe the endless lights of the city, disappearing into the river. Then I open the drawer of my writing desk and pick up the Greek coin that Lucía gave me, and its slight weight is like the slight weight of memory.

I think that one of these days, in the afternoon perhaps, I might make up my mind and go down to the loud and feverish city to walk through the crowded streets and, after skirting the avenue, cross Plaza de Mayo and leave it in the same place Russell had left it in his replica, safe and half-hidden, off to one side, on the cement path, concealed under the wooden bench. I sometimes think I must go looking for it. But the nights pass by and I do not make up my mind. I'll do it now, I think. When autumn comes and the first rains begin.

1 8

Diary 1967

The best thing to happen recently is a letter I received from Julio Cortázar in the conversational tone of *Hopscotch*; he comments on the stories he sent me and leaves me with a clear image of an everyday life without uncomfortable surprises, a life constructed according to his work.

I read some fragments of *Vertical Poetry* by Juarroz—close-fitting, as they say about the toreadors who strike the bull. (A definition that also works for some of the prose I admire.)

I looked through paper bins and drawers until I found the sheets I was looking for—enormous and ruled with lines. I'm going to write out the novel by hand this time.

I want to go back to the nights that, like these rooms, have long been locked off—or better still, like those cool and dark corners you discover as a child and use as hiding places. To enter the night that abets my escape and takes me to a personal territory, where I can work uninterrupted.

Today, I started the preliminary notes for the novel about the thieves who escape to Montevideo.

I am also captivated by the presence of a narrator who observes the events and is distantly implicated in them (as in Henry James, Conrad, and Fitzgerald): I would like for him to be the author of these notebooks, sketching the facts of my life with a clear and efficient style, from the outside, and made to exist through the ambiguous references of my acquaintances, who will speak about him as well (when referring to me).

Recently, the strange memory of a trip on the bus (maybe from Adrogué): uncomfortable, with my legs pushed up against my chest because of the wheel invading the seat, but happy because it eased my exhaustion from the journey halfway down a dirt road that I had made on foot, at nightfall, under the eucalyptus trees, after being with Elena in a hotel on the outskirts.

Also, an afternoon with Inés in La Plata, the two of us sitting under the cathedral, the dusk was waning and the night seemed to come from very far away, and no one could feel it because the sunlight still lit up the plaza and the flowers.

I always remember these situations and see myself in them, but I can't reconstruct the content of those memories, or rather the experiences that often precede the memories and others, their consequences.

Emotion persists in memory, feeling gives form to an image and assures its intensity; that is why the books I have read and the women I have loved endure: figures—or subjects—that resist forgetting. As it were: I only dream of birds and trains that pass in the night.

And now Julia turns over in bed, illuminated by the light of this lamp, and I can imagine her dreaming that she is sick, as I was a few days before. Events persist, evolving into images that never age.

There is a danger but also a grace in the dispersion that comes to me from the fragmented notes for the novel as I search for a tone in this notebook. I am looking for a mid-length prose, allowing me to escape from short forms.

Wednesday 4
Last night I worked until three in the morning, writing down some situations. Someone abets a robbery on the San Fernando bank. He settles an agreement so that, in exchange for information, he will receive part of the stolen money. The situation will not be told directly; only the effects will be visible.

Thursday 5
The admirable Thomas De Quincey, at the end of his homage to the crimes of J. Williams, uses a multiplicity of viewpoints and ambiguous and possible texts, which are recreated in bursts, a technique that owes something to journalistic reports and to the technique of the police genre, which recalls Truman Capote's "very modern" *In Cold Blood*, that is, the current methods of new journalism and the nonfiction novel. He reviews interviews, notes, reports, and news stories and recreates a "real" crime. There is a clear similarity in the tones and techniques through which the two authors approach the events they narrate, with similar deviations. If Capote disguises himself as a novelist in order to legitimize journalistic work, De Quincey disguises himself as a journalist in order to legitimize his work as a novelist. And that is, precisely, what I envision that I want to do in a novel.

What leads from De Quincey to Capote is what leads from my novel to the real recordings from Oscar Lewis's *The Children of Sanchez*. Facing nonfiction, facing the novel-report, what I imagine would be a novel "disguised" as true fiction.

It is a technique that comes from far away, descending from illustrious forebears; the origin of the English novel is the false autobiographical document of a castaway who survives on a desert island and tells his epic, as Defoe imagines in *Robinson Crusoe* (and invents not only the story but also the method of narrating it as though it were a real document). The same thing occurs in Borges's best, "Tlön, Uqbar, Orbis Tertius." The strange thing about this apparent verism is that, using "true" events, it legitimizes an imaginary account. They are decidedly antirealist writers (De Quincey, Capote, and also Borges), who use the technique to traffic in radical stories. I am searching for a tour de force, to create a real world and base myself on events that have really happened in order to create a novel in which everything is imaginary except for the places, some events, and the names of the protagonists.

Going back to the action novel, passing through some antiromantic tendencies that turn the story into a subject of investigation and journalistic inquiry. The greatest success would be, as in the case of Borges's Pierre Menard, for the first critics to review the novel as a book of nonfiction.

The point, in short, is to create a real universe through the narrative technique, as real as the events it recounts.

In the novel that I'm imagining, the greatest difficulty is in conveying the interiority, or rather the consciousness with which the characters live through the events. The greatest challenge will be to recreate and imagine the personal worlds of characters who are completely different from the novelist and from the readers. To try to write a novel that goes far beyond the habitual experience of the people who read it and the person who writes it.

I am thinking about a possible title for this imaginary novel: *Campo de batalla*, and an epigraph from William Faulkner that I translate here: "The field only reveals to man his own folly and despair, and victory is an illusion of philosophers and fools; *el campo de batalla está en todos los sitios para revelar al hombre su propia locura, y desesperación, y violencia.*"

After having published "Desagravio" in 1963, I encounter this passage in Thomas De Quincey: "To conceive the idea of a secret murder on private account as enclosed within a little parenthesis on a vast stage of public battle-carnage is like Hamlet's subtle device of a tragedy within a tragedy; *concebir la idea de un asesinato secreto por un motivo secreto, incluido en un pequeño paréntesis en la vasta escena de matanza en una batalla general, se parece al sutil artificio de Hamlet de una tragedia en una tragedia.*" (My translation.)

Something other than the same. Reality cannot be represented inside a novel except by means of very complex artifices. Therefore, narrative technique becomes a central element in the development of the plot. It is necessary to invent witnesses, make the protagonists speak; reporting is necessary, pieces of news to ensure that the fiction survives the mediocre cloak of the journalistic cult toward true facts and real events. Today, the novel struggles against the wave of false reality produced by the mass media. Everything seems real and the fiction is ever more devalued by the common general feeling. Lies grow in the world, but readers are ever more skeptical and demand stories that are equal to life (as though the poor reality and the lives they lead were not enough).

That is what interests me, narrating the story as though I didn't invent it, as though the history was already there, had already taken place in reality, and I had to meet the protagonists and witnesses face-to-face in order to understand it. In short, I have to act as a historian. What interests me is that this perspective defines the method upon which the reader's belief will be founded.

Saturday, January 7
Every time I walk through Buenos Aires, I let myself be swept away by forgetfulness and nostalgia (which is false memory). I forget the facts but remember with needless clarity the feelings that come back to me, resurfacing along with the places that bring up "personal stories." For

example, today, the wide sidewalks, the tree-lined boulevards of Cerrito, with tables in the streets, sitting in the open air and drinking beer. The same with the nocturnal walks and the dinners at daybreak, men and women who live out of phase and act as though the night never ends, walking between bars and seeking the morning that never comes; along the slope down Corrientes toward the river, the lights enclosing Plaza San Martín and the distant sounding of bells from Torre de los Ingleses; or the bookshops that stay open until dawn (the bookshops I imagine stay open until dawn).

Jorge Álvarez seems excited about the stories. There will be a "tribunal" appointed, presided by Walsh, to judge them. I like that metaphor because it alludes subtly to the literary danger that I want my writings to possess.

Tuesday 10
Suddenly, like a music, like the ticking of a time bomb, I start turning over the first sentence of the novel. "It was a way like any other to let the time pass by, leave the cell, cross corridor and line up in the dining hall, all looking forward, with tin plates in hand."

The central episode of the novel is the standoff; they go three days without leaving the apartment in Montevideo. Suddenly the police arrive and begin the siege and the battle that lasts all night.

Thursday 12
I have only six hundred pesos, which need to last until who knows when, but I am only interested in today. I have a kilo of peaches for refreshment and expect to work until nightfall. Today I am going to write the beginning of the novel and the chapter from the recording.

La Razón (1/12/1967) AFP. Havana. "Writers here from several Latin American countries have issued a declaration advocating for the urgent

343

transformation of literature in Latin America and appealing against the armed conflicts. Julio Cortázar and David Viñas sign for Argentina; for Perú, Mario Vargas Llosa." There is no explanation of whether literature will be urgently transformed by the armed conflicts, or whether literature will narrate the armed conflicts. Nor is there a clear understanding of the direction in which it must be urgently transformed.

Saturday

The tense unrest of Donatelli, the veterinary student who lives in one of the rooms in the house, whose girlfriend left him for a *"negrito*, a thirty-year-old loser, a bohemian who doesn't know how to do anything but play the bandoneon." He is nervous, can't sleep at night, and thinks that "insanity is contagious" and that his girlfriend is sick. "She's crazy," he says. "'I'm bored of you,' she said. 'Don't you get it?'" As crazy as a different girl, also from Lobos, who hung out with another veterinary student and left him, and a while later ended up dancing at the Club Social, one Saturday night, barefoot with a stranger.

Or the police officer whose wife had left him and who had to stand guard on Saturdays at the Club Social dance where she would go with other men. He watched her dance and go out with others, stony, never speaking, until one night he put a bullet in his head.

Or the clown who worked at children's birthday parties in the town, whom a man threatened with a revolver, demanding that he entertain him, and since, after several attempts, each once more desperate and useless, he failed, the man shot him in the left knee. "There, *rengo*, that's how you'll entertain people."

And also the brother, owner of the whiskey bar in the town, who laughed at how ridiculous it seemed to him to spend youth studying, saying, "I start work at six in the afternoon, *viejito*, and pay attention," and he showed him the roll of money on the table. "But you," the other asked, "what do you do for the town?" "Get it drunk, querido, I get it drunk. I am as necessary as the hospital."

And as he went on speaking and telling stories about his town, I leaned back against the wall, I looked at my face out of the corner of my eye in the wardrobe mirror and tried to find an interested expression. I let him talk because I needed the five hundred pesos that I'd asked to borrow.

Sunday 15

The danger in Norman Mailer's literature (*The Naked and the Dead*) or in Sartre's novel, which becomes unbearable in David Viñas, is the reiteration of the meaning of the actions being narrated. The motivations are always thoroughly explained, and logic or intelligence are not employed toward suggestion, toward ellipsis and the unsaid, but rather are shown in the explanation of the events narrated in the book. You have to analyze the ways that Vargas Llosa ruins his novels through excessive "intelligence" in the structural tricks (for example, hiding the identity of the Jaguar in *The Time of the Hero*).

Monday 16

Regrets, for me, are always abrupt; I ended up on Sunday with eight pesos, forced to walk to the post office today. My grandfather sent me a money order for 18,885 pesos. I call him on the phone to ask why that figure and he tells me, in his sharp and amused voice: "I calculated the hours and minutes that you worked with me, straightening out my archive." He wants to know when I will come back, maybe this Saturday. He has decided to organize the documents and letters into different boxes. It makes the house look like a museum. On the door, he has hung up some handwritten signs: "Isonzo," "Fosalta"—places where he fought during the war. In a larger room, at the back, he has put up "Last Mail"; the letters from the dead soldiers are in there. He has laid out the maps in another part and has left only the books dedicated to the war in the library. He imagines that he is the only one who can tell the truth. "My truth," he says. Sometimes he wants to write a book, sometimes just an open letter to the Pope in the Vatican.

I drank a few beers on the sidewalk under the awning with fat Ferrero, whom I have assigned to keep me in touch with Spanish poetry from the Generation of '27. Jorge Guillén, Pedro Salinas, and Luis Cernuda. Ferrero knows the poems by heart and recites them to me on command. Today he played a little trick, he recited a very good sonnet to me, I hesitated, couldn't remember which of those poets had written the sonnet. Finally, he told me that the poem was his own. It was called, or rather, is called "La luz del día." He writes *inside of* a tradition; his poems are and are not equal to the poems by the poets he admires, but they are surely better than what he could write alone, without references.

Tuesday 17
The novel. The gangster and the girl, a love story. But behind the scenes, secretly, she was sleeping with others, pushed away by him. In the end, she dies with a bullet in her back. Almost by chance; the bullet rebounds and kills her in the bathroom. Love, then, romantic, and at the same time, of course, as perverse as ever, between the Englishman and Moira, her death in the end, when they start to hate each other and only remorse is left.

It rains without ceasing. I suffer the consequences of last night's alcohol. I can see a little blue crystal ball that seems to float precariously on the lip of a bottle. Blurry vision. When I close my eyes and open them again, the ball slides to one side and smashes against the floor and shatters the harmony of the image.

A true story. I saw La Pléiade's edition of Flaubert's novels in the afternoon. I decided not to buy it; it seemed too expensive to me, even though I had the money, so I went on doing the things I had pending. I was in Tortoni for a while and, while there, felt for some reason that I had to have that book.

I went back to Hachette, but they had already sold it . . . Unbelievable. I am going to spend my life thinking about the book that I wouldn't buy; it will last longer than the memory of all the books I have in my library.

Thursday
I have been in La Plata for a few weeks because of Julia. But today Lalo Panceira came to see me, and I felt once again the happiness of living in Buenos Aires. I will be here until the end of summer and then will return to the city.

Thursday 26
The club or gang of kids who play with the town's deaf-mute, at the station bar. They threaten him with a revolver to get a reaction, to "see how he reacts"; in the end they kill him. "A bullet got away from them."

The married couple who separated long ago and now rent a hotel room in the city and lock themselves up there for a week. The sister tells the story.

Tuesday, January 31
I reread old notebooks in which Inés appears, here and there, until she leaves and never appears again.

I spent twenty thousand pesos in fifteen days (without going to the races).

Wednesday, February 1
I balance certain virtues with my flaws (40 and 60 percent, let's say), and I am certain of my ability to write what I want and how I want it . . .

Dostoevsky contends that our notion of reality is at fault if we find events "exceptional" or unbelievable (in his novels).

Knowledge in literature is considered a loss of innocence. For the story-teller, this represents a paradox; you lose something once you learn that it isn't worth the trouble to narrate "like someone singing." That conviction must be present in the prose. Fear of that knowledge can make us diverge from "the adventure" and turn from the path to avoid meeting the dragon.

Thursday 2
Last night, a very entertaining gathering at Edgardo Frontini's house. Tensions between Rubi and Julia, which Antonio Mónaco and I witness like people watching a famous scene in a film they are seeing for the first time.

"You can depict wine, love, women, and glory on the condition that you're not a drunkard, a lover, a husband or a private in the ranks. If you participate actively in life, you don't see it clearly: you suffer from it too much or enjoy it too much. The artist, to my way of thinking, is a monstrosity, something outside nature," G. Flaubert, *Correspondence*.

Irony is a hopeless method for the left. Too much solemnity, too much seriousness in its goals. All of them take what they say with too much gravity. Only those who have nothing to lose can laugh at themselves.

Friday 3
The novel as investigation of reality. Separate from the traditional story, as in the novel without plot, when the story is already in the realm of reality and you have to be able to recreate it and narrate it as though it were not your invention. Reality is not being copied; a fictitious story is being copied—transcribed—told as if it were true, or rather, made to pass as real.

Saturday
A strange experience today. A funeral for the daughter of a colleague who works with Julia at the laboratory. Then a walk in the cemetery in the sun. The pain of daylight.

Two sudden ideas about death. A base idea, happiness at being alive. A metaphysical idea, there is no experience in death; anguish is for the survivors.

To be immortal would be to lack emotional bonds, to die without anyone experiencing the pain of your death. Dying, then, would be a leap into the void.

The tone of the prose in these notebooks derives from the inversion of the act of writing consciously. There is no preparation; you sit down abruptly and write a few words about something that has happened, or that you remember, or something you have thought; everything happens in the midst of life and action. To write a diary is to establish an interval, a personal temporality, defined by the chronological entries. Writing down the date is the only formal sign that identifies a diary. Everything written there is truth; it is a contract, yet, nevertheless, you often write what you believe happened and reality contradicts it. You have to overcome inertia, sit down at the table and write. That is all, just a movement of the body, an intention without a clear aim or antecedent.

Monday
Carnival. There is a parade down La Diagonal and I watch it from the window. Before, I was filled with excitement by the days of guaranteed freedom; I would go to the dances, disguised so that no one would know who I was, and I could imagine myself having other perspectives and other words. But that has passed, and now I lean out from the balcony, hear the racket, watch pathetic buskers pass, and analyze it with the certainty that I am someone else while I write.

Tuesday
Last night on the sidewalk at Teutonia, Ricardo W.'s confessions reminded me of that party in the Villarreal sisters' house, the cries about "the end of the left"; life no longer has meaning, they say, what can be done? We

will never know if it is lucid thought or comedy. In any case, the story of desperation always leaves an impression (whatever it may be).

And when we went down Corrientes and crossed Abasto toward Once, every night, and then on Medrano, her walking ahead and me wanting her.

One of Beckett's most repeated motifs is that of the ending of all possible self-expression: the end of language is the end of the known world, as though the characters—Molloy, Malone—had come to the edge and looked out from there at the inhospitable and silent desert.

Saturday 11
An enjoyable meeting in Edelweiss on Wednesday with Jorge Álvarez, who thinks that my book is "the best book of short stories in recent years, the best one I'll publish." He wants to print eight thousand copies but also wants an exclusive contract for everything I write in the five years after this book. We discuss possibilities for work: publishing a story in *Adán* magazine in May, an article on Malcolm Lowry for *Marcha*, a volume of collected essays on Hemingway, and the introductory notes for an anthology of stories from the USA.

Monday, February 13
At eight in the morning I am awakened by the bell from the street. A postman with a telegram from Casa de las Américas. "Your book long-listed for Casa Prize. Will be released in the coming months. Congratulations."

Doubtless, I know it better than anyone, this kind of happiness is always uncomfortable, too "social," and worthless at heart. In any case, it is what I wanted, what I looked for; an arrival, a bridge into "literature" understood as a territory distant from writing. You could say that I'm two people, the one who writes and the one who hopes to be published. For the second one of us, some affirmations have now appeared: a prize (which is not a prize, just a mention) and a double publication promised: the book will come out this year in Havana and in Buenos Aires. I hoped for that approval (the telegram arriving at eight in the morning to announce that you have been "mentioned" in the literary world) even before writing the book. Maybe because I took it for granted, I don't understand now whether it has meaning beyond this vague sense of unreality. Things have always been given to me with too much "ease"; it seems that there really is a star watching over me, the superstitious conviction that I will always be safe.

But it isn't as magical as I would like it to be. If I look carefully at the book, I discover the reason: a concrete book, with terse poetics, not easy or complaisant.

In Buenos Aires, a long time traveling through the familiar area and several close-up shots: the bookshop, Plaza Lavalle, friends. I meet Ismael Viñas and also Álvarez, who celebrates the honor. Tata Cedrón is happy but hints that it was unfair not to give the prize to Miguel Briante's book as well. I agree. These competitions, I tell him, are a lottery with few winners; luck helps more than the quality of the prose.

Later, in Politeama, an encounter with Castillo's *troupe*; Battista is there, too, and he also received a mention. We play at being celebrities and devils. They thought that when I left their magazine literature was over for me . . .

Tuesday 14
I am writing the mini-biographies for all of the American writers. Almost a book, with introductions or portraits going from Sherwood Anderson to James Purdy.

Pirí is organizing an anthology of stories selected by writers—Borges and Walsh, among others. What would I choose? Two kindred stories: "The Death of Iván Ilyich" and "The Snows of Kilimanjaro." "The South" also belongs to that series. What does a man do at the point of death? How do we look at someone's life if we know that he will die soon?

351

Thursday

Yesterday, long walks with Lucho Carneiro, who has discovered the Sergi winery and is still able to find some bottles in the suburban markets. Everything is part of my friends' celebrations over my book of stories.

Sunday

On Friday, a considerable journey through Buenos Aires, alone at first because I missed a date with Inés, who had sent me a telegram congratulating me on the prize. Finally, another meeting with Castillo's crowd at Tortoni, like the old days in my youth. We went to the Hormiguero afterward to listen to Mercedes Sosa, a young folk singer with a beautiful voice. We ended up eating breakfast at La Cultural as the sun rose. The same circular (triangular?) conversations that we had three years ago . . .

The list of writers influenced by William Faulkner is shocking: Onetti, García Márquez, Rulfo, Sabato, Dalmiro Sáenz, Saer, Rozenmacher, Miguel Briante. I keep myself away from that wave, seeking a laconic and elliptical prose. In that, at least, I am unique in the rhetoric of these times.

Tuesday 21

I am working on writing amusing and erudite biographical sketches of twentieth-century American authors, almost a panorama of modern narrative. I began with Truman Capote. In a quick visit to Jorge Álvarez, I made fifteen thousand pesos for those notes. I proposed a translation of *In Our Time*, the book by Hemingway that is not yet available in Spanish.

The Sun Also Rises is by far Hemingway's best novel, but it doesn't achieve the splendor of "Macomber" or "Kilimanjaro." Just as his novel about the Cuban fisherman is a pale version of "After the Storm."

Thursday 23

I discover my natural talent, so to speak, for writing portraits of writers I admire. They have something of what I attempt in essays (they are narrative), but they are threatened by brevity and have echoes of Borges's prose. I wrote about Truman Capote, Hemingway, and Scott Fitzgerald.

Friday 24
Signed inscriptions have an infallible technique: dedicating the book as though you were praising the merits of *someone else* (that is, of the person to whom we deliver the book in writing).

Oh, the bursts of happiness are brief, intense, possess something luminous and lucid. They never last; when I want to preserve them, it is because they have already gone. But I still possess the memory—for example, just now in the armchair with Julia. Then you aspire toward that momentary happiness, and its immanence—or its promise—is what keeps us alive.

The narrator must express what all men have once felt or will feel. That is, he must be able to convey emotions that we have once experienced or imagine to have been our own.

Monday 27
I used up the thirty-five pesos I had left on a half kilo of grapes and came back home on foot. I put the bunch in a bowl of ice and was eating them on the patio, an indefinable cadence; each one announced the next, as though the bunch contained an invisible rhythm—or shape—that organized them. I write or try to write about James Baldwin, while Julia is gone at the pawnbroker, trading all of the music of Brahms, the Deutsche Grammophon records, for money, because we need cash to make it to Friday.

Hunger is an insatiable feeling, it makes you become monothematic, it is impossible to work or want to think about anything else. The grapes now finished, I wait for Julia, who has still not returned, even though it is four in the afternoon.

Thursday, March 2
I work for hours and hours without stopping; American literature has *too many* writers. I have already written about five authors and have seven or eight more waiting.

Imagination also possesses a dark side; I am used to imagining catastrophes with the same austere ease with which I imagine plots or biographies written on commission.

Saturday 4
Yesterday I saw Tata Cedrón and his brothers in Boca. I share lamentations about the injustice Miguel Briante has suffered—not considered in the Casa de las Américas competition, not even by the publisher Jorge Álvarez, who rejected his book (a stain that cannot be erased). No one can use a friend whose prose I admire to confront me or to insinuate literary injustices that I agree about but have no connection to.

Earlier, a walk with a photographer from *Primera Plana* who makes me fervently uncomfortable, placing me against walls with antique textures to take photos of me that I don't want to see or remember. In the middle of the exposure, I lose my fountain pen. I'll buy another, more expensive one, and if I lose it, I'll buy myself another one, more expensive than the second, and go on in this way, wasting money on the objects that are my only real fetish. Later, I meet Álvarez and we adjust and put the final touches on *Crónicas de Norteamérica*.

Tuesday 7
I managed to settle the debt of sixteen thousand pesos that had been weighing on me for days. In total, I earned, for the notes and the prologues, twenty-six thousand pesos, instead of the seventeen thousand I had calculated.

I write about Sherwood Anderson and then write about Faulkner, the best of all of them.

Thursday 9

I am writing this with another Parker fountain pen, a petty and auspicious gift from Julia. "Don't lose it," she said, "because then you'll lose me, too."

Last night a long talk with Dipi Di Paola, always witty, he tells great stories about what he has experienced or imagined. One afternoon, euphoric, he went out to buy paint on credit in the hardware stores in Tandil because he wanted to paint blue the fronts of the houses on the block where he lives. "I wasn't crazy, I was just happy." His father went after him, trying to cancel the sales and refill the containers with blue paint that he had to pay for himself if they had already been used. Dipi and Briante and Saer are the closest friends whose literature I have as much faith in as my own.

I am at a bar, very lofty, in the building where the editorial office of *Primera Plana* is run. It is the fourteenth floor; below is the city and further below the river. I come here with my second personality, the one who publishes and performs the formalities that writer detests. All of my contemporaries believe that appearing in that magazine, written in high-sounding and Borgesian prose, seems like glory. I laugh at that pretension; the weekly production obliges Cousté, and the mediocre people working under him in the cultural section, to discover or invent a new genius weekly, whose literary life will last a week.

I worked then for a month on the brief portraits of American narrators. They were fifteen-hundred-word texts, in which I synthesized everything I know and everything I have read in the last ten years.

Friday 10

At *Primera Plana* magazine, Mastropascua, the photographer from the film club in Mar del Plata, gave me the copies of the photographs they took for me a few days ago. I am going to use one of them in the book.

Pirí was surprised because I cut my hair very short before taking those photos. "I want to look like anything other than a writer," I said. At the publishing house, Álvarez put me in charge of *Crónicas de Latinoamérica*. I'm going to write about James Purdy now, the final writer in the series, although I'm still missing Nelson Algren, Thomas Wolfe, John Updike, and Ring Lardner.

A possible short story. It was a completely normal sensation at first. Who has never felt, in the face of an event (in the face of any event) that he has already lived through it? The feeling that you are repeating a previous moment of your life has an unexpected vehemence. It is not a memory, there are no images, it is only a state of grace, like returning to a room you have missed from childhood. Thus begins the story: the narrator lives concurrently in two distinct times; gradually the feeling of déjà vu grows and dominates his entire life. He knows what is to come, because he has already lived through it and cannot avoid it. (Maybe it will be the story of a crime the protagonist commits in order to escape from that imprisonment, platonic reminiscence or reincarnation.) In any case, the story does not explain at any point why the double temporality and the repeated life are taking place.

Sunday

I was thinking recently about the notion of the *interval*. Having a time frame, a future frontier that cannot be avoided; in English, they are called, very accurately, *deadlines*. They are not distinguished from the imagination of what is to come, but they have the peculiarity of being decided by a stranger. Someone gives us a definite time frame in which to do something, to fulfill or settle an agreement at a future time. Is it possible to believe in the deadlines you have assigned yourself? Difficult, whereas the other assignments or due dates seem inevitable or inexorable. Then time takes on another dimension and it is very hard to "let yourself go," to live out the days in themselves and not as the promise or sentence of something yet to come. This feeling is embodied culturally in the myth of a deal with the devil. "What a long time you set for me," as they say in the Spanish play *Don Juan.* (The notion of *expiration.*)

Those who knew me from before can't seem to forgive me for having accomplished what I desired—so to speak. As a result, there is a certain anger and a certain aggression that I perceive in old friends, who see me as different from how they had imagined me. Those who know me now only see what I'm doing as a virtue, not as a surprise that makes them anxious, faced with a stranger who nevertheless still remains, to them, "familiar."

If there is no God, all we have left, then, is the justice "of others."

A night in Edgardo's house; mental speed and lots of whiskey. In the middle of the racket, like a flash of light, the subject of a novel occurred to me, a man who lives his life as though it belonged to someone else. He tries to conceal his false life, etc.

Monday, March 13
Anyway, the summer has gone now; the sun turns pale and weak this morning and a freezing wind comes in from the south.

I have realized that, in writing about the American writers, I have defined or glimpsed my own lives through them. These texts are my tribute to Steve R.'s friendship.

Pity is a terrible feeling. They speak of the passions of love, but pity is worse than passion. Adolescents do not commiserate with one another. Compassion is a passion of adulthood.

Tuesday 14
The cold, between us. Once again, I confirm an old supposition that the best way to think about a problem is to investigate it through concrete

work. Synthesizing everything you have discovered and deepening it, as though it were something remembered. That explains my rapid journey through American literature (I knew it before).

Hemingway attempts to turn the reader into a contemporary of the action, while the novelist writes in past tense. Yet it is not about the tense of the verb, but rather an alteration of the story's syntax.

Something that has started happening to me is that my friends or acquaintances confess to me that, beyond their concrete lives, what they want is to be writers. These days, Frontini, West, Lacae. Literature seems to be a way out, within reach of anyone who has learned to write in school. Obviously, writing is not the same thing as composition. I agree that anyone can be a writer; I don't believe in "chosen ones," only that there will always be great writers and terrible ones as well.

In many cases, the recourse of literature as a way out, or as salvation, is an effect of the crisis of the left or the beginnings of adulthood. Confronted with skepticism, they think that this disillusioned view actually turns them into writers. Nevertheless, it is impossible to write without enthusiasm and trust in what lies ahead.

Long ago, I dreamed about a journey by train in the middle of the night, in one of the old sleeping cars on long-distance trains. I imagined an almost endless trajectory, the stations lit up along the countryside, the towns rapidly passing. I remembered that hope to be separate and yet in motion, just now, looking at the picture window in my room as though it were the little window of a stopped train.

Now I have come to fear *surmenage*, the image of a blank mind, without memories, a lagoon glittering in the light.

Wednesday 15

I still don't know my limits, must begin staking out the boundaries of my life. At times, I imagine being a machine that carries out every function. And yet the only machine that I know first-hand is the Olivetti I use to write; it is there that I must test my reach.

Friday 17

A long march for two days through the city, in the middle a room made of angles, a skylight above and Julia daydreaming in the succession of whiskies she drank, one after another amid the storm that also lasted for two days. Pirí proposes becoming my literary agent and taking responsibility for my stories. Later, I met with Dalmiro Sáenz, who brought news of the competition; my book was in first until the end, but then they awarded it to the Cuban Benítez. In any event, they still decided to publish it at Casa de las Américas this year.

Saturday 18

Yesterday with Dipi Di Paola; we remembered old times, old projects. He is melancholy because his woman, a Lolita with a Japanese look, ran away with his best friend. I remembered the boardinghouse I shared with José Sazbón in 1960: Dipi brought me the Italian translation of a novel by Gombrowicz; back then everything was dark for me. A few years later I lived on a block with Briante, Constantini, Castillo. Nowadays, I think I work better and know what I'm looking for, and I feel that I'm at the vanguard of the writers in my generation (though that is not something I would say out loud, ever—unlike the others, who boast about their genius to anyone who will listen).

Just now, a surprising appearance by Ramón T., who started to say goodbye to me "mysteriously" and vanished, passing over into his secret life. I left him in a taxi, and as we said goodbye he let me know, without saying so, that he was going to "join the revolution." I thought I would never see him again. In the middle of it, Celina, helpless, tense. But I didn't take advantage of my friend's distance, even though she would easily have come with me, safe in her choice to live her own life (and not become a guerrilla fighter herself).

Wednesday

I passed the night without sleeping, working on the novel until morning. Just like that I picked up my main project again.

A subject. A woman chastises her lover for failing to do what he promised her. Gradually, it becomes clear that the conversation is about suicide, which must never be stated but must become present in the gravity that their conversation develops. It would be a subjective version of what happened on Saturday, when Celina realized that Ramón was leaving and she would likely never see him again. Surely, she would prefer that to seeing him get out of the taxi and say he was renouncing his political ideals to stay with her.

Thursday

My most dependable erotic dreams are very entertaining: I make love to the daughter in front of the mother, all amid laughter and jokes about the Greek tradition.

After many years, I read *Cantar de ciegos* by Carlos Fuentes once again; a good book, but no, in no way is he "a better short-story writer than Cortázar" (as Dipi says). Good control of insignificant and frivolous situations, but grisly and sensationalistic resolutions.

Friday 24

I look critically at certain life decisions I've made in service of the future of my literature—for example, living with nothing, no possessions, nothing material to bind and coerce me. For me, to choose means to discard, to cast aside. That way of living defines my style—stripped down, swift. You have to try to be quick, always ready to leave everything behind and escape.

Now I am looking at the galley proofs for my little history of American fiction, which has high points but is uneven.

As always, I live with a provisional calm; I won't have any major economic difficulties for the next six months. After that, we'll see.

March 27, 1967
I am at Don Julio in La Plata, such a students' bar, half a block from the College; it provokes introspections that I have denied myself lately in order to live more actively in this beautiful summer, not stopping to think. But here I sat seven years ago, and once again the memory takes on the form of a snapshot in which I see myself back then, but at the same time I am the one seeing the image. I was in an unknown reality then, living alone and yet accompanied by a web of new relationships, and also confused, not knowing clearly how to find what I sought but sure of my ultimate triumph. That certainty, which had no guarantee or logic to it, held me steady in my new life. Now I have almost everything I could have wanted back then, but I'm at a new crossroads. I say this as a joke: things are not really that clear, and, in the end, I only wanted to recycle the coincidence of an image from memory and my presence in the place remembered.

Tuesday, March 28
The fear of breaking your eyeglasses "because I've had them for a long time" is strange. Why not use the same criterion for everything? With relationships, for example, time is the same as decay. We can think of someone, in love with a woman, who starts to be terrified because they have had years of perfect relationship so far. That terror makes him turn against the woman; he starts to harass her, tries to find signs of disinterest and boredom in her, ends up metaphorically smothering her. She cannot stand this harassment and leaves him. The relationship breaks apart as he expected. I trust that the case of my eyeglasses is different from that fate. I almost left them behind on a minibus the other day. If it hadn't been for the fact that I wanted to put them on as I was entering the College,

I wouldn't have discovered their absence. I left hastily, got into a taxi, went off after the bus; we kept up alongside it, I made signals for it to stop at the corner, got out of the taxi, got onto the minibus, and found them in a corner of the back seat. When I got off the bus, my eyeglasses on, the passengers applauded as though the company had sent me there to entertain them during the trip. A *live show*, as they say.

I set a meeting with my parents here. Every new visit with them is an estrangement: I meet myself from twenty years ago yet again, take a cruel leap while trying to break free from that image and be myself, opposing them. My mother amuses herself and understands the façade of my life, and then, to show that she knows what it's all about, she calls me *Nene*; my father, on the other hand, observes me with a certain anger because I have not become—like him—a Peronist doctor, ready to give "my life for Perón."

Wednesday 29
Unpleasant premonitions and dreams about my economic future, always uncertain and increasingly out of my control. The fear has been bearing down on me ever since I left the University, after Onganía's coup, and I joined the others who renounced their fellowships and thus cut off the possibility of stable work. It makes little sense, is absurd to worry myself over a future extending further than six months ahead. I have to live with an economy that guarantees me a few secure months, not my whole life—that would be ridiculous. I have the book of stories ready now and two hundred thousand pesos (as an advance for the publication). These ideas surface because I used up 22,500 pesos on an Italian coat that I bought for myself yesterday.

Technically, Borges is connected to the cleanest narrative in the English language: the same reasoning behind the narrative material, the clear presence of a common narrator in all of the work (Borges himself), the framework that primes the action. His intelligence consists in

362

erecting complex and unreal worlds upon those structures of meaning. Another of Borges's qualities is that reality is never presented; it is always obscure and intriguing, and therefore it becomes the object of an investigation, giving rise to the searches (most often bibliographic ones for him) that conclude the events. His "humility" turns him into a perfect transmitter for books written by others, for stories that don't exist, for fantastical characters whom he encounters, recreates, and displays. The greatest example of this method is "Tlön, Uqbar, Orbis Tertius," the best thing Borges has written. A small bibliographic reconstruction leads into a parallel world. The story, painstakingly put together with chronometric precision, is blended, falls into the void, into unreality, into dream and nightmare. The most valuable part of Borges is the path that climbs up the hillside of the world toward that unreal, magical confirmation.

Yesterday, my parents gave me their unedited vision of Inés. Suffering, very anxious, speaking about me too much, came to the house three times, repeating that she really loves me, that the relationship is over, that "they must love Julia," etc. Just like on *Radiolandia* but, at the same time, the surprise of an affection that she wants to exhibit.

Thursday 30
Yesterday my cousin Horacio appeared; he is almost my brother, we were born just days apart in the same year and grew up together. Often, I have thought that he is my double; he stayed and lived in the same house where he was born, got his degree in medicine, as my father wanted me to do, and doesn't leave the area where we lived as children. I have always thought about his as the life I would have led if I had stayed in Adrogué. Whenever I am in hard straits, I think about him and the life he leads, like a sanctuary I chose to abandon. If I had stayed there, I surely would have been the same as him. I suppose he sees me in the same way, the adventurous brother who broke away from the family to make his own life. He comes to see me every now and then, and the conversation picks

up the fluidity of two friends who see each other all the time. He is back from some vacations in Brazil; I catch him up about my new situation. I have separated from Inés, I tell him, and am now living with a woman in Buenos Aires, Julia. He, on the other hand, married his childhood girlfriend and stays true to the passions of his youth. We go out to eat and then go in circles around the city, ending up listening to Rovira at Gotán. It was almost sunrise when we said goodbye, and once again I felt that he was living the life I could have lived, etc.

I will try laboriously to correct the book of stories and prepare the final version. It is a moment when you can, with the same decision, send the book to the press or leave it in a drawer forever. Impossible for me to make a value judgment. What I like most about the book is that it is written contrary to the current stylistic fashion (which owes everything to Borges); in my case, I'm too interested in that work not to try to distance myself from it and start over, with a language that has no connection to "literature" as Borges has imposed it. I have to revise the story "Tarde de amor" in particular. It is the most daring, and I sometimes think that all of its deficiency hangs upon a well-placed comma and a rhythm resembling music. I am thinking of "touching up" the book while I copy it again—that is, copy it out once more and, as I transfer it, look for ways to adjust it.

April
Yesterday I met with Miguel Briante in Florida bar; long conversations about the book he has finished writing, which I like very much. It is called *Hombre en la orilla*, and I hope to be able to publish it at the Estuario publishing house in the coming months. We stop at Jorge Álvarez quickly, and I give Miguel a copy of my book, even though he knows all of the stories except for the last two. Earlier, I received three thousand pesos and checks for twenty thousand to cover next week. It's the first work I've gotten since I left the College. At the moment, I'm preparing a collection of classics and planning a police series.

Monday 3

Last night we listened to Edmundo Rivero at Nonino. He has great talent and manages to disguise his decline. He sang "Mi noche triste" in a wonderful way, a medium tone with lots of "interpretation." A great feel for captivating the audience, which led him to perform a more rabble-rousing and noisy repertoire. There were several friends in the audience, the women I have loved: Cecilia pregnant; Vibel uncomfortable, trying to be seen; Susana M., married.

A short story. A long-distance phone call, a man and a woman talk, confusion, silences. "What can we say to each other?" etc. She is in California and he in Buenos Aires; the dialogue has several possible interpretations. In the end, it is revealed that she is not his wife but his cousin—his sister?—whom he has loved ever since one afternoon, now many years ago, at the hour of siesta, in a country house, when he found her—encountered her—naked in a tub set out on the patio, and with whom he had a passionate and impossible romance.

Wednesday 5

A talk with Noé Jitrik today about a possible course focused on American fiction. We will begin in July. I am thinking of opening with Thomas Wolfe and closing with Kerouac and the Beat Generation.

Thursday

While I make progress on the final version of the book, doubts arise, as expected, about the style. That always happens when you analyze the isolated sentences and lose sight of the general tone of the story. For me, that is the distinction between a decorative literature, which only thinks about isolated effects, and a more direct writing that works on the style in blocks, building it up the way someone raises a wall with different-sized stones. In fact, I end up typing out the book again, feverishly, as though someone were chasing me, anxious about changing phrases or words without running the risk of altering the prose. Curiously, no one reads books with as much detail as the writers themselves.

Friday
A day of steady and happy work in the afternoon at the Lincoln Library, reviewing American fiction, developing theories about the books that I began thinking about nine years ago, when I started with Hemingway's first stories and then continued with Fitzgerald and Faulkner.

Hemingway understood that, after what Joyce had done with the English language, he had to begin from zero. In 1938, Ezra Pound would say of Hemingway, "He has not spent his life writing anemically snobbish essays, but he understood at once that *Ulysses* was an end and not a beginning." He sought a conceptual, elliptical prose, "more difficult than poetry," and in his first book he achieved it.

Sunday 9
Although periods of intense work distract me from these notebooks, it is certain that, at some point, I will have to search for a tone—even here—that unifies this record of my days, to go against an immediacy that impels me to note down what comes into my head, without deciding or choosing. Although, sometimes, I think that spontaneity must lie at the center of these diaries.

I turn things over and change the order of the stories in the volume. The first will be "Tierna es la noche" and the last will be "Tarde de amor."

Tuesday 11
Resolved to move once again, the journeys through rooms for rent in hotels and boardinghouses force me to traverse the city like an adventurer seeking a place to settle down. Suddenly I need to change my neighborhood, and now I've decided to abandon the room on Riobamba and Paraguay and look for something further south. In the end, after going

in circles around Barracas, I find a spacious and brightly lit room on Montes de Oca and Martín García, near Parque Lezama.

Wednesday 12

Once again, amid papers strewn on the floor and suitcases, the strange feeling of changing places, always experienced as an escape. The figure of the man without a fixed residence, a hero for me in the contemporary world. Without property, without rules, without settling down anywhere, yesterday, a magical encounter with a beautiful place in Barracas. Julia looked in the paper, because someone had walked by selling it a minute before, and she discovered this address, after we had almost decided to rent another with less light. It's amusing to see that the room costs thirteen thousand pesos per month, that we will move in on the thirteenth, and that the room, of course, is number thirteen.

Friday

Carrying suitcases that feel like they're filled with lead, (almost) escaping without paying for the other room in La Plata. Entering the city gradually, with a certain economic insecurity and a great urge to start something new here. I write in this incredible room over the avenues, with a large picture window, filled with light. Literature, for me, depends greatly on the place where I write. I could imagine a superstitious man who, before writing a new book, changes neighborhoods, opens a map, points to an area by chance, moves there, and lives for a few months until he finishes a novel and then undertakes the same ritual once again.

Monday 17

Against this balcony over the city, dampened by light rain, I start to work. Worried about Julia, who will live in La Plata for part of the week.

Some discoveries: The white whale represents evil for Captain Ahab. The central subject in Edgar Poe is vampirism (of love).

A little while ago, I went over to see Jorge Álvarez, who calls me on the phone and confirms my work as coordinator of publications in exchange for twenty thousand pesos per month. I will continue with the collection of classics, make some anthologies, and plan the police series. Jorge suggests three hours per day at the publishing house. We'll see. Economically secure, set up in a place in the south of the city now, I can finally start writing the novel about the robbery of the armored bank car in San Fernando.

Tuesday

Going through old notebooks, I found a subject that I want to transcribe here once again. The indifferent man, detached from everything, who sees someone in a plaza about to fall from a tower he has climbed to do repairs, and, as he sees him descend and step on a broken rung, he doesn't warn him, lets him fall. A meticulous story in which nothing is said about the central theme, the character of a man who, in a certain moment, *does nothing*. Murder by indifference.

Wednesday

Yesterday at the Ver y Estimar art gallery; some exhibitions of Argentine pop art and kinetic art. Best, conceptual works by Jacoby and Carreira. Also a Víctor Grippo installation. I see Patricia Peralta and Alicia Páez, friends from another era, or, should I say, from another geological period. Both of them studied with Inés at the College, and we would see each other very often. You break up with a woman and lose half of your friends and half of your library.

Borges like Hemingway. They ask him: What is your greatest concern before writing a short story? To imagine an action or series of actions honestly, Borges answers. And he adds: To forget what has already been written about the subject and hope that another imagination claims it. And to the question "What is your technique when you write short stories?" he answers: To intervene as little as possible. To omit, for the sake of brevity, some part of the things I have imagined. That will lend it feeling in some way. And Hemingway, referring to one of his first stories, says the same thing: "It was a very simple story called 'Out of Season' and I had omitted the real end of it which was that the old man hanged himself. This was omitted on my new theory that you could omit anything if you knew that you omitted and the omitted part would strengthen the story and make people feel something more than they understood."

The key for an artist, we might say, is meditation on necessity. Not needing more than you have in order to live. Forgetting "necessities," you have to learn to live in the present.

Overcast and cold once again; a while ago I ate a bit of ham with a glass of wine, and now I feel the harsh and burning flavors of the ham and wine in my throat and that memory, persisting in the present, distracts me from reading Katherine Anne Porter.

Thursday 20
It is still raining, and I kill time waiting for noon, when the pawnbroker opens, so that I can leave the camera in exchange for the money I need for the rest of the month.

I could describe the morning today like this. I slept until ten and shaved slowly and stayed in the shower a while, and midmorning I drank a double espresso at the bar downstairs while reading the paper disinterestedly, and finally I walked out down the damp streets of the city looking for the pawnbroker.

Friday 21
I go to La Plata to give Julia company, and in the College hallways I encounter the same commotion as always, and once again a memory comes up like a gust of wind. When I came in on the first day, I saw Jiménez, my professor from high school in Mar del Plata, and I avoided him without any greeting despite his friendly gesture. As always, I see the scene as

though looking at a photograph, and, as always, I wonder what exists in the memory that I cannot see in its image.

Saturday 22
"How can the prisoner reach outside except by thrusting through the wall?" H. Melville.

In the writers I admire, for example Osamu Dazai now, what I like most is that everything is narratively justified: the story is supported on documents—notebooks, diaries, letters, confessions—that the writer makes available if you wish to interpret them. I am trying, therefore, to write a story based on Pavese's diary, narrating his thoughts, dramatizing them.

Dazai is in the same vein as Pavese: "In the final analysis, my suicide must be seen as a natural death. A man does not kill himself for his ideas alone," he said.

Sunday 23
Meetings with David Viñas in his apartment in Bajo, over Viamonte, and then in a bar on Calle Florida with José Sazbón.

I am working on the prologue for *Crónicas de Latinoamérica*. Essentially, I'm interested in creating a record of experimental writers. You have to remember that the often-mentioned crisis of the novel is nothing more than the crisis of the nineteenth-century novel, and that short writing forms were already more innovative than novels (Poe, Bierce). I am fascinated to read Guillermo Cabrera Infante, Fernando del Paso, Vicente Leñero—redevelopments in method and the search for new forms.

Monday, May 1
The city half-empty, the streets deserted and, on July 9, from Corrientes to Córdoba, a crowd watching an assailant's desperate defense, surrounded

by police at the top of a building. As though the day, vacant and with no work, had prepared them for a live spectacle, ready to be spectators to a man's death.

Tuesday 2
The room filled with light and eight hours of peace ahead to work on the new story, tentatively titled "La torre." It begins like this: "Sometimes standing at the lookout, with the wind crashing wild against the tin, I have felt the tower alive, as though it were an enraged animal."

Saturday
Yesterday a meeting with Roa Bastos; we talk a while about his projects and mine as well. He is a novelist who, because he is exiled, now has his narrative domain defined: all of his writings are set in the place he lost. In my case, I tell him, exile is the subject: the narrator is trapped in his territory and yearns to live like a stranger, lost off in another country. On this subject, Roa asks me for an explanation of the chronicles of another country (Conti, Moyano, Saer). Well, what connects them? A certain monotony in the way they tell stories, a certain interest in marginalized areas of life and the provincial world. I don't have anything to do with that poetics of slow and descriptive prose, and I don't claim to be—or brag about being—an interior man.

Monday 8
Last night at Gotán we saw *La pata de la sota*, a new work by Tito Cossa. Some changes in his poetics (always floating, the mother reading the Bible), which aren't able to resolve the internal conflicts of realist theater, once again a priori. Drawing from a concept in order to arrive at the same concept (the crisis of the middle class reflected in a work that focuses on the crisis of the middle class). Good control of situations, dialogue. Leaving the theater is like leaving after a family visit: nothing happens, and that is everything.

Prologue to the Latin American short stories. The encounter with the spoken language of each country (Cabrera Infante, Rulfo, Cortázar, etc.), even as it separates us from the supposed mother tongue (Spanish), refines and unifies the literature of Latin America. Tendency toward linguistic realism and the mimesis of orality.

Tuesday 9
Perhaps the initiation rites should be institutionalized in Argentina; at least that's the impression I have after seeing how a juvenile culture develops, connected to rock music in certain styles of dress, defined by their own laws and codes.

Regarding the relationship between life and literature, you have to pay attention to where you put the positive sign: to look at literature from life is to think of it as a closed and airless world; in contrast, to look at life from literature allows you to perceive the chaos of experience, the lack of form and meaning, allowing you to endure life.

Wednesday 10
After Cacho's arrest in February of last year, I went into a spiral, or rather a confused whirlwind, and hit rock bottom; in August "The End of Something" led me to move in the darkness and search for the light, which only now has started to shine. When you think about yourself and attempt to recreate naturally what you have lived through, you use a narrative and link the events with causal logic—but life doesn't obey those rules, and everything comes about confusedly, at the same time.

Monday 15
I worked all weekend long, half-sick with the flu, but just a little while ago today I finished the note on youth for *Extra* magazine, in exchange for five thousand pesos.

Tuesday 16

An affectionate meeting with Haroldo Conti and then an interview for Venezuela; they asked me about authenticity, and I answered, "To be sincere, you have to be insincere, think about technique, avoid confessions. You have to be genuine with the reader by means of a convincing style (but it isn't necessarily sincere, or spontaneous). Technique, as Ezra Pound said, is the test of the artist's sincerity."

I am working on the anthology of Latin American literature. Old themes are rewritten but given another setting. The creation of a manifold literary language has begun, connected to the breakdown of Spanish predominance.

Briante's second book is written in a borrowed language that never becomes personal. That doesn't stop his book from being very good, but I think it hinders him—or will hinder him—in moving forward and writing other books.

Saturday 20

In Florida bar, always an oasis in these places, at once anonymous and familiar. I regain some peace after the confusing turmoil today with Julia; neither of us have any money, and she is now alone in the place. I am reading a book about American film noir. Narrating a police interrogation as though it were a scene of jealousy (in general it happens in reverse: What were you doing last night? Where were you? Who is the other woman or other man? Tell me, admit it . . .).

She devotes herself to a ferociously exclusive love and dedicates all of her energy to tying him down forever, but, of course, her efforts only serve to lose him.

As night falls. A woman, almost crippled and tied to her bed, isolated in a vast and empty house, makes a telephone call to the outside, trying to find her husband. It is ten at night. By chance she interrupts an anonymous conversation: two men, two voices really, are planning a crime that will take place an hour later. After many calls to different places, each time more anxious and more frightened, the woman comes to realize—or imagines—that the murder will be her own.

Tuesday 23

Long travels since Sunday. At six in the afternoon, with forty pesos to my name, a call came from Pirí Lugones inviting me to a meeting at her house. I put together some books and sold them at a used bookshop for three hundred pesos. Then I went to her house in Flores and stayed there all night. A meeting with Rodolfo Walsh, Ismael Viñas, Horacio Verbitsky, arguing about the police, based on Paco Urondo's sentimentality. Returning at six in the morning with Carlos Peralta, some conclusions. According to Carlos, the invitation may have to do with the idea of producing a version of *Marcha* magazine in Buenos Aires.

Carlos shares some information with me and I copy it down here, somewhere between surprise and embarrassment. For Ismael Viñas, "E. R. is the most brilliant, the only writer from the new generation who matters." According to Urondo, this year Casa de las Américas, in Cuba, will invite me to Havana at a request and recommendation from him, Noé Jitrik, and César Fernández Moreno.

After so much whiskey, I get up at noon and go to the pawnbroker. Two hours of waiting, my attempts to pass out. I went twenty-four hours without eating, plus the sleepless night with whiskey. In the end, surely after looking at my face, a policeman stops me to interrogate me about where I got the camera that I have gone there to pawn. Nothing serious, just arrogance. Finally, around three in the afternoon, I order a piece of chorizo with fried potatoes at Pippo, after a scattered and extremely lucid vision—due to hunger, exhaustion, and alcohol—of the city: everything seems vast, the sky is made of glass, and the buildings all have blinds and locked shutters. Vision modifies reality, the crisis of urban certainties. Now I want to work, all in one go.

I worked fairly well all afternoon, ended up with the prologue for the anthology almost ready.

Friday

No money once again. Now I'm working on the mini-biographies of the writers I selected for the anthology. Since it is coming out in Buenos Aires, I didn't include Argentine writers. León R. reproaches me for it when I mention the criterion: "You did that," he says, "so you wouldn't have to include David . . . " "Well," I answered him, "I'm not including Borges either."

Cortázar: when he stops being Borges, he's a naturalist (the same thing happens with Bioy Casares).

Anyway, the worst thing is always this insane activity that keeps me tied down at the table, tapping away at the typewriter like a sleepwalker, with the idiotic feeling that I can't stop. Entire days working without leaving the room, and when I lose the thread, I find a series of pages written passionately, which I can't read again until a few days have passed. I've written two chapters of the novel, the biographies of the American writers, the impossible article about what it is to be young, the prologue for the Latin American anthology, the corrections and rewrites of the stories in *La invasión*. But maybe I am making myself blind and the only thing that matters is the activity itself, without false utilitarianism and without seeking results.

Saturday 27

Ready to draw something from the well of the stories from *La invasión*, I work them over doggedly, but I have to learn to hold back when I sit down at the typewriter, to stop myself from writing a different story every time I revise what I am going to publish. I am trying to create a progression for the stories in the book, to give them an organic structure.

Sunday 28
A slow walk through the suburbs of Constitución with Julia. The dark little plaza, the cut-off street, the low and yellowish houses, the memories of returning to the station at various points in my life, first from Adrogué, and then from La Plata, and always a feeling of defiance in confronting the city, the insane desire to conquer it. As though literature were also a weapon and a way to stake out my place in Buenos Aires.

The Tower (Diary of a soldier). Sometime I let myself be dragged along by a foolish hope and want to think I am alone on the tower, the sea behind me. You can see the coming night, as though suspended between the mountains, because there is no twilight to the south; the shadows fall and, in an instant, everything is darkness.

Monday
Long walks around Buenos Aries, looking for *Historia de la literatura latinoamericana* by Anderson Imbert to help finish the articles. I went to the National Library, the Institute of Literature, the College of Philosophy and Letters, and *La Prensa* newspaper. It felt like I was looking for a nonexistent book and, even if its content is fairly nonexistent, I don't understand why I couldn't find it.

I saw a young man running down Viamonte, crossing through the puddles in the street; he was drenched but didn't stop running and turned his head back fearfully toward where a woman with a mesh bag in her hand was screaming, and the young man went on running clumsily, now pursued by a policeman, who trapped him halfway down the block.

Tuesday

Yesterday an encounter with Edgardo, a neurotic intellect. What does he mean to say? A kind of thought—thinking—that is sinuous, menacing; he always seems to be on the brink of announcing something he will never say. Circular, self-centered, concentric.

José Sazbón lent me a thousand pesos that I hoped would make it to Friday, but last night six hundred of them got away from me. Now I'm freezing, don't have the money to turn on the furnace; I put on two pairs of pants and two sweaters, and want to finish the anthology of Latin America.

Thursday, June 1

I am in La Plata, at the library of the University I know very well, where I manage to find everything I'm looking for. Dazzled by the books I have to read, by the magazines and publications lying on my table now.

These places urge me toward old memories, and sometimes I feel that I am several different men, or rather, sometimes it seems as though I were several different men. An intense, intimate experience, which leads me to see alternatives and realities based on who I am in a given moment. Something of the truth about my life lies in that impression, a *printed* man, as it were, a man who can read his life in different registers, or rather, in different genres. It isn't a psychological confusion—although those abound in me—but rather an illuminating experience.

Sunday 4

"The greatest magician would be the one who would cast over himself a spell so complete that he would take his own phantasmagorias as autonomous appearances," Novalis.

A frozen Sunday, two degrees below zero, the room warmed by the furnace, where we set a stew in the afternoon, while I was finishing the prologue and the biographies of the Latin American writers, and Julia cried from time to time, raging with a cold that held her down in bed for the whole weekend.

Monday 5
I'm working on the book of short stories. Just now, dead from cold, I finished the last revision before the galleys. I have grown too tired of these stories.

It's remarkable, but every conversation, no matter whom it is with— recently, for example, Pirí—becomes a misunderstanding for me, I misinterpret what they say; nevertheless, conversation is a surprising example of our capacity for using language at a moment's notice. Speaking over the phone and then connecting with a disembodied voice is a very interesting exercise; by not seeing the gestures and expressions of the person on the other end, you can carelessly misinterpret the meaning of what you hear. It would be best to talk in front of a mirror and practice making the gestures and assuming the expressions that accompany the words we hear. When I speak, on the other hand, I feel myself propelled forward and don't know where I will go; when I manage to be precise and effective, as I did just now, I immediately have a feeling of happiness because it seems that the language has worked to perfection.

Tuesday, June 6
In Florida bar, with blasts of wind, because this table near the window is right next to the swinging door. I stubbornly tried to warm up the room by force of patience, but the concierge at the hotel took advantage of an oversight to slip in and open the windows and clean and turn my work place into an igloo. That's why I am now in this bar, so cozy, working calmly on the letter to Cabrera Infante. Yesterday I started reading *One Hundred Years of Solitude*, the new novel by García Márquez.

I switched tables because the woman who was sitting opposite me left and I was able to take the best place at the bar. I have great experience in the layouts of the cafés where I sit down to work. For me they are annexes of the place where I live, a mixture of writing desk and living room. I know the times when the bars are empty and you can stay in them without a problem, enjoying the tranquility and a clean and well-lit place. As always, in such cases, I come only with the novel that I'm reading and a book of notes, and that's enough for me to pass the afternoon. And so I am reading García Márquez, smelling the unmistakable aroma of coffee, the dull noise of the street behind and a cheerful feeling of happiness with time stopped before me, convinced of the "goodness" of my life these days.

On some level, still undefinable for me, García Márquez's novel reminds me of Borges in *A Universal History of Infamy*. Here it is about the universal history of the world's marvels, an optimistic novel, maintaining the mythical and astonishing perspective and distance between the narrator and the heroes, which is also the case in Borges's book. The protagonists are heroes, for happiness here and for disgrace in Borges's stories. They have that in common, characters who are already given and act according to conventions that only the narrator knows. For example, García Márquez relates the everyday as though it were fantastical (for example, the excursion to see the ice) and relates the extraordinary as though it were trivial (women fly without any problem).

Thursday 8

Sitting here now, the same table as four years ago at Teutonia in La Plata. At that time, I was with Susana M., about to take my final for "Medieval History" with Nilda Guglielmi, Hemingway's smiling face on the cover of *Época* newspaper. Nostalgia is an almost dreamlike feeling for me. As I have already said a couple of times, the images from memory sometimes come attached to places and other times senselessly, as though someone were sending them to me from the past, the same as a postcard of a German-style bar, and on the back someone has written the note that I just finished writing here.

379

In order to understand the notion of "figure" in Cortázar (links between different characters coincidentally connected in a shared space), it is enough to sit down for a half hour near a public telephone and listen—by chance, inadvertently—to the most intimate and varied conversations, and, in this way, witness the single-stringed weaving of destinies, meetings, dates, breakups, disagreements. Because it is oral, that fabric is inevitably "literary": the world is recreated based on the language and the speech of a heterogeneous ensemble of fragmented and unknown narrators.

Friday, June 9
I am at the College to get my salary from the first part of last year, before my resignation due to the military government's takeover of the University. I receive half of the money they owe me and a promise that they will hurry with "the case," as they call it. The funny thing is that, except for the high authorities of the University, so to speak, the secretaries and administrative staff of the College are still the same kind people that you meet when coming in as a newly arrived student. My commitments to Jorge Álvarez and my new work with him have come to replace my academic life, which seems to have ended once and for all. I have gone from being a professor to being an *editor*, in the English sense of the term—that is, an editorial adviser who directs collections, writes reader's reports, but works at home, *freelance*, another English term that has no translation in our world.

Sunday, June 11
I have been making notes on *One Hundred Years of Solitude*, the novel everyone is talking about, which I read too quickly and with uncertain feelings. On the one hand, it seems too—professionally—Latin America to me: a kind of celebratory local color, with something of Jorge Amado and also of Fellini. The prose is very potent and also very demagogic, with calculated punchlines for the paragraphs to produce an effect of surprise. I am writing a review of the book for *El Mundo* and hope to

finish it tonight. Yesterday afternoon I killed time at Noé Jitrik's house; he wants to organize a study group (with Ludmer, Romano, Lafforgue, etc.) on Argentine literature. The point is to create an alternative to the University, now taken over, where all of the professors have resigned, and to build an alternative institution, the Institute of Arts and Humanities. In any case, today I have not moved from this room, where freezing air filters in, trying to finish my pending projects.

I would also like to quickly finish this notebook, filled with so many events and, for that very reason, so strange and elusive to me. Moving, new neighborhoods in which I move like a stranger, renewing my interest in the city. Barracas for a while now; the old factory buildings—Bagley, for example—which abound around here, along with the warehouses near the old port that give it its name. Also nearby is Parque Lezama, which has a serene atmosphere, some very pleasant old bars and restaurants. I always have the experience of having no money and getting to know the city by walking, looking for cheap places, traveling by bus, a more direct experience, more conflicted, not mediated by the magical quality of money that alleviates all unawareness of reality, because there are no mysteries when you can buy everything. (You might think that García Márquez's novel is appealing because it recounts the life of a large and penniless family whose relationship with reality is archaic, precapitalist, and therefore—for the media—romantic and magical.)

I could make a list of the things I did, which would be a way to recount how I earn my living (for example, the review of GGM's novel in exchange for two thousand pesos), and see that the novel remains static and that my personal world (my passions) must be financed alone—that is, separately, outside of literature and life as I want to live it.

Sometimes I think I shouldn't publish the book of short stories yet, wait a couple years longer and see what happens, but I have to follow the enthusiasm it has earned from some readers and my conviction that the book has nothing to do with what's being written in Argentina now. That, for me, is a virtue, even if no one realizes it. I am certain that the volume is on the same level as the best works published in the genre in recent times (*El inocente*, *Palo y hueso*, *Cabecita negra*, and *Los oficios terrestres*), but of course that means nothing or, anyway, I don't know if that's enough to legitimize it.

While looking through this notebook, I find a file card from the National Library, which I will transcribe as a trace of my life at this time.

National Library – Buenos Aires – May 29, 1967

Title of work: *Tratados en La Habana*
Author: José Lezama Lima
Número: 339,260
First and last names of the reader: Emilio Renzi
Address: Martín García 896
ID Card Number: 186,526
Date of birth: November 24, 1941

On the back of the card is this information:

Collections of the Library, as of December 31, 1959

Books, magazines, newspapers, and periodicals . . . 496,604
Folders 110,495
Archives of the Indies copies 6,000
Maps. 6,555
Plates 1,995
Music 36,112
Photographs. 366
Microfilms 68
Total bibliographic items 658,155

Comparative quantities

Collected from 1810 to 1934 . . . . 276,477 bibliographic items
Added from 1934 to 1952. . . . . . .376,908 bibliographic items
Added from 1953 to 1959. . . . . . . .44,947 bibliographic items
Total . . . . 698,332 bibliographic items
Manuscripts subtracted 40,177
Current total . . . . 659,155 bibliographic items

Monday, June 12
I went to the magazine to get paid for my notes on youth—four thousand pesos. Then I went to the destitute National Library, came back home with my shoes broken, not from too much walking. Now I'm ready to read Onetti's short novels.

Last night Julia tells me with an indifferent tone that the essence of my notebooks is that, by writing them, I imagine I can change reality; reading them, then, will be a way of living in the present once more. What is memorable is not the boring motion of sitting down to write them: only the future justifies them, according to her.

Tuesday 13
An incredible cold, several degrees below zero in the city. I unsuccessfully try to warm up the room.

The current debate predicting the disappearance of the novel, erased by the popular voracity of the *mass media*, holds some truth. Part of the public leaves the novel behind and seeks fiction in the movie theater or on television. At the same time, the novel can be an impoverished bastion of resistance and negation of the state of things. A culture of opposition can emerge, isolated from the "industry" of propaganda. Precisely because of that, a writer can embark on a venture of resistance, keeping his separation and attempting to cut away from what he is given. Although formal techniques and discoveries are universalized, the novel can preserve a passion for free experimentation.

I am not refusing the possibility of pop being included in the literary tradition. The other issue is that, as writers, we live "pursued" by politics. We can't forget that, in its own way, and before anyone else, literature has narrated this tension, or rather the consequences of this persecution (Stendhal was the first to perceive the problem).

Of course, this discussion originates with the strong presence of Marshall McLuhan, philosopher of mass-communication media, who wrote, "Our technology is, also, ahead of its time, if we reckon by the ability to recognize it for what it is. To prevent undue wreckage in society, the artist tends now to move from the ivory tower to the control tower of society."

In other words, in the electronic age, books (very primitive machines for the diffusion of thought) will disappear and writers will turn into technocrats. The issue, of course, boils down to knowing who will control the system of the mechanisms for diffusion.

An example of the industrialized and impersonal standardization of prose is the style connecting all of the articles in the magazine *Primera Plana*: everything comes from Borges—surprising use of adjectives, indecisive verbs, baroque structure. An example is seeing what journalists from the magazine write or have written in other times or places—for example, Silvia Rudni in Issue 8 of *Mundo Nuevo*, or Ramiro de Casasbellas's old notes in the newspaper *El Mundo*, Tomás Eloy Martínez's notes on cinema in *La Nación*, before they learned to write the generalized prose that comes from Borges.

Sunday 18
Yesterday, a disjointed conversation with Noé Jitrik that concluded with a reading of each other's short stories—and, as always, the certainty of my intuitive advantage in literary standing.

Wednesday 21

Taking refuge in the National Library, between baroque walls and chill air, I read Mansilla.

"Only great minds can afford a simple style," Stendhal.

Monday 26

I am in the National Library. After walking down Corrientes and selling *Point Counter Point* by A. Huxley, *La Bâtarde* by V. Leduc, several history books, and several police novels, I got back five hundred pesos to make it to the end of the month. Then, at Jorge Álvarez, I signed the contract for the publication of my book of short stories. He had already put me in charge of an anthology of Latin American stories in exchange for twenty thousand pesos. Earlier with Pirí Lugones, a veiled reference to a possible literary magazine with Walsh, Gelman, and Rivera. And a meeting with Allen, an American critic whom Beatriz Guido and Walsh introduced to my short stories. Then a meeting with Viñas, who offered for me to lead a *reading* on new Latin American literature. As we were leaving, José Sazbón appeared and the three of us ended up in the Japanese café. Viñas half-deaf, insulting Sabato and going in circles about Argentine literature.

Tuesday 27

An amusing conversation with Beatriz Guido, who inundated me with generous suggestions and "obliged" me to send a story to *Mundo Nuevo*, according to her after "begging" from Rodríguez Monegal, who is "crazy" about "Las actas del juicio," and she arranged a meeting for me with that guy Allen, an American professor who came to study Argentine literature. At the end, I mentioned my problems with work and she automatically asked me, "Do you want *Primera Plana*?" . . . these *relations* make the (new) world go round.

Wednesday

At night in Jorge Lafforgue's house I am meeting with a study group about Borges, directed by Noé Jitrik, connected to the attempt to create an Institute of Arts and Humanities as an alternative to the University taken over by the military.

On Sunday, at Beatriz Guido's house, I met Juan Manuel Puig, the author of a novel that Edgardo Cozarinsky got for me. Today with León Rozitchner, who offers to have me direct a collection of Argentine literature for Lautaro. Then with Jorge Álvarez, who raised the amount he is going to pay me for putting together a chronicle of Latin America to twenty thousand pesos and, finally, in a bookshop on Corrientes where I got *Holy Place* by Fuentes, before running into the very friendly Horacio Verbitsky on the subway.

Wednesday 19

Yesterday, a meeting in Rozitchner's house with people from the Lautaro publishing house, very interested in my plan for a collection of *nouvelles*. A good possibility for work.

Monday 24

Today I finally signed the contract for *La invasión* with Jorge Álvarez. Three years.

On Friday, a meeting with everyone on the left: Ismael and David Viñas, Rodolfo Walsh, León Rozitchner, Andrés Rivera, Roberto Cossa, putting together a magazine that I would help direct.

Today I submitted the prologue and notes for the Latin American anthology.

Several meetings lately in Pirí's house, discussions about Peronism and culture with Ismael Viñas and Rodolfo Walsh.

Meetings with Beatriz Guido and L. Torre Nilsson. I go with them to watch rehearsals of the work by Pinter that they are putting together.

Borges's style is a colloquial one, written and not spoken (like the kind I'm looking for). The route for me is *Martín Fierro* and *Los ranqueles* by Mansilla.

A list of things I want:

> Swim in the sea.
> Clifford Brown with Max Roach.
> Go through the antiquarian bookshops.
> Listen to *A German Requiem* by Brahms.
> Policastro's painting.
> Borges's prose.
> Aníbal Troilo playing at Caño 14.
> Ignacio Corsini singing "Pensalo bien."
> Go to the cinema during the day and come out while there's still sun.
> Sergi wine, '40 vintage.

Pirí calls me, she has the proofs of *La invasión*.

Wednesday 30
A long talk with Haroldo Conti, going south down San Telmo.

After an opinion from Pirí Lugones about my security in the future, I started thinking honestly about my work. It seems that, at some point, I said to Rodolfo Walsh, "In ten years I will be the best Argentine writer." Careful, then, because it's too easy for me to assume the success of what I'm trying to do. We'll see what I think about these chaotically written lines after a while.

Thursday 7
The outbursts begin, the fury. Rodolfo Walsh reminding me, too pre-
cisely, about my prophecy (forgotten by me) that I will become the best
Argentine writer in ten years. Esteban Peicovich goes ahead and says
I am "the best Argentine short-story writer." My book has come out in
Havana and has been confirmed as the best book in the competition.
Álvarez has decided to publish ten thousand copies of *La invasión* and is
talking about my book to everyone.

I propose Miguel Briante's book *Hombre en la orilla* at the Lautaro publishing house.

Romberg, B. *Studies in the Narrative Technique of the First-Person Novel.*

Monday, September 4
Last night, in the building with the golden dome on Carlos Pellegrini,
on the other side of Rivadavia, after ascending a spiral staircase that
rises from the street, an event organized by Álvarez and Pirí Lugones to
honor García Márquez. Many people, many friends, Tata Cedrón sang
some tangos, lots of whiskey, very little space. In one of my circuits
around the apartment, I found myself face to face with García Márquez.
Rodolfo Walsh introduced me to him, playing the competitive game, à
la Hemingway, and announced me like a national boxing prodigy, as
though I were a welterweight with great promise and a secret mission
to defeat the champions in the category, García Márquez and Walsh
himself among them. A friendly and "male" way of demonstrating the
ruthless competition that defines the world of literature. I suspect that
is also García Márquez's style. The fact is that, after his sporting pream-
ble, we found ourselves talking about the results of the Primera Plana-
Sudamericana novel competition, in which the Colombian had been a
judge. They gave the award to *El oscuro* by Daniel Moyano, but García
Márquez said he had gone back and forth a great deal because he liked
El hacedor de silencio by Antonio di Benedetto, but hadn't given it the

award because it was a *nouvelle* and not a novel. But that doesn't make sense, I said, more or less, *Pedro Páramo* or, if you'll allow me, *No One Writes to the Colonel* wouldn't have been considered in a novel competition either, to everyone's embarrassment. The conversation grew interesting because we started to distinguish between short forms, medium-length stories, and novels. García Márquez entered the discussion eagerly; he knows the methods and techniques of narrative well, and for a while the conversation focused exclusively on literary form and we set aside Latin American demagoguery, the subjects that are specific to this region of the world, and we spoke about styles and methods of storytelling and made a rapid catalog of the great medium-length writers, like Kafka, Hemingway, and Chekhov, and of the problems with the excess of words needed to write a novel. A conversation about literature between writers is something unusual for us these days, so I was very interested in our discussion. Walsh also suspects that the novel is a form without control. (As for García Márquez's novel, Borges, who is always abreast of every- thing, apparently said to Enrique Pezzoni, "It is good, but there are fifty years too many.")

Monday, September 11
Some choices present themselves clearly; I just rejected the work that Esteban Peicovich offered me at *La Razón*—thirty-eight thousand pesos per month in exchange for a nine-to-five schedule. I told him no, despite my economic uncertainties, my salary of twelve thousand per month. I prefer being responsible for myself. I have abandoned so many things for literature that continuing down this path is now a kind of destiny. The initial choice defined all the others, and, as always, that choice was unexpected and surprising. "So, what are you thinking about studying?" E.'s sister asked me once, having said that she was studying French at the time. "Well, I'm going to be a writer," I said; I was sixteen years old and had the same odds of being a writer as being a pilot or a mercenary. Treating literature as a destiny in life doesn't guarantee the quality of your work, but it insures that you have the conviction needed to choose

at every moment. You live the life of a writer because you have already chosen it, but then your work has to be up to the level of that decision.

This all sounds sentimental, but it is the result of always finding myself with no security other than what I create for myself. I guess that, someday, I will have time to remake these notebooks, recover the rhythm of the years being filtered through my hands. In the end, if the diaries are all that remains, it will be possible to see them as the endeavor of a person who first decides to be a writer and then starts writing a series of notebooks, before anything else, in which he records his devotion to that imaginary profession. One day I'll try to shape it into something and leave behind a loose thread, clear and strong, from which the spool of my life can be unraveled. Maybe that is why I write them; sometimes they bother me, but I go on ahead as though there were a contract, the meaning of which will become clear at the end (of what?). In my literature, more clearly than anywhere else, you can see something I'll call overthinking "my personality": I seem very rational and aware, but I'll never know why I chose to dedicate my life to literature, nor do I know what forces or winds allow me, once in a while, to produce some acceptable pages. I allow myself to be led by a very nineteenth-century instinct: I have chosen some women or left them, I have made sure to study something else at the College (history) so that nothing can disturb my impromptu readings—and therefore, when faced with decisions that demand clarity, I am not disturbed and make up my mind spontaneously and instinctively, without hesitation. Instead I uproot myself from this blue table by the open window in the breeze that heralds the summer and, to avoid new confused outpourings, I stand, light the fire, put on the kettle, and prepare some yerba maté.

All stories that leave their mark are constructed based on something dark: for example, in "Streetcorner Man," Borges hides the crime—at least, he hides the result of the fight—and does not narrate it; it happens in the darkness and is never seen, and everything is hinted at imperceptibly.

In this case, it deals with an action that is snatched away; I have to think about which other elements of a story can be removed for its implicit contents to become greater. In Pavese's "The Leather Jacket," the boy narrating is only half-aware and is recounting the story of his sadness at losing his friend; the real story (centered around the woman) is not told but is woven secretly underneath the other.

Kafka: "Goethe's diaries. A person who keeps none is in a false position in the face of a diary."

When Kafka reads in Goethe's diary that he spent an entire day occupied with his concerns, he thinks that he, personally, has never done so little in a day. In the future, someone will be able to read my reflection on the diary and then will see Kafka's reflection on the diary and also Goethe's reflection on a day in his life.

In Pavese's diary, the "subject" seems to be the impossibility of suicide ("I will never be able to do it, it's more difficult than a murder"). R. Akutagawa: "Isn't there someone kind enough to strangle me in my sleep?" Working on diaries, fragmented narrative, open ending.

As for *La invasión*, I have started to move away from the book more and more, imperceptibly. I have complete confidence in its future, but that can't help me now. You are once again defenseless when you start another book, whether you have better control over technique or have learned to be more spontaneous; regardless, it won't help you much in the moment you start over again.

To write a story about madmen, a story of madness, it is essential to avoid the hallucinatory stereotype. Therefore, I hope to be able to tell a logical, geometric story, in which everything is organized in such a way that the frenzied wind of insanity only passes through in the final scene. That doesn't mean a surprise ending, but rather a wind that begins as an imperceptible breeze and grows amid the events until it turns into a sort of whirlwind, making all of the words fly.

Tuesday 12
I am reading Virginia Woolf's diary.

In the novel that I intend to write, I would like to recapture that same slightly irrational impulse with which I wrote the short stories, all in one sitting. The closest thing to inspiration I had was that night in the house in Boca, where I wrote three stories, one after another.

After finishing the book, my relationship to books written by others has changed. More and more, it has become difficult for me to read "disinterestedly"; it's impossible not to start editing them or thinking about how I would have written them.

Wednesday 13

A list

Call Noé Jitrik (book of criticism).
Sara Goldenberg (rights for "Isabel Watching It Rain in Macondo" by GGM).
Juan Gelman (piece about the new world for the magazine).
León Rozitchner (message Sra. de Jorge).
Miguel Briante (he's calling Martini about publishing *Hombre en la orilla*).
Marta Gil (prints ready tomorrow).
Juan de Brasi (cancel the meeting).
Finish going over the Rozenmacher recordings.
Version of Salinger story.
Correct the proofs.
Prepare for lecture.

I can't figure out what it is that bothers me in "The Pursuer": all of Cortázar's themes are there, but the contrasts between Johnny's mysterious genius and the biographer's pettiness, between Bruno's greed and the artist's insane brilliance, seem too demagogical and trivial, and irritate me.

Tuesday 19
I stop at Beatriz Guido's house to look for materials about Salinger. She is kind, amusing, not painting due to a cold. She tells me that they've offered her one hundred thousand pesos at the magazine *Atlántida* for a report with or on the jockey Irineo Leguisamo, *New Yorker* style. As for me, satisfied with the corduroy pants I bought this morning in Giesso.

A recent phantom apparition of two policemen looking for the thief. It isn't clear what was stolen. They rang the bell, talked to me, but raised their heads to see the layout of the place. The uncomfortable, knowing way in which the officer addressed me, to which I responded dryly. We have always distrusted the police and have always felt ourselves to be offenders of the law (no matter which), so that any encounter with someone in uniform turns into a complex scene. This leads to a possible meditation on "conditioning."

"The Robbery" is, we might say, a messy story, because everything changes in the escape. Narrating it in plural, with a chorus, but without anyone who decides the meaning of the events. They plan the robbery of the armored car in collusion with the police and then escape, breaking the deal.

Hemingway's iceberg theory doesn't suggest a poverty of information, but rather an absence of explanations. To put it better: the facts are there but the nexus is missing.

Thursday 21

According to a sudden call from Marta Gil, the cover for the book is ready. It is yellow, with white lettering. Last night, paper proofs of *La invasión*.

Sunday 24

I correct the proofs and let myself embark on the ambiguous attraction of my own stories, trying not to see their deficiencies. Kafka says, "How much time the publishing of the little book takes from me and how much harmful, ridiculous pride comes from reading old things with an eye to publication . . . In any event, now, after the publication of the book, I will have to stay away from magazines and reviews even more than before, if I do not wish to be content with just sticking the tips of my fingers into the truth."

In some way, the central story of the novel has come to be the characters' process toward insanity. A madness that could be called heroic; excess, surplus, hubris was a mortal sin for the Greeks.

Monday 25

"El laucha Benítez." Plan. His face contains the story (describe it), show something he keeps under his clothing, a newspaper clipping. Boxer. Archie Moore. Never falls. His handsomeness. The first time they threw him, he fell to the ground out of surprise, shook his head, and moved his face without understanding. After that he started looking around strangely. Fighter. El Vikingo. Club Atenas. El laucha Benítez.

I woke up with Julia at six in the morning. I let the day gradually light up the room while I drank maté, bathed, and then read the paper.

I will never manage to understand where these things come from, but the fact is that just now, suddenly, I found what I was looking for in the story of El Vikingo. Everything hinges on Laucha's death, which he wanted, and therefore it is told again and again. Just now, I can say that I resolved how to write the story.

Tuesday 26
Last night the launch of Walsh's book. Many people piled up, great confusion, too much whiskey. In any case, I want to remember the friendly and warm conversation with Rodolfo W. and Haroldo Conti before I left for the city and came back home.

Novel. It has to be narrated by the chorus, that is, it must be viewed from its destiny ("I told him that if he was leaving, etc."). The voices of the chorus (witnesses, friends, accomplices, police) are superimposed on the investigator, the reporter and the narrator.

Wednesday
The facts could be listed. 1. He started boxing. 2. The highest point of his career . . . Look for an objective, informative tone.

It is two in the morning. I'm fairly tired and decide to leave the end of the story for tomorrow. The furtive feeling bothers me, writing at night with the machine echoing in the silence, creating a strange relationship with the people who live in the room next door in the boardinghouse, whom I sense are awake and alert.

Thursday 28
After ten days of work, I have the first version of "El laucha" ready. I makes me remember the cold and distant way that I worked on the story about Urquiza.

October 2
Sometimes I think I should publish the book under a different name, thus sever all ties with my father, against whom, in fact, I wrote this book and

will write the ones to follow. Setting aside his last name would be the most eloquent proof of my distance and my resentment.

I caught up with delayed commitments: letter to Daniel Moyano, interview with Rozenmacher, translation of the Hemingway story.

Wednesday 4
I cannot, of course, write anything about my book; I spent a few days turning over the back-cover text that Jorge Álvarez asked me for, but in the end I found the solution, helped by Haroldo Conti's friendship and enthusiasm. He will write the introductory text. I'm going to Di Tella in a while, and then I'll get the photos for the book.

Tuesday 10
Greetings from Pirí Lugones last night. Martín Fierro on television. A meeting with friends: Miguel Briante, Dipi Di Paola, Vicente Battista. Talking about money, mandatory work, the excuses that each of us invents.

Friday 13
If it's true that they killed Che Guevara in Bolivia, something has changed forever in my friends' lives and also in mine. A messy week, confusing news. It did not stop raining. I remember going down Calle Libertad with Ismael Viñas, jumping over puddles of water, crossing improvised bridges, when we heard the news. Great commotion.

Monday 16
Fidel Castro confirmed the death of Che Guevara. The issue now is why Guevara left Cuba and why he went to Congo and then, without any support, launched guerrilla warfare in Bolivia. The other issue is why the Cubans didn't rescue him from the field when the army started to uncover the whole plot and their contacts in La Paz fell, their only source of provisions. It's obvious that a special group could have rescued him and taken him to the border, but we won't know anything until we have

direct news from the two or three guerrillas who survived the trap and saw when Che was arrested and, subsequently, coldly executed.

Monday, October 23
Ramón T. called me just now; it has been almost a year since that afternoon at the taxi stand on 1 and 60 in La Plata, when we said goodbye and I realized, without either of us saying anything, that he was going to Cuba to prepare for a new guerrilla adventure, which I now see was connected to the contacts in Argentina that Che expected to follow him in Bolivia. We said nothing of this, but I noticed that Ramón was troubled and distant.

Wednesday
Plan: finish "El Vikingo." Prologue for the book about Hemingway and the anthology of Latin American short stories. Letter to Daniel Moyano. See Beatriz Guido, Jorge Álvarez (Sartre).

Sunday
A recent call from Pirí, a preview of the book in two magazines, expectations, plans. I'm not thinking about a book launch and I don't want one, I told her.

The novel about the heist will be called *Among Men*.

An oppressive day; only a plate of noodles in oil, because there is no money.

Tuesday, October 31
I suddenly remembered, as always happens to me, an image of myself, newly arrived in La Plata, six years ago, sitting at the París café with Alvarado. Memories, in which there is something in play that I can't glimpse, always take the same form: a snapshot, a flash that passes before me like a bolt of lightning, and I see myself in the scene of the memory. As though I were simultaneously viewing the scene and taking part in it. It isn't Proust's involuntary memory, instead it seems more like a sort of

private cinematography; from time to time the projector starts running and I see a few scenes from my life. It happens when I'm not prepared and don't know what has given rise to the appearance of the image.

Today I earned twenty thousand pesos from Jorge Álvarez, with which I will be able to survive until December with some security and without too much stress. Meanwhile echoes of the book arrive, news of the publication of *La invasión* in Havana, Andrés Rivera comes from Montevideo bringing me a pamphlet from Casa de las Américas with news about the book, a review and photo in which I see the cover of the book printed in green. The first book is the only one that matters; it takes the shape of an initiation rite, a passage, a crossing from one side to the other. The importance of the thing is merely personal, but you can never forget, I'm sure, the emotion of seeing a book of your writing printed for the first time. After that, you have to try not to turn into "a writer."

Thursday, November 2
On Guevara. The commotion around his death is dissolving the purpose that brought them this far. His critiques of the Soviets and, therefore, certain lines of the Cuban Revolution resolved him to renounce his position and return to the struggle once more. Some of my friends (Elías, Rubén, Ramón T.) have that same conviction, as though they took responsibility for an ethics of their own, or rather, an ethics that finds its meaning in the future. After so much time suffering from secularization and the end of transcendent ideas—or the death of God, as Nietzsche said—some have found a way to restore this lost sense in history. The possibility of that meaning, which in another way defines life itself, obviously justifies their risk of death.

Tuesday 8
A confusing weekend at Pirí Lugones's house. She suggests that we come to live there; her house is large and she rents out one of the rooms to offset her spending. Ismael Viñas, who has been living in the house, announced

that he was moving somewhere else and she is offering us the free room. On Sunday, Walsh interviewed me (between liters of whiskey and ridiculous discussions) for his notes about new writers in *Primera Plana*.

Now, leaving behind the excitement of this time of great festivities, I set out once again, writing about Hemingway's stories.

"Wash Jones" (which I will include in the collection of stories). Faulkner's story anticipates and retells the central theme of *Absalom, Absalom!* and lends another meaning to Colonel Sutpen's life. Faulkner's characters (Quentin, Shreve) imagine what they don't know, what no one has told them, what hopelessly admits no variations or allusions. They could even predict the death of Quentin Compson. The technique is simple; it consists of attributing knowledge about things a third-person narrator usually doesn't know to various narrators—distinct in time and space. Not affirming anything as definitive truth, making all of the action potential.

Monday, November 13
National Library. In my hands, *Tristram Shandy* by Laurence Sterne: *born on the 24 of November, 1712.* (He was born on the same day as me.)

Wednesday, November 15
In terms of style, there seem to be two paths (if you want to escape, as I have done in *La invasión*, from the gravity of Borges's prose). A neutral, impersonal, transparent tone, not forceful, but full of nuances and false syntactical simplicity. Or a style that copies orality, very subjective. In both cases, there is an attempt to erase the written signifier, through brevity or through a colloquial verbalization. For me, at heart it is about an art that intensifies synthesis and that, on the other hand, signals that it is a book, not a reality, but rather an artificial object that has been proven as real.

RICARDO PIGLIA

In a surprising way, the story about Lazarus Morell from Borges's first work presupposes, divines, suggests Sutpen—through his geographical sphere, through his lineage and through his "activities"—before he reaches the territory.

Friday 17

A meeting for the magazine. Rodolfo Walsh ponders *La invasión*, "a very good book, very even, the best ones are: 'Tierna es la noche' and 'Mata-Hari 55,'" "great formal construction."

"The very noise of his words, of his sincere declaration, reflected his conviction that language could serve no purpose to him," J. Conrad.

Conrad and H. James define a kind of storytelling in which the vision matters more than the story. The imagination doesn't draw from a conventional story, already completely made, but rather from an ambiguous situation that never ends up being understood.

Thursday 23

Now settled into Pirí's house, in this room over Calle Rivadavia, full of light, with large picture windows. As always, I adapt with difficulty in the face of changes. Yesterday with Jorge Álvarez; final proofs of the book that will come out "at the beginning of December."

Thousands of things to do and I'm stuck in a lethargy, as though everything had paused, spaced-out, with no desire to go back one last time to the boardinghouse on Calle Montes de Oca and get the things we left.

Monday 27

A furious call from Juan Gelman just now, asking me for a preview of the book in *Confirmado*. "Excellent book, very well written, dazzling," he pointed to the phrase from "En el terraplén"—"the chief of them all"—as an exemplar of synthesis.

400

It is curious, but Onetti's best works, always so excessive, so verbal, so Faulknerian, are his short histories ("A Grave with No Name," "The Pit," "Goodbyes").

December 2

I have a proof of the book cover here on the table—straightforward, yellow, with my own face.

December 11

In El Rayo bar, ancient, dark, and cool, facing the train station in La Plata. I spent many nights here drinking gin and watching the shady life that is amassed in terminals. The girls from the bar—showgirls, entertainers—came to the tables of students like me and immediately established a rapport, because we were separate from the "clients" they went with to turn their tricks in the hotels surrounding the area: business travelers, public employees, people leaving the racetrack. Afterward they returned and sat down to talk with me, at a table reading. "What are you reading, *corazón*? You're going to hurt your eyes." They put their hands over the open pages and invited me to leave with them. Sometimes I would wait for the bar to close and invite them to have a coffee in a Japanese bar on Calle 1, and sometimes I also spent the night with one of them, only to hear them tell their bizarre stories with dignity.

December 12

Another day of waiting, reading Carlos Fuentes's stories, killing time, paralyzed. Sometimes a tranquility in the face of the futility of these expectations, distance from the book and nostalgia for the gentle ease with which I wrote the stories, efficiently and without thinking too much.

Among Men. These are the first results of a broader investigation I have begun based on the experiences of Oscar Lewis (*The Children of Sanchez, Life*). As we know, Lewis has innovated in the field of anthropology based on the use of the tape recorder, with the goal of recording life stories, real events, and at the same time narrating them through the voices and styles of the protagonists. I am interested most of all in raising some considerations here. As we know, the use of the recorder changes the level of exploration of the experience and creates a distance in the way the events are told. We try to strengthen this criterion; in this book, I have reconstructed the events that occurred, basing it on the assault on the armored car from a bank in San Fernando and the criminals' subsequent flight to Montevideo, where they were finally surrounded by the police in a trap caused by betrayal. My first contact with the protagonists of this story took place on January 11, 1965, after reading news of the assault in *La Razón* newspaper. After that, I interviewed all of the witness and participants in the events and gained access to a radio amateur's recordings of the conversations between the lowlifes while they were resisting the police attack. There's no need to tire the reader by narrating the difficulties I had to overcome to conduct the recordings and achieve a personal rapport with the protagonists. Several interviews were necessary before I could manage to understand the facts in any detail. Finally, I was able to join a group of five witnesses, initiating the first conversations without a recorder in order to establish a level of trust with them, and, by the time we finally began working with the record of their account, we already had a very smooth relationship.

Wednesday 13

Work to do, several matters. Plan for the novel. American and Latin American anthologies. Series with Editorial Estuario. Projects with Editorial Tiempo Contemporáneo. I make my living as a publisher, or rather, as a director of collections, which means I am a professional reader.

Friday 15

Yesterday a surprising call from Francisco Urondo, announcing an invitation from Casa de las Américas for me to travel to Cuba. There is already a ticket in my name. Desolation with Julia. According to Pirí, the book is coming out today.

December 17
The book is finally in my hands, and also the issue of *Crónicas de Norteamérica*. I can't travel with Julia, and it makes no sense for me to stay with her either.

Monday
Jorge Álvarez book. Then Germán at Florida. Then Ludmer at noon. Sara, expecting the meeting at the publisher's. Passport today at six (call Paco). Conti.

For the better, this month has turned out to be very Argentine, and I'm reading autobiographies of writers and other heroes to organize an anthology centered on first-person narratives. I'm going to include a variety of texts, letters, confessions, fragments of personal diaries, and I'm working with a very wide register that includes politicians, adventurers, writers. *The I*. That will be the title of the book. The idea is that the autobiography is a genre that we all practice at some point, deliberately or not. We can't live if we don't pause from time to time to make a narrative and tangential summary of our lives. Finding those moments, wherever they are written, will be the concept of this anthology. Catching the protagonists in the moments when they refer to themselves.

Tuesday
Introduction to the book of stories by Torre Nilsson.

In the National Library. I spend the afternoon looking over old books, creating a new version of the concept of the autobiography. New, because I imagine the writings connected by genre and not by the incidental notion of "literature." Personal writings surpass that category and, in fact, put themselves forth as testimonies. The other issue is that, usually, only fictional texts are considered literary (whatever their direction may be).

Argentines for themselves. An anthology of autobiographical prose. "It seemed to me that they all committed a great error: they conducted themselves very well with the erudite class, but disregarded men of the lower classes, those from the country, who are men of action. I noticed this from the beginning and thought that, during the critical points of the revolution, the same parties had to account for that class conquering and causing the greatest damage because there is always a known willingness in which there is nothing against the rich or upper classes. It seemed very important to me, then, to gain significant influence over this population in order to contain it, or direct it, and I resolved to gain that influence at all costs, for which I had to work with great perseverance, with many sacrifices, to become a gaucho like them, to speak like them and do as they did, protect them, make myself their representative, look after their interests, in short, spare no work or methods to win their opinion." Juan Manuel de Rosas, December 9, 1829, the day he is elected governor of Buenos Aires.

(Peron thought in exactly the same way and did the same thing as Rosas, in another context, but with the same paternalistic popular concept.)

Tuesday 26
The situation is like this: I will travel with León R., Rodolfo W., and Paco Urondo; París–Havana route.

Buy
  Agenda. Black notebook. Shirt. Buttons. Canvas shoes. Gillette. Shaving cream. Toothpaste. Shoes. Suitcase. Clothes. Handkerchiefs. Books (Álvarez).

See: Miguel (boots).

Ticket (Tucumán seven thousand).
  Vaccine.

19

Who Says I

As linguistics teaches, the I, among all of language's signs, is the most difficult one to control, the last that the child acquires and the first that the aphasic loses. Midway between the two, the writer has developed the habit of speaking about himself as though referring to another.

In spite of it all, one tries, in some books, to forget that mask; in these, a concrete subjectivity shows its face, is accepted.

Exorcism, narcissism; in an autobiography, the I is all spectacle. Nothing manages to interrupt that hallowed area of subjectivity, someone tells himself about his own life, the object and subject of the narration, the only narrator and only protagonist; the I also seems to be the only witness.

Nevertheless, by the simple fact of writing, the author proves he is not speaking to himself alone; if he were, "a kind of spontaneous nomenclature for his feelings would suffice, for feeling is immediately its own name." Forced to translate his life into language, to select the words, the problem is no longer lived experience but rather the communication of that experience; the logic that structures the events is not that of sincerity, but that of language.

It is possible, having accepted that ambiguity, to attempt the task of deciphering an autobiographical text—trying, in short, to recover the meaning that one subjectivity has let fall, illuminated in the act of telling oneself. Mirror and mask, that man speaks of himself when speaking of the world and, at the same time, shows us the world when speaking of himself. It is essential to corral these elusive presences into all corners, to know that certain prestidigitations, certain emphases, certain linguistic traditions are as relevant as the more explicit "confession."

Like no other text, the autobiography requires the reader to complete the circle of its expression; closed in on itself, that subjectivity is blinded, and it is the reader who breaks the monologue, who bestows meanings that were not visible before.

It is enough to review some of the pages included in this anthology (the ways in which Borges or Macedonio Fernández tackle the problem, Mansilla's attempt to establish a natural dialogue with his reader, etc.) to understand that, behind the tone and rhythm of a voice, behind a circumstantial reference to money or to literature, behind the narration of a political incident, it is possible to glimpse not only the density, the climate, the dreams of an epoch, but also the speaker's level of awareness (of himself and of the world), the way in which reality has been experienced, internalized and remembered by particular people under particular circumstances.

Far from wanting to exhaust a literary form that has such a fertile tradition in Argentina, this volume tries to suggest the possibility of a meaningful reading, and, for this reason, texts have been included that, although not intentionally written as autobiography, preserve that aperture, that respiration weighed down by signs and subtexts, that complicity that ultimately cuts down the distances, compromises the cold blood of ideas in the warm density of life. In that sense, they may be read as chapters of an ongoing autobiography.

2 0

River Stone

Stories proliferate in my family, Renzi said. The same ones are told over and over again, and through being told and repeated, they are improved, refined like pebbles honed by water in the depths of rivers. Someone voices a song, and the song rolls around, here and there, over the course of years. My mother, for example, now lives with my brother in Canada, and if I want to find out something, I have to call her on the phone, and then the story lacks the secret meaning of gestures and, most of all, of my mother's gaze, her sky-blue eyes, slightly unclear but still very expressive, which comment on events and impart other meanings. My mother was, for years, the most faithful repository of our family stories, and those stories were great because they were held up on personal understanding. There were permanent figures—my uncle Marcelo Maggi, for example, someone to whom the stories always returned, and who could never be forgotten.

She, my mother, one afternoon, during the time when we were burying my grandfather, suddenly, on the patio under the vines, in the shadows, decided to reveal the secret to me—that is, the truth of Emilio's life, as she called it, something always slightly uncomfortable because I had the same name as my father's father, which caused her a kind of rage, as though she imagined or feared that the similarity of the names would affect her son's destiny. Because of this, she only called me *Emilio* when she was angry or irritated and then would modulate my name like someone scratching glass to produce an unbearable screech: *Emmiliiio*, she would call me until I was deafened. But the rest of the time, before my grandfather died, she called me *Em* or *Nene* or simply nothing; she talked, without naming me, in a caring intonation that made my presence inevitable in the sentence directed at me. No one could doubt that my mother's favorite son was the one she never called by name. Not calling me what everyone else called me, she instead made a slight pause—a silent modulation—in which our intimacy was clear. As soon as my grandfather died, that very afternoon, she started calling me *Emilio*, with a new cadence, and straightaway, as though she wanted to erase the death from the scene, she went on to tell me the reason, or rather, the motive that caused my grandfather to enlist as a volunteer in the First World War. An insane decision that, for years, was the greatest proof of his courage and manhood to me. Because Nono went to the Italian Embassy in Buenos Aires and asked to be shipped off immediately to the battlefront. As he was an educated man, and was at his peak physically, they made him an officer, and he took on responsibilities as soon as he arrived at the front lines.

Emilio Renzi was, then, in the same bar where he went every afternoon, sitting in front of the same table, in the flat corner against the window that opened onto the intersection of Riobamba and Arenales, and he seemed to have discovered, or remembered, a lost event from his life that better enabled him to understand his grandfather's experience.

The worst part of the war, as my grandfather would say, Renzi continued, was the stasis, buried down in the trenches, in those caves, flooded, muddy; you had to keep still and wait. Wait for what, my grandfather would ask, Renzi said, and keep silent, his gaze lost in the flowers on the patio, seemingly attentive, but he had gone astray in the memories. The history of my grandfather, who had gone off to war, was one of the key stories in the family novel, told in chorus, for which my mother was the essential narrator. She had been steeped in the dense collective mythology because she was the youngest of the siblings, the smallest and the one who, in batches, with each new generation, would receive the story or stories. Sometimes one of these histories would be told over the course of months: for example, the actions of her nephew Mencho (her brother Marlon's son), who, when his father died, had tried to save him from the darkness, stricken as he was that night, hours after his father had been deposited in the family mausoleum in the town cemetery, a crypt, although it was not a crypt but rather the structure destined to be the place where dead family members would be deposited. Mencho left in his pickup truck, forced open the gate to the burial ground, and then advanced along the wide interior streets until he passed next to the funerary structure and, with the key that each relative possessed, granting the right to open the iron and beveled glass door, which was also engraved, that door, with white steel filigree to resemble a tree. My cousin entered, crossed himself, and took out the coffin with his father's body, bore it on his shoulder, and lifted it with delicate care into the bed of his truck, constantly speaking to the cadaver under the light of the moon. He crossed town with the body, with his dear father, and stopped beside the lake, unable to bear the idea of his father being alone that night. The story of the man who stole the casket and took it down the street for a ride until, at noon, the police found him by the lake, where, sitting next to the coffin, he was talking aloud with no one to hear what he said—it was told with a smile, as though it were a comedy. Because my mother would tell that story with grace and respect, yet also with a certain irony. The boy, my mother would say, knew how to honor the specter of his dead father. Don't you think so, dear, she would say to me, suggesting with her gaze, full of light, that I also must do the same when, in short, she passed on, as she would say, *to a better place.*

The history of my father's imprisonment also had a principal place reserved in everyone's official version of the past, even though my mother would tell it with sarcasm, taking away everything epic about it, and, on top of that, the reconstruction of events would take place with my father in the room. But he now no longer worried about denying this version, and let his wife's narration flow.

The difference, in the case of my grandfather Emilio and his adventure in the war, was that my mother kept an ace in her sleeve. My grandfather was assigned to the fortified line in the Alps, a series of trenches set into the heights of the mountain range. It was impossible being there—a terrible chill, narrow paths among the frozen rocks—yet, nevertheless, they held the position for months and months.

That story was told jubilantly behind my grandfather's back, when he was not around, because his version of events was fragmented and terse; actually, it was centered around his assignment in the Second Army post office, the experience that had scarred him and almost driven him to insanity. But my mother was capable of protecting the secret for many years, because that was her style, always very faithful to her promises. My grandfather trusted her, and I inherited that trust, although my grandfather never told me why he had decided to leave everything behind and enlist as a volunteer in that war. I have told part of his story in one of my novels, disguised under the name of Bruno Belladona. He was the station chief in a desolate part of La Pampa, and he founded a town and was political chief and commander of the place, and he bought lands and grew rich, helped along by his political contacts, and, in the town, his decision to go to war was understood as an example of patriotism and valor. At that time, many young people imagined that going to war was a way to acquire an experience beyond what any of them could dream of in civilian life.

Renzi paused a moment and looked at the street, almost empty that summer afternoon, and then went on talking with the same enthusiasm with which he had started to tell the story. If I became a writer—that is, if I made that decision that defined all of my life—it was also due to the stories that circulated in my family; it was there that I learned the fascination and power that hides in the act of recounting a life or an episode or an incident for a familiar circle of listeners, who share with you the references behind what is being told. Therefore, I sometimes say that I owe everything to my mother, because for me she was the most convincing example of how to be a narrator who dedicates one's life to always telling the same story, with some variations and detours. A story that everyone knows and that everyone wants to hear again and again. Because that is part of the logic of the so-called family novel: repetition and knowledge of what is about to happen in the chronicle of life, which everyone began hearing about in the cradle, because one of the most persistent exercises in my mother's family was telling those terrible stories to the children, about alcoholic and beautiful women, like my aunt Regina, Mencho's mother, who at some point decided never to leave her house and spend the days smoking and drinking whiskey and listening to a Uruguayan radio station that spun Carlos Gardel records twenty-four hours a day. My aunt listened to the tangos and soliloquized in the house in front of the terrified or perhaps fascinated eyes of her son Mencho. That story, for example, came out of that closed-off nucleus: a beautiful alcoholic woman who does not leave her house and only listens to tangos by Carlos Gardel. Why she never leaves, why she locks herself up, does not become clear, ever, said Renzi. It never would become clear, because he knew very well how a story is told; an event or image is taken—for example, a beautiful woman smoking and drinking in her house and listening to the radio—and that event would be retold and refined like the stones that the water transforms into hermetic jewels, but the causation behind it is never explained. It is only told and left there, in the clear afternoon air, floating along like a dream or an apparition. That was what I learned from the family stories my mother used to tell: the persistence and the lack of reason.

All the novels I have written come from here, narrate episodes of this family epic. The first one began with the story of my uncle Marcelo, who left everything behind for the love of a cabaret dancer. Then, when I pick them up and tell them again, the plots change; they contain nothing auto-biographical, but I could never write a story that did not have a personal experience at its root. Without this, he said, without any trace of my life, it is impossible to write, or at least I can't believe what I am narrating if I am not personally implicated. Afterward, everything consists of erasing the tracks and blindly following the feelings that come back to me from the stories I have been told.

The most entertaining part was that you were inside the stories being cir-culated. You not only listened to them and knew them, but you could even be among them. I have spent some afternoons in my aunt Regina's house and have talked to her and have seen her move here and there through the rooms without ever going out to the street, while Gardel sang on the radio. Sometimes, she would even sing some tangos in an impassioned voice that I have never been able to forget. That is, it was possible to listen to the story, to know its variations and changes and the conjectures circulated concerning its dark core, and at the same time enter, see them living, see them acting, just as the familiar plot dictated them to do. One spring afternoon, for example, I remember it as though it were today, I went to see her and sneakily started to invite Regina to go to the Plaza with me for an ice cream, and then I watched the curious way in which she eluded the invitation, without refusing, but stubbornly, with trivial excuses. At that moment, just then, she had to wait for a phone call, and even though the call did not take place, she could refuse to leave without giving any further explanation. That unique quality of being inside and outside of a story, and watching it as it took place, left a mark on all of my literature and defined my style of narration. The experience of the plot is unique; the story exists there and you are at once a witness and a tangential protagonist. In some cases, I would take part in the story and I, too, was one of her heroes. For example, I went looking for my uncle Marcelo in Concordia, in Entre Ríos and was, in that way, able not only to participate in her story but also even to transform it.

In this way, there are personal stories in which you are the protagonist, which are never too interesting for the one living them, and there are also personalized stories in which you participate without anyone seeing, as though you were only a guest, an intruder, but you feel the defining emotion in your body. Because narrating, he said, my dear, is transmitting an emotion. That's what narrating means, he said, suddenly furious; transmitting a personal emotion from the stories that you have lived through, intimately and barely. Just barely, he said, you don't need much for the emotions of a story; it's enough to find your mother kissing a stranger to then write *Anna Karenina*. Is that clear? he asked, now smiling. Yes, it's perfectly clear, he said then; you have to live and not live, to be there and pass unseen, to be able to narrate a story as though it were your own.

Now, for example, I have a Mexican muse, a friend I love a great deal, with whom I shared some years at Princeton; she was my colleague there, and I did many things with her in those days, and we write to each other every so often. She, Lucía, mailed me, if you can say it like that, sent me, one of her daughters, just as beautiful as her, *bella como ella*. He paused: "bella como ella" is a verse, a poetic alliteration, rather. And her daughter, María, came to Buenos Aires because her mother couldn't put up with her there any longer, and she really did it all—said hurtful things, made rude gestures, was indifferent and sarcastic—until her daughter, offended, tired of her mother and her mother's gloomy suggestions, decided to escape and come to the most extreme point of the continent, all the way to the south, and ended up in Buenos Aires, intending to carry out a field study examining the singularity or personal nuances of language use in distant territories. In Mexico, said Renzi, who seemed to have begun to diverge slightly, as had been happening more and more frequently with him since he became sick—not "sick," he never used that word; he was, to say it in his way, "in a bit of a fix," or he would say, while mad from panic, "I don't have any pain, just a bit of a disruption in my left hand, which is my good hand, or rather, was my good hand, as I'm left-handed; other than that, and a fatigue that seems to have come from the beginning of time, I am perfectly well." For that reason, he had to hire an assistant to dictate his diary, the notebooks he had accumulated over years and years. He thought that dictating his life just as it was written in those miserable notebooks could entertain him, but above all might help him search for the cause, the motive, the reason for which he had started to feel that his body was alien to him. That expression, "my body is alien to me," abounded in his diaries; ever since his distant youth, he had lived in someone else's body. "That is why I became a writer," he said, "to keep it at bay and carefully observe the stranger who had taken ownership of my body." I will use a metaphor, a simile: There are so many idiots in the world now, with their little cell phones, who walk down the street, talking alone. It has happened to me many times, where I think a passerby has gone insane and is talking, alone on the street, and sometimes laughs and often says, "I'm on my way there," and even, sometimes, provides his coordinates, as the idiots now seem to do to prove they are in some place, and then they say, I've heard them say "I'll give you my coordinates, I'm at fourteen hundred on Malabia and going that way, give me two." Renzi was outraged because those idiots, instead of saying, "I'll be there in a while," said, still say, because this goes on happening, "I'm two," to say, to mean to say, "I'll be there in two minutes." They say, "Give me two," because the decadence of worldwide culture has reached its end. I know many places, I am a sedentary man and for that same reason have traveled constantly, always indifferently; the more sedentary a man is, the more he travels. In the same sense, a nomad only wants to have a place to live, a site of his own, but you see, the nomads only want to keep still, while the sedentary ones like me go on traveling. I am distracted by what they call cultural tourism, and also academic excursions; therefore, a writer like myself, who only longs to be alone in a room, travels a great deal, because there are international congresses, colloquia, keynote addresses, visiting professors who are always on planes, looking over those lowly papers that they will read in the classrooms, lecture halls, amphitheaters, which are always the same, there is a platform and a microphone and a poster that says, for example, "Emilio Renzi," because there are so many lectures that it is necessary to give them a distinguishing mark, it is often a laminated card with a photo of the delinquent who is about to speak, and below the photo his name and origins. I have been around many cities on those trips as a visiting professor or invited lecturer, and in all of them have come across people who go down the street talking alone, gesturing and smiling. It surprised me at first; I have thought they were talking to me and paused in the middle of a sidewalk and said, "Excuse me?" as if they had said something to me or knew me, but no, they went on, walking quickly, with their smaller and smaller little devices, usually with a microphone over the lapel that lets them continue the phone conversation while making gestures with both hands as though the person on the other end could see them, or as though they could remain in the old culture, when people spoke in person. Maybe they don't think that it's a metaphor and that when I say, "I'm living in someone else's body," it is just so, just like that; they are literal, take everything at face value, so I mean to say that I have the *sensation* that my body does not obey me, that I am not sane, lucid, to put it that way, but my body is out of order. Nothing serious; you don't need to be alarmed, I tell my friends. I am a casualty of war, a veteran; I have lived in Argentina and many of us, my friends, my comrades, have died on the battlefield, young, their lives ahead of them, gravely injured or killed because writers in this country, but not just writers, are always in the danger zone; we set ourselves on the psychological frontier of society and from there report back what is happening. We send messages, write books, are the correspondents of an imaginary, brutal, bloodthirsty war. My friends—Miguel Briante, one down, Juan José Saer, one down—on the long list of those killed in the charge, in that no-man's-land where battles have been fought for years. "We have to strike straight inland / towards where the sun goes down," Renzi, touched, said, reciting the verse from *Martín Fierro*. Waiter, he said, then, and with difficulty raised his left hand, made a very imperfect circle in the air—it turned out closer to a square, or rather, a parallel-epiped—and said, "A bit more," looking toward the counter of the bar. "In Mexico," he resumed the sentence he had left hanging, suspended,

415

like a trapeze artist waiting, stunned, for his partner's signal, to throw himself though the air without a net, in a fatal double jump that comes to a climax when he grabs his assistant's waiting hands, suspended above, from whom he hangs, as they say, in the air. And that is what narrating means, he said then; to throw yourself into the void and trust in some reader to catch you in the air. "In Mexico, as I said a moment ago, the women are more intelligent than the men. *Much more*," he emphasized, "more intelligent and faster and more astute than the Mexican individuals of the opposite sex."

And so, he continued after the waiter served him another glass of white wine, and so I am now working with my Mexican muse. I dictate, and she of course writes something else, improves what I say, barely understands. She speaks a pure Spanish, and to amuse me will sometimes say phrases or make jokes in Nahuatl. She, María, daughter of Lucía, understands what I tell her in my Buenos Aires slang, made worse by a certain alcoholic pronunciation, because nowadays I can't work if I'm drunk at all, so she writes down what she thinks I'm saying. Not so fast, she sometimes says, but I can't speak slowly, have to hurry to be able to put up with what I am saying, and she gathers my words and writes them as she feels them, so that, when I ask her after a while to read what we have written, she, in her clear Spanish, reads some pages in which what I've said is barely a gray shadow amid the pure and precise words with which she has improved my narration of things written by hand in my notebooks, from many years before. Where I say "poems," she writes "problems," where I say, referring to my Alfonsinist friends, "civics," she very properly translates it as "cynics." There does not always need to be a synonym; sometimes María, my Mexican assistant, transforms and improves what I say. For example, I have dictated, "In those days of creative loneliness . . . " and she, who cannot stand those self-praising expressions, stifling a smile, corrects it to "In those days, a lonely criminal . . . " and I am enchanted by the solution she has found, go forward from there and dictate: "In those days comma a solo criminal is worth more than two hundred grieving Argentine writers

colon in italics with a capital: *That is how it is.*" But there are other times
that she, a qualified typist who writes without looking at the computer
keyboard because she is watching my mouth to be able, as she says, to
read my lips and so, as she moves at top speed, sometimes looking at the
screen, sometimes at my face, and sometimes at the window that opens
on the garden, all without stopping her rhythmic typing, some confusions
occur. For example, if the nurse who takes care of me is in the room next
door and I say, "Margarita, please put a blanket over my legs," though it
sounds strange but not impossible, could without batting an eye become
a paragraph with a surrealist tone in the diary of an Argentine writer who
is a bit of a snob. The exclamation "Come in" also often appears in my
diaries as well as the sentences "It's raining outside" or "Isn't the phone
ringing?" They are all copied down promptly; since she's a vocational
linguist, nothing surprises her. On the other hand, María, daughter of
Lucía, has a contagious laugh and laughs sympathetically at everything,
at me in the first place, and also sometimes at herself or at what is happening in the world. Therefore, within my diaries, in which I try not to
put people's real names, I call her "the Thracian woman," a reference to
the young peasant girl who laughed when she saw the philosopher Thales
walking, lost in thought, observing the firmament and trying to capture
the hidden truth of the universe, and falling into a well. And many have
said that there is more philosophy in the cheerful laughter of that girl
washing her hair in the water of a spring than in the profound thoughts
of the philosopher who fell into the bottom of a hole for failing to look
where he was going.

We had returned from the cemetery that afternoon in August or
September 1968 and entered the family house where my grandfather
Emilio had lived alone for ten years, and where he died, which had been
prepared room by room until it was transformed into an archive of the
Great War in which he had fought; rather, he had created a personal
museum in the house, almost in secret, with documents, cards in glass
cases and maps on the wall, with little flags indicating the positions of

the armies facing off in the tall frozen mountains of the Austrian border. There were also many photographs; the war of '14 was the first war to be filmed and photographed, once and a thousand times over by army cameramen and by professional or amateur photographers. In the museum, there was a great store of images of battle, the trenches, the offensives, the no-man's-land, and my grandfather curated them with great care, and once brought my cousin Horacio, Susy, and me together to project, onto an improvised screen, scenes from the war, which he explained to us, identifying the places, speaking from behind the projector, behind the white light, as though his were the voice of a ghost, a specter of the war, and sometimes he would read us letters from the dead soldiers or battle dispatches that the confused general dictated and declared, although they never ever said, my grandfather would say from the back of the room, that they had gone too far, that they did not know what to do, because the officers failed, and there were thousands of deaths every time that a general, from his office in the high command, gave the order to attack, that is, to advance cross-country toward the enemy fortifications. In this way, the war, my grandfather would say, was swamped; all the military tactics went to the devil in the face of frighteningly effective modern weapons. The war conquered the generals, who, in the end, did nothing but hold their positions in the infected wells where soldiers died like flies, so that, my grandfather would say as the terrible images appeared on the wall, the war stagnated and transformed into trench warfare, and it was there that the Germans began to experiment with toxic gasses, a new way they found to kill enemy soldiers in the trenches, like throwing poison in a rat's den or a hornet's nest.

And that afternoon, once all of my grandfather's relatives and friends and acquaintances had gone, with that strange and ambivalent sensation that burials leave and the long sleepless hours through which the dead man was accompanied on his first night of death, a certain sorrow but also a certain relief, and the disturbing feeling of happiness at being alive that you feel at such times, and after my father had gone, rather numbed by the pain that his father's passing or disappearance had caused him, my mother and I stayed there alone, on the patio. Susy came to bring us some tea and sea biscuits so that we might recover from the endless night, and we were there, in that beloved place, under the vine, sitting in canvas chairs in front of a round marble table, and then my mother, unexpectedly, as was her style, changed the calm tone of our trivial conversation and started talking about the situation that had led my grandfather to enlist as a volunteer in the war.

The first sign of trouble, said my mother, Renzi explained, was his idea of sending his pregnant wife off to Italy to have her son, your father; he wanted his son to be born in Italy, can you believe it? And not just in Italy, but, more specifically, in Pinerolo, the town where your grandfather was born and where my scatterbrained ex-husband was born. The Italians are excessive, my mother said; they seem very emotional but are also cruel and Machiavellian. She paused to have a cup of tea and look at the flowering garden, with her beautiful and haughty face turned toward the country jasmine with its white flowers and unforgettable perfume and said, it's nice here. I've missed this garden for years and years, when we had to leave for Mar del Plata so your father wouldn't get arrested again, the thing I always missed, she said, was the perfume of jasmines in the afternoon air. And then, after pausing, in her swerving way of speaking, she went back to what she had been about to tell me, the secret she was on the verge of revealing. Your father was born in Italy in September of 1915—that's to say, that if your mother set sail already pregnant, or if she was *heavy* then, my mother said, because she enjoyed out-of-fashion words, was heavy, she said again in a happy tone, that means, Nene, my mother said, that your grandfather traveled by train from the town in La Pampa where he lived and went to Constitución and from there to Puerto Nuevo so that his wife could set out and have his son, your father, in Pinerolo, that is, if you do the math, in December of 1914 or January of '15. And she paused, incensed. I mean he sent her on a ship to Italy once the war had already started, months before, and the German submarines were sinking or trying to sink the ships that crossed the Atlantic. He was crazy, my mother said, smiling, completely crazy. Who would think of sending his pregnant wife to Europe once the war was already sparked? Insane, incredible, mysterious—call him what you will. A deliberate decision, because your grandfather, dear, was very intelligent and very rational and would spend his time calculating each one of his moves.

My mother, Ida Maggi, had a virtue as a narrator that I have always tried to use in my literature, because the key, or one of the keys to the art of writing, is not to judge the characters. My mother never judged a family member's conduct; she narrated the events but did not condemn those who belonged to the clan, whatever they did, and therefore, I think, she waited until my grandfather was no longer in this world to tell his life's secret. She did not mean to condemn, and now, this afternoon, recounting my grandfather's incomprehensible actions, so as not to have to judge him, she had waited until he was dead. Or maybe she and my grandfather had made a pact of silence about this crucial issue. And, when she resumed the story, she remained objective and direct, with some ironic footnotes intended to indicate the surprising quality of my grandfather's decision to send his pregnant wife to war-ravaged Europe. What could his motive have been? She said nothing about that now, limiting herself to narrating the events, and saved the explanation for the end, or rather, the description of the reason why my grandfather had done *that*, as she called it. She imagined the scene at the port, the goodbye, the woman, young and pregnant, climbing up the ramp to the ship, and my grandfather, waiting on the dock and watching the ship depart and then slowly grow distant and disappear from sight. It was possible, according to her, to imagine the scene and see my grandfather standing on the dock, dressed in an English suit with a vest, thin and tall, very elegant, wearing a thin-brimmed hat that he might have waved in his hand as the ship moved out from the port, a greeting or maybe a final farewell.

He returned, afterward, to the town and resumed his routine work, but when Italy entered the war, in April or May of 1915, things rapidly became complicated. He lost contact with his wife, the letters did not arrive, the military censors registered all correspondence and, on top of that, worse still, he couldn't send money to his wife; the money orders that he sent her would return rejected, the ties with Italy were severed.

My father and I had decided to save my grandfather's archives. I was going to be in charge of organizing them, as my grandfather had left a bank account intended to provide me with a salary so that I could spend my time organizing his documents to eventually publish them and make them public. And so, on the very night of the wake in the Lasalle funeral home in Adrogué, at sunrise, only my father and I, unable to sleep, and half-intoxicated by the coffee we drank on and off and by the cigarettes we smoked one after another, decided not to sell the house and, if we rented it out, leased it, as my father said, to do the front only, leaving the rooms in the back, with the archive, free and available for the work of conserving my grandfather's papers.

And there we were for hours afterward, my mother and I, sitting on the patio in the shadow under the vine, after my father had already gone and all the so-called mourners had retired as well, surely to celebrate because it was not they, this time, but my grandfather who had been called away. He, who would always say to his grandchildren and the kids in the family with a wicked smile, he said, surely no one will reveal the truth to you, how to live life intensely, because, my grandfather would say, they're all dead, with permission, and he stressed the phrase *with permission*, and the children listened with a certain uncertain fear and without understanding all of the warning, perplexed, in front of that man, tall, clear-eyed, who said such strange things and spoke to them in a personal way, and of course none would forget that sentence, engraved into their minds like a riddle that they could only decipher with any clarity much later, once grown up and after having suffered sufficiently. My grandfather spoke

421

like that, death and misfortune surrounding us. "Don't forget that, kids,"
he would say, without a trace of bitterness on his face; he spoke to us happily, like someone sharing good news. I remembered those things, said
Renzi, and told them to my mother, because the day after the death of "a
dear soul," as they say, when the sun shines again and you feel pain from
the loss and the hangover from the vigil night in your body, it is natural
to speak of the person who is gone and remember him in order to keep
him on this side, with anecdotes and sayings that, in a fragile way, keep
him alive. And I remember how, when I dictated a version of the distant
afternoon, remembering my grandfather, to my Mexican muse, María,
the daughter of my colleague and friend Lucía, she started talking about
a dog that the pre-Hispanic inhabitants of Mexico would bury with the
dead so that the animal could guide them on their return to the land of
the living. The dog was a Xoloitzcuintle, an extraordinary name, unpro-
nounceable, a sacred dog, a sort of seeing-eye dog that guided spirits
returning to life. And, as though I wanted some relief from the pain that
overwhelmed me as I dictated the day after my grandfather's death, in
order to distract me, she quickly searched on the internet for an image
of the guide dog, a bizarre animal, a mixture of cat and dog, similar to
the Egyptian figures that you see on the pharaoh's tombs. But, on that
afternoon, my mother and I had no hope that my grandfather, so dear
to us, would return, guided by some magical animal that would let him
visit us and thus relieve us of the pain caused by his death. Maybe this
was the reason that my mother, who was a narrator of great sensitivity,
very attentive to conveying the emotions of the story she told, decided to
create an anticlimax and bring me out of the sorrow caused by the death
of my grandfather Emilio.

Afternoon was falling and they had lit the lights in the bar, even though
outside, on the streets, the sun was still shining and a dying light burned
in the city. Renzi paused, took a breath, and then resumed the story with
new spirits. My father had already gone, had divorced my mother, so the
two no longer spoke, avoided each other, as happens in such cases, when

two people who have known each other intimately separate and try to forget. And so it was that my father left that day and my mother came to the family house and sat with me on the patio and revealed to me the secret that explained or, in any case, allowed a glimpse of the reason why my grandfather had fought in the Great War. He had another woman. Your grandfather sent his pregnant wife to Europe because he had a lover, had fallen in love with an upper-class *criolla*, the young daughter of a local rancher with whom he kept up a clandestine relationship for months. He could not get separated, did not want to get separated, and he imagined he could keep a lover, have two houses, two families, make a double life, as was fairly common out in the country at that time, but the girl, Matilde Aráoz, would not allow it, and, when she found out that your grandfather's wife was pregnant, she summoned him; she was a determined woman and was not prepared to support the lies of your grandfather, who always promised her that he was going to get divorced, but, as is common in those cases, never did it. She did not want to see him, she swore at him; some people say that, one afternoon, when your grandfather came down the dirt road in his car, a shiny new Ford Model T, between the poplars, the girl, very calm and beautiful with her riding pants and tall boots, went as far as the cattle gate with a shotgun and told him that he could turn around because she was going to shoot him if he didn't.

The afternoon was cool and my mother paused, amazed at the image of the girl walking toward the road and aiming a shotgun at him because she loves him and is not going to put up with new excuses or pretenses. She pushed him back from the other side of the gate and your grandfather turned around and went back home. It was then, my mother explained, on the route from the Aráoz ranch to the station near your grandfather Emilio's town house, that he made the decision to send his wife to Europe. It is characteristic of the men in the family; they never make decisions, they don't have the courage to do what they want to do, they try to keep all of their alternatives open, to put things off. Your grandfather was that way, and your father was the same, and you, too, Emilio, you're the same way—indecisive, insecure, not in terms of what you think, but what you feel. You are all unable to let yourselves be led by the truest emotions. And so your grandfather thought that if he sent his wife to Italy he could continue the double position at the same time. Surely, he thought, I'll see what happens to me with Matilde, and if that doesn't work out, I can always bring back my wife, but if things are going well, I'll leave her in Italy and let her relatives look after her. Like he could see it happening, my mother said. Driving the car, both hands clinging to the wheel, thinking about possible solutions and throwing away one after another until he discovered the possibility of deceiving both of them. Telling one that he had separated from his wife, who had already decided to return to Italy, and telling the other, with feeling and genuine expression, that his hope was for his first-born son to be born in the town of his birth, in Italy. A real idiot, like your father and like you, too, if you aren't a little careful, Emilio.

My mother described the situation, and her condemnations and her invectives were given in the name of one of the story's protagonists; she, Matilde, must surely have thought so, and my mother used free indirect discourse to speak with the voice of one of the characters in the story she told. She actually displaced herself that afternoon and suddenly went off and started recalling her brother Anselmo's experience. A doctor, very well-liked, very sociable—he was at that time president of the social club where the town's elite met; not just anyone could go there, and he was the president, the most prominent and visible figure in the place. But he quickly started to become reclusive, did not make himself visible, neglected his practice, stopped going to the hospital and attending the family's social meetings and started talking to himself, murmuring that he was sick, that he had something wrong with his skin. My mother returned that afternoon to tell the story of the man who had retired, had guarded himself because he thought he had some affliction on the skin of his face, which had turned him into a monster.

The first sign of his illness or disease was that all of the mirrors, and even any surface that could reflect a face, vanished from the family house. In this way, all vestiges of the personal image that might have been found in the place were taken out, covered, or erased. I knew the story because my mother had told it to me already and I knew my uncle well; he always visited when he came to town for the summers, and he took me to the lake many times to swim. I loved him, and so one afternoon, a Sunday, I insisted on visiting him and went to the house and there he was, shut off, as they say, in one of the interior bedrooms, actually a whole wing of the residence; only my uncle's trusted nurse could enter, serving as a link to reality, a kind of secretary, shall we say, who spoke in his name, attended to his matters, and sometimes, after consulting with my uncle, prescribed some medication for the nurses who insisted on still dealing with El Doctor, as they called him. The truth is that I went to see him one afternoon; I was fifteen and wanted to see him, and he received me. In fact, I was received by the nurse, a short man, thin and swarthy, with an Indian face, dressed in a white smock. He was called Estévez and had the name on a little plaque on the chest pocket of his nurse's uniform. We crossed one room and then another and passed through a greenhouse and ended up at my uncle's bedroom. A vast room, with large picture windows and high ceilings. My uncle was facing away, looking out at the patio, and when he turned around I saw that he concealed himself with a white cloth that completely covered his face. He held it up in front of himself with both hands. We had a trivial conversation, and he spoke to me in his usual jovial tone but never referred or alluded to the fact that he held up a white cloth in front of him with both hands, concealing his face. And so it was a rather strange conversation, because his voice came from behind a kind of private curtain that he held a certain distance from his face so as not to be seen by anyone. I was slightly inhibited by the sensation of speaking to a phantom or to a death mask, softly trembling with the afternoon breeze or the slight shaking of my uncle's arms, already tired from holding up the cloth. As I left, Estévez, the nurse and secretary, told me, confidentially, that my uncle was taking a period of rest in his personal chambers.

In this way, when my mother told me the story, I was up to date on the matter and knew that a year or a year and a half later, my uncle, El Doctor, returned to his normal life, the sickness he imagined having passed, because, as my mother clarified in concluding the story, Anselmo's face had no mark or symptom or disturbance that could have justified his refuge. He was perfectly well, my mother said that afternoon, but he felt that his face had transformed into a swollen and formless mass. He thought that, my mother said, or rather, she added, he believed that, and when someone believes something, it's difficult to change their opinion; my mother neither judged nor explained my uncle's behavior, only recounted the events, but that afternoon, on the patio under the vine, she told me his story as a way of speaking tangentially, changing the subject, which is what my grandfather Emilio must have done as a result of the pain he had caused two women and the changes he had suffered in his life by enlisting as a volunteer in the Italian Army and going to war, the fault of a history of poorly resolved love. As soon as he reached Italy at the end of 1915, my grandfather was sent to the front and could not get permission to see his family and meet his son, meaning my father, and he was in the Army until 1919, when the war ended, and he spent months in a military hospital, making reports about the soldiers affected by the trauma of war. Terrified men who ran to hide under the hospital furniture whenever they heard a loud noise or, sometimes, in some cases, not even that much—their own thoughts were enough to make them think they were back in the trenches, under constant bombardment, and they would set off running and throw themselves under a table with their hands over their ears and a heartbreaking groan on their lips.

A man goes to war for personal reasons, and he sets off on an epic for sentimental reasons. It is an extraordinary story. It sounded like the life of a romantic hero who achieves impossible feats and fights, over the course of years, for private and sentimental reasons. A new type of hero, the interior man, the impassioned and sentimental man who faces battle and is wounded by a bullet and returns to combat for the love of a woman. Of course, he concluded, we will never know whether that passionate feat was dedicated to his wife—that is to say, my grandmother Rosa—or was done as a tribute to or atonement for his Argentine lover, the beautiful Matilde Aráoz.

Renzi was silent, went a while without speaking, looking at the night now fallen over the city, and then he smiled. An extraordinary story, isn't it, he said. A man who goes to war for emotional reasons. He turned silent again and then called a waiter, paid the bill, and we went out to the street. It was cool outside; the heat had left a trace, like a mist persisting on the walls, but the night air was agreeable and light. I transcribe my diaries without following any chronological order; that would be terrible, and very boring, he said. I travel through time, picking up the notebooks by chance, and sometimes I'll be reading my life in 1964, and a short while later, I'm suddenly in the year 2000.

We went down Riobamba toward Santa Fe, and Renzi went on describing the experience of dictating his notebooks to an assistant, who copied them down as he read them. He could not write them all again—it would be impossible, there are pages and pages—but reading them aloud to a girl is something else; it felt like we were spying on the life of a stranger moving in circles through the city, or rather, moving back and forth, from one side to the other, lost in the life. We paused before crossing Santa Fe, waiting for the traffic light to change, and then Renzi spoke again to say that he would like to have a coffee at Filippo, on the corner of Callao. And once more he utilized that pause, standing at the counter of the bar, to put an epilogue on the story he had told that afternoon.

His mother, a couple years after his grandfather's death, wrote in a letter to Emilio about Matilde, the young woman his grandfather had loved and for whom, in a sense, he had gone to war. It was the *criolla* girl, in short, who troubled him and forced him to make the decision, at once heroic and foolish, to go to a war, one that would completely turn his head; he would return delirious, half-insane, obsessed with the experience of being the messenger who gave a family the letter announcing the death of a son, a brother, or a husband who had died on the front. He had to write these letters by hand, with his elegant writing, that of the student of a Jesuit school, where he had been educated, where he had spent interminable afternoons doing calligraphy exercises, rather, copying pages and pages using different types of writing, sometimes Gothic and sometimes cursive, so that his letters were written with great elegance; he expressed himself with great rhetorical skill, treating each letter as though it were personal, not a bureaucratic or superficial message, but rather a letter, brief but heartfelt, announcing the terrible news. He also had to send them the soldier's personal effects and even the half-written letters found in the soldier's rucksack. That work deranged him, Renzi said, looking at his face in the mirror along the bar.

In that letter, his mother had said that she knew the whereabouts of Matilde Aráoz, the woman his grandfather had loved. And, one afternoon, Renzi went to visit the girl, who by then was already an old woman and was institutionalized, or rather, lived in a rest home on the outskirts of the city; his mother had noted down the precise details for the address of the house where the girl was settled, waiting for the end. Emilio had recorded the visit in his diary of May 1972, and, that night in the bar, he retold the encounter with the same emotion as the first time.

It was, said Renzi, far off in one of those *petits hôtels*, or large mansions, in a type of garden that abound in the northern part of the city, close to the river. The woman was disoriented, without any memory; she was very beautiful, and age had refined her features, and in her eyes burned the same passionate light that had dazzled his grandfather Emilio. She sat in a woven rocking chair and moved rhythmically and spoke in a delightful and happy tone, and her monologue was both foolish and very beautiful. She seemed to live inside of a specific day from the past, a day she recalled in full detail. One day in the countryside, at sunrise, a group of her father's friends—young people from the town and two English girls recently arrived, whom they had brought along to go around the ranch—had gone out on horseback, and they had camped in a grove of trees near the lake and laid out a red gingham tablecloth, on which they set out sandwiches, pastries, and crystal glasses; they had brought two bottles of white wine, which they put in the clear water of the lake near the bank to chill. Renzi listened to all this, but the woman ignored or confused him, he thought, with the doctor or with a ranch hand who was there with her, in the country, in her youth. And so, every now and then, the woman gave orders to Emilio, asking him, for example, to go and get the hat she had left on a post of a corral where they had let the horses loose. It is fairly common for someone who has lost the notion of time and space, as a result of age, to reconstruct a day of life as a refuge and to recall it with total precision, in such a way that in order to remember it, or rather, in order to live through it again, they require an entire day. What they recall lasts twenty-four hours, and it therefore occupies the space of the present day, which lasts as long as the day being remembered, which, on the other hand, Renzi clarified, is repeated endlessly, never ceasing, and seems akin to happiness, because the day being remembered is a beautiful or perfect day from their life that survives and orbits eternally in the unreason of extreme age. And so, she was content, was entertained, happy, going back to live an unforgettable day from her youth. But then something happened that Renzi recalled with astonishment, and also with horror. He realized that, inside that afternoon in the country, they were waiting for the girl's suitor, who was going to arrive late, directly from the station; Renzi managed to understand it from what the woman was saying aloud, conversing with absent and long-dead others. And suddenly Matilde heard the noise of the Ford T's engine as it came down the road from above and parked by the edge of the lake. And she asked them to comb her hair and paint her lips, told her friends that she had not brought

429

a mirror and they had to help her prepare herself for the rendezvous with the man who had come in the car. And Renzi saw her smile excitedly, seeing him for the first time, as though she had never seen him before, because she moved toward him and took his hand and said, Emilio, how you make yourself wait, my dear, and then, in an intimate whisper, with her mouth very close to his face she said, I will kiss your body, my love. And then Emilio understood that the woman had confused him with his grandfather, and the likeness was so strong that the girl managed to think that, on this empty day of her old age, the young body of her lover could have appeared. I realized, he said, that she had taken me for him because we were so alike and that I was, or seemed to be, the same as he had been at my age, when he and the girl were in love.

We left the bar and went down Santa Fe toward Ayacucho. Walking calmly through the night, we paused a moment to look at the display window of the Ateneo bookshop, and Renzi took advantage of the pause to go back to critiquing the state of the world, using the books exhibited in the glass as a pretext. They're the same insubstantial books from the same idiotic authors who only write so that their books will be exhibited in the windows of bookshops around the world. You know, at this very moment in London or Paris or New York, the same horrible covers of the same insubstantial books are being exhibited. And the same authors, the photographs with the faces of the same idiots can be seen at this very moment in all of the airports, supermarkets, chains of bookstores and newspaper stands. And he became furious, repeating the names of all those despised writers as though it were a litany.

He took me by the arm and literally dragged me away from the place because he suddenly feared that someone would recognize him and see him standing outside a bookshop as though checking to make sure his own books and his own face were being exhibited, and they might think his anger was due to the fact that none of his books were there on display, not even as a joke, he said. Therefore, we walked at a lively pace to get away from the lights of the sidewalk next to the business, as he said, and even though he moved with some difficulty, a slight limp impeding his movement, we still turned, quickly, down Ayacucho toward Marcelo T, as he would say, in disdainful reference to the street where his study was.

That is why I am transcribing my diaries, because I want people to know that even now, at seventy-three years of age, I still think in the same way, criticizing the same things that I criticized when I was twenty. Now I am surrounded by converts who change their minds with every season to adapt to the common general mood. They have abandoned their convictions and their libraries again and again, while I remain faithful to my ideas. By reading my notebooks—if I publish them—they will be able to know, or to guess, or to imagine what my life has been. I already have close to nine hundred pages copied into a file on the computer, and we, the Thracian woman and I, have made several backup copies. Several, he repeated excitedly, on different pen drives, what can only be opened by entering a password. Even María advised me to send my diaries to what she called "the cloud," a virtual space, in the air or in the atmosphere, where you can send what you write and leave it there and take it down when you want, but I refused, of course, because I was horrified by the idea that some idle navigator might infiltrate my place in the cloud and dedicate himself to reading the true story of my life.

We are copying them without following a chronological order; I move through time, as I have already said; for me, they are the mechanism of time. They are, he said, and paused in the door of a Chinese or Korean supermarket, and he would later say, when recording, in his diary, our conversation at the bar, El Cervatillo, and then in Filippo: *I am studying the behavior of Chinese or Korean supermarket workers. Today, I confirmed, as I paused angrily in the doorway of the business, that the cashier, a very short Asian woman, listened to what I was saying with great attention. So, I have to be careful,* he wrote in his notebook a few hours later, *about what I say out loud when I go to buy a bottle of wine at the little market.* They are, he repeated, returning to the present time of the conversation, they are now, for me, the mechanism of time. I move from one period to another, by chance; I keep the notebooks stored in cardboard boxes, without any hint of dates or locations. And so, he said, I open a box blindly, as you might say, and sometimes I am back in the distant past. Nineteen fifty-eight, for example, let's say, and a while later I am reading about what I did last year, in two thousand and fourteen. At one point, he had decided to go traverse a day in his life, any day, let's say the June 16, and see what happened on that day, year after year. It had been a scheme, attempting to organize his life based on an order that was not chronological.

By then, we had left the Chinese supermarket behind, and, after turning down Charcas (ex-Charcas, as he would sometimes say, obstinately), we crossed, always with a determined but slow pace, the eighty meters separating us from the building where Emilio spent the majority of his time. He made me go up and accompany him to the tenth floor, where his apartment was. In the elevator, he started explaining to me why he wanted me to come with him; he wanted to show me, he said, if I can find it, he added, the second part of his future autobiography. He was going to publish the first part of his diaries now, based on what was written in his notebooks from 1957, when he started, until 1967, when he published his first book and when his grandfather Emilio's death was looming. He looked at me in the mirror and explained that he thought it would be the second part of his self-published diaries. "By me," he said. "The happy years of my life, which go from nineteen sixty-eight to nineteen seventy-five, seven years," he said. "A magic number. There are many stories within those notebooks." He stopped. "You'll see how they go." He made a sign and looked at me. "It will continue," he said, as we got off the elevator. "The story will continue," he said, and paused. He searched for a silver key on the key chain that hung at his waist, and, after a few attempts, managed to insert it into the lock. "If I don't die first," he added, smiling, as though announcing some news that filled him with happiness, and opened the door.

432

GLOSSARY OF NOTABLE FIGURES

Alem, Leandro (1842–1896)
Argentine politician who served as National Deputy and as a senator, later founding the Republican Party in Argentina.

Alterio, Héctor (1929–)
Argentine theater and film actor, known for a prolific career in both Argentina and Spain.

Álvarez, Jorge (1932–2015)
Argentine book publisher and record producer, a key figure in promoting literature in Argentina in the 1960s and '70s.

Amado, Jorge (1912–2001)
Brazilian writer associated with modernism, whose novels were praised by such pivotal writers as Albert Camus and Jean-Paul Sartre.

Amaru, Túpac II (1738–1781)
Leader of an indigenous uprising in Peru against the Spanish colonial authorities, named after the last indigenous Inca monarch.

Anderson-Imbert, Enrique (1910–2000)
Argentine literary critic, novelist, and short-story writer, known for short fantastical stories, who became a professor of literature at Harvard University.

Aricó, José "Pancho" (1931–1991)
Argentine writer and socialist philosopher, influenced by the Italian theorist Antonio Gramsci.

Arlt, Roberto (1900–1942)
Argentine writer of novels, short stories, and plays, whose use of brutality and colloquial language proved a major influence on the 1960s Latin American "Boom" generation.

Asquini, Pedro (1918–2003)
Argentine theater actor, director, producer, and teacher who worked for Argentina's National Endowment for the Arts.

Astrada, Carlos (1894–1970)
Argentine philosopher and university professor who studied in Germany under Max Scheler and Martin Heidegger.

Battista, Vicente (1940–)
Argentine writer, translator, and screenwriter, honored with the 1995 Premio Planeta.

Bayley, Edgar (1919–1990)
Argentine poet, translator and essayist, considered a major figure in avant-garde poetry.

Barba, Enrique (1909–1988)
Argentine historian who served as director of the Historical Archive of Buenos Aires Province and the National Archive of Argentina.

Baroja, Pío (1872–1956)
Spanish writer and one of the leaders of the Generation of '98, an important influence on Ernest Hemingway.

Benedetti, Mario (1920–2009)
Uruguayan novelist, poet, and journalist, a major figure in Latin American literature and one of the leading writers from the Generation of '45.

Benedetto, Antonio di (1922–1986)
Argentine short-story writer and novelist, best known for the existential novel *Zama*.

Benítez-Rojo, Antonio (1931–2005)
Cuban novelist, short-story writer, and essayist, considered a major figure in Cuban literature.

Bioy Casares, Adolfo (1914–1999)
Argentine author, journalist, and translator, a friend of Jorge Luis Borges, best known for his fantastical novel *The Invention of Morel*.

Blomberg, Héctor (1889–1955)
Argentine poet, playwright, and journalist, known for co-writing a number of famous songs with guitarist Enrique Maciel.

Boero, Alejandra (1918–2006)
Argentine stage and film actress, winner of the Konex and Molière awards.

Borges, Jorge Luis (1899–1986)
Argentine writer of short stories, translator, poet, and essayist, considered one of the most influential figures in Spanish-language literature of the twentieth century.

Bosch, Beatriz (1911–2013)
Argentine historian and geographer, mainly specializing in the political history of Argentina and the province of Entre Ríos.

Briante, Miguel (1944–1995)
Argentine author, screenwriter, and journalist who wrote for a number of magazines including *Primera Plana*.

Briski, Norman (1938–)
Argentine stage and film actor, director, and playwright, known for work in such plays as *Rosencrantz and Guildenstern are Dead*.

Cabrera Infante, Guillermo (1929–2005)
Cuban novelist, essayist, critic, and translator, compared to James Joyce for his literary experimentation.

Cambaceres, Eugenio (1843–1888)
Argentine politician and novelist, best remembered for the novel *Sin Rumbo*.

Cancela, Arturo (1892–1957)
Argentine critic and novelist, known for humorous works and portraits of life in Buenos Aires.

Canclini, Néstor García (1939–)
Argentine anthropologist and academic, known for his theories of hybrid cultures.

Carpentier, Alejo (1904–1980)
Swiss-born Cuban writer, essayist, and musicologist, best known for his novels, often dealing with the subject of Afro-Cubanism.

Castillo, Abelardo (1935–2017)
Argentine writer and essayist, regarded as one of the best novelists of his generation.

Castillo, Alberto (1914–2002)
Argentine film actor and performer, known for recordings of popular tangos.

Cedrón, Tata (1939–)
Argentine guitarist and composer, best known as a tango performer and for musicalized versions of literary works.

Cernuda, Luis (1902–1963)
Spanish poet from the Generation of '27, exiled to the United Kingdom and then Mexico due to the political climate after the Spanish Civil War.

Costantini, Humberto (1924–1987)
Argentine writer and poet, the son of Italian Jewish immigrants, who was an active member of the political left.

Conti, Haroldo (1925–1976)
Argentine screenwriter, novelist and professor of Latin who disappeared during the military dictatorship.

Corsini, Ignacio (1891–1967)
Italian-born Argentine musician, vocalist, and lyricist, known for folk music, tangos, and waltzes.

Cortázar, Julio (1914–1984)
Belgian-born Argentine short-story writer, novelist, and translator, known for his innovative novel *Hopscotch* and Spanish versions of Edgar Allan Poe.

Cossa, Roberto "Tito" (1934–)
Argentine playwright, considered one of the most important figures of his generation in theater.

Cozarinsky, Edgardo (1939–)
Argentine writer, essayist, and film director, known for mixing elements of personal reflection and documentary.

Cuzzani, Agustín (1924–1987)
Argentine playwright, a critic of capitalism, known for combining satire and farce in his plays.

Di Paola, Jorge "Dipi" (1940–2007)
Argentine novelist and short-story writer, a disciple of Witold Gombrowicz.

Droguett, Carlos (1912–1996)
Chilean novelist and short-story writer who escaped to Switzerland to avoid Pinochet's military dictatorship.

Escari, Raúl (1944–2016)
Argentine writer and avant-garde intellectual who studied in Paris under Roland Barthes.

Favio, Leonardo (1938–2012)
Argentine actor, director, screenwriter, and singer, appointed Argentina's Ambassador of Culture near the end of his life.

Fernández, Macedonio (1874–1952)
Argentine short-story writer, novelist, poet, and journalist who mentored and influenced Jorge Luis Borges.

Fernández Moreno, César (1919–1985)
Argentine poet, writer, critic, and diplomat who founded important publications including the literary magazine *Contrapunto*.

Ferreti, Aurelio (1907–1963)
Argentine playwright, particularly known for farces and satirical works.

Franco, Luis (1898–1988)
Argentine poet and essayist who founded a socialist party in Argentina and remained outside of the literary establishment of Buenos Aires.

Frondizi, Arturo (1908–1995)
Argentine lawyer and politician who served as President of Argentina from 1958 to 1962, following the coup that overthrew Perón.

Frondizi, Silvio (1907-1974)
Argentine lawyer and leftist intellectual, brother of president Arturo Frondizi, who taught as a professor of law in Buenos Aires, Tucumán, and La Plata.

Fuentes, Carlos (1928-2012)
Mexican novelist, essayist, and short-story writer, considered one of Mexico's greatest writers.

Galli Mainini, Carlos (1914-1961)
Argentine doctor, known for creating a reliable pregnancy test involving a frog.

Gálvez, Juan (1916-1963)
Argentine race car driver who won more than 50 races before being killed in an accident.

Gandini, Gerardo (1936-2013)
Argentine composer, professor, and pianist, known for performing with Astor Piazzolla.

Garay, Juan de (1528-1583)
Spanish conquistador who founded the permanent settlement of Buenos Aires in 1580.

García, Germán (1944-)
Argentine novelist, essayist, and psychoanalyst, founder of the Fundación Descartes.

García Márquez, Gabriel (1927-2014)
Colombian novelist, short-story writer, and journalist, awarded the 1982 Nobel Prize in Literature, best known for the novel *One Hundred Years of Solitude*.

Gardel, Carlos (1890-1935)
French-born Argentine singer, composer, and actor, one of the most famous tango performers of all time.

Gasalla, Antonio (1941-)
Argentine actor, comedian, and director, known for roles portraying female characters.

Gelman, Juan (1930–2014)
Argentine poet, awarded the Cervantes Prize, whose work was influenced by the political turmoil in Latin America.
Girri, Alberto (1919–1991)
Argentine poet and intellectual, known for translating major English-language poets including T. S. Eliot and Wallace Stevens into Spanish.
Gombrowicz, Witold (1904–1969)
Polish writer exiled to Argentina during and after the Second World War, known for his extensive diaries.
Goytisolo, Juan (1931–2017)
Spanish novelist, essayist, and poet, known for works opposing Francisco Franco and Spain's nationalism.
Grippo, Víctor (1936–2002)
Argentine painter and sculptor, recognized as one of the first conceptual artists in Argentina.
Groussac, Paul (1848–1929)
French-born Argentine writer, librarian, critic, and historian known as a significant influence on Jorge Luis Borges.
Güemes, Martín Miguel de (1785–1821)
Argentine military leader who fought against Spain in the Argentine War of Independence.
Guido, Beatriz (1924–1988)
Argentine short-story writer, novelist and screenwriter, an outspoken critic of Perón's government.
Guillén, Jorge (1893–1984)
Spanish poet, scholar, and critic, a central figure in the Generation of '27 and recipient of the Cervantes Prize.
Güiraldes, Ricardo (1886–1927)
Argentine poet and novelist, best remembered for the 1926 novel *Don Segundo Sombra*, examining the figure of the gaucho.
Hernández, Felisberto (1902–1964)
Uruguayan writer, known as a major influence on writers such as Gabriel García Márquez and Italo Calvino.

Jacoby, Roberto (1944–)
Argentine sociologist and artist, known for creating some of the first conceptual art exhibitions.

Jitrik, Noé (1928–)
Argentine writer, considered one of the most prominent literary critics in Latin America.

Juarroz, Roberto (1925–1995)
Argentine poet, admired by contemporaries including Octavio Paz and known for a body of work he called "vertical poetry."

Kelly, Guillermo Patricio (1922–2005)
Argentine activist and left-wing politician who led the Nationalist Liberation Alliance from 1953 to 1955.

Kohon, David J. (1929–2004)
Argentine director, screenwriter, and cinematographer, three-time winner of the Premio Cóndor de Plata.

Kuhn, Rodolfo (1934–1987)
Argentine film director, writer, and producer who served as a judge at the 1974 Berlin Film Festival.

Lafforgue, Jorge (1935–)
Argentine writer, literary critic, and professor of philosophy who has taught and lectured throughout Latin America and in the United States, Europe, and Asia.

Lamport, William (1611–1659)
Irish Catholic pirate and adventurer, put to death after attempting to lead a rebellion against the Spanish Crown in Mexico.

Leguisamo, Irineo (1903–1985)
Uruguayan jockey, well known for his races both in Uruguay and Argentina.

Leñero, Vicente (1933–2014)
Mexican novelist, playwright, and journalist, known for a stage adaptation of Oscar Lewis's *The Children of Sanchez*.

Lewin, Boleslao (1908–1988)
Polish-born historian and professor who fled to South America in the 1930s to escape the pogroms in Europe.

Lewis, Oscar (1914–1970)
American anthropologist, known for studies of poverty and living conditions in Latin America such as *The Children of Sanchez.*

Lezama Lima, José (1910–1976)
Cuban writer and poet, a major figure in Latin American literature, known for developing a baroque style.

López Jordán, Ricardo (1822–1889)
Uruguay-born Argentine politician and soldier who led a series of unsuccessful revolutions against the government of Buenos Aires.

López Merino, Francisco (1904–1928)
Argentine poet and writer belonging to the Committee of Young Intellectuals for Yrigoyen, led by Jorge Luis Borges, and who committed suicide at the age of 23.

López, Vicente Fidel (1815–1903)
Argentine politician, lawyer, and historian, remembered for important texts on the history of Argentina.

Ludmer, Josefina (1939–2016)
Argentine writer, literary critic, and professor, won several awards for contributions to literary theory.

Lugones, Leopoldo (1874–1938)
Argentine journalist, poet, short-story writer, and novelist, known for historically detailed works such as *La Guerra Gaucha.*

Lugones, Pirí (1925–1978)
Argentine writer, editor, translator, and journalist who disappeared after being kidnapped by the military dictatorship.

Luna, Félix (1925–2009)
Argentine writer, professor, historian, and lyricist, known for several important books examining stages in Argentina's political history.

Lynch, Marta (1925–1985)
Argentine writer of short stories and novels whose books became popular bestsellers throughout Latin America.

Madariaga, Francisco (1927–2000)
Argentine poet influenced by surrealism, widely anthologized and translated into several languages.
Mallea, Eduardo (1903–1982)
Argentine critic, writer, and diplomat who served as editor of the daily newspaper *La Nación*.
Mansilla, Lucio (1831–1913)
Argentine military general, politician, and writer who served as governor of the province of Chaco.
Mariani, Roberto (1893–1946)
Argentine short-story writer, novelist, and poet, known for his anarchist works and critiques of elitism.
Mármol, José (1817–1871)
Argentine writer, politician, and librarian who served as director of Argentina's National Library.
Martel, Julián (1867–1896)
Argentine writer, poet, and journalist, associated with modernism and naturalism, who completed a small number of works before dying of an illness in his late twenties.
Martínez Estrada, Ezequiel (1895–1964)
Argentine poet, biographer, short-story writer, and critic, known for his opposition to Perón and support of the Cuban Revolution.
Martínez, Tomás Eloy (1934–2010)
Argentine writer, journalist, and professor of literature, director of major publications such as *Panorama*.
Masotta, Oscar (1930–1979)
Argentine critic, essayist, and psychoanalyst, known for extensive studies on the work of Jacques Lacan.
Molina, Enrique (1910–1996)
Argentine poet and painter, known in both media for works influenced by surrealism.

Mondolfo, Rodolfo (1877–1976)
Italian philosopher who escaped Europe in 1938, becoming a professor
in Córdoba and Tucumán, Argentina.

Moreno, Nahuel (1924–1987)
Argentine revolutionary leader, actively involved in the Trotskyist
movement.

Moyano, Daniel (1930–1992)
Argentine writer and literary critic, forced to go into exile in Spain in
order to escape the military dictatorship.

Nieto, Chango (1943–2008)
Argentine singer-songwriter and folk musician, both critically
acclaimed and prolific, recording over 600 songs.

Onetti, Juan Carlos (1909–1994)
Uruguayan short-story writer and novelist, a key figure in Latin
American literature and member of the Generation of '45.

Onganía, Juan Carlos (1914–1995)
Argentine military officer who became President of Argentina from
1966 to 1970 after leading a successful coup d'état.

Orgambide, Pedro (1929–2003)
Argentine writer, playwright, and essayist, forced to leave for Mexico
to escape the military dictatorship.

Ortega y Gasset, José (1883–1955)
Spanish liberal philosopher, professor, and essayist, known for his analy-
ses of politics and culture during a period of political upheaval in Spain.

Ortiz, Juan Laurentino (1896–1978)
Argentine poet, known for works exploring poverty and the landscape
of his home province of Entre Ríos.

Palacios, Alfredo (1880–1965)
Argentine lawyer and socialist politician, known for passing labor
reform laws while serving as a senator.

Paso, Fernando del (1935–)
Mexican novelist, poet, and essayist, winner of the Cervantes Prize,
known for developments in the historical novel.

Peicovich, Esteban (1929–)
Argentine poet, critic, and journalist, known for conducting important interviews with figures such as Juan Perón and Jorge Luis Borges.

Perciavalle, Carlos (1941–)
Uruguayan actor, producer, and comedian, performing in such works as *La Cage aux Folles*.

Perón, Juan (1895–1974)
Argentine officer and politician, considered a dictator by some and a populist icon by others, who served as President of Argentina from 1946 to 1955 and from 1973 to 1974.

Peyrou, Manuel (1902–1974)
Argentine novelist, short-story writer, and critic, a friend of Jorge Luis Borges, known for works exploring the detective genre.

Pezzoni, Enrique (1926–1989)
Argentine poet, translator, writer, professor, and literary critic, known for important essays on the literature of Latin America and the United States.

Piazzolla, Astor (1921–1992)
Argentine composer and bandoneon player, known for his virtuosic performances and his major impact on the genre of tango music.

Pivel Devoto, Juan E. (1910–1997)
Uruguayan politician and historian who served as Uruguay's Minister of Public Instruction from 1963 to 1967.

Poletti, Syria (1917–1991)
Italian-born Argentine novelist and short-story writer, remembered particularly for her stories for children.

Pucciarelli, Eugenio (1907–1995)
Argentine writer and philosopher who taught in Buenos Aires, Tucumán, and La Plata.

Pugliese, Osvaldo (1905–1995)
Argentine musician and composer, considered an important figure in the development of the tango genre.

Puig, Manuel (1932–1990)
Argentine writer whose early novels, influenced by film and television, bear similarities with pop art.

Rivera, Andrés (1928–2016)
Argentine writer and journalist, known for historical novels dealing with Argentina's political history.

Rivero, Edmundo (1911–1986)
Argentine singer, guitarist, and composer, known for his contributions to the tango genre and international touring performances.

Roa Bastos, Augusto (1917–2005)
Paraguayan short-story writer, novelist, screenwriter, and journalist, a recipient of the Cervantes Prize, known for works dealing with political upheaval in Latin America.

Rodríguez Monegal, Emir (1921–1985)
Uruguayan scholar, critic, and professor, known for founding the publication *Mundo Nuevo* and teaching contemporary literature at Yale University.

Romano, Eduardo (1938–)
Argentine writer, poet, literary critic, and professor, teaching classes on popular culture and literature at the University of Buenos Aires.

Rosas, Juan Manuel de (1793–1877)
Argentine military officer and politician, known for wealth and authoritarian power, who served as governor of Buenos Aires Province from 1829 to 1832 and 1835 to 1852.

Rovira, Eduardo (1925–1980)
Argentine bandoneon player, known as a prolific composer of tangos and chamber music.

Rozenmacher, Germán (1936–1971)
Argentine writer and playwright, known for novels such as *Cabecita negra* that dealt with Peronism and Jewish tradition.

Rozitchner, León (1924–2011)
Argentine professor and philosopher, known for works on politics, psychoanalysis, and religion.

Rulfo, Juan (1917–1986)
Mexican novelist, short-story writer, and photographer, known for the stories in his collection *The Plain in Flames*.

Sabato, Ernesto (1911–2011)
Argentine writer, physicist, and painter, a major figure in Latin American literature, who led CONADEP in investigating crimes committed during the military dictatorship.

Sáenz, Dalmiro (1926–2016)
Argentine short-story writer, novelist, and playwright, known for sarcastic and absurdist works.

Saer, Juan José (1937–2005)
Argentine novelist and scholar, the son of Syrian immigrants, considered one of the most important writers of his generation.

Salas Subirat, José (1890–1975)
Argentine writer and translator, best remembered for completing the first Spanish translation of James Joyce's *Ulysses*.

Salgán, Horacio (1916–2016)
Argentine tango musician, considered one of the central figures of his generation in popular music.

Salinas, Pedro (1891–1951)
Spanish poet, critic, and professor, part of the Generation of '27 and an important influence on Jorge Guillén.

Sánchez-Albornoz, Claudio (1893–1984)
Spanish historian and politician, an important figure in the Second Spanish Republic.

Sánchez-Albornoz, Nicolás (1926–)
Spanish historian and professor, son of Claudio Sánchez-Albornoz, who was exiled to Argentina following Francisco Franco's rise to power.

Sánchez, Néstor (1935–2003)
Argentine writer and translator, a friend of Julio Cortázar, known for an extravagant and experimental style.

Sarmiento, Domingo (1811–1888)
Argentine politician, writer, and intellectual who served as Argentina's seventh president, from 1868 to 1874.

Sazbón, José (1937–2008)
Argentine academic and intellectual, known for his work on Marxism and German literature.

Solar, Xul (1887–1963)
Argentine writer, painter, and sculptor, a friend of Jorge Luis Borges, known for creating imaginary languages.

Sosa, Mercedes (1935–2009)
Argentine singer, known throughout Latin America for popular folk songs.

Szpunberg, Alberto (1940–)
Argentine poet and political activist, exiled to Europe after the 1976 coup d'état.

Torre Nilsson, Leopoldo (1924–1978)
Argentine film director, writer, and producer, known for screen adaptations of *Martín Fierro* and works by Jorge Luis Borges and Adolfo Bioy Casares.

Torres-García, Joaquín (1874–1949)
Uruguayan-Catalan painter, sculptor, and writer, considered a major figure in avant-garde art, whose work included collaborations with architect Antoni Gaudí.

Troilo, Aníbal (1914–1975)
Argentine bandleader, bandoneon player, and composer, known for popular tangos and dance music.

Urondo, Francisco "Paco" (1930–1976)
Argentine writer, activist, and essayist, assassinated during the military dictatorship.

Urquiza, Justo José de (1801–1870)
Argentine politician and military general who served as president of the Argentine confederation from 1854 to 1860.

Vargas Llosa, Mario (1936–)
Peruvian writer, journalist, politician, and professor, awarded with the 2010 Nobel Prize in Literature.

Verbitsky, Horacio (1942–)
Argentine writer and journalist known for documentations of violence during the military dictatorship.

Viñas, David (1927–2011)
Argentine novelist and playwright, a critic of authoritarian government and director of the Institute of Argentine Literature.

Viñas, Ismael (1925–2014)
Argentine writer and critic, brother of David Viñas, known for important works analyzing Latin American culture and politics.

Vítolo, Alfredo (1910–1967)
Argentine lawyer and politician who served as Minister of the Interior during Arturo Frondizi's presidency.

Walsh, Rodolfo (1927–1977)
Argentine author and activist, considered one of the first writers to develop investigative journalism, murdered during the military dictatorship.

Wernicke, Enrique (1915–1968)
Argentine short-story writer, playwright, novelist, and journalist who also worked for many years as a puppeteer.

Wilenski, Osías (1933–)
Argentine film director and Juilliard-trained composer, known for his film adaptation of Julio Cortázar's "The Pursuer."

Yrigoyen, Hipólito (1852–1933)
President of Argentina from 1916 to 1922 and from 1928 to 1930, known for activism in improving education, voting rights, and labor conditions for the working class.

ABOUT THE AUTHOR, TRANSLATOR, AND INTRODUCER

RICARDO PIGLIA (Buenos Aires, 1940–2017), professor emeritus of Princeton University, is unanimously considered a classic of contemporary Spanish-language literature. He published five novels, including *Artificial Respiration*, *The Absent City*, and *Target in the Night*, as well as several collections of stories and criticism. Among the numerous prizes he received were the Premio de la Crítica, Premio Rómulo Gallegos, Premio Bartolomé March, Premio Casa de las Américas, Premio José Donoso, and Premio Formentor de las Letras.

ROBERT CROLL is a writer, translator, musician, and artist originally from Asheville, North Carolina. He first came to translation during his undergraduate studies at Amherst College, where he focused particularly on the short fiction of Julio Cortázar.

ILAN STAVANS is the Publisher of Restless Books and the Lewis-Sebring Professor in Latin American and Latino Culture at Amherst College. His books include *On Borrowed Words*, *Spanglish*, *Dictionary Days*, *The Disappearance*, and *A Critic's Journey*. He has edited *The Norton Anthology of Latino Literature*, the three-volume set *Isaac Bashevis Singer: Collected Stories*, *The Poetry of Pablo Neruda*, among dozens of other volumes. He is the recipient of numerous awards and honors, including a Guggenheim Fellowship, Chile's Presidential Medal, and the Jewish Book Award. Stavans's work, translated into a dozen languages, has been adapted for the stage and screen. He hosted the syndicated PBS television show *Conversations with Ilan Stavans*. He is a cofounder of the Great Books Summer Program at Amherst, Stanford, and Oxford.

RESTLESS BOOKS is an independent, nonprofit publisher devoted to championing essential voices from around the world, whose stories speak to us across linguistic and cultural borders. We seek extraordinary international literature that feeds our restlessness: our hunger for new perspectives, passion for other cultures and languages, and eagerness to explore beyond the confines of the familiar. Our books— fiction, narrative nonfiction, journalism, memoirs, travel writing, and young people's literature—offer readers an expanded understanding of a changing world.

Visit us at restlessbooks.org